FOR SINNERS

AARON DRIES

POLTERGEIST PRESS

POLTERGEIST PRESS

'A Place For Sinners' © 2019 Aaron Dries

This is a work of collected fiction. All characters depicted in this book are ficticious, and any resemblance to actual events or persons, living or dead, is purely coincidental.

All rights reserved. No part of this book may be reproduced in whole or in part without the publisher's written consent, except for the purpose of review.

ISBN: 978-1-913138-01-1

Originally published by Samhain

www.poltergeistpress.com

This book is dedicated to multiple people and a single place. To Don D'Auria, who took so many chances. To Erin Al-Mehairi and Adrian Shotbolt, your support means the world.
And lastly, to Thailand. You were there for me when nobody else was.

The island waits, as it always has and always will, twitching, shifting, ever hungry and impatient. Her sugar-white sands hold on to the day's final burn, but loose their grip as the sun drops behind the mountains. She bruises in twilight. Soon her children won't be able to tell sky from ocean, and that is okay. That is the way things are meant to be. It is easier to hear her speak in the dark.

A sly shape between the branches, shadow against shadow.

Then there comes the music, reedy chords of loneliness and melancholy chiming together. It is a song that most don't live to dance to.

Avenues of trees and trodden path; galleys of lightning-charred branch and vine. She is a restless, always-stinking mother, and is without architecture or rhythm. Her tallest fruit mocks icy, distant stars.

Starved, half-blind animals prowl her orchardways. Spider eats mosquito; bird eats spider; monkey eats bird. There is the sound of tearing skin, a cough as bone catches in throat. It doesn't move her; she has no concept of mercy. She was old when the first men to stumble her shores were young, and she was not to blame for what happened to them, either.

Spider eats mosquito. Monkey eats bird.

There is laughter in her canopies when the sun dares touch her again. Fish swim in her veins, celebrating the new day. Moss steams. Last night's scat becomes the food of this morning's scavengers.

The island watches over it all. She is an impatient mother. Frustrated, she sometimes quakes and splits, but not often. There are long stretches of still silence. Silence interrupted by music. And like the twilight—like it all—it is okay. That is the way things are meant to be.

And so the sun sets again. So she continues to wait.

They will come.

Yes, they always did. All creatures seek retreat in the end.

PART ONE

PART ONE

CHAPTER ONE

Amity

1

A CAUL OF mist painted the world a dull, headache gray. It was just after six in the morning on June 8, 2000, and those who still slept did so in fits and spurts. The small Australian town of Evans Head writhed with concern, illuminated by the defiant torches of men and women who refused to give up their search with the coming of the sun. A little girl was lost.

"Amity!" called one voice.

"Amity Collins," called another.

Over and over they yelled, throats red-raw and eyes bloodshot. The night had been grueling; fatigue ran deep. Whiskey no longer calmed or fueled, only thumped in their heads, as incessant and violent as the waves against the shoreline.

Crabs ran sideways across the sand until snatched up by gulls, leaving behind disembodied claws and shells. A bloodied white feather. Sun fought unyielding fog.

Seven-year-old Amity Collins had wandered from the tent near Chinaman's Beach where she, her older brother and her father had been sleeping. They were a local family drawn from the comfort of their home on Yarran Street by mild adventure. Camping had been Amity's idea.

Janine Collins was at church, surrounded by friends, instead of searching for Amity with her husband. The room was cold. Knees ached against pews and the old wood groaned, the sound not too dissimilar from the group's murmurs. Both were tortured, in their own way, yielding weights unaccounted for in their design. The groans falling from their lips were indecipherable from the wood.

Janine's hair fell across her face, yesterday's makeup still on. She worked at the Saint Vincent de Paul Opportunity Store on Woodburn Street and found comfort in the oddities and used clothes. On that morning, as they entered the ninth hour of Amity's disappearance, she longed to go back there and make sense of those chaotic aisles of junk. It was soothing, in a way. And right now that was just what she needed.

The stained glass murals—timeless faces trapped in glass—splayed the church in a kaleidoscope of color. Rosary beads whispered between fingers. Father Lewis, whose eyes danced in the shimmering light, was leading the group in a search of a different kind.

"Holy Mary, Mother of God, pray for our sins now..."

The Collinses' house was dark with all the doors and windows locked tight.

White roses wilted against the lip of a vase on the glass dining room table; photographs lined the walls. Amity's older brother, Caleb, lay in his parents' bed upstairs. The home phone rested on the pillow next to him, the cord coiled around his fingers.

A family friend had escorted him home earlier but hadn't stayed. Caleb was alone now, content with exhaustion, lingering in that nowhere place between nightmares lived and those that were only dreamed. He remained there until seven, when the alarm clock blared barbs of music.

The tent was swallowed up by mist.

Inside: empty sleeping bags and a Raggedy Ann doll, the button eyes staring off into nowhere. Wind blew hard off the ocean, vomiting sunshine into the clearing. Dead trees full of spiders, their webs outlined in dew, shook and quivered. The tent flap stirred and a sliver of light cut across the doll's face, and then was gone, fleeting as hope.

2

Amity Collins didn't go anywhere without her transistor radio; she kept the palm-size unit tied to her wrist with a blue shoelace. The antenna almost stretched the length of her arm, and there were *My Little Pony* stickers—that she'd fished from a box of cornflakes—covering the battery hinge.

She loved the pop stations, with their carousel of bubblegum melodies and all of the funny talk between the hosts, even if she sometimes didn't understand what they were blabbering on about. And then, just as thrilling, was the noise between these stations, sometimes little more than a captured squeal of frequency pinned by a fingertip against the dial. Ghost sounds. Once, she'd even heard the voices of highway truck drivers, their conversations full of naughty words. That had been cool, a random glimpse into a life outside of Evans Head, the (uncool) east coast town she'd lived in her entire life.

Amity wanted to be Carmen Sandiego when she grew up, the red-coated wonder woman from her favorite cartoon who crossed the planet in the name of mystery solving. This titular character would pop up in random locations, in dangerous situations, and Amity would applaud, jumping up and down and clapping in front of the family television set. Watching that program had gifted this child with the sense that the world might just be bigger than she had imagined.

Like those truck drivers whose ghost voices she heard if the dial of luck clicked in her favor: Where were they going? Where did they come from? Wondering at the wonder of it all—it was enough to make her head spin.

She'd been humming the Carmen Sandiego theme song when she wandered from the tent. The tune didn't last long. And the radio was now shattered into pieces.

The dogs were huddled around the cave, three of them, shaking their matted fur and fighting with each other. Accordion ribbed and bound whole by countless scars-on-scars, Amity thought they must have been wandering the scrublands for a long time. Ropes of saliva swung from their jowls as fleas hopscotched back and forth among them. These were creatures from the dead trees, from the part of town where little girls were not allowed to go, and yet somehow, here she was—the kind of places where the wolves in her picture books were as real as the hands that turned the pages.

Despite pain, Amity wondered, *Are they older than me?*

The dogs bared their teeth and growled every time she scrambled close to the jaws of the cave.

"Pa! Pa, please! Help me! *Help me!*"

She felt like a bone the animals had found and claimed as their own. It terrified her to think it, but she believed that her blood—now candying their maws and tongues—was a taste they found favorable. Sweetness forbidden until today. They were desperate for more.

Amity was trapped, her back flat against the cave wall. The dogs glared at her with candle-flame eyes that flickered with the potential to burn and cause pain, or perhaps just blow out and die.

3

The door to the Collinses' house swung open and Caleb came running out—only to trip over one of his father's boots. This was no surprise; his mother had predicted this would happen if the family continued to ignore the rack she'd brought home from work. And Caleb had to admit that he was just as bad as the rest of them; he owned more scuffed and battered running shoes than all of them put together.

"It looks like there's an army staying here," his mother would say. "It's a pig's breakfast!"

Yeah, if I got a dollar for every time I heard that one.

"This place is a bloody brothel," was another popular turn of phrase, although Caleb didn't quite understand what that meant. Weren't brothels places where men went to have sex with prostitutes, like Cherry's Retreat, that grungy joint on the road to Lismore (not that he was positive it was a whorehouse, though the schoolyard speculation had been fueled by a reliable source: the year eleven student who worked as a pizza delivery boy in town)? *Brothel...* How could his untidy room, with the sports posters hanging off the walls from where the Blue Tac had peeled away and his bedsheets knotted on the carpet, resemble such a place?

Whatever.

"I'm so angry, I could just *spiflicate* you!"

That one confused him too, but there was no mistaking the venom in his mother's threat, or how Caleb or his sister should react: *Dummy up and run as fast as you can. She's on the warpath.*

"Do it, or I'll wear your guts for garters!"

He could see himself on the floor, legs splayed, ribbons of blood dripping down the walls. The image made him come over all shivery.

Caleb wondered if that was where Jack the Ripper got his ideas from: *Momma dearest.*

Nah—Janine Collins, for all her weirdness, wasn't so bad. Sure, there were times when Caleb hated her as only a son could, or was scared by her restlessness and mood swings, but there was also a lot of tenderness in the woman.

Her arms beneath the folds of her winter nightgown, which she wore every night, regardless of the season, wrapping around him. Mumbled comfort.

"You'll be right."

"Come on, chin up."

"Things get better. You'll look back on this someday and laugh."

Caleb wasn't so sure about that last one. Monday to Friday, between nine in the morning and three in the afternoon, his days were full of guys who wore their pimples with pride, trying to flog his ass at handball, and girls who lived to bitch. Caleb didn't *want* to look back on them and laugh. In fact, he didn't want to look back on them at all.

No way, José!

But the boys he could handle. They were puppies, just like him, longing for affection, which was kind of endearing in a way. Hell, even borderline cute. The pimples, however, those they could keep to themselves, thank you very much.

It was the girls, with whom he associated more often, that dealt the fiercest blows. They were forever armed with endless tests and impossible-to-meet criteria.

If you're really my friend, you'll do this. You'll do that.

Boys were a lot easier to handle, which was a shame, because he just didn't find them as fun to hang out with. Caleb couldn't stand it; the pressure was incredible. Were one person to fuck up, it threatened to drag down the reputation of the entire group. For some reason, that person always ended up being *him*. And Caleb was no idiot. He knew they never had his best interests at heart, but that wasn't the point—it couldn't be—the moment it did was the moment it all started to hurt, the slowly penetrating blade plunging deep. Yes, his friends were selfish, and yes, he still longed for their approval.

Sometimes, Caleb envied his younger sister. To be seven was to see the world as nothing but marvelous. It was so unfair. Situations that would stop Caleb's heart filled Amity's with wonder. She was free.

Caleb's jump from the front door to the bottom step was misjudged. He landed on his knees, pain crawling as skin peeled back to welcome gravel. "Don't cry! Don't. Don't."

Was I just spiflicated?

The fog had thinned, but the end of Yarran Street was still obscured. He limped past the family Holden and caught a glimpse of his reflection in the driver's window. The sight of his warped, manic expression shocked the breath out of him.

4

The dog's teeth were bared. Black gums. It stank of the ocean, of fog.

Watching it inch closer was like watching a storm roll in off the sea, and Amity didn't like storms. She'd watched a movie on television about them, and had felt naughty the whole time because it was rated M and she knew she wasn't allowed to watch anything over G. G was safe, it was *Toy Story* or *Barney's Great Adventure*. M, on the other hand, meant "old". In the film about the storm, a man had been sucked out of the cellar in his backyard by the strength of the wind alone. There had been flashes of lightning and hail pelting down. Screams—the shriek of a grown-up.

Men weren't supposed to scream or cry; those were the rules.

Day comes after nighttime; men marry women; girls wear dresses and boys wear shorts. Guys don't cry. Or scream.

Rules.

Every time thunderheads crawled across the coastline, the image of that man being lifted up into the air came back to her with chilling clarity. Could such a thing happen to Pa? And if it could, did that mean that she was at risk too?

Little girls don't die. She knew this as much as she did anything. The world protects its children.

"Doggy, don't!" Amity screeched. Hands clenched tight. The shoelace that had tied her transistor radio to her wrist now hung around her bones, loosening, as was her defiance. She half smiled at the monster; maybe it was nice after all. Smiles always made people feel happy, didn't they? So who knew, perhaps they made doggies feel better too—

It snarled, leaped forward and snapped its jaws down inches from her fingers. Amity screamed and jumped backward, cutting up her shins on the rocks and oyster shells.

Seagulls rode the wind outside, dropping scat and cawing.

"Stop!" Amity screamed, pushing her palms against her ears. The radio lay in pieces before her, sprinkled with beads of water and blood.

Waves crashed below, shaking the earth and dislodging rocks. The dank cave filled with the stench of natural gases, making her eyes water. Each breath filled her lungs with dust and mold spores. Each cough, a stab of pain. Cockroaches spilled from a crack in the ground on a thoughtless tide of legs and shiny backs. The dogs raised their heads and barked as the waves struck again, throwing fans of water up into the air. Only the water was full of eucalyptus oil from the weeping trees along the shore, turning the froth red.

Caleb walked the cold church aisle, passing under the stares of religious statues, immobile enemies waiting to strike. Their vacant eyes didn't move, though he was certain that they saw.

His chest seized, squeezing out his breath. *One of the marble figures held a dagger.*

He stumbled; the ceiling stretched high above him, vertigo sweeping in. Nausea hot on its heels. A similar sensation had overcome him the prior summer, when he and his clique of female friends had visited the Ballina Pool.

He'd climbed to the top of the highest waterslide but had been too frightened to go down it. He watched the water rushing down the blue fiberglass alley as the sky drained of color overhead. The blowing wind tried to make wings of his scrawny arms.

Jump. *Slide.* Fly. *Fall.*

His friends, whom he was always desperate to impress, had laughed.

Later, as the girls walked to the bus stop where they were to wait for their ride back to Evans Head, Caleb realized that he was walking on his own. Neither Mindy nor Sharon had told him to fall behind, yet somehow the order had been passed.

Caleb looked up at the statue again. The cold saint wasn't holding a dagger as he'd thought at first. No, the weapon in its hand was nothing more than a crucifix.

Whoa. You gotta keep your head on straight.

His mother sat among a small crowd in the front pew, watched over by Father Lewis, a man who scared him, despite being soft-spoken and mild. There was something in the way he held himself that Caleb found unnerving. He appeared so *removed* from everything. Owlish. It was as though he were waiting for something that anyone who didn't fawn over him wasn't enlightened enough to know about.

Caleb cleared his throat, silenced their prayers. They turned to face him and the pews creaked protest. Father Lewis raised his eyes. They were the color of the ocean around those parts: steel blue, but threaded with imperfections, the wavering silhouettes of sharks.

"Ma?"

These people were strangers to Caleb, even though he knew them by name and went to school with their children. He knew they were the kind of folk who didn't connect with those who contradicted their views.

Doubting's as good as sin, he'd been told by his mother, a woman who took her faith straight up, no chaser. And Caleb could tell that they smelled that doubt on him. Were the words I'M NOT REALLY SURE IF I GET THIS ENTIRE RELIGION THING tattooed across his forehead? Caleb figured that they might as well be, as there was no sympathy to be found in any of their expressions.

"Ma?"

Caleb knew that a lot could be said with very little, as the day at the Ballina Pool had proved. Like the girls he'd tried so hard to please, his mother didn't have to say a thing. She'd already turned her attention back to the one thing that counted in her books: the Book on her lap.

Crucifixes sometimes become daggers.

Wind blew hard off the coast and flowed into the church through the big open doors. Father Lewis's smock billowed, revealing the outline of his wiry frame; the goose bumps prickling thirteen-year-old Caleb Collins's arms had nothing to do with that breeze.

"You're not coming with me, are you?" he asked.

5

Dean Collins, an imposing man with a handlebar mustache and a gout-ridden leg, noticed that his daughter was gone from the tent just before sunset. The search had taken its toll. He leveled sugarcane for a living, and his body was as though carved from stone. It now looked half its size. Withered by fear.

He'd circled Chinaman's Beach and was almost back to where they had begun. From his current position, crouched in the V between two boulders, he could see the blue tent behind the fence near the cliff face. State Emergency Service volunteers were to his left, two baby-faced police officers on his right—local boys whom Dean had known for years. Boys refusing to look him in the eye.

A violent storm had thrashed the coastline two weeks

prior, and as a result, the landscape looked either half-destroyed or only half-built. *The kind of place God just don't care about no more,* Dean thought. He shook his head and watched tendrils of mist curl around his ankles.

The shotgun was heavy in his hands, cocked and fully loaded. His breath blew over the double barrels, making a faint tooting sound. "Please, *please,* bring me back my little girl."

A hand landed on his shoulder. Dean tensed but didn't jump. He faced Clover, a man his own age who just happened to look a hell of a lot older. His huge, dark-skinned hands were covered in scars of different sizes, care of snakebites and saw wounds. And yet whenever Clover opened his mouth to speak, a thin and uncertain voice wavered out, with all the strength and substance of smoke. He'd been born Gordon Dunne, but christened Clover by his mates. He was "Shamrock Aboriginal", a heritage he was very proud of, hence the nickname.

"Dean-o. We've checked long and hard. I don't think she's here."

"You're wrong."

"Mate—"

"I said she's *here.*" The wind howled, flapping the thin remainders of what had once been Dean's proud, thick hair. "Girl's got grit. I guess it's easy to see what you don't got in yourself when you see it in others, 'specially kids."

"Dean-o, settle down."

"She's still just a kid. That's why she strayed; it's what they do. Damn it, Janine and I have lost her half a dozen times in shopping centers. It happens to everyone. You can't be everywhere at once."

"You're only one guy."

"She's smart, Clover. That's why she's alive."

"I know. I never said she wasn't, it's just—"

"I was reading in the tent," Dean said, flat and stern. "Caleb was still sleeping. The sun was going down. I called out to her but she never came."

"We'll find her and bring her home. You should turn in. Go to the missus and your boy."

"I'm staying put, Clover."

"Listen to me. I've known you for twenty years. You's family, through thick and thin. You've helped me out when nobody else gave half a shit, not even my folks. Everything I got, I got you to thank for. So now it's my turn to ante up, okay? Mate, I know you don't want to hear this, but you've got to let me make this easier for you. Go home. You shouldn't be here."

"Fuck you, 'I shouldn't be here'. Pftt!"

You don't want me here because you don't want me to see her body on the rocks. Or facedown in the water, pigtails floating around her head.

Clover stepped close enough for Dean to smell his odor: part sugarcane, part alcohol.

"Mate," Dean said, clutching the gun as though for life. "In '65 my parents parked their XK Falcon on the shoulder of a road, just out of Evans. You know the road. They stopped to poach a rabbit that'd ducked out in front of them. The old girl took a burlap sack out of the back and stood near the car, while my dad loaded his pistol with buckshot. It'd rained the day before and the earth was sloppy. Stupid bastards, shoulda known better. The car slid in the mud and rolled, killing her first. Dad didn't stand a chance. Fuckin' rabbit got away."

"Dean—"

"My girl's out here, lost somewhere. Clover, I'm coming back for her. I don't want her to think I've left her, not even for a second. I'll never stop. Not now, not never."

6

Trees sheltered a path overgrown with lantana vine, whose bright flowers were inked by darkness. Amity spared a quick look over her shoulder at the tent where her sister and father were sleeping and stepped forward. She didn't take the time to think of where she was going, or what might happen to her if she got lost.

"Gonna go exploring, it's gonna be fun. Fun, fun, de-dum-de-dum," she mumbled as she stepped through the hollow of scrub. The wind rattled the vines around her. Amity screwed up her face; the lantana smelled like cat pee.

Thinking about fairies and singing about Carmen Sandiego helped her take her mind off the musky stink. And then, without warning, a cloud of orange dust exploded from beneath her feet and shot up her nose. The ground had given way. A landslide of soil and scattering ants carried her through the cloud and into open air. Rocks. Flashes of gray waves. Screaming seagulls. Amity slammed against a narrow outcropping, cried out. Her little fingers scraped against the boulders. Barnacles lent grip to her sneakers. She shivered. Petrified. Amity felt the crevice of the cave's opening on her right and shuffled inside.

Before she had a chance to brush the ants from her hair, kamikaze bats began to squeal, flying circles in the small space before crashing into the rocks and dropping to the ground. Twitching and broken. Survivors flapped their leathery wings and jittered out into the dark.

Once Amity had wiped the dirt from her eyes and saw that the radio she kept tied to her wrist was now in pieces between her knees, she began to whine. Picking up the shards of plastic, one by one, paved the way for tears that carved lines through her soiled cheeks.

Amity didn't wonder where she was, didn't think about how she was going to escape—there was only the fresh sting of awareness: her most cherished possession had been destroyed, and not all the king's horses and all the king's men would ever put it back together again. As far as she was concerned, it was the end of all music. And what did she have to show for it? Just some broken plastic. A shoelace tied around a wrist that now served no purpose, other than reminding her of this, the great loss of her life.

"Oh no, no, no."

The lead bitch bounded from the dark and latched its jaws onto her thigh. Teeth sank through her denim jeans and tore at *the flesh beneath. Blood squirted up onto the pink frills of her torn shirt.*

Pain.

Pain unlike anything she'd ever imagined.

Pain so strong she saw it as a very real, very distinct color. And that color was RED. It was like looking into the sun; it blocked out everything else. The cave was gone, as were the broken pieces of radio, even the dogs. There was only RED, boiling and alive.

Amity wondered, where was the Papa-Jesus she'd heard so much about? Her mother always said that he was everywhere and in everything, but that was so hard to understand. Wasn't Papa-Jesus an old man with a long white beard, as he was in the pictures she saw at school? An old man like that couldn't be everywhere at once—that was just silly, just like the name "God". Papa-Jesus made more sense to her, even if his absence did not.

So maybe he's a ghost.

But ghosts were mean and hung around old houses, so that couldn't be right.

What about Baby-Jesus, then? What's the difference between Baby-Jesus and Papa-Jesus? Baby-Jesus was a real person once, wasn't he? So he's like a friendly ghost? Like Casper. Does Baby-Jesus help his pa get around, kind of like the elves that help Santa in the North Pole? How does he hear everyone's prayers?

Wait, Santa Claus isn't Baby-Jesus, is he?

It was all so confusing. But through this confusion— through the RED—came that frightening question again: if Papa-Jesus was everywhere, then where was he now?

He's not playing by the rules, she told herself. *And I know that 'cause little girls aren't supposed to get hurt.*

7

Caleb sprinted through his house and into the kitchen, stopping at the table in the middle of the room. Envelopes with phone messages scribbled across their faces, shopping receipts and old bills that his parents had doodled over—all went flying through the air. Though his face was flushed bright red with panic, his eyes were dark and focused.

They aren't here!

He dragged a chair to the refrigerator, stood on the seat and reached up. Magnets that had been holding newspaper clippings and report cards in place shook free and scattered across the linoleum.

Be careful, boy. You shouldn't be doing this. You were told to stay put.

Caleb stretched over the top of the refrigerator, shuffling dust and forgotten trinkets—a Vegemite jar full of sewing needles, a ball of twine. He heard the jingle of keys brushing against his fingertips before he saw them.

Gotchya.

He limped down the hallway toward the front door. He'd left it open. Leaves waltzed across the carpet, carried on the wind.

Don't go any farther, whispered a little voice in his head. *You're going to get in so much trouble.*

But he didn't listen—he hardly ever did—and ran into the still-foggy morning instead. Caleb saw the limbs of neighboring trees fading out of the gray wash, the sliver of the dark road. The Holden was still in the driveway. He hobbled over to it, slipped behind the wheel.

"Holy shit!" he said, looking down at the dashboard, knowing the word was something he shouldn't say. But it didn't matter; the guys at school said far worse things. They even dropped the f-bomb sometimes—the dreaded word that got you sent to detention quick-smart.

His fingers were shaking so hard he struggled to get the key in the ignition. *I've seen Ma and Pa do this a thousand times—it can't be that hard!*

"Stop fighting me," Caleb told the car. He closed his eyes, took a breath and funneled all of his focus into his fingers. Then, as though the key had been listening, it slid into place with a satisfying *click*. Caleb turned it so hard he could hear the crack of his wrist bones. "I did it! I did!" The engine revved and roared. He lifted his foot off the clutch and the Holden lurched. Stalled.

Caleb peered in the rear-vision mirror and saw his reflection hunched over the gigantic wheel. It all looked so *wrong*. He was a teenager doing something that teenagers should never do—it was so much worse than swearing. He was driving a car without ever having been trained. And he'd seen enough episodes of *Degrassi Junior High* to know what happened to kids who drove without a license.

Can teenagers go to jail? I'm not sure, but I think so.

The engine rolled again. Sweat dripped over his lips and onto his tongue.

He saw himself in a white room, face lined with shadows from the window bars. Sitting on the bed. Bound ankles. There were no sports posters on those walls. And even worse: no telephone.

The car zoomed backward at an angle, ran into the garden and bounced over the curb. The postbox cracked in half and twirled through the air.

He had no idea where the second car came from. Where seconds before there had been just a blank slate of fog, there was now a wall of rushing metal.

The station wagon clipped the Holden's tail, sending it spinning into the wattle tree near the property line. The sounds were intense: screaming tires, folding metal, the tinkle of glass fragments bouncing across bitumen. Pollen stained the mist. Leaves blanketed the windshield.

Caleb's heart thrashed within his chest. There was no pain. Yet. He straightened himself and looked in the rear-vision mirror again, the scented pine-tree card arcing back and forth beneath it. A jet of hot blood squirted across the dashboard. His nose had been punched flat.

8

Dean Collins followed his daughter's cries. Clover was close behind. Crabs scurried from their hiding spots as the two men forced themselves between the rocks. The shotgun was gripped tight in Dean's hands.

Emergency volunteers crept down the incline—not an easy task, considering the fog glare. Wind whooshed off the ocean and carried the stink of salt and rotting things over their heads and through the town.

Clover watched his best friend draw closer to the cave. "Go slow, Dean-o!"

They were descending at such a speed that it would make stopping difficult. He'd only seen Dean run like this once before, and that was on the morning of Caleb's birth. They had been cutting cane in Queensland—a rare freelance stint, cash in hand—when the call came through that Janine had gone into labor. Clover would never forget the shock on the man's face. *I knew this would happen*, that expression seemed to say. *I knew this would happen but I took the job anyway. What kind of husband am I?*

"Slow down!"

Between the swooping birds, the slimy rocks beneath their feet and Dean's gout-ridden leg, it was no surprise that his best friend fell. Clover heard Dean's ankle snap and watched, helpless, as the bone shot up through the skin. Dean toppled to his knees, and in an instinctive jerk that would cost him his life, drew the shotgun close to his chest.

A fist-size burst of light sparked so bright in Clover's eyes that it lingered when he blinked, dancing in the dark. Dean's head was gone. A mushroom cloud of skull pieces and brain exploded through the air, carried by the wind. It painted Clover's face.

The corpse rolled over the outcropping, fell ten feet and landed on hard-packed sand, ass first, as though sitting upright. The spine snapped in half and stabbed up through his shoulder. Twin fans of blood and shit burst from each trouser leg. Dean's body slumped to the side, convulsed and went still.

Clover could feel life draining from him, and watched the wavering hand at the end of his wrist, the fingers curling inward. Defeated. "Dean," he said. Flat. Toneless. There was blood diamonded in his whiskers. The dogs in the nearby cave started barking again, more ferocious this time.

"*Help me!*" came a voice.

The shotgun, slick with gore, was wedged between two rocks five feet away.

The feral dogs yelped, snapping their heads toward the gunshot. Amity was still fighting the cockroaches; their pursuit of warmth was relentless.

The lead bitch swung around to face Amity and lowered its head. She saw its long, stained teeth. The gunshot had distracted the dog from its desire to possess the girl-meat, but not for long. This wasn't the first animal the pack had cornered and toyed with before the sport wore thin and that desperate need to eat took over.

Amity watched the shadow plunge over the cave entrance and sat upright, still scratching cockroaches off her arms. Wind blew again, creating a vacuum within the narrow crevice that made her hair flare around about her head. She forgot about the dogs, the cockroaches, the RED pain, and the shattered radio, which she missed above all else. There was just that shadow, too big and well defined in that pale light to be anything other than a man.

"Pa!"

The two dogs near the entrance leaped and snapped, thrilled by the excitement. Nothing worked them into frenzy quite like defending something. The lead bitch refused to take her piercing green eyes off the meat. Her

26

hair stood on end, hindquarters tensed in readiness to pounce. She'd made the small pink creature fear and tremble—and that was good. Fear shook the meat from the bones.

It made them sweeter.

Amity watched the heavy industrial torch twirl through the air and snap one of the two dogs across the nose. It howled and turned, its tail between its legs, and ran into the rocky labyrinth outside the cave. It didn't make it very far before its long, untended claws lost their grip on the barnacles and it dropped out of sight.

The torch shattered against the cave wall. Cockroaches swarmed over the bulb shards and plastic casing, too dumb to recognize their disappointment when no warmth or food was discovered.

Amity wanted to scream again, only out of happiness this time. *Someone's come to rescue me!* She wanted to jump up and down, to clap her hands like she did when her first grade teacher told her class that prizes would be awarded for the best crayon drawing—but she didn't. The doggy's eyes were still locked on her. And even worse, she could only see the man's lower half, which raised a question she hadn't considered before that exact moment: *were those even her pa's trousers?* Maybe, maybe not. He did wear big, heavy boots like those to work, but there was something about the way her rescuer walked that struck her as decidedly not-like-Pa.

But doubt didn't matter, not in the end. "Help me, please!" she screamed anyway. "I'm in here! *Wait, watch out—*"

The dogs leaped at the person who might or might not be her father. She watched those boots—which might or might not have belonged to the man who had said yes to her camping requests, who had vowed to keep her safe when she woke up at night, afraid of the monsters living in her closet—rise up and strike the smaller dog in the stomach, driving it from sight.

The bitch knew that they were not alone, but no longer cared. There was only the meat. She would rather die than let someone else come along and snatch it away.

Clover hunched down, inserted the gun into the yard-wide crevice and took aim. "Wolf, ya fuckah!" he yelled. A chill crawled through him. Random memories crashed around in his head.

Dean Collins running through the sugarcane field, his skin blackened by dirt.

His two-bedroom house on Cashmore Lane. The renovations that never seemed to get finished. A series of tarpaulins forever fighting northwesterly winds.

Janine Collins at church one Christmas Eve. She'd been fanning herself with a doubled-over community newsletter. They had made eye contact, only Janine had turned away.

Clover pulled the trigger and the dark cave bloomed white. The dog flew against the wall, its intestines spelling words in the air before splattering against a bed of insects. "I got you! I got you, bitch!"

He stuck his head farther into the cave and saw the girl huddled on the floor—moving. Only now did he realize the dice he'd taken the risk of rolling. Had he aimed a little to the right, it might have been little Amity Collins lying there in a bloodied mess and not the wolf—

Not a wolf, Clover. There ain't no wolves on this land. This was a dog. A big, mean fucker, too.

And you killed it. You tore it a new asshole. You're a fucking hero.

Clover stepped back into the gray and stood, those bones that were just too stubborn to align right cracking again. "Down here, fellas," he called. "Goddammit, I found her." Clover's hoarse voice broke on the final word.

Her. Amity—whose father was dead.

His blood's all over me. Christ, Dean-o's gone.

The cloud of blood floating toward him like a slow-moving shadow, only once this shadow had passed over him, he didn't feel the familiar cold that shade brings. Instead, it had been warm.

"We're coming!" Disembodied calls coming from nowhere, from everywhere. "Hold in there!"

Clover crawled back into the cave. *Stinks of rot in here.* And even worse was the reverberating thrum of the ocean, the sound distorted into something almost soporific; he struggled to keep his eyes open. All he wanted to do was escape into the fresh air, lay his head against the rocks and sleep, but he forged on instead, the cockroaches parting before him, scurrying back into their dank hiding spots. And then he saw Dean's little girl, lying on the rock, facing away from him with her hands cupped to the sides of her head.

"Amity?"

Clover touched the fatherless child's arm, his hand so dark against her sugary skin, only to have her shy away. The small part of him that believed in the good of the world, in fairness and in justice, withered inside him and was never known to live there again.

The girl faced him and he saw her eyes. They were wide. Confused. Hands plastered against her ears, blood gushing from between the fingers.

A ray of light so strong it glimmered on the ocean floor drew fish into play on the surface. It was like Papa-Jesus himself had wiped away the fog—as though it were little more than a layer of dust he could breathe life into later—to reveal the blue beneath.

9

There was no sound; there was nothing.

Amity Collins was on the rigid hospital bed, the sheets wrapped around her. She held her shaking right hand close to her ear, clicking. *Clicking.*

There was no sound; there was nothing.

She could tell that she was humming, could feel the vibrations in her throat, buzzing and then stopping. The fact that she couldn't hear anything didn't stop her from doing it anyway.

A year before, Amity had explored the crawl space under their house. It was a dusty wasteland of moldy cardboard boxes, bricks and rotting planks of wood. She always thought it was fun to explore there, despite being frightened the entire time. It was the kind of place where monsters might live, like those on the covers of the *Goosebumps* books her brother was always reading, or the kind that came out of her closet when nobody else was looking.

But there might be fairies too. That concept had made her smile.

Amity had been about to carry her grimy self out of the crawl space when she noticed cobwebs quivering between the wooden beams above her head. There were dead bugs trapped in the cottony strands. Amity touched the wood, and even though she couldn't hear the washing machine in the laundry, she knew her mother had put in a load on account of the vibrations.

The vibrations in her throat felt the same way.

There was no sound; there was nothing. And she was afraid.

Her mother's lips were moving, but she couldn't make out the words. Amity got the impression that she was being asked a question, so she nodded anyway. *Does Ma want to know if I'm okay? Is she asking if I'm scared?* She didn't want to answer that one. All she wanted was to be back in her room and play with her toys, maybe doodle in her coloring-in books. She was halfway through *The Hamburglar Gets Away*, which her pa had bought for her at the McDonald's in Lismore. Amity liked going outside the lines, adding speech bubbles, and didn't care that she sometimes used the wrong colors, that sometimes her skies were pink, and Ronald was blue and green, not yellow and red.

A PLACE FOR SINNERS

Click. Click.

Amity was beginning to understand that she was deaf. She was easing into the concept, wielding a childlike acceptance no adult could match.

Amity had no idea how long she'd been inside the hospital. It felt like years. She wondered when she would have to go back to school, if people would recognize her. Would all of the other kids still ask her to go and hide with them in the Love Tunnel at the back of the playground near the gum trees they'd carved their names into, or play afternoon hopscotch on the footpath while they waited for their bus to arrive, or ask her over for sleepovers where they would watch the same movies over and over again, and dress up in their older siblings' clothes?

All she knew was that her bandages were starting to itch the skin beneath. She wanted to rip them off, but the doctor-lady had scolded her the last time she'd tried.

Amity longed for a distraction. Anything. The collection of toys her mother had brought in no longer worked its spell; the same with the boring, dog-eared books that one of the nurses had given her. There was a television in the corner of the room, but the volume must have been switched off because she couldn't hear the sound.

No, it's not. You just can't hear anymore, silly-billy.

She sighed, playing with her Raggedy Ann doll. One of her button eyes was gone.

My ears are broken.

Amity with her ear pushed flush against the perforated speaker of her radio, toying with the My Little Pony stickers she'd stuck to the back to keep the battery hatch closed. Music flowed into her ears, into her body. She breathed the lyrics out.

Time had slowed, and she guessed it would only get worse now that she would never hear music again. She tried to remember the last song that she had listened to but couldn't remember.

31

Amity wondered how old the woman sitting next to her mother was. She looked youngish, but had an uptight quality that betrayed her smile. It aged her.

Maybe fifty? Nah, not that much.

Seven-year-old Amity Collins was of an age when any adult was either twenty or fifty. These were the numbers that stuck; it didn't occur to her that people could be anything but. But she was inquisitive. So she asked.

She could tell from the look on their faces that the words were coming out wrong. Amity thumped her hands against the mattress and scrunched up her face. Sometimes, all she wanted to do was cry, but she refused to crumble. She wasn't in kindergarten anymore; she was a Big Girl now, and Big Girls don't cry. Those were the rules.

The younger woman leaned forward in her chair. She held a set of cards in her hands.

Is this a game? Well, I don't want to play. So there!

Amity exhaled, crossed her arms. She studied the row of purple bruises across her skin, as pronounced as the flower print on the "good skirt" her mother insisted she wear to church every Sunday. She hated that skirt. Amity liked her pink one much better. A smile flirted with her face—there was at least one good thing about being stuck in hospital: she didn't have to go to borin'-ole-church!

A hand landed on her ankle, and Amity flinched, unable to help it.

The lead bitch, her lips pulled back to reveal her black gums. Teeth.

The image of the dog receded as her mother stroked her ankle. Amity looked at the worn face attached to the hand, watched the overpronounced nod. A forced, draining grimace.

Ma is magic, Amity reminded herself. *She makes the bad stuff go away.*

Clouds passed over the sun and the room dimmed. The television had been switched off for the meeting;

there were grimy handprints across the black screen. A ring of dying flowers and get-well notes circled the bed, a barricade from truth.

The young woman, who might have been old—maybe twenty but *na-aaahhh*, not fifty—lifted the placards in her hands, and with a tilt of her head, cracked the bones in her neck.

SNAP.

I heard that! Amity brightened, gripping the bedsheets.

No, you didn't. You think you heard it, is all.

It was then that Amity understood that there was a link between what she saw and what she had been programmed to hear. The memory of a sound—its echo— didn't cut through the silence; it was linked to something on the other side. And that felt wonderful. Amity was positive it was its own kind of magic, a quiet kind.

The woman held up the card. It read: **HI!**

Amity gave a halfhearted wave. The woman smiled and handed the card to her mother.

AMITY read the second card. The woman pointed her index finger at the little girl.

Ah-huh. That's my name, don't wear it out. I know how to read, you know. And I can write my name too. But I get the T and Y confused sometimes and I switch them 'round. I've got my name spelled out on my desk at school, so I can lift up the lid and double check. You know, just in case.

The woman handed the second card to her mother, who dropped it and began to cry. Amity wanted to cross the linoleum between them and give her a hug.

Please don't cry, Ma. Please.

The woman held up a third card: **L-U-C-Y** and then pointed at herself. Amity saw the letters floating around in her head and concentrated hard, screwing up her face. She felt the random shapes fall into form, creating a name.

Hi, Lucy, what are you doing here?

Amity liked sounding out words. It made her smile.

Lucy, are you going to make the sound come back so I can listen to my music?

A fourth card: a picture of an ear. A fifth: a picture of an ear with a red line drawn through it.

Lucy pointed at Amity, who understood but could only blink in response. Amity took a deep breath and held it, cupping her mouth.

She wished she were swimming with Caleb at the Ballina Pool. Caleb was the best brother in the world. She imagined herself leaping into the shallow end—even though she knew she wasn't supposed to—with the big blue rushing up to meet her. And then there would be the splash, a bolt of cold water exploding around her. The chlorine would make her eyes sting. And then she would be floating, weightless. Silent. Caleb would be right there beside her, making sure she didn't go under.

Lucy produced a sixth card: A heart stencil, which the woman pointed at and then followed with a gesture toward her mother. Amity could see that the twentysomething's hands were shaking.

A seventh card: A Xeroxed photograph of Amity's father glued to the board, the adhesive warping one corner.

A bolt of longing shot through the seven-year-old, the kind of longing designed for daughters to feel for their fathers. She wanted his big, calloused hands to snatch up her own, wanted him to squeeze her fingers. His stubble brushing against her as he kissed her between her eyes. She loved how she never had to work for his affection; he made her feel brave enough to wander on her own.

"There's no such things as monsters, sweetheart. And even if there were, I'd catch them all up for you and lock them away. I'd keep you safe as houses."

"Pa," she tried to say.

Again, a cloud passed by outside and the window burned bright. It didn't last. The wind blew and the clouds rolled back. A draft plucked wilted petals from the older flowers, scattered them.

Amity could tell that the woman named Lucy didn't want to be there; she almost looked angry.

Please, let me go home, Amity wanted to say to her. *This place scares me.*

Lucy shook her head and laid the final boards flat across her knees. Her mother's movements were quick and finite, and reminded Amity of the giant cobra in the movie *Aladdin*—a favorite rewatch among the sleepover crowd. *I want to get in a blanky and sit in front of the TV and watch cartoons all day. I'm sick. That's what sick kids do. Oh, maybe someone will get me some ice cream from the shops down the street!*

Her mother snatched up the two remaining boards from Lucy's lap and flipped them over, causing the twentysomething to scowl, get up and prepare to leave.

Oh, don't go. I like you. You have a friendly face and pretty hair and you smell nice.

Lucy stopped, one hand on the door frame and the other rubbing the flushed underside of her neck. Amity thought the woman looked like she was going to cry too. She hoped she wouldn't; that would make her very sad.

On the second-to-last sheet there was another photocopy. This one of Baby-Jesus, bearded in black and white, with his eyes cast upward. Amity watched her mother's finger point at the image, her face stern and pale. Tears were now growing fat at the tip of her nose. Amity tried so hard to understand what was being said, but couldn't make sense of the goldfish *smack* of her mother's lips.

Pa, where are you?

The finger moved from the image of her father and the image of the Son.

Stop. I'm scared—

Fingers slammed on the pictures in frustration. Dean to Christ, over and over.

Ma, I don't get it.

Dean to Christ. Back and forth, each strike harder and faster.

Pa and Baby-Jesus. Wait, Pa is Jesus?

STOP!

Pa's with Baby-Jesus? What, is that what you're trying to say?

Amity flinched, even though she couldn't hear the shrillness of the adults' voices. She pulled the funny-smelling sheet across her knees up to her chin. *Why am I in trouble? What did I do? MA! Make it all go away.*

Amity couldn't tell if she was screaming the words out loud or if they were only bouncing around in her head. Nothing made sense. She couldn't feel the vibrations as she had before.

Amity watched her mother get up out of her chair, drop the final card to the floor and leave the room. Her bulk slammed against the woman named Lucy as she forced herself through the doorway. Amity peered at the floor and saw the final upturned placard on the linoleum. It was another image of a heart, in color this time. And that color was RED.

10

A little girl lost in the fog. A story for the gossipers of Evans Head to spin.

Dean Collins was buried in a closed coffin, watched over by hundreds of the town's population crammed into the narrow church pews, spilling out the front archway onto the footpath. There was a swarm of television crews that a group of locals chased off.

"Show some respect for the dead!" they screamed. "Leave us alone."

Us. The tremors of the tragedy had rippled through them, and as a result, they had come together. The people of Evans Head were sometimes mean, they sometimes schemed, and like most folks in most places, being judgmental came easy. But on the other hand—and oh what a hand it often proved to be—they could be beautiful.

Amity watched them, just as she had watched the coffin lid, with a reverential eye. The wood of that strange man-sized box had been so dark, almost stony. She knew what was inside, meat with all the meaning scooped out. And although she had caught herself looking around for her father amongst the crowd once or twice through the service, Amity understood what was happening, even though her mother didn't seem to think she did. This was Pa's funeral and all of the people around her were crying for *him*. Each held an image in their mind of who and what he was to them—the workmate in the sugarcane field, the beer-buddy, the best friend. None of these impressions were wrong and all should be held up and honored, but not a single one came close to who the dead body in the coffin was to her.

Pa. Just Pa. A single syllable, a world entire.

And he was gone. The stony coffin lid was not going to rise, revealing him sitting there with a cheeky grin on his face as he yelled "Gotchya, ya silly buggers!" Not a chance.

She understood.

Father Lewis bent down to stare Amity in the face after the ceremony and spoke words that she didn't have a chance of understanding. She watched his lips, saw the glint of his teeth. His tongue was in there too, like a piece of half-chewed-up meat. Amity felt fear closing in, and its presence made her breath quicken. She clung to the hem of her mother's skirt. The clouds had grown thick and heavy, and Amity wondered if it was going to storm.

Will the winds blow and rip off people's roofs?

Will the headstones shoot up into the sky? That would be weird.

Only no, it wouldn't just be weird. It would be scary. So scary that Amity caved in to her own rules and began to cry. Terror was the wind: just because it could not be seen did not mean it was not there.

What if the storm rips up the ground and pulls Pa out of that box?

Amity nuzzled against her mother's side and was disappointed when all she received was a cold pat to the top of her head. She'd been hoping for a hug, a kiss. So Amity asked for one aloud, but she had no way of knowing that the words were indecipherable, or that her mother was embarrassed by her attempt.

Amity turned to Caleb. He was hugging himself. His bandaged face looked wet.

I think he's been crying too.

It was all so hard to understand—her father was dead and was with Baby-Jesus. Wasn't that a good thing?

Isn't this what's supposed to happen?

There were no answers. There were just all of those faces bending down close to hers. They came at her from every direction, each bringing with them different scents. Sweat. Cologne. Huge hands grabbed her shoulders and spun her around. Wet eyes. Crooked, yellow teeth. Sour punches of breath.

She pulled away from them and ran through the cemetery, a veil of rain chasing close behind. She was no match for its speed, and the storm doused her to the bone. Amity wondered if she was steaming. Everything felt too hot. She took off her shoes and threw them at an old angel statue on her right. They bounced off cracked, unflinching features. Amity gasped.

Drowning. Drowning.

Fingers touched her elbow. She turned and saw her brother, panting and afraid. He glared at her as though he didn't know what to say or do. So he simply pulled her into a hug instead. Amity felt his pulse on her cheek.

Isn't this what's supposed to happen?

This final question wouldn't be answered until the seven-year-old returned to school, as she watched the wave of parents coming to pick up the other students. There she would stand, the only one left on the hopscotch squares, head slightly tilted to one side. Not all the longing in the world would make her father walk through that gate, not all the longing in the world. This wasn't what was supposed to happen. She was different now and always would be.

CHAPTER TWO

Caleb

1

THERE WERE STORIES about Dean Collins in a number of the newspapers, and the same photograph from the social worker's flash card wound up next to all of the articles. One by one, Janine scissored them into Memory Lane albums she kept in her closet, which was still full of her dead husband's clothes.

Photographs from Amity's first communion were also within the albums. The faded yellow wash of the Polaroid didn't do her daughter's dress justice. So many people had commented on how beautiful she'd looked that day, with Janine nodding through their remarks, accustomed to hearing their thinly veiled pity.

On another page: Caleb's sports ribbons. Strips of cheap cotton in a spectrum of colors trapped under wax paper.

There was another cutout, only the edges of the trim were not as neatly aligned as those of the other stories. This article looked as though it had been excised from the newspaper in a hurry, or in secret. The story was about Dean's best friend, Clover, whom Janine never spoke to again. And it wasn't as though she'd never had the opportunity. He'd approached her at Dean's funeral, only to have her turn her back on him; he'd turned up drunk at their house in the middle of the night a week afterward. Janine had seen him through the parlor window, caught a whiff of his whiskey funk, and ignored his weeping. She'd almost called the police. Resisted. It was hard to articulate why she never wanted to see him again; the man had saved her daughter's life, after all. Perhaps it boiled down to Dean's relationship with the drunk, to her jealousy—that old, deep pain. But then again, maybe it was just because she didn't much like black people.

Clover hung himself from the rafters of his neighbor's shed. No suicide note, no good-bye. All he left behind were a series of unfinished renovations and the few tattered blue tarps shielding them from the weather.

Other photographs were tucked away in an old Quintero 25s Panetelas cedar cigar box, which had a rendering of a small island overlooked by a dawning sun on the lid. She had found it in the deposit bin at work and hadn't even bothered putting it into the inventory. The moment Janine laid eyes on the delicately painted palm trees, those exaggerated and almost biblical rays of sunshine, she'd known it would be perfect for hiding ugliness. The photos themselves were fading, unlike the scars they depicted. Doctors at the hospital had taken them during Caleb's stay, post-car crash. There had been no lasting damage to her son's nasal cavity or upper palate; just the crooked nose remained.

The cigar box collected dust in the bottom drawer of Janine's tallboy. She had only opened it three times. Once to tuck away the photos; again to throw in Dean's wedding and engagement rings; and another time to tuck away his weathered Sunday missal, which she found in the garage two summers after his death.

Janine never tossed anything away. Not then, and not in any of the following years.

Her small world was now crowded with trinkets, books and oddities, and it didn't take long for the Collinses' home to look like the back room of the thrift store she still worked in. Despite her children's protests, she continued to bring home other people's trash and make it her treasure.

"Ma, one of these days we're going to come home and find you buried under a collapsed pile of shit," Caleb had said more than once. "It's chaos in there."

"It's not shit. And it's certainly chaos," she would reply. "It's memories."

"Yeah, but Ma, only a portion of those memories are yours."

2

The counselor's office was crowded with messy papers and coffee cups. Motivational posters plastered the walls, screaming at Caleb to TRUST himself, to STOP WISHING AND START DOING. He both hated and loved coming to this cramped warren in Lismore's seedy backstreets, which was a half-hour drive from where he lived, still with his family on Yarran Street.

It was May 1, 2013. Caleb was twenty-six, and his father's headstone had been lost among the tumbleweeds and dusty fake flowers of the Evans Head graveyard for thirteen years. This was the same number of years that he'd been seeing help, starting with psychiatrists, continuing with court assigned social workers, and now community counselors.

"When Ma gets all distant, she might as well be in another country." Caleb knotted his hands across the taut pull of his tattered blue jeans; he'd bought them at his mother's thrift store because he couldn't see the sense in dishing out a hundred bucks for a new pair. The way he was dressed in general, with his signature plaid shirts and the Converse Chucks bound together with gaffer tape, not to mention the designer stubble, all contributed to an air of ruggedness that was instantly undermined by the fragility in his voice.

"Kids at school used to call me Monster Mash. And there was this one guy, Steve Grafton—who's now got three kids and a wife with a drug problem, by the way. Steve. Man, what a piece of work. He'd press a finger to his nose and would bend it sideways like it was the funniest thing ever. Strange thing was that everyone laughed anyway."

"Did you ever confront him?" the counselor asked.

"Confront him? I punched him square in the jaw!"

A cloud of dust on the sports field. Two crying kids, one more beaten than the other.

Caleb found a puppy on the way home from school that day. It was shivering and afraid, just like him, huddled in an alleyway near their house. It looked sick. He picked it up and cradled it. The puppy stuck out its pink tongue to lick his hand. It had only known him for two minutes and loved him already, leaving Caleb to wonder why people couldn't do the same. Did the dog care that his nose was out of joint, that he didn't fit in? No, it didn't.

He made it a bed out of cardboard boxes and lined it with some of his father's old T-shirts. The dog would live in their garage, and as far as he was concerned, his mother never need know. He fed it water from a Tupperware container and tried to get it to eat a couple of leftover sausages, but with no luck.

Amity kept her distance through it all. The little girl didn't like dogs very much. Caleb couldn't blame her.

"Well, if you're going to confront your mother, do us all a favor and don't punch out her lights, okay?"

"Dude, I so feel like doing it sometimes. Don't worry; I'm all talk. But I'm going to tell her about it tonight. It. Or maybe I'll wait until tomorrow. She gets in these moods after work. Oh, bugger, I don't know."

His counselor, Danny, looked tired—not bored. And to be honest, that was increasingly rare. Seasoned visitors to the Australian Mental Health system became very good at differentiating those who were good at their jobs from those who just didn't care.

Danny was different. There was nothing artificial about him, or controlled, plus he was relatively young, which helped. He was also kind of cute in his own nerdy way. But it was his deep, melancholy eyes that Caleb responded to the most, empathy without effort, leaving him to wonder if Danny was one of those counselors who entered the field because he'd once required the service of a counselor. Yeah, he'd met those kinds of people, too.

"What do you think her reaction's going to be?"

"Oh, Jesus. She's going to—damn, I don't know. Crumble." His voice faltered, but he straightened in his chair. Defiant. "It wouldn't be the first time, trust me. I don't care. But the tickets are booked. We're going."

"You really *don't* care?"

"Well, of course I do. I just say I don't." Rain pelted against the small window. "How can you sit in a room like this all the time, Danny? I'd go batshit crazy."

"You get used to it, and I don't know if I'd want anything more, really. If I had a bigger window I'd only end up staring through it all the time. Not a good habit, you know. Focus." He crossed his legs and laced his hands over one knee, an effeminate gesture.

Caleb smiled. "Can I ask you something?"

"Sure."

Caleb wanted to ask—despite his instincts being sharp and often correct—if his counselor was gay, too. Of course Danny knew about him, it was just that Disclosure Street, to his frustration, appeared to be a one-way road. Not that Caleb was *interested*, and it certainly didn't bother him, but he couldn't help but imagine that some of the other clients he passed in the hallways might find it uncomfortable, to say the least.

"Do you ever just want to cut and run?"

Danny smiled, semi-coy. "Not anymore. I'm a getting a little long in the tooth to start over again."

"Again?"

"We reinvent ourselves all the time. It's just that sometimes we make a decision to. It's a necessary evil. It's not running away, if that's what you mean, or are afraid of."

Lightning flashed so close the community center shook.

"Christ, that landed right outside," Danny said, and then returned his attention to his client. "You're not going away for forever. Your ma will survive."

He bent down to kiss the dog goodnight. It looked up at him with wide, shaking eyes. It didn't understand anything, and for that Caleb envied it. The next morning, he woke and tiptoed into the garage with a saucer of milk. The dog was dead.

"And you better get used to this rain, Caleb."

"Why's that?"

"Thailand would be coming close to its wet season, right? At least I think so."

"You've been there? Awesome. When'd you go?"

"God, a long time ago. Just after high school. I haven't traveled since. I find it very easy to admire those who do. Bottom line: color me green."

"Come with us, Danny! You, me and Amity, dancing in some sweaty bar, fighting off the lady boys and drinking Red Bull and vodka from a novelty-size bucket."

"Watching me dance is like watching one of those wacky, inflatable guys you see on those car dealership ads. It isn't pretty, trust me."

"Ah, don't worry about it. Being yourself means never having to be pretty," he said. Exhale. A short laugh. A beat of silence. "Tell me things are going to be okay with Ma. She wigs out easy, and when she does, she's like that crazy chick in *Misery*."

"Caleb, if I had a crystal ball I'd sit here and predict your future. And I'd charge you through the nose for it, too. But I don't, mate. Sorry, it just doesn't work that way. All I can do is look you in the eye and recommend that you be honest with her. That, and dump any sledgehammers you've got lying around. Pronto."

"Ha. You want to talk about honesty. Well, *honestly*, this is all a case of now or never. The timing is perfect. Amity and I are both single, so we're not leaving anyone behind. She's a graphic designer who works from home, plus she's managed to save up some funds; and my bosses have traveled in the past, so they totally understand and are flexible; they get that this is something we *need* to do. And that's such a blessing. Ha, and to think I ever doubted working at their Lismore practice."

"So how is work going at the moment?"

"It's good, but physiotherapy kind of plateaus out, you know."

"I'm sure it's a case of the people you work with keeping things interesting."

"Oh, for sure. And you know, they're good to me, which is a first. And even better, my job is secure. *See*, that's what I mean! Both Amity and me, the stars have aligned, but that won't always be the case. Gee, it makes me feel all butterflies-in-the-stomachish."

"Caleb, if I only had a mirror right now I could show you your face, and you'd know, beyond a doubt, that you're making the right decision."

"Thanks, mate. Mirrors, crystal balls, you got nothing, mate. Budget cuts, hey? But you're right. I know you are. What's the saying? The world is my oyster!"

"So don't be surprised if it makes you gag once in a while."

"True! Well, it doesn't have to be easy; it just has to happen. And what's the alternative? Staying in Evans Head forever? Not bloody likely, thanks. I really can't express how much I hate that place. Even the mention of our names gets all the old biddies chatting. '*Don't you go wandering, or you'll end up like poor Amity Collins.' 'Don't drive when you know you shouldn't, or you'll end up like crooked-nosed Caleb.*' It's awful. Oh, you wouldn't really get it—"

"I do, trust me. Some people are just too big for small towns. They don't understand that you and your sister didn't ask for your histories. So let them gossip among themselves, and feel safe in knowing that they live lives that are about as big as that damn town. Okay? Just don't snap and king-hit them like you did Steve Grafton. Biddies break easy."

Cool blue shadows ran the length of Caleb's face, over the crescent curve of his nose. "I think I'll miss our talks."

"You can always come back. That's the good thing about choices: you can always make the right one."

"I don't know if I will, Danny. There are very few people, besides Amity, that I really trust, and you're one of the... select few. And that's great! It's awesome having someone to talk to, but I, I, really don't like how, well, dependent I've become on it."

His counselor stilled. Nodded.

"Danny, you don't need a mirror to show me that I'm doing the right thing."

"So say it."

Caleb took another deep breath and his smile faded, revealing the serrated edge of emotion beneath. "We're going away, Amity and me. We're going to go away for six months, all through Southeast Asia, starting in Thailand. Our tickets are booked. You can't change our minds."

"Good," Danny said, punctuating the word by slamming down his coffee mug. He crossed the room in three strides and opened the door. "Now go tell your mother that."

3

Moths beat at the window, hungry for light and desperate to escape the rain. The electronic clock beside Amity's bed splashed a soft, red 10:48 p.m. across her face. She sighed, rolled onto her side and stared at a crack in the wall.

The day had been hot and the roads steamed when the rain arrived, forming an eerie mist that stunk of wet earth and ozone. As it crept in through her bedroom window and into her lungs, it unlocked memories hidden inside with shapeless fingers.

The echo of a gunshot. A hurt that never healed.

She traced the crack with a fingertip as lightning flashed, throwing enormous, writhing moth shadows over the wall, over the calendar on its hook. Landmark dates branded with crosses: a dentist appointment, the last of her pretravel vaccinations. She didn't bother marking down her twentieth birthday; it was still two calendar pages away. After all, there would be no big party this year, not in Australia anyway. Amity dropped her hand and studied her fingernails, each of which were painted a different color, as though in an attempt to express a facet of her personality she couldn't enunciate with her voice.

Fights were the hardest conversations to understand. Hand signs lost in waves of emotion, forcing her to have to lip-read, which she *was* good at—within reason.

Mouths opening and closing, cracked lips pulling back to cry as hand-signals floundered in the air and died.

Uu. Annt. Eee. Mee. These were the syllables she'd caught. "*You can't leave me.*"

These silent words cut through her. Guilt for blood.

Eeee.

"*Please.*"

Amity and Caleb's conversation with their mother about their upcoming travel plans had not gone well, culminating in Janine's storming from the kitchen. They hadn't really expected otherwise, just hoped. Caleb had reached across the table and taken his sister's hand. A little "stay strong" squeeze. And Amity had needed the reassurance as she stood and stalked down the hallway into her mother's room, the labyrinth of junk. The stench of old newspapers and musty boxes clawed at her sinuses, sending her into a sneezing fit she couldn't hold in.

There were old dolls with missing eyes and beaten-in faces. A mounted deer's head lay sideways across a harpsichord that no longer worked. Hundreds of books piled high in crooked towers. Records. Odd shoes. Paintings, all of which looked as though drawn from the same sun-bleached palette. It all didn't just make Amity angry; no, it went so much further than that. It depressed her.

The four-post bed sat in the middle of the room. It was rare that Amity ever saw it made, and that night had been no exception. Her mother sat there, surrounded by tissues, the Memory Lane volumes on the knotted blankets beside her. Rosary in hand.

It took five minutes for her mother to soften; only then did the book close. The stalemate was over.

Sitting there, saying nothing, Amity was reminded of the first few signs she'd been taught in those Auslan lessons they had taken as a family.

Left hand palm up, as though receiving Eucharist. The fingers of the right hand touching slightly. Thrust forward.

This was the sign for "help".

Palms up. Thumb to fingers pinched together. The knuckles of each hand just touching. And then let them go and drop.

The sign for "lost".

Lightning flashed again, illuminating the bookshelves in Amity's room, where titles like *Living in Silence*, *Hearing for All*, and *The Quiet Place* were on display. There were work concept sketches on butcher paper (Amity was best when using charcoal and ink; paints could be so messy), a corkboard pinned with photographs from her years at Saint Catherine's School For Hearing Impaired Children.

A car drove by outside, sending the room into swirls of light.

Amity couldn't remember what vehicles sounded like, but she knew she missed it. She sensed this absence every day, and that loss had a color.

BLUE.

She pulled her cell phone out from under her pillow and scanned her e-mail account, making sure there weren't any work offers. There weren't any, just a winding ream of spam that made her feel inadequate about her penis size— and she didn't even have one! Discovering nothing of worth in her account was okay—she had enough jobs lined up to carry her through the four weeks before leaving—so she logged onto Facebook instead and swiped through her news feed. She had 1,251 friends, and only half as many followers on Twitter, but she didn't mind. It felt good to be liked, even by strangers. The important thing for her was that she didn't know any of these people.

Amity was very careful to never add schoolmates, coworkers or relatives, and it also helped that the majority of them had jumped the Facebook ship and now bled their hearts out on Kik. All good with her. Minimize the risk. It was important that none of her "friends" or "followers" knew that she was deaf. Online, she was no different from anyone else. Only once had she ever disclosed the truth to someone in that murky cyber swamp, someone whom she went on to meet in person, which was an indulgence she'd never allow herself again.

The family photograph was gathering dust on her bedside table. Her father, his face bathed in red light from the clock display, looked happy. Amity was sitting on his shoulders, the sun in her eyes. This photograph was always the last thing she saw at night, except for the dark, and the *things* it sometimes brought.

Eyes peering from a dream. Moonlight glimmering against sharp, wet fangs.

4

Their travel backpacks were open on the floor, the contents strewn like innards. Music bopped from the small radio on the windowsill, but the song was lost on

Amity, who only knew that the radio was on because its little red light was watching them pack.

Amity and Caleb's matching blond hair was highlighted in the dusty beams of afternoon light stabbing through the back room windows. They were of similar build, lithe and athletic, but Amity lacked the sculpture her brother had accumulated after years of track and field events. Caleb moved like a dancer, with a grace Amity couldn't match, but on that day, the Thursday before flying out for Thailand, they both carried themselves with a degree of confidence that seemed almost rehearsed.

The packing of those two overpriced backpacks was one of many rites of passage they would indulge in before leaving Evans Head.

Amity's fluoro rubber wristband shone bright in the light as she tapped the spread laid out before her. A silent checklist.

Assorted clothing in plastic and drawstring bags, including a rain jacket and bandannas. Fully stocked toiletries in a rubber case. Three tubes of Chap Stick. A portable hard drive to download movies off hostel Wi-Fi networks. Her Kindle. Her camera and its spare batteries. A first aid box full of bandages, Band-Aids, antifungal cream, DEET mosquito repellant, painkillers, constipation and diarrhea pills. She kept her tampons in a waterproof carrier inside her makeup case. Water bottle. Bottle opener. Locks. Passports. Credit cards. Money belts. Just-in-case Ziploc baggies. A pocketknife. A universal sink plug and portable clothesline with detachable pegs. A travel adapter. Umbrella. Earplugs. Eye mask. A small box of laundry powder. One by one, Amity packed it all away. She slipped her drawing journal into her shoulder bag.

The light had drained from the day, the autumn heat subsiding.

Caleb straightened up and the bones in his back cracked; it felt good. The concept of cheap Thai massages sounded mighty appealing right now, but of course, all good things come to those who wait. He stretched his arms over his head, exposing a tattoo on his right forearm. The elegantly rendered script ran from a few inches above the wrist to a few inches short of his elbow crux. Printed there for the world to see were two words. They were simple. They were stark.

Family love.

The front door opened. Caleb dropped his arms and listened to the signature noises of their mother's arrival home from work.

Slam. The tinkle of car keys being set upon the hallway armoire. Feet shuffling over floorboards, drawing nearer and nearer.

Caleb tapped his sister on the shoulder and gestured toward the kitchen. They watched their mother step into the dimming light. And stop.

"Hi, Ma," Caleb said. "How was your day?"

"What's all this, then?" Janine asked without signing, but Amity understood. As with the night they told her they were leaving, neither son nor daughter had expected their mother to deal well with this confirmation, which would only confirm that *yes,* they hadn't been lying; they were leaving. *For real.*

"This is all our stuff, Ma. We've got everything organized from top to bottom. Visas, clothes, electronics— the lot."

"And you two didn't want any help from me, then? Is that it?"

"Well, we didn't think you'd want to, is all."

Janine Collins's expression turned cold. She stepped back into the kitchen and flicked on the ceiling light, the bulb flinging a slash of white across her children's matching sea-green eyes.

Caleb listened to his mother at the sink, thumping dishes and clanging unwashed knives and forks. Each sound was a slap to the face, a misfired discipline.

"I'm so sick of this place," Caleb whispered, clutching

his clammy arms. He felt Amity's look burrowing into him, but no translation was required. *The shaking head, the quivering of her lower lip...*his sister heard things best when nothing was said at all.

"Fucking joke," he spat.

"What was *that?*" came the shrill voice from the kitchen, followed by the dramatic thump of footsteps. His mother reappeared in the doorway, her purple gloves dripping suds onto the floor.

"Nothing."

"I'm not the deaf one around here, Caleb."

"Whatever."

"What did you say?"

"Nothing. Jesus, Ma. Chill out. It's just not worth it."

"Not *worth* it? Oh, 'not worth it', he says."

Amity watched their volleying mouths. All she wanted to do was get up, walk away and lock herself in her room. There she would throw some butcher paper across her bed and scratch away with sticks of charcoal. There wouldn't be beauty in whatever she poured out, but at least it would be raw. Emotion bled onto white.

"This doesn't need to be so hard, Ma. It isn't hard for *other* people, *other* families."

"If you like *other* families so much, well, go have dinner over there. Sleep in *their* beds."

"Are you even listening to yourself?"

His mother retreated to the sink again, and Caleb took this as his cue to leave.

Amity sat on the bulge of her backpack and rested her chin in her hands, chewed on a fingernail and toyed with her wristband. She turned her head toward the darkening windows, toward huge clouds painted in evening colors, and saw the portable radio on the sill. The pinpoint of red light winked at her like a distant, mocking star. A song that couldn't be heard continued to play.

We're doing the right thing, Amity told herself. *Going away will be the best thing that has ever happened to us. To us all.*

5

Amity often visited him, more out of habit than anything else. There was something soothing in bending down to yank the weeds from her father's plot, knowing that they would only grow back, scrambling like buried hands seeking freedom.

Caleb was with her. Their loss was something they both could share, though they had to admit that time was taking its toll. Amity hardly remembered her father anymore, even though he made appearances in her dreams, brief nightmare cameos.

Heat sucked the moisture from her skin and Amity could feel herself beginning to burn. They wouldn't stay for much longer, just long enough to say good-bye.

A plastic bag floated through the air and snagged on the corner of the headstone. Amity leaned forward to remove it, only to have the wind do the job for her. She watched it bob away on its inelegant journey through the cemetery.

Bye-bye, Pa, she wanted to say. But didn't. Not yet.

Her mother had stopped coming to visit the grave years ago. Amity wondered what state it would be in six months from now, without Dean Collins's children there to tend to it. The weeds were merciless.

Don't think about it. Just pick up your shit and don't look back.

CHAPTER THREE

Sycamore

1

THE TWO MIDDLE-AGED women exchanged a US dollar for a handful of grimy córdobas from an old man with a lesion on his face. Lynn knew the conversion rate was way off but didn't care; it was an act of kindness from a stranger, soothing the burn of their evening. Their flight had been delayed for eleven hours, but they had finally arrived in Managua, the Nicaraguan capital.

She was near the luggage turnstile, waiting, and could see a large group of people bearing signs and flowers outside the airport windows. They had broad, toothy smiles bared for their families, setting off the first ache for her own that she'd felt since leaving. It wasn't long before children started approaching her with handmade bamboo flowers, asking for money.

It was midnight and she was drenched in sweat. Enough was enough.

Lynn felt alone, despite traveling with her best friend, Stacey. They had invested so much in this trip—that it had started off on the wrong foot brought a lump to her throat.

She wondered what Ray, her husband, was doing.

Probably sitting around, letting the dishes climb to the ceiling, Lynn thought. That image would have angered her under any other circumstances, but right then, in the hot Nicaraguan air, the concept of her kitchen and a passed-out Ray on the living room La-Z-Boy sounded just fine to her. It sounded like home.

"Well, I finally found a working phone," Stacey said, trotting toward her. Her smile was broad yet strained. "I got in contact with the guy who owns the villa. He sounds fantastic, although I think he might be a little nuts. But I'm sure he'll be a hoot. We'll stay there for two days and then we're off to Granada. After that, Costa Rica, as planned."

"Thank God. But how do we get there?"

"Tristan—that's the ex-pat who owns the place—is picking us up. What a doll, huh? Look, we're tired and stressed. We just got off the flight from hell. Take a big, deep breath with me, okay? No, I'm being serious... Yessum, that's it. And another... Good. Now, look at me. Get ready to have some fun."

2

Tristan's pickup wove through the traffic, dodging families on motorbikes and stray oxen that had wandered onto the road. Lynn drank up the sights, her heart racing. She saw graffiti-covered buildings, power lines that sagged to eye level, knotted in some places, often dangling sneakers. Trash burned on every corner, while children ran through makeshift houses. Adults cooked on open grills, billowing acrid purple smoke.

If Tristan's driving was anything to go by, she believed the man had well and truly shaken off the restraints of his North American conservatism to run free in a country where there was little law. This made her smile.

The moment they entered the villa, the blast of cool, conditioned air made Lynn go weak at the knees. Cheering, they stumbled over the threshold and tossed down their bags. The door swung shut behind them, blocking out the drone of crickets.

"Thanks so much," Stacey said, hugging Tristan while reaching around to squeeze his ass. They laughed, high-pitched cackles shattering silence.

"We're just in the door and you're already throwing yourself at him," Lynn said. Any other time and she would've been embarrassed by her friend's behavior, but like Tristan before them, Lynn could feel the real world melting away. Revealed was an attitude that was as raw and inviting as the streets they'd sped through.

"Oh, you little devil!" Tristan said, slapping her hand away. "Well, aren't we three just the desperate housewives of Managua!"

He was a tall, thin man, with neat hair and kind, worn features. He looked *happy*–something Lynn admired him for. Showing them their rooms didn't have the air of rehearsed, tired formality that she'd expected; if anything, Tristan seemed to be enjoying it. "And there you go, girls. The villa's empty except for us at the moment, so you've got free range of everything," he said.

"You're a life saver," Lynn said. "The thought of being in that airport for much longer—"

"Yeah, you two *did* kind of stand out like a sore thumb."

"I've never felt so pale. Stupid, I know."

"Oh, *pfft*! I buzz back and forth between here and Minnesota. Trust me, I *know* what pale is. So you gals said you're from Seattle, right?"

"Yeah, and it's gorgeous, but we just had to get out. Live another life for a month. I still can't believe we're here. We didn't even have passports five months ago!"

"And Nicaragua, Jesus! Of all places. Out of the pan and into the fire. I love it here. I tell ya, it's like having a split personality. Back home I go to church and here I go clubbing. We're free."

3

The backyard perimeter fence was ten feet tall, embellished with bale wire and broken wine bottles. Palm trees swayed in the breeze as though dancing to the Latin music playing next door. The air smelled of papaya and cooked meat. Lynn and Stacey tanned in silence by the villa's pool. They were happy.

Lynn was wearing the two-piece she'd bought for the trip. She knew she looked good for her age, even though being a mother, wife and secretary did take its toll. Her pre-vacation workout had been successful, although camping out on the sofa with *Judge Judy* screeching from the idiot box was far easier on her ankles.

Lying there, her thoughts turned to the two families she'd seen walking past the villa earlier that morning—a group of stocky men and women, all with bulging stomachs and thighs. "Different, isn't it?" Tristan had said to her. "Here, if you've got a tummy it means you can afford food, and that's important. It means you're not poor."

Lynn didn't know how *that* made her feel.

When it came to her weight, her greatest hurdle was her husband, who insisted on buying every fat-inducing product at the local IGA. It also didn't help that whenever she proposed "shopping healthy", Ray gave her this condescending once-over that undid her every time. He didn't like change and that made dieting almost impossible. In fact, getting *anything* done at home was a challenge.

But things would be different when she returned. *Screw Ray.* The cans of paint she'd bought a year ago would be pulled out of the garage and the contents slapped on the living room walls, all in preparation for selling. Getting their house on the market was something Lynn had wanted for years. Change was on the rise, and it'd arrive by hell or high water.

4

Fever-warm night fell, intertwining its moonlight fingers with the shadows of the trees, telephone poles and buildings. It lit upon the villa's doors, but did not knock; touched the abandoned caipirinha cocktails on the deck, but did not bother to shoo away the mosquitos buzzing around them. But those silvery fingers were barred from Stacey, who was on her bed watching *Grey's Anatomy* in her nightgown. Tristan was out of reach too, as he was in the living room sending drunken e-mails to all of his friends back home. The moon would just have to be satisfied with Lynn, who was walking between the palm trees that flanked the path leading to the pool.

The rich loam of soil, the fabric softener her towel had been washed in—it all beat at her senses, which had already been dulled by the alcohol she'd downed. The motion-activated toy bird on the rafter of the poolside shelter began to sing "Don't Worry, Be Happy". It flapped its wings and shook its little robotic head, which brought a smile that wouldn't last to her face.

"Ah, the bird. Meh, I've had enough of you. I'd much rather the bees," she said, stopping at the pool's edge. It was lit from below and cast ghostly trails over the hedges and walls. She slipped out of her blouse and tossed it over the arm of the reclining chair she'd sunbathed on earlier that day.

Lynn stepped into the warm water and dived under.

Beautiful silence. And yet it wasn't silent at all. Every bursting bubble was like thundering footsteps drawing nearer and nearer. She arched her neck and saw the sky, wavering and uncertain through the ripples. Pressure bore down on her lungs, forcing her to surface.

Lynn waded over to an inflatable raft and pulled herself onto it. She struggled at first but found her balance. She kicked aside the beach ball floating beside her foot and stared up at the stars, trying to pinpoint the constellations.

It had been years since she'd *really* looked at the sky. The stars shone bright, with no detracting city glow, and their dark backdrop seemed darker, more *penetrating* here. As weird as it sounded, she could almost sense its depth, a universe stretching off into nothingness, farther than any man or woman could ever imagine.

Her head swam in the best possible way. The drinks Tristan had made were wonderful; she made a mental note to ask him for the recipe. Lynn liked the idea of cocktail hour once a week after work, in her clean and freshly painted house.

Images drifted through her mind. Ray in his La-Z-Boy recliner, watching television, a bowl of yogurt-covered raisins on the table next to him. Ray in the shower, staring out at her and pulling faces as she brushed her teeth. For every bad thought, there was a good one; for every ping of sadness, an opposite. No; she might not be happy, but she certainly wasn't *unhappy*. In her short time at the villa, Lynn had come to realize that whatever was wrong in her life could be fixed.

The bird sang.

Lynn sat upright, splashing her face. Chlorine lingered on her tongue. There was nothing under the shelter, nothing except the singing toy. It fell silent.

"Stacey?" she called out. "Tristan, is that you?"

There was no response. She scanned the hedges around the pool; from her low angle they seemed as tall as the cement fences behind them. Nobody was there, either.

Lynn looked at the bird again, so still and poised, its dead eyes staring off into nowhere.

Oh, don't we spook easy? said a voice in her head. *The batteries must be winding down, is all. Don't they say they burn harder just before they die?* That calming voice ushered her heart from her throat and back into her chest, where its beat returned to normal.

Lynn laughed and sat back down on the raft. The sky continued to stare down at her.

There was movement against the trees. She splashed again, freckling her face with water. Breath escaped her, some hidden weight forcing against her breasts, but after a few slow-moving moments, it lifted. Oxygen. Panting.

There was nobody there.

It was just the beach ball drifting past the underwater light at the end of the pool. Its shadow was projected against the hedge, a crescent of darkness creeping by.

Lynn didn't laugh this time, just a half smile. *You're giving yourself the willies*, said the voice.

"No shit."

You're literally jumping at shadows.

"I don't want to go back inside. I'm enjoying myself." Her own words didn't sit right in her waterlogged ears. "Stop talking to yourself."

Lynn lurched back on the raft, her skin screeching against the rubber.

The water was calm now, and she floated across its surface, eyes closed. The lingering alcohol buzz took the edge off her fear. Lynn chose to focus on Costa Rica instead. *If I'm having this much fun at a random villa on the outskirts of Managua, just imagine how much fun I'll have at my resort.*

She thought about drinks with novelty umbrellas, of waves on the shore and the salty ocean air, talking to her husband on the telephone when she arrived and telling him—

Something rustled.

This she *hadn't* imagined. Lynn inched the length of the pool, her chin just below water level, eyes wide. Staring.

The hedges. The trees. The walls. The shelter. The bird. The chairs. The gap among the palms that led back toward her room.

Nothing.

Okeydokey, I've had enough of this bullshit.

Her husband and Costa Rican beaches—even the stars themselves—were forgotten as she paddled closer to the shallow end, facing the villa. Her feet brushed against the bottom of the pool, toenails snapping backward as they flicked the pebbled cement. It hurt a little, but she pushed the pain aside and waded through the water, forcing her upper half into the heavy air.

There was an electric crackling. She stopped.

Behind the bird, suspended on a wire at the very rear of the bamboo shelter, there was a bug zapper. Lynn hadn't even noticed it was there, just as the insects themselves continued to beat at the cage, unaware of the ashes of their kin.

Adrenaline pumped through her body. Lynn was at the end of the pool, her knees doubled up underneath her. She felt exposed now that she was out of the water. The handrail leading up to the recliners was on her left—almost within reach. She chanced a final glance around the yard.

The back fence. There was nobody under the shelter, in the wicker chair or standing under the bug zapper. *Nothing.*

Lynn spun around and looked at the palm trees, and then below them at the dark, knotted hedge. Moonlit water lapped at her sides. There was nothing near the hedge on her right, so she glanced down at ground level. Beneath the branches of the hedge were roots and a thin glow from the lights at the rear of the villa. There, she saw the man's face.

Lynn gagged and flailed backward.

He was lying flat against the ground on his belly, snakelike, with eyes as dark as buttons peering out at her. Water shadows wreathed across a manic smile—only it wasn't a smile, not really: the lips were pulled back to reveal the neat white teeth beneath. It was a grimace at best, something pained, although maybe—*just maybe*—born of pleasure. Lynn recognized the high forehead, the sunburned cheeks.

Tristan.

"Oh, fucking Jesus!"

There was only one way back to her room, and that was through the palm trees at the side of the shelter. Meaning that she had to *near* Tristan to access the door.

She wasn't wondering about why he was spying, or how long he'd been lying there—her only thoughts were of getting out of the water and back to her room. If he was playing a joke, then she didn't find it very funny. The fright in her system boiled over into anger. She snatched up her towel and pushed it against her chest.

Another insect exploded in the bug zapper.

She ran, feet slapping against the tiles, moving so fast the parrot didn't even detect her presence. Earlier, she'd passed through the palm trees, their leaves tickling her skin, and the scent of the earth and loam had enticed her. Now the leaves felt like perverted hands grabbing at the fat she couldn't work off fast enough, no matter how hard she tried—

(it's not my fault! I keep on trying to get Ray to buy healthy, but it all makes him fit to be tied)

—and the soil reeked of decay.

Lynn rounded the corner and saw two doors: the closest one led to Stacey's room, the second to her own. She slipped, her legs sliding sideways, and landed flat on her stomach. She'd snapped her head to the right to avoid breaking her nose, which was lucky in one way.

Unlucky in another.

There was no time to register pain, but the terror was as immediate as electricity. Tristan was right next to her, peering out at the pool. Only he ended at the neck. Insects had crawled out from under their rocks to climb into his mangled throat muscles.

Lynn tried to get up. Her hands and upper arms ran scarlet. She could smell copper, could taste it on her tongue. She'd slipped on a puddle of blood. Garbled, messy sounds erupted from deep inside her, noises she'd never expected to hear because she'd never expected to make them.

She skidded to her left and saw Stacey's door. Crawling, screaming. Her palm slammed against the wood and the door flung wide; it had been open a fraction the entire time. She saw the sheets, the almost-black blood. A lifeless hand dangled over the edge of the saturated mattress.

The bird started singing again.

Lynn snapped around. A patter of boots against the tiles as the shadow descended on her, swooping down low. And then there was nothing.

5

At first there was the throbbing, a slow-lolling thing inside her head, but once she managed to open her gummy eyelids, there was the stink of blood and chlorine. It sickened her.

Ropes bound her to the chair, the same chair that she'd sat on for breakfast earlier in the day. Only now Lynn wasn't in the kitchen, or at least she didn't think so; she had to push aside that terrible throbbing to see where she was. Shuttered windows. A closed bamboo door. Humid condensation dripped down the walls.

She could hear a soft hissing coming from somewhere in the dark before her. The jade screen of the CD player, which was stuck between stations, peered at her—a glowing, unblinking eye from the ocean ink.

They were in the back room near Tristan's bar, and it was hot. Swampish. Sweat pooled in the hollow of her collarbone. She wanted to scream, but could manage little more than a whisper.

"*Quiet,*" came a voice.

Christmas lights sprang to life with a spark of electricity. They were wrapped around the body of the speaker, the woman who had attacked her. The woman who had taken a blade to their host. To her best friend. She looked as though clothed in the stars she'd admired from the pool, her form revealed in the glow. A bloodied machete was in one hand and a tumbler of alcohol in the other. Every breath, a wet rattle in her gullet.

The stranger stood, the wicker chair she'd been sitting in crying relief. She wore toothpaste-bright Reebok running shoes. Unscuffed. Unmuddied.

"Stacey," Lynn moaned.

The hand, draped over the side of the bloodied mattress. It had ended at the elbow.

Sobs wracked her body, but she fought against them as she fought against the ropes. Her screams were powerful now.

"*Quiet.*"

The stranger shuffled forward, careful to not loosen the Christmas lights from her body. The cord uncoiled out behind her. Lynn could see that she was white, maybe in her late thirties—could see strength radiating from her body like heat. The woman's face was cold, with skin cast tight over its high, prominent forehead, casting eyes into darkness and pronouncing the baldness of her skull. Without the definition of eyebrows, she looked as though crafted from devil's porcelain, a half-made china doll that didn't break with ease.

The CD player continued to hiss.

Lynn's scream ran dry as the stranger drew close. Her slick right arm reached out at her. Touching her with rubber-gloved hands. She snapped at her, teeth clamping down on air.

"No, no," she said, her voice a parody of kindness. The words were knowledge, a narrative laid out between the two of them, as plain to see as the floorboards beneath their feet, depicting yet another life about to end in agony.

The woman smiled, seeming to despise her prey, and reached out again. She still held the drink, a lime wedge floating on its surface. She bent low, the cord pulling taut behind her. The two-pronged plug clung to the socket; soon it would fall out and they would be swallowed by the dark. The concept sent Lynn into screams again, lashing out—but missing every time. Exhausted, she slumped against the chair. Lynn glared at her from under a blood-caked brow, but the fire brimming in her eyes didn't last. The cool of memory. She wondered where her children were and what her husband was doing right now.

Paint tins in a basement somewhere, collecting dust.

6

She fucked her with the machete and left the body to the mosquitoes. A cold shower followed. For two hours straight, she wiped down every surface that she'd touched through a blurred cataract daze. Muscles rippled under her layer of freckled skin as she buffed the door handle with a rag. Even though the night was cooling, even though she'd showered, the sweats still came, tickling as they trickled down her ribs, down her spine.

The soiled rags thrown into the burlap sack she'd brought with her. Inside were used tissues and two chewed-up ears of corn that she'd nibbled on over the three-hour period she'd been hiding on the property. Waiting had been tiresome but worth it—the payoff too, as it always was if she didn't rush things.

Got to make it last, baby doll. Last real goo-oood.

She wasn't always quite so disciplined, but on this occasion, she'd impressed herself by just how long she'd managed to hold out. It was hard not to get too excited when they squirmed and fought and screamed the way these three had, and in the throes of the pièce de résistance (that oh-so-silken beat), glazed over and realized that no, they weren't going to get out of this alive. That the last things they would hear would be the intonations of her British accent; the last things they would feel would be the ropes about their limbs and the burn of her blade.

She'd stumbled across the two women and the man at the airport and followed them home from there. Trolling had paid off.

Carnage was laid out before her.

A smirk.

She dropped the sack beside her foot, stretched the knots out of her back and rolled her head. Bones cracked and fell into place. A smack of her lips. *Cluck.* She touched her tongue to the roof of her mouth. She'd kill for another drink—that hideous desire reaching out to her, like the arms of a persuasive dead friend wrapped in fetid, warm rags—but didn't dare touch any of the taps now that she'd wiped them clean.

A great burden had been lifted from her body; it wouldn't be long until it returned. And when it did, she would have to troll again, which meant more waiting. They were exhausting, these yearnings. Soon, the aches would come. But she had to be patient. The way she figured, patience was like one of the many muscles in her body: a part of her that would grow soft and spent if she didn't work on it with at least a little discipline. It was hard but rewarding.

She lifted both hands and framed the scene with her fingers.

"Click," she said. The picture lingered in her eyes as a bright flash sometimes bruises the eye. This was all she would allow herself, as taking real photographs was just too risky, but were she to have indulged—just one harmless shot each—they would have totaled eleven.

Eleven people. Eleven cries for mercy.

She spared a moment for number twelve. What would it be like? How would it taste? And what then of lucky thirteen?

These thoughts were candy colored. It made her smile, even though those aches were now starting to creep in. It always would.

She would never stop. Couldn't. There was no choice, no option. She had to keep moving, keep trolling. If she stopped, went back to the United Kingdom and put away the blade, she was certain that she would die.

The sack made her hands itch, but she didn't care. She left behind the slaughter, stepped outside and climbed onto the rented motorcycle she had hidden among the trees, watched over by agonized faces in the bark. Along the way, she passed two small children dancing around a pile of smoldering trash. The sting of longing for some other life, some other time. They waved and laughed at the color of her skin, making her feel insignificant again. She kick-started the motorcycle and rode into the night, stopping only to weigh down the bag and throw it from a bridge and into a river.

Her room-for-hire was tucked away on the outskirts of Managua, and stank of mold and wet paper, fueling her hay fever into overdrive. It didn't matter. It couldn't. "Got to keep moving, keep moving," she said, over and over, as she packed up her clothes and toiletries, sweat rolling down her face and beading off her nose.

The passport was on the bed, and inside it was a name next to her picture: SUSAN SYCAMORE, it read. She was thirty-nine years old and, as illustrated by the swirls of multicolored ink stamped across the pages, had been on the road for nine months. Beelining it from one developing country to another wasn't easy or cheap, but like patience (like making it last *real goo-ooood*), it was worth it.

CHAPTER FOUR

Amity and Caleb

1

PALM LEAVES GAVE way to reveal the elephant's wizened face. Its trunk arched upward and trumpeted red dust through the air, hazing Amity's and Caleb's matching imitation Ray-Bans. Their legs were draped behind the animal's huge ears, tapping its guitar-string hairs. They hugged chest to back, unharnessed on the crest of the elephant's neck.

The air reeked of jungle stench, elephant funk.

It was their sixth day in Thailand.

"This is fan-fucking-tastic," Caleb said, wiping the soil from his face. It didn't matter that Amity couldn't hear his sentiment; they both knew how the other felt. Their bodies were electric.

The elephant trod over rocky outcroppings, pushed though the boughs of *nareepol* and banana groves, startling birds and whatever spirits the locals believed lived there. They crested a hill, and the ocean off Phuket Island opened up before them, twinkling sunlight on a bed of blue.

Amity laughed and gestured at the ground, where two

toddlers played peekaboo around a television-size mound of elephant dung. Their parents, the owners of the animal rehabilitation center, stood close by; father toyed with a large black spider as though it were nothing more than a yo-yo.

"It's all so strange."

Caleb's eyes were wide beneath his 150 baht sunglasses. He covered his mouth with the back of hand as though embarrassed. *Strange*—it was such a simplistic thing to say, stupid really—but hell, he didn't care. And besides, who was around to listen and judge? Certainly not his sister.

"Wow. Somebody pinch me." The wonder of being overwhelmed was addictive.

"Coo-ooooee!" he announced to the landscape, so shrill and loud his voice cracked. An echo answered back, just as enthusiastic, and it confirmed to him that yes, *this was all real*, and that he shouldn't be ashamed of the little tears of happiness caught in his eyelashes.

Evans Head had never been so far away.

Amity thumped against the bed, her belly full of the rich and spicy foods they had bought from a street stall on their way back from the reservation. Whatever plans she'd mapped out for her day would soon be sacrificed at the altar of sleep. She had a mean case of almost-Christmas-Day-esque lethargy going on.

It's hot, I've gorged on mountains of food and now all I want to do is have an afternoon nap. Thank God for air-conditioning.

Their resort room was crisp and cool, a stark contrast to the tepid humidity clogging up the Phuket air outside. She rolled onto her back and stared at the ceiling, at the skittish refracted light from the balcony wind chimes, and thought that there was one upside to the high temperature: *I've got to be sweating off whatever weight I'm putting on, and that's totally fine by me.*

Smiling, she shifted onto her side, restlessness keeping her awake. There was a stack of soiled clothes heaped near the bathroom door; her brother was showering.

A PLACE FOR SINNERS

To distract her from ever-tempting sleep, Amity slipped her iPhone from the pocket of her cutoff jeans and logged into her Twitter account. She thumbed out a quick status update that simultaneously appeared on her linked Facebook homepage.

Amity Collins @agirl93
#Thailand rocks and is beautiful. Crazy place. Having an amazing time!!!!! YOLO.

And YOLO was right. You only live once, so why not make the most of it?

Their two-week resort visit was to be the first and last significant monetary splurge of their six-month trip, and Amity could already tell how much she would miss the creature comforts around them now. And it wasn't just the poolside cocktail bar, or the beach massages, or even the buffet breakfast (although it kind of *was*)—it was the joy of an air-conditioned room, the convenience of a decent Wi-Fi signal. They would soon be staying in a string of hot and overcrowded Thai backpacker hostels—with the weird toilets they couldn't put paper into, with the showers that didn't work.

Creature comforts. It was very easy to feel guilty for indulging, but unwinding felt even better. *It's the bomb*, she thought to herself. *YOLO; so why not do it in style while you can?*

She'd read that hostels were great, though hard work for those who didn't want their trips to be dictated by the allure of the attached bar or the balcony parties going off every night—neither of which were a socially manageable feat for a deaf girl. Amity suspected that she'd be lost without Caleb by her side. And day after day, his by-her-side reliability was a lot to ask.

It'll be fine, you dope. Stop stressing. ENJOY YOURSELF. GO WITH THE FLOW. BELIEVE AND YOU WILL SUCCEED! You know, do all those things you read on people's bumper stickers!

Her cell vibrated. The comment she'd just posted was already being retweeted and favorited by many of her online buddies, sending her heart aflutter.

Luce Goode @lbgoode
@Amity Collins Gr8 2 hear ur havin a blast. Photos plz!
We R living thru u!

It hadn't been until she'd stopped working that Amity realized just how hungover she was from the past year, how intoxicated she'd been by the long hours, jobs and deadlines. It had left her a paler shade of herself, and only now was that color returning to her cheeks. Smiling was easy to do when your day wasn't full of indecisive clients, when you weren't fighting for payments and drafting invoices between online university classes.

Defer everything. She smiled, giddy.

The sacrifices were over—for a while, at least. She was here, in her room, with the sensation of cool bedsheets against her sunburn. It made every effort worth it, and yes, helped to balm the blister of having left people behind. People like her mother (who, despite herself, had taken them to Ballina for their connecting flight to Sydney).

Amity tried not to think about it. That memory evoked a color, and that color was RED.

Corby Hans @Vdrinkaddict
@Amity Collins Jealous much? Take me next time!

Earlier that day, Caleb had signed to her, "You look healthier." And that too had made her happy.

You've earned this. Put that on your bumper sticker, buddy.

Amity eased her mind back on a pillow of disbelief and was asleep within three minutes.

2

Phuket Town, in the southeast corner of Phuket Island, was unlike anything Caleb had ever experienced before. Natural warmth emanated from the locals, who emerged from their homes and businesses in the mornings to light incense and tokens for Buddha. They would then stroll into swarming traffic as though everyone on the road weren't driving under their own regimes.

Their trip from the airport to their resort had been the first of many culture shocks to leave Caleb shaking with equal parts excitement and fear. They had torn through a chaotic landscape in an overcrowded minibus at an incredible speed, leaving him clutching for a seat belt that wasn't there.

"Do they always drive like this?" the middle-aged woman sitting next to him had asked.

Caleb hadn't answered—he was too frightened. *He could see his head crashing through the windshield, glass flying everywhere, and the splat of his brains across a road he couldn't even pronounce.* "I think I'm going to have a heart attack!" It was a half lie, dismissed with a laugh.

Weaving through traffic, veering onto the opposite side of the highway, just missing trucks toting livestock. Families of six perching on a single motorcycle. Telegraph poles teeming with beards of tangled wires that sagged so low they flirted with the ground. Smoke billowing from open barbecues in the blur of passing hawker stalls.

"This is a whole other world," Caleb told his mother during their first Skype call after arriving. "It's weird, you know. Now that I've arrived, I can't wait to come back here! I guess that sounds strange, but it's true. And Ma, you're totally coming with us. I don't care if I have to strap you to the wing of the plane."

"Well, I don't think there's much of a chance of that," she replied, bent close to her webcam for fear of not being heard. "I don't like flying."

"You've never even been on a plane."

"Oh, Caleb. I'm from the old school."

"For crying out loud. Ma, you'll be fine. Trust me. I'll slip you a glass of Lambrusco with a crushed-up Tylenol in it and you'll be out like a light. A couple of hours later, *hello Thailand!*"

"Look, if God had intended us to fly, he would have given us wings."

It was one mountain Caleb knew he couldn't climb; when it came to his mother, it was becoming easier and easier to give up. And why not? In many ways she had given up on him. She thought he was going to hell, after all. In her book, it wasn't just unloved gays who burn.

"*Sawadee kha-aaaaaa,*" the local women would say to the two of them in greeting. A bowed head and palms pressed together as though in prayer. Caleb loved the sing-song sounds of the language, the way it bounced along, syllable by syllable.

"*Sawadee krup,*" he would reply for them both, his voice wavering and unconfident. When he'd booked their elephant ride at the reservation, Caleb had been forced to use Google Translate on his iPhone to get his request across. "*I don't know how people used to travel before the Internet,*" he'd signed to his sister.

The Mango Coco cocktails they'd ordered on their first night out in Patong (a fifteen-minute *tuk-tuk* ride from their resort) arrived in oversize carafes shaped like nude women. Semifrozen packaged towels to wipe the sweat from their faces accompanied every meal.

"*I need a shower,*" was Caleb's most frequent sign.

Phuket's scent was a delicate mix of spice and sewage, a Molotov mixture that was by turns alluring and repulsive. One minute, Amity would be walking near the food stalls while scanning the market T-shirts, and the next— *bam*—she would be hit in the face by the stench of shit, so warm and tangible it was as though someone had slapped her with a fecal blanket. A flurry of hands and then it would be Amity signing that *she* was the one who needed a shower.

Between the smells, the traffic, the constant offers for cheap tailoring, and locals identifying their nationality by their footwear, they were on high alert—in the best possible way. It was almost a joke, really; a lurid penny dreadful in which their lives were the punch line. Amity would wonder, much later, if their lives had been mapped out in advance by some great power or entity. If they had been lured in and laughed at, as plans fell into place and they began to fall, one by one.

3

Caleb jumped on the bed and pretended to smother his sister with a pillow. They faux-fought and tumbled to the floor. The laughter of one fueled the laughter of the other, a round robin of bleats.

Amity reconsidered putting on makeup; sweat would only strip away her efforts. So they settled for vodka shots at eight, and within half an hour, the *sawng tiew* they'd called for at reception screeched to a stop out the front of their hotel. They took photos of each other with their iPhones, pausing to look at each image before taking the next. Caleb searched for a Wi-Fi signal to upload the photographs to Instagram but had no luck.

Shop owners called to them as they walked the busy street. "Helloooooooo! You want dancing? You from Australia, yes?"

Patong's neon lights burned bright. Men and women played Connect Four with waitresses in open street bars. Sad-faced children approached them, trying to sell roses.

The world spun, drink after drink, leaving Amity fumbling with her Thai baht at the bar. Caleb swept in to help, snatching the money from his sister's hands and paying on her behalf. "*Khob-kun-Krup!*"

Local men flicked nudie cards at the male tourists as they strutted the street, high-fiving each other and tugging at their Chang Beer singlet tops. There were Australian women just off the main drag, vomiting into gutters near a busy nightclub, faces feathered with streaks of running mascara. "I can't believe he did that to me! The *fuggin'* prick," Caleb heard one woman say.

"Tracey, you're so much better than him," said the other, who was now holding back her friend's curls as she doubled over to lurch up her dinner. "He's a prick, but her, oh she's nothing but a bogan slut!"

More drinks. More baht slammed down on the bar.

Cameras flashing. A whip crack of flame seen through an open kitchen window.

Amity watched her brother twerk on an empty dance floor, swinging his arms through beams of blue light, spearing clouds of smoke. Amity thought he looked happy, and that made her happy.

Tobias approached them at midnight.

4

It was two o'clock in the morning and the city still swung, assuming it ever wound down. Amity watched it all from within her fishbowl silence. Children giggled as they passed by on their bicycles; white, middle-aged men held hands with their rented Thai teenagers; Tobias Schubert's lips bounced as he told some story in his semicharming, broken English.

To Amity, deafness was like one of those black-and-white drawings in a coloring book: it was stark and honest—only the child didn't have any crayons with which to bring the picture to life. Deafness was to be incomplete in a world that demanded completeness. And Amity had half expected Thailand to do nothing but accentuate such feelings, but in reality, it helped. Being unable to speak the native language was giving her brother a little taste of what it was like to live without the ability to communicate with others. Amity sighed; it was cruel in a way. Cruel, but necessary. It was plateauing their relationship.

Amity *almost* felt normal. And then Tobias had started talking.

The three of them sat on the curb out the front of the nightclub, half-eaten meat skewers in their hands. Caleb had given up on translating what the black, twenty-four-year-old German was saying.

He drank up the sight of him. Tobias.

This stranger was tall and thin, an awkward melding of nerd and handsome. Hair as dark as his skin surfed across his brow in a halfhearted quiff, framing eyes marked with imperfections. "This all happened last week," he began, dulcet tones hazed by alcohol, his clunking accent. "And I was so scared. You may think I am tough and fit, but I am like a kitten."

Caleb laughed, trying to ignore his sister's gaze.

"I was staying with this guy in my hostel in Phuket. He was nice, but man, he was crazy and liked the drugs. His name was Matt, and he was from Ireland. All the time, he was asking, 'When are we going to find party?' 'I want to go party tonight, Tobias'. It got on my nerves. I like to party, but not all the time. I've been traveling for two years. I've got no money sometimes."

He paused midstory to take a bite from his meat skewer and a sip of Red Bull.

"So we go to the market together. He wants to buy a suit, because here you can get one made for you. Very cheap. Good quality sometimes. If you want to get clothes, you should be careful; people try to rip you off all the time. Very bad.

"We were walking down the street together and this man, he calls out to us, 'Sir, you want to buy suit?' We go into his shop; it all looks very nice. Silk and the cottons, all of the good things. I don't want a suit 'cause I'm, like, almost broke. But he measured me up anyways—it's good to be polite. And Matt, he says to them straight out, 'Where can I find some drugs? Like pot?'"

"Hell no!" Caleb said, hastily signing to Amity in the hopes of not excluding her. "You hear horror stories about that kind of thing. Young tourists—just like us—sent to prison and left to rot. It's a nightmare."

"Very scary. But Matt, he is dumb. But the funny thing is that the, *uh,* man who makes the suit, *um*...what do you call this person?"

"The tailor."

"Yes. The tailor says, 'Yes. I have some pot. Very good. Good for tourists'."

"Please tell me you guys hightailed it out of there, quick smart."

"I wish. The tailor, he takes Matt out the back door into an alley. And my hands were shaking—just like this. *Shake-shake-shake.* But I can't leave him, can I? So I go out the back with him and see this man. A huge guy, very big for a Thai. He's got this machete in his hands."

"Oh, good God!"

"Yes, this is all true, I swear. And in front of this huge man is this block of wood with a brick of hash on it. You know, good stuff. I could smell it: *black licorice.* And Matt is like, 'Yeah man, this is the shit. I want some'. But I was like, no way. And I know that as soon as that guy cuts the hash, we're going to have to pay up, and I've got no money and I know Matt doesn't really have any either. Matt's crazy, he loves to risk, you know? One day he will kill someone, or himself."

"So what did you do?" Caleb asked. He had edged his way along the curb during the story, and his shoulder now brushed against the not-so-stranger. His back was to Amity, which Tobias noticed and rectified by shuffling forward.

"Well, the man has this machete, and he's bringing it down. I'm seeing it all in slow motion, like in the movies.

So I run across and grab him by the wrist, just before the blade is about to cut into the hash. My eyes must have been popping out; see, his arms were the size of my head!"

"Just incredible. I can't believe I'm hearing this."

"Oh, it's very real. I was like, oh, Matt, you are a fool."

"What happened next?"

"Well, I told this man, 'Please, no. We cannot have any pot. We'll go now'. And wow, this man was very shitty with us. He was like, 'You will go tell the police now'. You will do this, you will do that. I was scared. And so I jump back and grab Matt by the shirt and pull him back into the shop. Man, we ran and ran. The tailor was screaming at us, 'You come back and buy suit, okay!' Matt thought it was so funny. I didn't think it was so funny, though. *Shizah*."

Caleb picked up Tobias's Red Bull and put the can to his lips. He could taste the musky tang of saliva around the aluminum rim, sending nervous wings fluttering about inside him. He would never have been so brazen back home, but there was something about being in a country like Thailand, where there were no expectations or limits, that fueled him on. He was his own worst avatar.

"I didn't talk to Matt again, and I left that hostel. Besides, he was very racist. To all peoples."

"Really? Did he ever give you shit?"

"Not really. But one time we was in a pub, having a good time. And this man comes up to him and asked him if he was American. Matt got very mad and screamed at him, 'Don't you fucking call me an American, you prick, you bastard'. Terrible. Yes. I do not miss him."

Tobias's story ran itself dry, and Caleb watched him wilt under the silence left behind. Despite his lanky build and the deep bellow of his voice—despite the size of his calloused hands—there was a vulnerability to him Caleb couldn't deny being attracted to.

"You're cute," Caleb told him. Regret settled in the moment the words were aired.

"Well, I think you are cute too."

"You do?"

"Sie sind sehr attraktiv."

Amity watched them kiss, their faces bleached by flashing neon. Flakes of confetti twirled around them as a tide of drunken tourists walked by, not caring. She thought this was nothing more than luck. Though the company they shared, the alcohol in their systems, had freed her brother and this stranger, it frightened her to think that others on this street may not be quite so enthusiastic about, or liberated by, their public display of affection.

Every eye was upon them. No eyes were upon them. It hurt to be caught between.

And it wasn't as though Amity hadn't seen her brother hook up before. There had been a string of guys before Tobias—kisses at house parties, university balls, a discreet embrace in the back of the Evans Head Bowling Club. But the flutter of anxiety within her had nothing to do with this. It was some ingrained fear—institutionalized, maybe—that she bore for him. The fear that one day, he'd meet Mister Not-So-Right and Caleb would be infected with AIDS; or that he'd become too confident for his own good, as he was now, and some stranger would come out of the crowd and take him down in a rain of punches. Once, she'd witnessed a grown man stab a friend with a broken beer bottle on New Year's Eve at the local pub for far less.

Glass, drops of blood, laid out like a reward of undeserved diamonds.

You're being stupid, Amity.

No, I'm not.

Yes, you are.

Caleb's back faced her again. The envious throb Amity had been fighting since Tobias's arrival now began to knit itself within her chest—the needle stinging when his thick fingers caressed Caleb's neck. Twisting through his blond hair.

No, I'm really not being stupid. Caleb isn't as tough or as strong as he'd like to think he is. Sure, he's got a bit of muscle behind him, and some big, burly fucker with a grudge to prove would have a hard time kicking Dean Collins's eldest to the curb, but I still worry. Just because Caleb is confident and quick on his feet doesn't mean he is undefeatable. And despite the stubble he seems to wear with pride, day after day, regardless of the plaid shirts and bargain-store jeans he insists on living in, I just don't think my brother is as masculine looking as he'd like to believe. Especially when he drinks, when those cringe-worthy and obvious macho barriers start to drop, one by one, and all of a sudden, the way he shifts his head seems to scream insecurity, the way a drunken laugh escaping him sends his hands into an effeminate clutching of the mouth.

It's the little things. They all add up.

Every eye was upon them. No eyes were upon them. She was alone there now.

Amity turned away. *I'm a ghost.*

5

They left Phuket Town behind with their backpacks heavy on their shoulders. *Good-bye, creature comforts,* Amity signed to the air, something she did only when alone. *You will be missed.*

Tobias went with them.

Together, they dived into island life, snorkeling through schools of fish in Raya's crystalline waters, sleeping in beach hammocks on Naka Yai and Naka Noi, each with a copy of *Fifty Shades of Grey* in hand. They just missed out on Koh Phangan's Full Moon Party by a single night, which was a disappointment, arriving in time to discover the wreckage left behind: twisted bonfires, grimy beer bottles, broken glass and the bodies of unconscious tourists in puddles of their own vomit. Thai emergency medical staff buzzed around. When the tide rolled in, unopened condoms glimmered below the surface like coins in a wishing well.

"Damn it, we came all this way for nothing. What the hell do we do now?" Caleb had asked.

"We keep on moving," Tobias replied. "Never stay still. There is so much more to see."

Amity read his lips and nodded in agreement. They high-fived. Day by day, his presence around her became easier. They even managed to teach him some basic sign language on the long bus trip north to Chumphon, the lesson continuing in their foul-smelling Prachuap Khiri Khan hostel. But a lot of the ground made up between them was somewhat undermined when Amity caught him sneaking into Caleb's bunk bed in the middle of the night.

It was a rare thing for Amity to be grateful for her deafness. These were such occasions.

Three weeks slid by, a contrast of speedy days versus painfully long, hot nights, with the downpours offering little relief. Amity spent many of those hours on her iPhone, waiting for her Facebook to load, or drawing in her notebook. Sketches were still magic, casting off bad mojo.

Doing a four-hour round trip to see a handful of dinosaur bones in a van they just knew was going to break down going both ways became the norm. They crossed gray mountains washed in low-lying clouds and smoke from locals who were back-burning during the wet season, through drizzling rain that no poncho or raincoat could shield them from.

And their soundtrack to all this was the voices of the tourists on the road with them. The ignorant Australians and Americans, who left Caleb feeling embarrassed with their cultural assumptions. He was of the opinion that a responsible backpacker should, at least, conduct a little background research on the country he was visiting, thus becoming familiar with what was and what wasn't respectful. The number of times he'd witnessed some grimy traveler with dreadlocks patting a Thai person on the head, or refusing to give up a seat for monks on public transport were numerous. He'd overheard a British couple buzzing about heading into the country's northwest and embarking on a 650-kilometer journey to the "Bermuda Triangle". That had made him laugh. "Um, I'm pretty sure it's the Golden Triangle, guys," he'd mentioned to them.

Their weeks together taught them that, above all else, the local people loved: their families, Buddhism, and most importantly, their king, whose image could be found in restaurants, hotels, shops, department stores, people's homes, night markets, on the sides of buses, on the backs of motorbikes and in toilets. Also, when they'd gone to the cinema to escape the humidity, they'd had to stand for the Thai national anthem, which was played before the feature with robust fanfare, while images of the king cross-dissolved back and forth across the screen. Later they had learned that not standing was not just disrespectful, but a criminal offense.

"I think we should go to Hua Hin," Tobias suggested over breakfast one morning while loading up his backpack with bread rolls he'd taken from the buffet table. "Get away, go somewhere more quiet. Away from..." He gestured to the little card table next to them with a flick of his quiffed head, where two girls sat rolling a series of cigarettes for the day ahead. "Everyone else."

"Where?" Caleb asked, taking out his Lonely Planet guide and thumbing through the index.

"Hua Hin. It'll say that it's a beachside city. Some guy told me it is where the Thai royal family goes for a holiday. Very cool, yes?"

"Oh, here we go. Hua Hin. It says it's full of cheap night markets, good food and 'a laidback lifestyle to complement the tourist traps of the south'. I'm okay with that. I feel like chilling, anyway."

And it would be an hour and a half drive from Hua Hin, off the coast of Bang Kao, on the tiny island of Koh Mai Phaaw, where sugar-white sands would run red.

CHAPTER FIVE

Robert

1

THEY DIDN'T CARE if they slept or not, whether they were happy or sad. They only understood one thing, and that one thing kept them alive. Robert Mann came to respect them for this, although he'd suffered by the time his judgment had turned.

Feed without remorse and escape intact; Robert almost admired them for their efficiency. They were coldhearted bastards, but then again, he'd been accused of being just as callous in his fifty-three years. He and they were not so different.

But only in *some* ways. Robert, for example, had the capacity to sympathize, to show mercy.

They only knew of one thing: their desire to feed.

Robert guarded his secrets well, which was why nobody at work knew how unhappy he was. It was all high fives under pressure and unwinding with after-hours drinks. People looked up to him because he was so confident and commanding. Even when the economic red line that dictated their lives dropped low, Robert kept his cool.

"You're the Mann," his co-workers would say, thinking they were so clever. He let it slide. Sometimes, his Cheshire Cat grin was more rigor than sentiment. In truth, he was fucking terrified.

The marketing executives—dinosaurs that had been in the advertising business for longer than anyone alive, it seemed—watched the creative types like him, ready to unhinge the trapdoor beneath their feet should they slip up. And added to all this were the rookies—copywriters and graphic designers who didn't know how to piss without sprinkling their shoes, threatening to supersede him. The competition was as high as the risk, and the gain. A pulse and a little adrenaline went a long way on their stretch of American asphalt, just so long as the deadlines were met and the clients could be kept happy.

THE SECRET WORTH KEEPING.

These words, stamped across a page layout depicting rose petals against black and the smoothened surface of Your Secret version 2.0, a petite, mauve-hued clitoral stimulator. Robert's fingers hovered above the keyboard, ready to backspace his way to contentment should the scales of reason happen to tip that way. A sigh was all he could manage. He'd like to think that "This is what I've been reduced to, writing ad hoc copy for goddamned sex toy companies", but of course it had always been like this. There was money, as there always would be in sex, regardless of what he was selling.

THE SECRET WORTH KEEPING.

Nobody knew about his divorce, or about his bright and beautiful twenty-five-year-old daughter Imogen, who had to be coerced into talking to him. They didn't know that as a child he'd witnessed his old man getting mowed down by a pickup truck in Wichita, driven by a liquor-happy teenager who only served a fraction of his sentence.

No.

It was high fives under pressure. It was a cold stare, the twinkle in his green eyes.

THE SECRET WORTH KEEPING.

He backspaced his way out of the building. Only the dinosaurs knew that he had arranged to take his long service leave. That he wouldn't be back for twelve months, if ever. Deep down, he knew this was good-bye.

Robert stuffed his suitcase with shirts he wouldn't be caught dead in at work, not even when New York burned hot and people traded stocks for tans. He then watched the city shrink down to a tiny dot in the airplane window, and within hours had checked himself into one of Orlando's cheapest motels. There was a ticket to Universal Studios tucked into the pocket of his jeans.

He decided on the Days Inn because it promised a decent Wi-Fi signal and secured parking for his rental car. That was enough. It was all he needed. And that was the point.

The walls of his motel room were the color of nicotine-stained teeth, but the bar fridge at least appeared clean. The ceiling fan looked new, its polished blades incongruous with its surroundings. He turned on the air-conditioning and listened to the old machine groan. Robert kicked his suitcase under the writing desk, bumping the telephone off its cradle. It spun in half-circles at the end of its cord. He snatched up the receiver; it was cold and strange.

Robert laughed. "Landline. Fucking *love* it."

He wet his face and combed back his graying hair. He felt tired, fatigue running deep. He was spent without a smile to maintain, as pathetic as a used rubber floating in a toilet bowl. Not that he had used one in years.

The queen-size bed was covered in a tawdry duvet that he pulled back and tossed to the floor. Robert rolled onto the mattress and groaned. "Holy Moses, that feels good."

2

Universal Studios hadn't captivated him the way he believed it should have; yet Robert still felt an undeniable thrill on the rides. And he knew how pathetic he looked with his digital camera, dressed in his Hawaiian shirt, but he wasn't bothered. He had no room in his life for condescension anymore.

Rain on my day and you can go to hell.

He felt the first itch around midday. It started as a tickle that mutated into a burn. He lifted the sleeve of his shirt and saw four red bumps staring back at him. He scratched and the irritation faded.

But the itch returned in the line-up for The Mummy Experience. Only now, it wasn't *just* on his arm, but on the shin of his right leg too. He rolled up his jeans and saw six more bites.

The voices around him sounded too loud.

"And, like, the ride went up and woosh!"

"I just couldn't believe it when he told me. I'm a grown woman, for Christ's sake."

"Keep it moving, folks, we're all hot in here."

"Damn, is this line moving at all?"

He felt a flicker of panic; it was strong enough to suck the air from his lungs. The echoing laughter of the children took on a manic quality.

The lights dipped, and when they burned bright again, screams filtered from hidden speakers. The jewel-encrusted sarcophagus to his right swung open, revealing a mummy. Its mouth snapped open and he saw picket-fence teeth. It belched dry ice. Robert's heart skipped a beat, his sweat running cold. The fog dissipated and the crowd fell silent, waiting for a *boo* that didn't come. What crept from the speakers was not a squeal or a clichéd musical sting.

Just the scurrying of scarab beetles.

Robert returned to the motel, sunburned but happy.

He couldn't wait to upload his photographs to his desktop back home, and for a moment, it saddened him to think that he had nobody to show them to. He thought about sending some to his daughter.

"Mmmmm. Maybe not."

Although the itching had lessened, it wasn't gone. The bites hadn't been serious enough to detract from his day, but with the distractions of the park gone, the silence of his room seemed to beckon to them. Robert shook off his pants and inspected his legs. There were bites across his foot as well, plus one on the back of his left hand.

Something buzzed by his ear.

Robert chased the mosquitoes around the room for the next hour, disappearing into the bathroom to wash his hands after each little victory. The competitive streak in him bubbled to the surface. "Come on, you little shits. Come to papa-bear." He giggled as he bounced across the bed and slapped at the air, singing, "Yankee Doodle Went To Town".

Relieved that he'd killed them all, Robert slouched into the chair near the desk. He popped the can of Diet Coke from the back of the refrigerator and downed it so fast his eyes watered.

"I got you. I got you all," he said and wished for a cigar. "Fuck with the bull and you get the horns, ain't that what they say?"

Robert laughed and dug through his suitcase. He retrieved the tube of Sting Eeze antiseptic cream from his toiletries bag. He showered, dabbed the bites white and then dialed out for a pizza. When it arrived, he threw the door open, surprising the young deliveryman on the other side.

"Hi, my friend!" Robert said, unaware that he was scratching at his neck. "You're a lifesaver."

"Um, sure," he replied.

"Damn good night, isn't it? Jesus, *this weather!*"

"That's Florida for you. So, yeah, it's twenty-two fifty for the pizza and drink."

"Of course," Robert said, a little disappointed that the kid wasn't riding his high. In the creative studio they called it "surfing": you caught a wave and rode it back to shore. Robert handed over a hundred-dollar bill.

"Oh man, I really can't take that. I don't have the change."

"I don't expect any." Robert took the pizza and soda from his hands. "Do yourself a favor and pocket the tip. It'll only end up in the wrong hands. And spend the damn thing. Our economy needs it."

3

He opened his eyes, slow and cautious. It was just after midnight and the room was dark. Something crawled across his arms, across his legs.

The sensation had assimilated with his dream, which itself was crafted from memory. In it, he was having dinner with his ex-wife, Ruby. Above them was a huge chandelier, the bulbs in its limbs fizzling out, threading the air with acrid smoke. Their table was in the middle of their old Manhattan apartment, surrounded by furniture pieces draped with white sheets. His ex-wife's mouth was opening and closing, soundless and empty words. The lights continued to pop out, throwing their faces into darkness; there was just enough illumination for Robert to see how angry Ruby still was. She reached across the table and slapped his face, leaving behind a hand-shaped welt.

And that was when he'd first felt the tingling on his limbs, an out-of-context sensation. It was like swimming in a lake, only to have tendrils of seaweed wrap around your ankle.

The chandelier exploded. Windows filled with dust.

Robert rolled over in bed, reached into the dark, switched on the bedside lamp. It took a moment for his eyes to adjust to the sudden brightness. His ears were ringing. Tinnitus.

Black bugs—each the size of a grain of rice, if not smaller—were swarming all over him. Mouths so tiny they couldn't be seen uprooted from his skin. He watched them scatter, frightened and confused, their secret exposed.

Robert gagged, flailing his arms. He shuffled across the mattress and heard crunching sounds under his weight—exploded bugs in stars of blood mashed on the sheets. They clung to his stomach hairs, burrowed into his bellybutton. He stumbled, his foot landing on the remote control. The television blinked to life; *Dawson's Creek*, dubbed in Spanish, began to scream at him. Perfect-looking faces laughed to a bopping nineties soundtrack, mocking him. Fumbled for the off switch. Found it. The screen went black, a blink of fading light and then nothing. One of the bugs bit into the filmy skin of his eyelid, and without thinking of the consequences, Robert thumped his fist against his face. Yelping, he ran for the bathroom, clipping his shoulder on the door frame as he went.

Punched on the light. Legs went weak.

His reflection revealed a mask of crawling insects.

Weird, animalistic sounds escaped from him when the freezing shower water struck the crown of his head. The bugs fell off his body in droplets, popping under his feet as he jumped around the tub.

"Ah, you *fuggahs*! Fuggin—shit!"

Robert wasn't sure if he was imagining it or not, but he thought he could hear them chattering in their foreign tongue as he dug the insects from his ears.

He lifted a hand and saw one of the bugs sitting on the tip of his finger. It was flat along the top, a weak shell lending weak protection to the legs beneath. It bore a twittering little face that showed no compassion or fear as it drank from a bubble of his blood.

4

"Look, Robert. I'm not saying that you shouldn't be angry, but there's really nothing I can do. Bedbugs are horrible. Don't feel like they got you because you're dirty; unlike a lot of things on this planet, they don't discriminate. And it's not just run-down places that have them, you know. They're everywhere! It's a major issue in North America. Google it—"

"I have, Donald," he told his doctor of nine years.

Robert's eyes had the same spark and determination they usually showed in the creative studio, only they now stared out of a face littered with quarter-size bumps. And those welts didn't stop at his neck; they covered his entire body. They were on his scalp, under his arms. Even on his testicles.

"*Trust me*," Robert said. "I've Googled it."

There were a total of three hundred and four bites.

"Look, Robert. Bedbugs don't spread disease, and the bites'll settle down. This *will* go away. Give it two more weeks. You're on holiday, right?"

He slapped at his skin, a poor substitute for scratching but it worked. He had already torn up some of the inflammations with his fingernails. "I was planning to just cut free of all this bullshit, you know. And now here I am again, back in Manhattan. I feel so..."

"Just heal up for a week and go again. It's not the end of the world."

A melancholy shadow scored Robert's face. He lowered his hands into his lap; they were still strong, but were beginning to look like they belonged to someone else. He didn't understand why.

"You got your money back, right?" Donald asked. "From the motel?"

"Of course I did. And I've contacted my lawyer."

"Good luck. Bedbugs are like an act of God, you know. You can't control a storm or tidal wave, and no matter what the experts say, you can't control bedbugs. They're immune to pesticides. How can you prosecute against something that can't be helped?"

"Thanks for the comfort, Donald."

"Go home. Throw out all the clothes you took with you—"

"Done. And my suitcase. I had my doorman burn them in the incinerator downstairs."

"Good. Look, I've given you enough cream to drown yourself in. Put it to good use, okay?"

"Yeah. Drowning myself sounds like a fine recommendation right now."

They crept through the carpet fibers, seeking darkness. They had no comprehension of where they were or how far they had traveled. There was just the new day, which brought further promises of blood with it. Soon they found the mattress, and there they ran wild, laying eggs in caves of resin and foam. It was their kingdom now.

Flesh beckoned to them. Once they reached the wall of meat, they would scale its height until they felt the throb of his veins. Then they would feed, blood shooting into their stomachs.

At first there was resistance from their cow. It relented in the end. It even attempted to exterminate them. *Ha*— could the bugs appreciate humor, they might have laughed. But they didn't. Instead, they fucked and fed, growing fat in pools of useless pesticide.

5

Imogen Mann was twenty-five but looked younger. She wore thick, eighties-style glasses with plastic lenses—a simple fashion accessory, just one of the many things she had but didn't need. Sighing came easy that evening. She didn't want to be there, but it was too late to turn back now. Her visit was the climax of four months' worth of e-mails; and now there she stood before the door of apartment 201. Nervous.

Her knocking startled her. It was the first *real* noise she had registered all day. It sounded *hollow*, as though the apartment had been vacated. It was a familiar sound, and one she was attuned to hearing. Imogen worked in real estate. She wondered if he even knew that. The door creaked open.

"Hi, Dad," she said.

They sat at the dining room table, mugs of tea cupped in their hands. Behind them, the living room was devoid of furniture bar a single recliner, which was covered in a film of plastic. Imogen noticed that there were no curtains on the windows and that the only light was the afternoon glow from outside. Apartment 201 was cold and inert, unlike the tea, which at least was hot.

The room was like a hospital. Its morgue.

"What's going on?"

"Well," Robert began, "I'm on vacation—"

"I'm not talking about that. I'm talking about all *this*," she said, gesturing to the room.

"Oh. *That*."

Imogen saw the two tiny white scars under her father's left eye. She'd seen more on his hands when he'd wrung out the teabag. It made her wonder what was underneath the pajamas he was wearing. Did the pale network of scars and half-healed cuts extend up onto his chest? The thought made her shiver.

"What is it, Dad?"

Robert took a sip of his drink, distracted by the ring of tea left behind on the glass tabletop. "I should get some coasters."

"What?"

"*Bedbugs*." The word was flat.

"Bedbugs? *Oh*." Imogen was at a loss for words. "I'm sorry."

"Oh, don't be. Not for me, anyway. I don't deserve it."

She didn't like the way he was poised, as though he was waiting. The business about the bedbugs only made it worse, so she searched for another subject of conversation. "Mom's business is going gangbusters."

"That's good to hear. Does she still hate me?" Robert put the mug down, smiling.

"Yes."

"*Ha.* I admire your honesty. It's good to see that you haven't changed. I find that funny, considering all the lies around you."

Imogen watched him reach inside his loose-fitting shirt to scratch the skin beneath. There *were* additional scars across his chest. "Dad, are those marks from bedbugs too?" She reached out and touched his hands, a gesture that, ten minutes before, she never would have expected herself to impart.

"I'm glad you came to visit, Imogen. But you're going to have to leave now."

She pulled her hand away. Edgy. She slipped off her glasses. "Dad—" But the sentence was over before it even had a chance to begin. That one word—*Dad*—was a storm of emotion and power, only it had blown itself out. Just more wasted air.

"I like you better without your glasses."

It makes you look like the girl I fought for, he wanted to say but didn't. *Too corny. She'd hate me for it.*

Robert tapped his watch instead. "You have to leave. It's getting late and I've got a big day ahead of me tomorrow. I'm going away for a while, just so you know. It's up to you if you want to tell your mother or not. I'll be in Thailand, maybe Cambodia. It's just a ticket. That's all it is."

"Thailand? What? Why are you going there? Didn't you just get back from Florida?"

"You need to leave."

"But you hate dirt and fumes and, like, congestion— getting through the Lincoln Tunnel sends you into panic attacks. Thailand's, like, the Third World or somethin', you know that, right? And for a few months? Wait. What about your job?"

"Please, you need to go."

"Why, Dad? Tell me, what's going on?"

"You can't be here after dark."

"What?"

Flicking on the bedside lamp in the middle of the night and snatching up the compact mirror he keeps next to the bed. Putting it to his face and seeing the bedbugs under his eyes. Rushing into the bathroom in his underwear and picking up the razor from the medicine cabinet. A bug crawls under his eyelid.

Little red blood drops pattering on white tile. Torture tears.

They only ever come out at night.

Robert overturned both mugs. Rose-colored water ran across the glass tabletop and dripped onto the floor. Imogen bolted upright, toppling her chair; the sound of it striking the tiles echoed throughout the apartment. "I'm s-sorry," she stammered. "Oh, Dad."

Her father roared at her, lurching forward. His eyes twinkled beneath his scarred brow. "Out now!"

"Oh, fuck you, then! You want to scream at me, *huh?* Well, scream all you want. It's all I've ever heard from you. I came here because I was willing to give you a chance."

Robert clung to the kitchen counter, weakness threatening to overcome him. *Hold strong,* he told himself. *Don't go soft on me now. Get her out of here.* He looked to the window, at the skyline behind it shrouded in smog and twilight. Stray memories came out of left field, spearing him, poisoning his mind with their sentimentality.

A birthday party. Imogen laughing, her face covered in a beard of whipped cream.

"If you love me, you'll go," he said.

"I *don't* love you!"

"Stop it, Imogen. Please don't say that. Not after all this. *Don't* start lying now."

"I'm not lying. You're the liar. That's all you've ever done. You cheat and you steal and you lie." She was shaking so hard she struggled to put her glasses back on.

"Out—"

The ring that Robert had given his daughter on her eighteenth birthday tore a jagged gash across his cheek when she stepped close and slapped him. The moment she had done it, though, she began to falter, yelping, cupping her mouth. "Jesus!"

Robert fell to the ground as a familiar sickness reared its head. He could feel the pressure building inside him once more. His ears rang, stomach churning. "Go," he murmured.

"Daddy, I'm sorry. I-I didn't mean it."

Robert didn't blame her. After all, he *was* everything she'd accused him of. And maybe more.

She's still a little girl, he thought. *She's honest and doesn't lie.* Robert could taste blood on his lips and licked them clean. *And she's got a swing just like Ruby.*

Imogen reached out and touched her father's shoulder. The moment her hand landed on the lapel of his pajama top, he snapped his head up at her. "*Get out.*" His palms slapped the floor; the folds of his pajama top slid down.

There were more marks lurking under there.

She wanted to touch him one last time, to apologize for every bad thing she'd ever said to him, but didn't, couldn't. Imogen snatched up her handbag and ran from the apartment instead, leaving her father on the cold living room tiles, his silhouette a collapsing bulk against the window.

The city lights started to blink into life behind him, one by one.

She left the front door open but Robert didn't care. He had no plans to stay in this place for any longer. Hell, he'd change his flight and leave now, or as soon as the blood stopped flowing. He could afford the cancellation fee. The open door spoke more of opportunity than it did of heartbreak.

CHAPTER SIX

Tobias

1

TOBIAS WAS LYING on his back, dressed in nothing but his underwear. The ceiling fan chopped through the steamy evening air, stirring the mosquito net. His bed was just a blanket thrown across a broken door propped up on concrete cinderblocks. A gecko scuttled across the wall, stopping to stare at him.

"*Hallo,*" he said. "*Sprechen sie Deutsch?*" His hands were nestled against the Samsung netbook resting on his sweaty chest. "*Nicht? Schon gut.*"

There were screams of laughter from somewhere down the halls of the run-down Hua Hin hostel; a couple were in the throes of an extended fuck session in the adjoining private room. There hadn't been enough space in the dormitory across the street where Caleb and Amity were staying, and he could feel the ping of their absence rebounding within his chest.

Tobias thought that there was nothing better than finding people to travel with for an extended period of time. It relit a fuse that he was always worried was close to fizzling out: his enthusiasm. And their company was addictive, even though he knew that the inevitable separation would be difficult; Tobias had been down this road before. Someone almost always got hurt.

The sex continued to play itself out on the other side of the wall.

"Get it done, already," he muttered in English, not German, which didn't surprise him anymore. On the nights when his insomnia released its grip enough for him to sleep, even his dreams were in his secondary language.

If they're still fucking in fifteen minutes, I'm knocking on their door.

And what are you going to say?

Tobias exhaled and rubbed his sore, red eyes. Who was he kidding? He wasn't going to get up, put on some clothes and confront them. That was some alternate version of himself, the version aspired to yet never reached. So he plugged his headphones into his netbook and kick-started his iTunes account instead. Music whispered in his ears; the voices of the Brit pop singers were his oldest and most reliable friends.

His cell phone chirped against his ribs, tickling him, and he smirked when he saw the caller ID. Tobias took off the headphones and wrapped them around his neck, where they continued to warble their tin-can melodies.

"Hallo, Caleb."

"Hi. What are you up to?"

"Nothing. I'm sitting here in my undies."

"Ha! Sexy."

"Yeah, no. Not so much. I'm hot and the people next door are doing the fucking and the Internet keeps cutting in and out. Plus, I'm so tired but I can't sleep."

"I can't sleep either. I'm in the common room downstairs, snooping around for something to read, but all I can find are more of those *Fifty Shades of Grey* books."

"Oh, right. So, did you have fun today?"

"Yeah, but Amity's sick."

"Oh?"

"Yeah, so I'm going to camp in with her tomorrow, if that's cool. I really don't like leaving her alone. So you're flying solo."

"Yes, sure. It's fine. I've been traveling for three years now; I'm okay with being by myself for a day. Is she very sick?"

"Trust me. She's worse for wear."

"That's sad. I got very sick in Vietnam on an overnight train a couple of month ago. I got off and I shit my pants."

Caleb exploded laughter.

"It was bad," he continued. "Very, *very* bad. I went to the toilet at the station and there was no paper in the cubicle! *Oh-hhh*, it was bad. I bought tissues from this little old lady outside who was making pho in a big pot. She gave me a couple of sheets and I was like, 'Uh-hhh *no*, you're not understanding how serious this is'. I had to throw away my pants."

"Jesus, I've got tears in my eyes, Tobias! That's incredible."

"Yes, it is funny now. Not so much then. I wish Amity is feeling good soon. *Fit wie ein Turnschuh.* I hope you are also feeling fit."

"Thanks, mate."

The broadness of his accent stirred something in him, turning him on. But it wasn't just that... He was intrigued by the streak of self-consciousness Caleb always tried so hard to hide, the blemish on his character that would rear its ugliness every so often, flagged by a telltale silence and a slight tilt of the head. It only made him more interesting. He assumed it had to do with his nose, which was a little out of joint. He wanted to tell him to not worry about it, though he knew he'd hate to hear it.

You have no idea how sexy you are. And that's what makes you so sexy.

"Did you have fun today?" Tobias asked.

"Yeah. That cooking class was great. I don't know what it was that made Amity sick, though. I'm feeling fine and so are you... Oh well, who knows? I just wish we could just go ourselves next time. You and me. I guess it won't be long before you have to leave and continue on."

"I won't be leaving for New Zealand for a month. I'll make sure I see you as much as I can. You two are so much fun to be around, so much better than Matt."

"Christ, that guy. I wonder if he's still off trying to score drugs from tailors with machetes?"

"Man, he's such a crazy, crazy guy."

"Well, good riddance, Tobias. He's a bad egg, as we say back home."

"*Bad egg.* I like that."

"Have you heard from your host family in New Zealand?"

"Yes. They are so nice! They are going to pick me up from the airport in Auckland, and then they are taking me to the farm in Waiuku, I think is the name. But I do not feel like working, you know? It's been so long. But I have got no choice; my monies is running low and I've asked my parents for the last time. They are very generous, but I think they are getting sick of me asking for help."

"Tobias, you'll love working again. You're the kind of guy who makes the most out of things. Sure, it's a bit of a reality check, but it's still an adventure. And being on that farm, I'm sure you'll get really buff."

"*Buff?*"

"I mean, strong. Fit."

"Yes, this is true. I have got chicken arms. I'll look like the Terminator by the finish, yes? And then maybe I can come visit you and Amity in Australia, show off my muscles."

"I'd like that," Caleb said. "I really would."

They talked for another hour—not stopping to think how much the call must have cost—through the moans coming from next door and the couple's eventual snores; through the slamming of doors, the echoes of tourists stumbling home from the Soi Bintabath bars. Soon there was just the poised stillness that night brought, broken only by Tobias's whispers down the phone. At a little after one o'clock, someone started to pluck at the strings of a ukulele. This normally would have annoyed him at such an hour, but instead, he found it soothing.

Sleep came. It didn't last.

The outline of the door was a rectangle of light etched against darkness. There were no feet shadows along the bottom threshold, but the feeling that he wasn't alone, that he was being watched, was asphyxiating. A predatory wisp of air slid into the room from somewhere cold and alien, clawing at his flesh. Tobias shuddered. The draft wasn't just predatory, it was almost *hungry*—a parasite that lived only to chill those it wanted to immobilize, and then dominate.

Don't be stupid, he told himself. *You're imagining things. It isn't cold and nobody's there.*

But something was wrong, something *off*. And the moment he realized it, the more it seemed that it wasn't just the cool breath of air, nor the room itself or the hallway outside, that had slid off its axis—it was everywhere.

And yet nowhere.

Was that a sound he just heard, footsteps along the rickety hostel floorboards? His senses frosted over. Tobias knew he wasn't making this up. It was real, as real as the makeshift bed he had been sleeping on, as real as the feelings he had for Caleb.

I'm not alone.

It occurred to him then: had the sound come from the floorboards in the hall or from those on *his side* of the flimsy hostel door? A word formed in his throat, quivering and small, fearful of its power because of the potential answers it might draw from the dark.

"Hallo?"

There was nothing—no affirming response, no apology from some drunken tourist stumbling home in the middle of the night and unable to find his room. Just unfilled silence, which, the harder he listened to, was not so empty after all. It was haunted.

A flower of sound, blooming larger and larger, emerged from the walls around him. Unseen children began to sing, their discordant melodies clashing together in a round robin that drove Tobias from the bed, sent him running to the door, into the hallway.

He stood there, rooted to the spot, panting marathon breaths. Sweat dripped down his face and beaded off his almost naked body, pooled between his toes. Whatever chill had violated his room was now gone, leaving behind humidity so thick it could almost be cut with a blade.

A moth swooned around the exposed lightbulb at the end of the corridor. Besides it and its monstrous shadow, there was nothing to seen. The voices were no more.

2

Amity watched Tobias order dinner for the three of them. Over the years, she'd relented to the repetitive blows of her deafness, and it was during moments like these, when people had to do simple tasks on her behalf, that she bore it worst. Humiliation was violent—a serpent swimming in the pool of her emotions, breaching the surface in the hope of air, and only then, as its lifeless eyes rolled white and it parted its jaws, would she see its fangs.

Whatever. Don't let it get to you, Amity.

She distracted herself with memories. There had been the tiger-penis whiskey, the deep-fried scorpions served on little toothpicks—all of which made for fantastic photos. Many of her Facebook friends had already commented on them. And, of course, there were all the buildings: modern Chinese-influenced temples, Cambodian mound-like temples, Myanmar-influenced older temples, traditional Thai temples with pointed, triangular roofs, plus dome-shaped *stupa* that housed Buddhist shrines.

I'm totes templed out! read one of Amity's tweets. It had been favorited a dozen or more times. Looking back, she hated how she'd written it. *Totes.* In order to feel accepted, to ensure that her secrets wouldn't be revealed, she felt she had to learn and speak the lingo. A square peg forced through a circle hole; the compromise saddened her. She knew she was smarter than that.

I'm not that person, or at least I don't think I am... Totes fucking joke is more like it.

Their food arrived at their table. Amity wasn't very hungry.

Caleb grabbed her by the elbow and signed to her, "*Are you okay?*"

A stray dog had wandered in through the open door and sat next to their table.

Amity locked eyes with it. Her heartbeat quickened; she could feel it drumming against her sweaty singlet top. *If I'd never wandered from our tent*, she thought, *I'd be able to lie to you now and tell you just how okay I am. For real.*

She sighed. The dog was nothing but breeds and beatings. *Take me or leave me*, its tumorous face seemed to express. *Feed me or don't.* It was complacent with its fate.

3

The neighboring resort launched fireworks into the sky every night at eleven, dousing Caleb and Amity's dormitory in radiant color. Their room was empty now, except for them; the tourist trade was winding down in preparation for the rainy season. They had invited Tobias to change hostels and join them, but he'd declined, concerned that he was overstaying his welcome when it came to the third wheel among them.

The rest of your life is about to start, those fireworks seemed to imply—a wordless holiday campaign.

Caleb had been half asleep when he heard his sister begin to struggle.

"What the hell?" he moaned, wiping sleep from his eyes. His mouth tasted sour, as though he'd used vinegar for mouthwash before turning in for the night. Half-remembered images of Danny, his social worker back in Australia, started to fade. Those kind, melancholy eyes—*eyes that pierced with an understanding he feared he could never match*—had been the last things he had seen before the dream was cut short.

Another crack-bang explosion illuminated the bundle of sheets on the floor. A glass had been overturned, spilled water drying on the floorboards.

Amity writhed on her mattress. Tossing and turning in strobes of red and green and yellow. Her moans rose from the semaphore dark-light-dark.

"Oh, Christ."

Caleb tossed back the covers, ran across the room in nothing but his loosening board shorts and thumped down beside his sister's bed. A tormented face rolled toward him, the freckles of sweat glowing like shards of glass embedded in flesh.

"Come on, wake up, hon."

Amity's eyes bolted open—two reflected fireworks in the dim. Caleb almost fell over when his sister started thrashing again, unleashing a deep, tone-deaf screech that made his hair stand on end. Amity scuttled off the mattress and shuffled backward until her shoulders slammed against the wall. She buried her face in her bony hands and began to rock back and forth, humming. Caleb watched as she clicked her fingers together, searching for sounds that would never be found, just as she had done in those initial weeks after the accident.

The dogs had come for her again.

CHAPTER SEVEN

Robert

1

A **WILTING CIGARETTE,** a camera. These objects were Robert Mann's armory against a world that was abrasive, even shocking. Yet he couldn't deny how engaged he was. He was growing to spite the ever-so-logical voices in his head screaming at him to cave to pressure and admit just how shit scared he really was—*because buddy, you're wa-aaayyy out of your depth here.* But honestly, it was only thoughts of Imogen that threatened to undo him. *"I don't love you,"* had been among his daughter's final words to him, back in his almost empty Manhattan apartment.

Gray flakes of ash flying, twirling, falling.

He stared through the camera's viewfinder and was happy to find the white man in the crosshairs; he wore a shirt so garish it scorched Imogen away. Funny how he'd spent so much time and energy fighting for her, even when he didn't deserve to win, and just the thought of her now left him feeling hollowed out. Defeated.

This stranger was close to Robert's age, though softer around the middle, and was walking toward the marketplace. He held his daughter by the hand. Robert followed their route and only lowered the camera when the girl turned around and he saw that she was Thai.

Am I surprised? Really?

A deep groan, almost a roar, echoed from across the road.

Robert lowered the camera. His breath stilted. It was odd that none of the locals passing him by on the street had stopped at the sound, odd that not a single person had scratched his head and said, "Well, gee whiz, that sure was *mighty* peculiar". Hell, they hardly even seemed to have noticed at all. *Maybe the natives just don't care; what's weird to me may be normal for them. Yeah, that's it!* And then a wraithlike concept shrouded him: perhaps the roar had come from somewhere inside, some hidden part of himself that just might house such beasts.

The place where the bedbugs lived.

Robert waited for the sound again, but it didn't come. The cigarette dwindled down to the filter and burned his fingertips. This sudden pain brought the sounds of the street back with it, and for a moment, he was free of Imogen's grasp. He crushed the remainder of the cigarette under the heel of his sandal and shook his head. *What the hell was that noise, gawd-dammit?*

"You're losing it, old man," he said, unaware that he was scratching at the bedbug scars under the V of his shirt. He scanned the road and crossed the already busy street, approaching the bright blue kiosk on the opposite side. A man in an old straw hat with a feather through the leather strap was hunched over the window, a bored expression on his face. The sign above him read:

**GOOD TOURS. VERY CHEEP. ISLAND.
LUNCH.
FEED MONKEES. SNORKLE WITH FISH.
PHOTOS! PHOTOS! WELCOME PRICE.**

Robert rapped his knuckles against the wooden counter, and the man corrected himself, his face splitting open in a wide, toothy smile. "Hello, sir!" the proprietor said. He was dressed in a loose-fitting cotton shirt, speckled with grease, one sleeve rolled up to keep the packet of cigarettes in place. "You American!"

"Why, yes, I am. How'd you know?"

"'Oh say can you see'. 'Is that you, John Wayne?'"

"Ha, you do that well."

"Obama is very good. He's a black man, very funny."

"Thank you," Robert said, a little uneasy. "What kind of tours do you run here?"

"Oh, very good tours, sir. Very good price."

"That's good. What's the tour, though? Do we leave from here?"

"Yes, sir. We get on air-conditioned bus and drive to Bang Kao. About an hour, maybe a little more depending on rain. We go to very good restaurant there, right at the water. Good food, famous for four-hundred menu."

"Four hundred? Do you mean four hundred recipes? Four hundred options?"

"Yes, sir. Very good, authentic Thai food."

"Well, that sounds great. I don't want any of this whitewashed Yankee stuff. I like it hot and spicy."

"Ha-ha. Oh, you like spicy? You don't like spicy like Thai like spicy."

"We'll see. And what then, after the meal? We leave on the ferry, is that it?"

"No ferry. We go on my boat. Big boat, very safe. We go to Koh Mai Phaaw."

"What's that? An island? I've never heard of it. Is it in the *Lonely Planet*?"

"No, sir. Hua Hin is not famous for island tours. People go to Koh Phi Phi, near Phuket. This is same-same, but different. Special nature reserve, not many tourist. We go on special boat, to island, you feed monkeys on the beach for one hour. We take you to special cove for swimming with fish, and then we come back, have dinner at four-hundred restaurant. Lots of option; very good."

"Do I need to have a snorkel or anything?"

"We have all for you. And life jackets. And bananas to give to the monkeys, and drinks. We have everything for you. And a good tour guide, my brother. He is very good. You will like him; he love Americans."

"And how much all together then?"

"Uh-uhhhh... How much, for you?"

"Yeah, how much?"

"Five hundred baht. Very good price. Best price in all of Hua Hin. There is not very much monkey and island tour here, because of protection."

"Protection?"

"On waters. Protection for royal family on the water, along the coast. We have special clearance to go to islands off land. Very good. Very special."

"I haven't seen many kiosks like this, actually. Are there many tourists in Hua Hin?"

"Oh, yes! Tourist very good. But it is rainy season. And there is not any others like us, doing monkey and island tour. We are a special. A unforgettable experience. Very good price."

"Five hundred baht?"

"Yes, but I do special price for you because you are first customer of the day. You are good luck for me. I am good luck for you. We are friends now, see?"

"Now we're talking, how about four hundred baht?"

"Oh-hhhhh. Four hundred baht? That is not enough, sir."

"Well, I don't know. It just seems expensive to me."

"Okay! Okay. I do four hundred and fifty baht, just for you. You are first customer, and I need good luck. There are not very many tourist in Hua Hin at this time of year. You are lucky."

"It's a deal."

"Very good, very good."

"So, what is it you guys are called?"

"We are Unforgettable Experience Monkey Island Tour. We are an unforgettable experience."

"I'm sold!"

Robert handed over his money and put the receipt in his zippered fanny pack, which was cutting into the soft pad of his stomach. The humidity was already on the rise.

"So you come back tomorrow at seven a.m. in the morning time," the proprietor said.

"Wait, tomorrow?"

"Yes. In the morning at seven a.m. in the morning time."

"Shit, I didn't realize it wasn't today."

"Oh-hhhhh. Sorry, sir. We only go twice a week because of nature reserve laws, and only once a week in rainy season. Off season, sir. You come back tomorrow, yes?"

"Well, all right. I guess that'll be okay."

"Good one, sir! You are a good American. 'Hi-ho, Silver, away!'" the proprietor recited through bouts of laughter as he tapped the kiosk counter with the doubled-up baht.

"Yeah, that's the ticket!" Robert said, shaking the man's hand. "Hey, tell me this... Why'd you do that? The tapping on the counter with my money?"

"What this? I do it because you are first customer. First customer is always good luck."

2

Amity jogged down the hostel staircase, which for the first time since their arrival wasn't buzzing with activity. This didn't surprise her; it was before nine on a Monday morning. She stepped into the foyer with a notebook and a pencil case tucked under one arm and saw two young Thai women chatting near a sign that read:

NO VISIT FOR YOUR FRINDS AFTER 10 NIGHT.
QUIET FOR GUESTS AT SLEEPING
NO DURIAN.

The women's faces looked to have been whitened with an array of chemicals, the sight making her skin crawl. Amity tried to fight the feeling but couldn't overcome it;

she was disturbed, plain and simple. *Things are so different here*, she thought. *Having a tan is the norm back home, yet it's frowned upon here, especially for women. In Thailand, brown skin means you work outside. It flags you as a peasant.*

She'd bought a tube of overpriced sunscreen at a market alongside the Pran Buri River in the Prachuap Khiri Khan province a couple of weeks before. The label proclaimed it to be 80 percent UV protective cream and 20 percent whitener. Amity had been forced to use it, as there was no other alternative, and her skin now looked semitranslucent. Her empathy ran deep and veered into the pity she'd so often been dealt. It was, after all, human nature to mourn the wounded.

The tide was out and the beach was littered with ocean debris—a speckling of driftwood shards, jellyfish and trash. She sat down on an uprooted tree to the relief of her aching thighs, which hadn't grown accustomed to the use of squat toilets yet. A blue bird lit upon a hand-size seashell nearby, but it flew away before she could finish her sketch.

It felt good to have the pencil between her fingers again, pouring all of the sights she'd seen onto paper. A visual diary crystallized memories that she would otherwise forget.

She stopped sketching and glanced around.

It's great to be on my own. Even for just one morning.

Amity loved her brother, despite his tendency to cradle and coddle; and she knew that traveling Thailand would be impossible without his support. On her own, Amity suspected that she would be torn between a desire to explore and a country that refused to accommodate her disability—*and it is a disability*, she often reminded herself. Amity didn't appreciate people pussyfooting around the concept or trying to convince her otherwise. In order to accept the truths in her life, she felt it was important to first own them, and Amity had learned long ago that denial got you nowhere.

She glanced down at the page across her lap and was caught off guard by the face staring back at her. The rendering wasn't very accurate, or even articulate, but from within the messy lines and smears, there peered two perfectly captured eyes that she hadn't seen or thought about in two years.

His eyes.

She smiled, memory touching her inside. Down there. Her fingers were blackened by lead shavings.

Amity noticed the bright blue kiosk on the opposite side of the street and wondered what they were offering, glad for the distraction. *Probably bus trips out to the Huay Mongkol temple, or maybe just another cooking course*–but her train of thought was derailed by a glimmer of warm sunlight probing through the tall aluminum fence next to her.

A warm flicker across her cheek.

She put her eye to the hole in the rusty tin and peered through.

Amity drew back, a thin gasp zipping from her throat. A lock of her hair fell over her face as she stepped backward, a clutched hand thumping against her breasts. Warm wind wrapped around her.

Holy shit, you've got to be kidding me.

The grimy fence, caked in layers of ocher dust and exhaust burns, stretched back to the corner she'd just passed. A middle-aged white guy in a Hawaiian shirt was jogging with his young, female Thai friend across the intersection. He was pointing at the fence, announcing the sweat patches under his arms, while the girl laughed at his enthusiasm. They slipped behind the corner and out of view.

Amity followed close behind. Motorcyclists buzzed by so close she could feel the heat of their engines against her side; their shadows flickered across the path.

She caught the mismatched couple disappearing through a gap in the fence. A chalkboard with the words

GOOD PHOTO scrawled on it was hung near the makeshift door. Her chest tightened as she stepped across the threshold.

It can't be what I think. I've got to be seeing things. It couldn't be–

The two dead trees on either side of the door made a hollow of twisted sentries. She passed under their gaze and entered the lot, which was little more than a square of lifeless soil with a shanty on the far side. There, she saw the juvenile elephant in all of its glory. It had been tethered to a pole with a length of barbed wire; a local man on an old wooden chair sat in the animal's diminutive shadow.

By the time she'd crossed the lot, the tourist in the Hawaiian shirt had shoved a bundle of baht in to the Thai man's hands and was preparing to get his photograph taken. His sweaty arms wrapped around the girl's thin waist and drew her close enough to rest his chin on the crown of her head.

Amity could almost smell his breath brushing against her. Phantom hands on her flesh.

The tourist's lips separated in a smile—a parade of rotting teeth.

Amity couldn't hear the camera click, but she was close enough to see the starburst flash reflected in the elephant's gummy, bloodied eyes. A photograph captured. Money well spent.

She ran up the hostel stairs leading to her room, half-blinded by tears and choking on sobs, only to stumble across the top step. Dull pain lashed through her shin. The wafting smell of burning incense from down the hall gave her an instant headache.

She wished she were alone so she could swear out loud. Alone, it didn't matter if her words failed to make sense. Seeing the elephant in the vacant lot had scoured away the thinning layer of her defenses. She wanted to punch something, to pull at her hair.

Let me out.

Let me out of my fucking head!

Her fingers kneaded away at her shin, the pain receding. *Grab on to the hurt,* she explained to herself. *Let the anger go with it. Let the anger carry the RED away.*

But sometimes the RED lashed back. Sometimes, the RED had teeth.

The echo of a gunshot.

A bearded, hipster-looking guy clipped her shoulder with the guitar strapped to his back as she stood up and stepped into the hallway. He didn't even notice.

Jesus, watch where you're going, she wanted to say.

Instead, she said nothing. Of course.

Douche bag. You think that just because you've got a guitar, you're better than the rest of us. That you're more "in tune" with the traveling experience. You yuppie. You're a fucking tourist, just like me.

She couldn't shake off her bitterness and, with a sigh of resignation, stamped toward her room. Her hand latched on to the handle, turned it, and she stepped inside. A ray of light was pouring in through the open window, making it difficult to see, but she wasn't blinded. Not enough. She saw the flurry of movement through the fireflies of dust, saw Tobias's final thrust.

Caleb could feel him inside, forcing him into a pleasure-song he didn't know he could dance so well to. Tobias was making him a part of something he'd been excluded from for a long time: a place where Caleb had no control.

Sex left him stranded between that which was imagined and hoped for, and the reality of where he lay. Submitting, needing. To Caleb, sex was both the beginning and the end; it was his making, his undoing. And this was why he couldn't let go, no matter how hard he tried. He was afraid that letting go would break him, shattering the illusion of order in his life, his flesh. It was worth the risk.

The door opened. There was a shift in the room's airflow.

It sucked them out of themselves, a backdraft of awareness.

"Oh, Jesus *bloody* Christ. Tobias, stop!"

But Tobias's face was pressed close, ignorant—or perhaps he simply didn't care. There was a thread of his saliva across his cheek.

"The door!"

Caleb could see his sister's face over the landscape of Tobias's back. Before he could cry out again, the door had slammed shut.

3

Amity sat on the hostel's front step, her sketchbook and pencil case across her knees. Her neck felt tight—a week's worth of sleepless nights back to haunt her. She was chewing her fingernails again, one torn-off cuticle drawing a sliver of blood. This pain couldn't be felt over the churn of her bowels.

She looked at the picture, an attempt to cleanse what she'd seen and so the people on the street wouldn't know she had been crying. It was a sketch of Owen, the first man she had ever been with.

They had both been sixteen and went to the same school in Lismore. Owen was partially deaf, his left ear adorned with a conch-like aid that he'd never become accustomed to and was embarrassed by. He would take it off when they were out of class together, preferring to sign in silence, until the burn she sometimes ignited in him took over, and his hands would still, language left behind, as he inched his fingers closer to hers.

Were she to finish the illustration, she would have sketched broad swimmer's shoulders, tufts of curly Samoan hair, the curve of his brown belly. But Owen's eyes were all she needed, all she wanted.

A PLACE FOR SINNERS

She had ridden her bicycle out to the sugarcane fields on the outskirts of Evans Head, a place she rarely visited because it reminded her of her father. There, Owen worked with his uncle. It was night, the air cool but full of ash, the tread of her wheels carved through the fall.

They had been burning back the fields, the sky a mushroom cloud of reflected light against the smoke and billions of firefly embers flirting with stars. The closer she got, the more heat she could feel against her face. It almost got to be intolerable, but then she saw Owen's silhouette against the flames and stopped.

He left his uncle and the other workers, joined her. Together, they watched it all burn, inhaled the stink of boiling sugar. Owen, bare-chested and sweaty, was blackened by grit. He took her hand and kissed the knuckles and then led her away from the others. He pushed her bike for her.

They found a clearing, crossed it and lay down together near the trees. Ash continued to fall around them, coating their bodies as they removed their clothes. Flickering flame-shadows through the brambles, cast against his lowering body. He had been loving and gentle, and despite the initial pain as he played with her and slipped inside, she found joy. His eyes were open the whole time. Until it was over. His come splayed across the grass. And then he brushed gray ash off her shoulders and helped her back into her clothes. She was shaking. She was alive.

Owen moved away with his parents just under a month later, and when Amity's mother asked her what was wrong, why was she crying all the time, she'd picked up a tea cup and thrown it against the wall.

He was her first, and there had only been one other, an older man whom she met online. He had crooked teeth, calloused hands. This man was the only person from that other world that she had revealed her deafness to. Ever. Amity would never do that again.

Food stalls had been erected on the street in the five minutes since she'd been on the street. There were platters of chili frankfurters, carrot crêpes and deep-fried insects.

Hobbled women, bent double over their canes, bought MSG-coated cockroaches by the handful and chewed on them as though they were popcorn.

Jesus, that's the last thing I want to see right now.

She didn't know if she wanted to keep on crying, or if there was nothing else to do but give in and laugh. Amity didn't think this was a decision she could make; her body would cast that stone of its own accord. And until that point, she had no choice but to relent.

The street looked different than it had the prior day, or even when she'd woken that morning. The mechanics of the city had been exposed, unveiling the ugly, turning cogs of the tourist parade.

This is such the fucking pits.

What beauty there had been had been changed. A view appreciated and then deformed in an attempt to capture it. Something limitless and wild had been bound, and that sad fact made her want to vomit even more. A creature of beauty, little more than an infant, had been tied up with wire so people like her could make themselves appear more beautiful by just standing in its blood.

Well, we all need a purpose, said a voice deep inside. *Don't we?*

Fuck you.

Oh, the sharp wit! Yeah, so what's your purpose here, sweetie?

Shut up.

You're chaos.

Please, just don't—

You wander so others can get lost.

A hand landed on her shoulder. Amity knew who it was without having to look; her brother smelled of both yesterday's deodorant and that morning's sex. The awkward embrace of unwanted conflict tried to take hold of her as Caleb sat down on the step. Amity couldn't look him in the eye and nor did she want to. There were barbs under her skin, dragging her closer and closer to an anger she didn't want to acknowledge. An anger that was juvenile and pathetic, one she knew she had to keep to herself: *why had it been Caleb who had scored the guy—as always—and not her?*

"I don't want to talk," Amity signed. She could tell that Caleb was replying from the tap-tap-tap of breath against her neck.

Calm down, said that voice in Amity's head. *Look, why don't you just suck in some of this fresh Thailand air and try to work up a smile? Because you know what? It just isn't worth it.*

"Just drop it. Drop it. It's okay," Amity signed. "But just remember: nobody likes being the third wheel. Got it?" She handed over her sketchbook and pencil case. "I'll be back. Just let me cool down. I'll be fine."

Caleb rolled his right hand as though turning an invisible crank, the sign for "okay". "Just don't be long or I'll start worrying."

4

Amity fought the temptation to imagine what the buzzing street must sound like. These kinds of questions were aggravating, and she was upset already. This temptation was fueled by the part of her that reveled in her own pain; the part that enjoyed the taste of self-flagellation.

Why don't you torture yourself some more and think about him?

And I'm not talking about Owen, sweetie.

I'm talking about him.

Just stop, Amity told herself. *Please. Let go.*

She forged ahead with the taste of bitter pollution in her mouth, ignoring the crowd. It wasn't easy. It never was. She approached the bright blue kiosk, trying to avoid the aluminum fence on the corner, and laid her money on the countertop. She covered her ears with her hands and signaled to the proprietor in the straw hat that she couldn't hear the sale he was trying to spin. Reading his lips wasn't an option, either. That, he would just have to deal with.

He looked at her and nodded. His kind eyes expressed understanding, making her soul lifted.

See, I can do this. There's nothing that you all can do that I can't.

Amity watched the man's finger, all calloused and cracked, tap at the laminated price list and tour description in front of him. He smelled of sour sweat and leather; it reminded her of the elephant across the street.

You've got to stop thinking about it.

I can't. There's got to be someone around here I can report this to.

And who's going to listen to you? You're a thin-looking nobody who can't speak the language. Good luck with that.

Like the temptation to imagine the sounds around her, that voice, too, was difficult to ignore. She couldn't tell if it was male or female, only that it was very much there. It was seven years of faint, auditory recollections rolled into a single tongue, formed in the mouth of a belittled, jealous person. The voice was so easy to hate, yet difficult to fight.

I wish I'd been born deaf. That way I wouldn't know what I'm missing out on.

The urge to snatch up her cell phone was almost choking; her fingertips brushed against it through the denim stretch of her cutoffs. On the other side of that tiny screen she was normal—just like everyone else. But again, she resisted and focused on the proprietor's laminated tour description instead.

An unforgettable experiennncee. Meet here for trip to Thailands famous 400 meal restauraunt on beach for breakfast. We then go to Koh Mai Phaaw's where you feed monkeys. We then take you to special cove for snorkeling, swim with fishes!!!!! We then bring you back here for late lunch at Thailands famos 400 meal restauraunt. Very good price. Off-season depature time EVERY TUESDAY at 7 am.

Amity blinked and, in that millisecond of darkness, saw what Caleb's face would look like when she laid the tickets out in front of him: an expression Amity had longed to see for years. The shock of realization.

Guess what? I'm not the retard you think I am.

But you are, and deep down you know that. You're chaos, remember? Wait, didn't we go through this already?

No, you're wrong. I'm here so people can change the way they think. Just because I'm deaf doesn't mean I don't want to be listened to... I love Caleb to death, but man, he's got to realize that he's turning into Ma.

Never underestimate how much you can be underestimated.

The proprietor tipped his hat to her and reached forward to pluck up the money but stopped. He glanced up at her through heavy-lidded eyes. He pointed to the soiled baht on the counter and raised the index of his right hand to her. Only then did she realize that the finger ended at the knuckle.

Ticket for one? the gesture implied.

Amity collected her thoughts and cast her decision.

CHAPTER EIGHT

Sycamore

1

IT WAS THE eve of their arrival. Monday night was about to ease into Tuesday morning. Tickets had been purchased, and the paths leading the tourists to that sugar-white beach off Hua Hin's coastline were clearly etched, as defined and immoveable as a scar.

2

The Thai teenager was slight of build yet tall for her age, clothed in a pink shirt that pronounced the almond flush of her skin. Two beautiful brown eyes, once wonderful but now cold, slid under the greasy surface of the water. They did not blink.

She'd been split from the upper cusp of her vagina to her sternum; the putrid ink of her intestines darkened the sewer water. A haze of blood. Sweet mango rice escaped, grain by bloody grain, from the sideways knife wound.

Her final meal. Susan Sycamore had watched her eat it.

The girl had downed the dessert quick and fast, swallowing the gloppy mess with the complete trust that she would do so many times again before she died. The teenager didn't take the time to savor the sweetness of the fruit, the fresh tang of coconut cream.

"I see you," Sycamore had said over the lip of her beer.

She'd been just one of many white faces in the Chat Chai night market in Hua Hin's heart, sitting in an open-air bar with a hollowed-out pineapple crammed with chicken fried rice before her. A sea of tourists snapping photographs swarmed, too busy buying their ornamental trinkets and haggling for the best price on that perfect lobster to notice her.

Earlier that morning, she'd bought a pair of electronic hair clippers and reshaved her scalp bald. Tufts of sun-bleached hair fell from her head, landing on the porcelain rim of the washbasin. She'd swept the clippings into a plastic bag. Sycamore couldn't recall why she'd been so compelled to shave herself in the beginning—but compelled she had been. It was hard to tell why, but the act brought her closer to something. Something undefined, yet obtainable. And until she found it, until that shadow presence revealed itself to her, it would be the carrot on the stick that led her further and further into the dark. From country to country, victim to victim.

She'd watched the girl through the wavering heat waves of a hawker's barbecue.

"Gonna make it last, baby doll. Last real goo-oood."

And she had. But it wasn't enough to still her. It never was.

Sycamore's sport was almost impossible to get away with in the United Kingdom. She knew that if you spilled blood in the civilized world, you got caught. *Home turf crime, you do the time*, and all that jazz. But travel was a different game. Travel was freedom.

In London, she was just another nobody with dreams of reknitting flesh. Back home, she was a schoolteacher, a woman not in control of herself but controlled by laws, policies and expectations. It was a castrated life.

Freedom.

She lifted her bloodstained hands and formed a finger-to-thumb frame, trapping the dead girl within the square. "Click," she said. A photograph formed in her mind, though it was soon to fade.

3

Tobias and Caleb left Amity in her room, where she was bent over a series of postcards. They walked to the beach, and there, a crowd was loosing paper lanterns into the sky. Bright lights rode the waves of air. Lost shooting stars. Their hands were intertwined in the dark as they kissed. Teenagers laughed around them as they ran with torches, hunting for soft-shelled crabs.

"I am still so embarrassed about this morning," Tobias said. They were now close together, breast to breast, lying on a weatherworn reclining chair that someone had forgotten to take home after a day in the sun. Tobias's breath smelled of chewing gum.

Caleb nuzzled his face against Tobias's stubble, the brush of it against his skin sending ripples of excitement through him. "Please, don't worry about it. I spoke to Amity today, and sure, she was weirded out about it, but it'll be okay. She'll come around."

"Of all the times for her to walk in—"

"Ah! Don't even say it, Tobias! It makes me tense up just thinking about."

"But I feel bad."

"Why's that?"

"I don't know. I just do."

The brittle leaves of the palm trees clattered together in the stirring breeze. Lightning flashed over the ocean. "This place," Caleb said, "it's just so beautiful."

"Yes. It is, isn't it?"

Caleb loved the chunkiness of his accent; the way words didn't form in his mouth, they clashed. He was so *apart* from any world he'd ever envisioned being

127

intertwined with. "I really admire how you've just gone off on this huge adventure, Tobias."

"It's no big thing. Lots of people do it."

"No, not all people. And not for so long. Three years on the road—and then going to New Zealand. *Wow.* The concept floors me, honestly."

"It's important to do it when you are young, before you have a wife and babies and all of that stuff."

"Ha! Yeah. So you think you'd like to have kids someday?"

"Oh, yeah. I love the babies. I think I will be a good papa. Doing all the jobs and changing the nappies and that kind of thing. It'll be great."

Caleb saw the curve of his dark cheeks floating in lantern light. It made him smile. "You'd be a great father. And I can tell that you're going to make a lot of people very happy one day." A small lump formed in his throat, and the only way to stop its growth was to tighten his grip on his hand. "Your family must miss you."

"Yes, of course. And I miss them too. It is not nice missing important things, like birthdays and Christmas. I missed my older sister's graduation, and she was not happy with me. She is going to be a doctor. A good one too. My parents are very proud of her, and me too. Her name is Alina and she has very pretty hair, just like yours. I feel bad for missing her special day. And even now, after all this time, I still don't like being away from my little brother."

"What's his name?"

"Eldric. He gets so sick very easily. Down Syndrome."

Tobias looked as though he was going to say more, but fell silent again. Caleb lifted his hand and kissed the back of it. He didn't want to tell him how sorry he was to hear this—although he was. After all, he hated it when people said the same thing about Amity, because at the end of the day, their apologies on behalf of the universe, on behalf of all empathy, pretty much amounted to beans.

"You make me feel, like, *comfort*," Tobias said. "Is that the word? Nobody has done that before. And I think I need that comfort, after being alone for so long. After Matt as well, who was so bad for me. Do you know what I am meaning?"

Yes, he believed he did.

"Do you think I'll come back here one day and it'll all be just as awesome? Just as special?" Caleb asked. One of the lanterns in the sky caught alight and trailed toward the dark horizon in a rain of sparks.

"No."

"Really?"

"Caleb, it is never the same. I've been to a lot of places more than once, and it's never as good as the first time."

"Gee. That frightens me."

"No; don't be scared. Yes, it is sad, but it cannot be helped." Tobias cupped Caleb's face in the warmth of his giant hands. "The only thing that feels as good as the first time is home."

4

Sycamore was back at her beach bungalow by three in the morning. She stank of the sewerage the girl's corpse had been submerged in. The taste of shit was still strong in her mouth.

Lightning rolled in the storm clouds' bellies, granting enough light to guide her way toward the water's edge. The sound of the tide ushered her closer, ebb by ebb, step by step. It wasn't until she'd dropped to her knees to strip off her saturated shirt, until she felt the ocean spray against her brow, that she realized how all-consuming her thirst had become. There was heat glowing bright inside her, a ball of light.

The swallowed spirit.

There was nobody around to watch her strip naked and slip into the water. Gentle waves cusped the curves of her body, massaged her into moaning. Sycamore turned her head to the sky and watched the dull, throbbing strobe.

Thousands of bioluminescent plankton swam around her, a swarm of underwater fireflies.

She floated on the blade that divided ocean from sky, glowing in light from above and below. The teenager's oily blood formed a slick around her as the briny hands scrubbed her clean.

5

The island was surrounded by pitch-black water, reflecting the sky like the pupil of a teary eye. Her trees stirred and swayed in the tug of shifting winds. Ivory sand glowed in moonlight.

A hollow whistle sang from her heart.

6

Amity was asleep and sprawled across her bed, snoring into her pillow. It began to rain outside, bringing with it a sliver of cool that prodded at the three tickets weighted against her backpack with a mud-speckled Converse shoe. The tickets were covered in a dance of Thai and broken English writing, all under the misspelled heading: AN UNFORGETTABLE EXPERIENCECE.

A pen was propped between Amity's fingers, the point bleeding ink into her insect-repellent sheet. The postcard near her arm could be seen in the flickering streetlight from outside: a picture of the Hua Hin night markets on one side and a handwritten message on the other.

> Dear Ma,
> Having a great time. Ridden elephants, canoeing, swum lots, eaten heaps of food. Everything's strange/wonderful. I bought some

silk for you—you'll love it! We're in Hua Hin atm and tomorrow we're going to go to an island called KOH MAI PHAAW. It's a nature preserve and only a couple of boats go there at all!!!!! It'll be great to go somewhere <u>nice</u> where there are no tourists. Miss you love you can't wait to see you again.
xxooxx Amity and Caleb

7

Rain drummed against the roof of Sycamore's bungalow, the sound almost overcoming the cheeping of her laptop. A gecko dropped from the ceiling and landed on the keyboard, killing the swirling screen saver. It scurried away, leaving behind a wiggling tail, which Sycamore picked up and inspected before tossing aside. She dropped into her chair, naked, and wiped crusty sleep from her eyes. The blue phone symbol was flashing on the screen. Her Skype account was awake, even if she was not.

HOME CALLING...

A glance at her Rolex, sitting against the tabletop, revealed that it was quarter to five in the morning. "God damn it." She cracked her neck and stared at the laptop, through it, and imagined her little London home. *The diplomas on the wall; the yet-to-be plotted plants on the back step that led out to a square of garden; her father's old armchair in the living room.*

She saw all of this and felt nothing.

Sycamore tapped the enter key and was thrown into dark, limbo loading.

Her husband's face appeared in the pop-up window a moment later. She watched his eyes grow wide with surprise, watched the faces of her three teenage daughters light up beside him. Their joyful, high-pitched screams shook the laptop's warbling speakers, making her ears hurt. The women of her life were crowded around the Microsoft webcam she'd bought at Dixon's for thirty-nine quid last summer. As far as she knew, the receipt was still tucked away in her good handbag, which sat sideways in the crawlspace behind her bedroom wall.

8

Foil candy wrappers on the surf, reminders of the men, women and children who had visited the island the week before. The weathered boats, piloted by men in straw hats, had arrived in the morning, bringing with them the stench of food. But never enough.

9

Susan Sycamore was flat against the floor, absorbing the chill of the floorboards through her back. She hammocked the weight of her head in her hands and sniffed the bitter tang of her armpits. Geckos crawled over her naked body, flicking their tongues across her abdomen.

"I remember you," she said to the empty room.

Sycamore was talking to the ball of light inside her. It belonged to the girl she'd killed in the South African slum. She was a bright thing, her little black-bitch Tinker Bell. Her first. The girl had been playing in an alleyway near her hotel, toying with a dung beetle tied to a length of twine.

You were sweet. You were warm.

There was also the homeless woman in Buenos Aires. A drunk tourist in Chile, her head, breasts and hands cut off and dumped behind an abandoned house. The young shoe shiner who'd told Sycamore that she wanted to be a police officer when she grew up—eyes dug out and jaw torn from her face.

And they were only some of them. Her burning lights.

"I can feel you inside me," Sycamore said. She opened her mouth so wide her jaw began to ache, and allowed her victims to reach up through her body to pluck the strings of her vocal chords. A moan slithered out over her tongue, a deep, drawn-out word. *"Hel-llllp–"*

10

The wind dropped and the island's whistle ran dry, leaving behind silence. Almost.

11

The whale song playing from the iPod deck eased Robert Mann out of his sleep. A thin ray of sunlight crawled across his panama hat, the bag of pirated DVDs, lit his unshaven cheek. It tickled.

He bolted upright, the mattress thrusting against him. Hands rose to his face. Scratched his skin. "God damn it, you *fuggin'* bastards!" he yelled, leaping into the bathroom, clipping his shoulder on the door frame. The walls of the resort room shook under the force of the impact.

The bedbugs were crawling over him again, latching their barbed mouths into his flesh and biting. He was their kingdom now. They vomited up their meals into the scabs they had carved in him. Their tiny black faces, dank with his night sweats.

Robert slammed his fist against the bathroom blinds and stumbled to the mirror. He pushed his face up against the glass, grabbed the pucky skin under his right eye with a finger that still stank of the shellfish he'd eaten the night before and pulled down the lower lid. A pink kiss of flesh was revealed.

"Where are you?" His voice was wavering and girlish. Robert jumped up and down on the spot in frustrating leaps, sending his man breasts jingling from side to side. "You *fuggin'* fuggs, get *outtah* me! *Gah!* Out!"

But there was nothing there.

That ain't true. They're in there somewhere. The bastards are hiding in my hair, or they've crawled back inside my ears. I can feel 'em scuttling around, making burrows in the wax.

"Stop it," he told the gaunt-faced reflection in the mirror. That man, with his gray hair and lined face, was so much older than he really was. Heavy fatigue grabbed his arms and dragged him to the floor, where he pooled in an awkward bundle of limbs and fat. He sat there, chilled by the tiles.

12

The monkey, a male rhesus macaque, strutted out onto the beach from a teepee of collapsed trees. Its furless pink face was white in the early morning glare, except for its eyes, which were doll-button black. Its movements were sluggish, alternating between walking on its hind legs and using its forearms for balance. It left a curved trail of cleft shallows in the sand from its tail.

It was dressed in the tattered remains of a rose-colored tutu. Red earth had been used to rouge its cheeks, applied by its own hands. It had been brought to the island in a chicken-wire cage by men many moons and meals ago, stolen in the night from its previous owner, another man, who had trained it to juggle butcher knives, jump through hoops of fire and laugh on command. It did not think of that other life, nor did the others of its kind who had been stolen and deposited here on the sand.

The monkey stopped at the shoreline, tried to fish candy wrappers from the water. When it failed, it sat back on its haunches and stared at the ocean. Waited. It opened its mouth in a hiss that mingled with the thundering waves. It bore thirty-two razor-sharp, rotting teeth.

PART TWO

CHAPTER NINE

Transit

1

THEIR BOAT SLIT through the gulf, bleeding brackish water. Gulls swooped and cawed and shat, but only for a while. Soon they dipped low and nestled against velvety waves, traveling no farther.

"Do you think it is going to rain?" Tobias asked, shielding his eyes against the glare. Clouds dueled morning sunlight, shedding a striking glow. He'd given up on wearing the imitation Ray-Bans he'd bought for a couple of baht on the mainland. It was near impossible with the ocean spray and wind.

"I don't know," Caleb replied, dwarfed by the size of his foul-smelling life jacket. He stood in the rocking boat to take a photograph of the horizon, but the resulting shot was little more than a blurry streak of lines. "Bloody thing. We're going so fast I can't get a clear pic."

At the 400 Menu Restaurant they had eaten at before leaving, the boat pilot had told the group that his name was Nikom. "I'm thirty-one and my brother sold you ticket. I love the travel today. Many tourist is good for rainy season fun." Caleb, enamored by their guide's smile and broken English, had struggled to translate the intricacies of Nikom's name to his sister. He ended spelling out the letters in a slick of window grime with his fingertip.

A straw hat held down Nikom's shaggy locks of hair. Brown skin caught the sunlight like a multifaceted diamond, offsetting the same uninspiring blue work shirt his brother had been wearing at the kiosk. His Billabong flip-flops were worn down to a film of rubber. He steered the boat with one hand on the wheel, a gnarled cigarette in the other.

"Nikom," Robert called over the roar of the engine, "how much further until we get there?"

"You sick?"

"Well, it's pretty rocky."

"Fifteen minute. Very soon. You sick, over side of boat."

Robert nodded and sat back on the bench seat. He'd been overwhelmed by the 400 options on the restaurant's menu and had settled instead for a bowl of fried rice, which back home he'd never eat so early in the day. Savory breakfasts had never sat well with him, even as a child on those mornings when his father's mood swung in their favor and the old man cooked up bacon and eggs. But Robert ate whatever was placed in front of him anyway, regardless of how the rich smell of fat made his stomach churn. He didn't have the heart to tell his old man otherwise. Even little truths undo the biggest of men.

A dolphin breached the water, its side glimmering in the light before thrashing against the big blue. Amity was on her feet, pointing at the rippling swell. Her blond hair whipped around her face in messy tangles, revealing the contours of her smile. She almost thought she might cry. Nobody else had seen what she had seen.

It was just for me.

She thumped onto her seat and could feel eyes probing her flesh—it was almost instantaneous. Amity tried to focus on the three bright-blue coolers on the deck. *Just ignore her.* Easier thought than done, that was for sure. The woman was on her right, greasy eyes drinking her up.

2

Sycamore watched the girl turn away, exposing the back of her neck. Pink skin through flapping locks. Yes, this one was a tender thing—she would burn when hot and yield under a firm hand, should pressure be applied. The girl's red life jacket burned bright red, the color arousing something in Sycamore, and that something glistened in the pits of her eyes. It was the color of cancer—welts and bloodied sheets.

She thought maybe that someone she'd once known had died of cancer, but that was from another time, another life. If so, had that person been important to her, she wondered? Had they been kind? The few remaining memories were eroding away. Soon there would be nothing left, and of that, she'd be glad.

"Excuse me..."

The reed voice pierced her, scattering already scattered thoughts.

"Can you take our photo?"

A child, who seemed lost between seven and ten years old, stood in front of Sycamore, a waterproof camera in his hand. From the thick lap of his words and the dark soil of his skin, she figured the boy and his father must be Lebanese, maybe Egyptian.

"Why, sure. Let me grab that camera. This is a fancy thing."

"Thank you, miss."

"So where are you and your daddy from, then?"

"Beirut, miss."

"Beirut! Isn't that a thing!"

"Where are you from, miss?"

"London. Do you know where that is?"

"It's where the Queen lives. In a big castle. I've seen pictures in a book."

"That's right. You speak awful good English."

"We learn it in school."

"Dad," Sycamore said, addressing the man behind the child. "You must be proud!"

"Oh, yes. Yes," the man replied. "Will you take the photo, miss?"

"It'd be my pleasure."

Sycamore peered through the viewfinder. There, captured within the camera's crosshairs, were father and son with arms wrapped around each other. A tarpaulin veil from the boat's roof waved behind them, but the hazy horizon could still be seen.

Click.

Man and child become one in flesh and sinew. A slaughter embrace. Bones rise through meat to greet the day. Mouths wide in death screams.

"How did it turn out, miss?" asked the father.

"Oh, it's a keeper."

"Wonderful. *Obtenir la caméra*, Aban."

The child crossed the slippery deck—passing the three ice coolers and a tub of assorted snorkels—just as the boat rammed an uncompromising swell. The boy, lips drawn into a sudden O of shock, skidded sideways and fell. Sycamore reached out and caught the waif, felt the boy's warmth. Aban's young face was caught in the twin mirrors of Sycamore's sunglasses.

"I see your light," Susan Sycamore told the child.

3

There were nine of them in stagnant waiting, lulled by the rock of the boat. The engine snarled. The final two in their number were a Swedish couple in their late twenties.

They were on their honeymoon, the memory of their wedding still fresh in Judit's and Rolf's minds. Three hundred people had been in attendance, watching them enter the church, hand in hand. In accordance with tradition, Rolf had been wearing his ring since the night of their engagement. When the time had come for him to slip Judit's wedding band on her finger, she'd beamed. And it was then that he knew: *This doesn't just feel good, it feels right.* That moment was captured in the brilliance of a hundred flickering cameras. They left the church for their reception in a rain of rice and bubbles blown from lollipop rings. The toastmaster, Rolf's brother, eased them through the night with between-courses anecdotes. Judit's father wept into his handkerchief during his speech. Knives tapped against glasses, a sign that it was time for the newlyweds to smooch. When Judit left the room to powder her nose, Rolf was swarmed with kisses from all of the female attendees. Afterward, Judit kept her bouquet and asked her mother to have it pressed and framed while they were away. She wondered how those flowers would look on the wall of their Uppsala apartment.

It made her smile.

Her husband was by her side, knee to knee. Every time she felt his skin against her own, a tide of tingles rolled through her, reminding her of all they'd shared and the future that lay ahead. They would be the first to die, though others would bleed before them.

4

"Tobias, are you feeling okay? Amity wants to know. You don't look well."

"I am okay, Caleb."

"Are you sure?" He touched his shoulder only to have him flinch. "Jesus, you're shaking."

"I said I'm fine!"

Caleb snatched back his hand. "Have I done something?"

"No."

"Then what is it?" he asked as Amity nudged him. Caleb waved her away with a glib string of signs. *"I don't know what's wrong with him."*

"Did you ask?"

He shot his sister an icy glare. *Of course I fucking did,* Caleb mouthed. "Yeah, understood *that* one, didn't you?"

"Don't get snappy with me just because he's angry at you."

"Stop giving me shit."

"Give you shit? Do you have any idea how awkward all of this has been for me?"

"Just stop. I'm trying to enjoy the day."

"You're not alone on that one."

"I didn't even want to come. Think yourself lucky I'm here at all."

"Would you two stop?" Tobias asked, rubbing his forehead. "I hate it when you do your signs around me. I can't keep up."

"Well, just tell me what's going on."

"Nothing." He sighed and turned away, as though looking him in the eye was some kind of resignation. "Really. It's just I felt funny. *Seltsam.* Weird. Like, *furcht.* I don't know how to say it in English. It's been like this since we left, after breakfast."

Caleb chewed his lip. Had something happened earlier? He replayed the morning in his head. Nikom had piloted them out of the bay, passing fishing trawlers docking at a wooden jetty where children had been waving palm leaves. Pointing. Laughing. Amity had taken a quick photograph on her iPhone and tried to upload the image to Instagram. Caleb had shaken his head; of course there was no Wi-Fi reception out here. *Christ, that girl's married to her bloody phone.*

Uh-oh, I'm starting to sound like Ma.

Nikom spoke to them while steering the wheel with his toes and rolling a cigarette with his hands. The ocean opened up around them. Caleb hadn't realized just how quiet the group had become until there was a sudden roar of noise, like the stomach-churning roar of a passing subway train.

Then there had been a splash of water as the oncoming boat, which they had missed by inches, zoomed past.

One by one, the passengers had glared at their sheep-faced guide, who removed his foot from the wheel—nice and slow—and waved his hands through the air. "Welcome to Thailand!" he called, hoping against hope that his enthusiastic flourish would wipe away the memory of their brush with death. "Lots of adventure, *ev-ah-rie daiiiii!*"

Amity and Caleb had gripped each other's knees, understanding and yet not understanding at the same time, that they had all just come within a hand-span's distance of being ripped to pieces. Had the driver of the other boat not been paying attention either, their bodies would be chum for the coral sharks, assuming the boat hadn't exploded on impact, as they always seemed to do in the movies.

Caleb wondered if it was this event that had upset... his boyfriend. Because that was what he was now. So he touched his boyfriend's shoulder, and Tobias didn't flinch. That made him feel better. Tobias's cold shudder had felt like a betrayal, spitting in the face of everything they had shared, which, at least to him, had been a hell of a lot.

"You're sure it isn't me?"

"Ya. I'm sure," he said, rubbing his shoulder against Caleb's. "I am sorry. I am just weird. I just don't know why."

5

"What is in the boxes?" Aban's father asked, jiggling his son on his knee. The little boy was not quite awake, yet not quite asleep either. They had been in the boat for going on an hour.

"Very good question, sir. Very good." Nikom flicked his blackened cigarette into the ocean. "These boxes, they are called *eski*. That is what Australians say, right, Aussies, huh? Or a cooler, like in the Americas, right?"

"You got that right, Nikom," Robert said. "I've got a couple in my apartment. Not that I use them, mind you."

"Ah-ha. Very good. Cooler."

"Yes, I know that," Aban's father continued. There was an edge to his voice, a sharp reveal to the harshness of his character. "But what's inside them?"

"Open them up; it is okay."

Aban stepped forward, his sandals squeaking against the swaying deck. A glossy layer of saltwater swished back and forth across the wood, an echo of the boat's sway. He kneeled before the first cooler, gripped the lid and pushed it open on a greasy hinge.

There was no ice inside, just clusters of bananas—some ripe, some rotten—and piled six-packs of Coke. The glass bottles were covered in beads of condensation.

Aban yelped, clapping his hands together. "*Ce que je peux avoir un, Papa?*"

"Yessir, it is Coke," Nikom said. "You will be thanking me for this, because it's their favorite. You will share the drink and food with them. Sharing is very good, yes? Just like sharing tips!"

"Whose favorite?" Sycamore asked. Her voice was rough and waspy and dragged under the weight of her accent—as though every word spoken cost her comfort. In that voice, one heard the inner workings of industrial machines and the final gasps of the vermin crushed between their cogs.

"The monkeys, of course!" Nikom said. "I brought apples and Fanta with me on a tour one time, and boy-oh-boy, they weren't happy. *Boy-oh-boy*, very American expression, yes? I love America. Hi-ho, Silver, away!"

"Yeah, you and your brother do that very well," Robert said, crossing his legs. His fingers were buried in the soft pad of his forearm. He glanced down and noticed what he was doing—there were crescent moons of sunscreen under his fingernails. Though the itch had subsided, the scratch marks lingered. *Lines*. They followed him everywhere. The hard line; the bottom line; the economic line gouged through the bloody tissue of his home country. Robert wondered how the company was faring with him gone, if he and his talent were missed. The whole department

144

could be in ruin for all he knew, the dust coming back to claim him for making it out of the building alive the first time.

But Robert just couldn't find it in himself to care. Not for the time being, anyway. For now, there was only Thailand.

"There it is," Nikom said, standing up and pointing over the peak of the bow. The tarpaulin strung across the roof continued to flap in the wind—a crunching herald to the sight. "Everyone stand up and look now. Koh Mai Phaaw."

CHAPTER TEN

Koh Mai Phaaw

1

AMITY SAW THE island and her tongue cottoned
enough to make swallowing difficult. For a moment
she was tempted to reach down and snatch up one of
Nikom's Cokes, but didn't. No; she kept temptation
in check. There was some unspoken, hard-to-identify
kinship between those clinking bottles in the cooler
and the unease the island, despite its diminutive girth,
evoked in her.

It looked as though Koh Mai Phaaw was little
more than the piled bodies of giants buried alive with
pleas in their mouths, reaching for the sky. The tiers
of rock interwoven at its center were jagged fingers
crashing in prayer. There were serrated boulders, worn
down by erosion. The beach was an ivory grimace;
the island's victory against those suspected giants was
a constant amusement.

The boat drew nearer, waves breaking around them.
Nikom lifted the outboard motor and spun them 180
degrees, the stern aligning with half-uprooted vegetation,
trees caught in the act of trying to escape. Koh Mai Phaaw
grew before Amity's eyes, absorbing her into its landscape.

Come home to me.

She backed away, a hopeless gesture. Her backside pushed against the railing. Damp ocean decay filled her lungs, and yet she couldn't help being allured by it all. Scared, but seduced, as she had been when the door had opened to the run-down building, revealing the man from the Internet whom she'd agreed to meet.

The branches of those trees were extended in greeting, revealing glimpses of darkness beyond. Amity's heart sped. It was there, in that seedy blackness, that she wanted to go. It wasn't a new feeling, that was for sure. On more than one occasion she'd answered adventure's beck and call.

Nikom dropped anchor and lit up another cigarette. He stepped toward Amity and grabbed her by the shoulders, his face smiling into a network of interconnecting lines. Up close, she could see the cracks and blisters in his lips.

We're here, she read him say. *Let's go.*

Caleb dropped into the crystalline, knee-high water, a school of fish buzzing around his ankles. Ripples sent white shadows over his chest. "Ah! Little Nemos!"

"Can you help me down, please?" asked the female Swede—flagged by her telltale blond hair and lilting accent—whose face was lightly burned from their hour-long journey. Caleb had read somewhere, maybe in the *Lonely Planet* forums, that overcast days were just as bad for your skin, if not worse, than an hour in summer's hottest rays. His own was accustomed to the sting of Australian sunshine, at least. These guys, however, didn't stand a chance.

Caleb offered her his hand and helped her down. The Swede gave a delightful squeal as cold water splashed up over her swimming trunks. "Oh, it's so cold. Ha! Look at all the fishes."

"Yeah, cool, huh?"

"Thanks for the help. Nice tattoo by the way! The one on your arm. What's it say?"

"It says 'Family Love'. And it's no problem." Caleb gestured to the man behind her, who was climbing down over the side of the boat—a feat that was impossible to conduct with grace. "Is this your boyfriend?"

"My husband."

"Great. Would you like me to get a photo of you two in front of the beach?"

"That would be great! Rolf, *kan jag ha kameran?*"

"Here we go."

"Okay, so you two stand here. Oh, guys, that's just awesome. *Smile!*"

"Thank you so much," Rolf said, checking the shot. "It's very good. Some people they do not do nice photo, but yours are—" He gave him the thumbs up. "I'll get one of you and your friends, yes?"

Caleb pulled his sister and Tobias into a group hug. He could smell his boyfriend's savory underarms as he nestled; brilliant. It was a manly smell, arousing. Amity pulled away as soon as the photo was taken. The cold shoulder: an angry sister's best defense.

"I'm sorry," Caleb signed. *"I do want to be here. It's beautiful."*

Amity knew as well as anyone else that sometimes it felt good to hold on to your annoyance, to own your anger. But in the end, it just wasn't worth it. The day was too beautiful, even with the threatening clouds, to fight someone she cared so much for.

"It's okay."

Caleb embraced his sister and kissed her on the cheek. They stared into each other's eyes, nodding away the tension. Makeup hugs, as far as Caleb and Amity were concerned, were *the bomb.*

2

Sycamore watched them come, a current of bristling brown fur and wagging tails. The monkeys dropped from the braches of trees that looked as though blackened by lightning, scuttled out from between the boughs of great palms. Their emancipated faces flushed pink with excitement.

"Hello, little things," Sycamore said, deadpan.

Only many of the animals weren't quite so little. When the males stood on their hind legs, revealing their flea-ravaged stomachs and testes, they reached above Sycamore's hips. Infants swarmed among them; they were coming thick and fast from the jungle shadows, kicking up tufts of sand as they ran.

Pebbled with puckered scars, their idiot glares—it made Sycamore cringe.

Evolution left you behind, you fucks. Walking fossils. That's why you come to me for food.

Nikom thumped the bananas and Coke bottles into the hands of the nine tourists and watched them scatter across the beach. Raps of thunder sent a flock of birds into flight. *That sky's got some curry in it*, he thought and took another drag.

It would be another long day. Carting around tourists who had little qualms about showing off their wealth was monotonous and draining work. He was bored.

Crabs ran sideways across the sand and scurried into their conch shells. The light had dwindled. He noticed that the monkeys cast no shadows today.

"Holy shit, look at all you guys," Caleb said, offering a peeled banana to the animal waiting at his bare feet; he'd left his flip-flops in the boat. He glanced around for his sister and saw her standing at the jagged nimbus where beach and trees clashed together. A sting of longing.

All right, wander off then.

Wait, where's Tobias?

He wanted to share this moment with someone; the experience was richer that way. The monkey, impatient now, leaped up to snatch the banana from his hand.

"Whoa! You cheeky bugger!"

It was only then that Caleb really looked at the animal in front of him. His stomach tensed. This *thing* was a far cry from the cuddly creature he'd been expecting. Come to think of it, he wasn't entirely sure what he'd expected to interact with here on the beach—knowing only that *this* certainly wasn't it. He watched the monkey gobble the fruit down with fingers of articulate dexterity. But it was its misshapen face that chilled him. Its maw was made of scars welding its lips to its left eye socket, a constant sneer. Maggots squirmed in the hole where its nose should have been. He saw the flash of a pink tongue, the hint of rotten snaggleteeth. Finished, it rubbed its hands together and scanned his body for more food.

It was humid, despite the temperature drop, but sweat still hammered down Tobias's cheeks. Phantom tears. He gripped the Coke bottle, a nervous shade crossing his face. *"You've got a case of the jitters,"* as Mother used to say. *"Just like your papa."*

A niggling expectation—formless yet so very tangible—was undoing him. But the expectation of what, Tobias couldn't tell. Not then as a child, and not there on the beach.

When he was young, back when his view of the world was limited to what could be seen from his yard, his parents took him to a mobile carnival show. There had been the giant Ferris wheel, lit in golden bulbs and piloted by a man in a beaten-up top hat; clowns with manic smiles who twisted balloons into screeching, deformed animals; food vendors who gave out paper plates of *brathering mit bratkartoffein*—fried and pickled herring with crispy potato slices and onion rings; frosty plumes of breath caught and burning in writhing carnival light, fluttering like the ghosts of startled quail before vanishing.

But above all this, gigantic and imposing, was the roller coaster.

It was rare for Tobias's parents to take him to carnivals, but he'd been a good boy of late.

"Your brother is lucky to have someone like you by his side," she would say. His mother was a fragile woman with black fairy-floss hair, and plagued by melancholy. It was there in every desperate hug, in every tear. And Tobias knew it all could be traced back to his brother, who had aged her.

Tobias refused to see Jörg as any of the things the kids at school called him.

Jörg wasn't "slow" or "retarded". No; he just had Down Syndrome. Wasn't that enough? Tobias didn't get it.

And for some reason he was being rewarded for this confusion. As he saw it, he was just doing what had to be done. The things his brother dropped on the floor weren't going to pick themselves up; when Jörg pooped his nappy, his mother *had* to be told. What was the big deal?

But deserved or not, the carnival worked its charm. He was thankful. And scared.

It was the kind of roller coaster held together by rust and luck. Tobias somehow knew that it would be *his* turn—not the thousands of rides that had come before—that would rocket the carriage off the rails. He'd shatter against the ground.

Would it hurt, dying?

He wasn't sure if he wanted the answer to that one. When his mother asked him what was wrong, he remained silent. Seized by dread. But no, he'd survived, as had the fear.

A blast of cold wind shot through the carnival. Dust plastered his clammy skin.

A crest in the tracks. The eventual plummet. His stomach lifting into his throat and the tingle in his toes.

Tobias could still feel it now, surrounded by the hundreds of monkeys that were clamoring for his attention, snapping and snarling for the bottle of Coke he held in his hand, for the bright yellow banana in his back pocket. Their eyes were rabid pits of black and red.

They seemed to grow around him, rising up, rearing as a roller coaster crests. Their tiny yet strong hands ran over pronounced rib cages, making muffled rat-a-tat sounds.

The clatter of the carriage as it began to descend; screaming children all around him. Something was plunging him toward a dark place. A dark place where he was no longer alone. *The distant plucking of ukulele strings.*

The Coke bottle slipped from his hand.

Caleb went back to Nikom for another bunch of bananas, brimming with excitement. His toes squished in the damp sand; it felt nice. *We ain't in Kansas anymore, Dorothy*, he said to himself. *Or Evans Head.* He thought about his mother. Was she pining for them, or had she settled back into her labyrinth of trash? And trash was what it was—the sooner their mother realized that, the better. When the time came for them to return, things would have to change. Caleb would move, for starters, but he wouldn't leave without making a difference in his mother's life first. The bric-a-brac, the musty newspapers—it all had to go.

"Yeah, easy to say. Good luck, mate."

He approached Nikom, who was resting on one of the three coolers he'd dumped on the shore. He was rolling another cigarette. Caleb saw his gray tongue, speckled with tobacco rinds, running the length of the paper and wondered what Nikom's home was like, what treasures he kept and how they differed from his own or his mother's. What was important to him? What did he covet?

Every person has their pearls. Hell, maybe myself included.

His weakness was old letters.

Scrawled notes that had been passed around at school and pocketed later on. Love letters and empty valentines from boys and girls, all written by unconfident, shaking hands.

Caleb wanna be my BF?

If you think I'm hot tick either YES or NO. Please respond.

And then there were those *other* letters. The not-so-nice ones. Yes, he even kept these.

Caleb you're a fugly faggot. Poofter!

He had no idea how many hours he'd spent going through the shoeboxes he used to keep them in, bundled up with twine and rubber bands he'd stolen over the years. It wasn't unusual for him to empty them all out onto his bed, where he would then lie on his back with his ankles crossed and relive those years. The good, the bad, and yeah, even the fugly.

"Nikom, can I grab some more fruit?" Caleb asked, hoping the question would shake away the bullshit thoughts chain-lettering through his brain. They didn't. Not completely.

"Yes, sure. I will get it." He lit his cigarette with a Zippo; it was in the shape of a naked woman.

Caleb sighed. Their guide was alive with enthusiasm when addressing the group but acted as though every request were a backbreaking effort when caught on his own. Caleb gave him an awkward nod. *Working hard for your tips, I see.* Nikom's sweaty shirt lifted as he bent to the cooler, revealing his lower back, which was covered in furrowed scars.

Scowls in the fabric of his flesh.

Caleb cleared his throat and stumbled for a question. Any question. "So, wow. All of these monkeys. There are so many of them."

"Yes. Many. Here, take another banana."

"I'm cool for now. What kind of breed are they all?"

"Rhesus macaque. Very powerful. Strong. I saw one of them rip off a man's finger. Pop!"

"*Jesus.* Just like that, huh?"

"Ah-huh. Very bad."

"One of these monkeys did it?"

"One like it. A lot of these monkeys are...how to say? Natural."

"You mean, like, born here? Natural inhabitants?"

"Yes. That's it! 'Natural inhabitants', I will write it down later."

"But only some?"

"Ah-huh. Some were brought in from mainland, long time ago. For tourists. Clever monkeys from special monkey shows and circus. That way they could be very entertaining for visit. But now they are... dumb."

Steamy wind blew off the ocean, slicing frothy shavings from the waves. Caleb thought he heard a melodic note from somewhere within the jungle, a noise that cut through the hiss of swaying trees. He couldn't be sure. His arms threaded across his chest, a wounded gesture. He shook his head and tongued a filling at the back of his mouth.

Oh, I see what's going on here.

"Take another banana, sir. Take another drink."

"I, um, don't think I want to do this. I've read about tours like this. I'm sorry, it just leaves a bad taste in my mouth."

"'A bad taste in my mouth'. Ha, that's a good one. I will write it down too."

"I think I'm going to just go get my sister and we'll wait in the boat."

"But you have to give them banana and drink. It's their favorite."

"I said I don't want to. Look at them all, Nikom. They're all rotten and hungry and feral. It's disgusting. Besides, if you load 'em up with this shit week after week they'll forget how to hunt on their own. This is killing them; you know that, right?"

"If you don't give them what they want, they will get angry." He leaned forward and chomped his jaws together. His pearly whites snapped against each other, making a bony clap that cut through the chatter of animals and tourists alike. Only then did Nikom's eyes connect with Caleb's. Excalibur striking stone.

The cool of the jungle called to her, ran its fingers over her forearms until a skim of bumps rose. The wintry thrill of excitement. It was too strong to fight. Amity stepped into the clustered trees, into a world of vine and leaf and rich, loamy smells.

The bottle landed in the sand between Tobias's feet with a leaden thump. Glancing down, he saw the winking eye of the steel cap. A breath of light passed across the beach and then was gone, as though the sun were drowning beneath the ironclad clouds.

The roller coaster ride was over. His stomach was back in its place. The fear had died away.

A monkey scuttled forward, leaving behind a calligraphy of tail swirls in the sand, and reached for the Coke bottle. Fingers that appeared so humanlike and yet so strangely unrelated curled around the glass neck.

Tobias bent down and snatched the drink from the monkey's grip, sending it into a wide-mouthed cry that drew back its leathery lips, broadcasting rows of jagged teeth. "Gotchya, bitches," said the man who looked like Tobias, but wasn't.

Caleb crossed the beach in upset strides, passing the Swedish newlyweds, who were encircled by monkeys of varying size and color—one of which was dressed in the tattered remnants of a tutu and was clapping, pleased with its bounty of sugared drinks and fruit. It locked eyes with Caleb. A sickening stab of alarm seemed to splinter his bones when he saw the makeshift rouge dabbed upon its cheeks—makeup drawn from dried, red earth.

"Tobias!"

His boyfriend was still fifty yards away.

Why the hell did he wander so far? You'd think he didn't want to hang out with me.

A lump formed in his throat when he saw the Lebanese father on his left forcing his son to have his photo taken with a placid, silver-haired monkey. The child's face was mutilated by fear, eyes wide. Teeming. The animal near his chubby legs was well rehearsed and now happily fed; it sat back on its haunches, drinking Coke straight from the bottle in a haunting pantomime of human behavior. It didn't seem to care, or understand, that the child near it was afraid, or that its father was threatening it with a smack if it didn't stand still and smile like a good little boy.

No; the monkey just sat and stared. It had the prize it had emerged from the jungle to claim.

"Tobias," Caleb called again, drawing nearer. "I want to get back on the goddamned boat!"

CHAPTER ELEVEN

Matt

1

MATT OPENED HIS eyes, Coke bottle in hand. The monkeys were around him. He'd been watching as he always watched, waiting as he'd always waited, and fighting as he'd always fought. So much time had been spent in that other place, and he was never satisfied. Every minute was a minute spent scratching for the surface.

In the dark, he often fidgeted with his ukulele, but he knew, as any sane person would, that random chords do *not* a life make. They can't. He was now and always would be active by nature. Tobias, on the other hand, Tobias was the passive one, despite his strong clasp on The Body.

Tobias had to defy himself to trust others, to not assume that everything was dangerous. Despite what the others would like to think, The Body never would have embarked upon all of this travel if it hadn't been Matt doing the pushing.

Matt was a balls-to-the-wall thrill junkie. "God, walking on the wire's about as good as pussy," he would often say as he chewed on his trademark lollipop stick. "Danger's dope to guys like me," was another one of his well-used self-descriptors. But the attitude—from his swagger to the way he dressed in 1950s-inspired leather jackets, even the way he greased his fringe into a Tin Tin-esque quiff—was all icing on the proverbial cake. The menace was in his blood, and nobody, no queer black brother was ever going to exorcise it from his veins.

"You get only one go at this life," he'd say to the children. "One chance. You got to ride the rap, you know? 'Cause one of these days they'll drop the bomb and we'll all go Rocky Mountain high! You'll all be burned away, just like me. Nothing but ash'll be left."

It didn't take a goddamned rocket scientist to see that Tobias wasn't a good guardian, and Matt often wondered why Tobias insisted *he* stay inside and remain in charge of the children. Wouldn't it be better for them all if they traded places? At least Matt could admit that he wasn't alone.

Besides, he was a far better driver of The Body.

Even though Matt had tired of the music he sometimes plucked into existence, it kept the children happy. Without the music, they had a tendency to wander. One day, they would grow strong enough to climb The Tree and make their way to the surface. Until then, his calloused fingers had to keep plucking at nylon polymers that never broke or went out of tune. Over and over.

His little lullabies.

He could still remember the first time he'd broken through, that time on the roller coaster. Born of fear as they plunged. Matt's baptism was the screech of a carriage along rickety metal treads that twisted and turned without warning. He'd been dragged back into the dark again by the time the ride had come to an end, but in those moments Matt had seen and felt what had been denied to him for so long, and he would never stop hungering for it.

The second time he'd made it to the other side was on a day that Tobias had been left to look after The Ugly Thing. The creature who looked like a human and who seemed to think it was Tobias's brother—but who was neither.

I'm his brother. Something so ugly and stupid can't be like us.

That's why he had picked up their father's work boot and smashed it across The Ugly Thing's face, and why he'd laughed when the blood had started to pour. But it wasn't a victorious laugh, more the kind of nervous giggle people sometimes make when they hear bad news. He'd been shocked by how red that blood had been.

And how The Ugly Thing had screamed.

Teeth knocked in, pierced up through its slanted mouth. Stupid pig eyes glaring.

I can't believe it didn't see this coming. If it weren't me who did him in, it would've been someone else. Everyone wants someone to hate.

Even the children didn't like The Ugly Thing, but of course he'd had a lot of influence over them. Matt spent a great deal of time in the dark, whispering in their ears as they played among the tentacle-size roots of The Tree they hoped to someday ascend.

Thrashing the boy had made Matt feel alive. It was addictive, though short-lived. As soon as the steel-capped boot had thumped against the floorboards beneath The Ugly Thing's feet, he'd been dragged back into the dark. And he'd even felt a little bad about leaving Tobias alone in the room with the pulpy mess, whose cries echoed down The Tree's branches. Matt got over it.

You gotta move on, man. Keep on truckin'.

Suffice to say, there were no more surprise carnival trips for the Schubert's idolized boy. Matt had risen twice since The Body had arrived in Thailand. The first was in that tailor's back room, when the dope had been laid out on the table, when the machete had been within reaching distance. He'd almost snatched it up. It would have been so fun to swing it around, to hear the blade whistling through the air. But no; Tobias, a regular Captain Sensible, had decided then to shake off his passiveness and take control again.

Dude, I was about to go apeshit.

It'd been a long time since he'd gotten high, not since he was a kid. It had been with a girl who only liked to fuck when she was doped, but hey—that was just the times. Hell, they might have even been ahead of the curve on that one... Longing was easy. Being desperate for the past was easier still. It hurt to let go.

Drugs he could live without, which was why he hadn't driven his fists into The Tree over and over again, as he sometimes did when the thrill was yanked away from him. It was sex that he missed the most—and what blue-blooded guy wouldn't? The edgy excitement that courting brought on, of wooing hard-to-pin tail wrapped up so nicely in a pair of apple-bottom jeans. Not much compared to the buzz of fucking, and doing it a little too hard, plunging a little too deep. Pain was power, and there was no better place to enforce it than between the sheets, when you're doused in each other's sweat and she really doesn't expect it. She thinks she has your trust; you have, after all, got this far, and then *bang*. And while she's a-thrashin' you put your lips to her neck and sink your teeth in—not enough to bleed, of course, but enough to hurt.

Matt had almost climbed The Tree when Tobias had been with Caleb, back on the morning when they had been so rudely interrupted. He'd almost risen, fought through, and sunk his jaws into Caleb's shoulder. That'd teach him good. The commie queer. No, Matt was not too keen on the idea of man-on-man action; yet another reason to fight for control of The Body.

And just as Matt had persuaded the children to dislike The Ugly Thing, he'd also whispered to them about the perils of Tobias's sexual proclivities.

"Brother above's borrowing time, don't you know it?" His voice was a purr. "Sinners end up in hell. When you're all grown, you've got to help me take back The

Body, to save it. Because if Satan reaches up and takes Tobias, he takes us too. Innocents burn just as fast in hell as they do under the bomb."

The children had been shocked. All seven of them.

There was Mariama, age eight, a young African girl with AIDS, a disease that didn't make sense to him. There was Joe Mccormack, a white Australian of ten years who insisted on being called by his full name, and his twin brother Gus, who peered with identical sets of dim-witted eyes. There was Apolonia, Polish, also age eight, who spoke in a language Matt couldn't understand, though he sometimes thought she was making up all of those funny-sounding words on the fly. There was Uwe, who was five and German too, but who was always scared and often pissed himself. Uwe was closest to Maëlle, a French twelve-year-old whom Matt suspected had several other personalities clamoring within her skull, only one of which seemed to enjoy her own company. Finally, there was Paw-Paw, a two-year-old who never spoke and was always dressed in a soiled Spider-Man onesie, whose ethnicity was a mystery to them all. Paw-Paw, like Matt, was a biter.

2

And just as he had stood over them all, now here he was, standing above a crowd of feral monkeys. Matt laughed; he couldn't help it. "I can't goddamned believe it!"

The monkey roared at him, or seemed to. Though its mouth was wide and snarling, that guttural screech wasn't coming from it. No; that sound was coming from the *other* monkey. The one shooting out from between the trees, tearing up the sand, ruffling its silver fur. Matt was taken aback by its speed, let alone its size. He saw its short, pendulum breasts flicking back and forth as it skidded into a pounce that shot it through the hot, humid air. Toward him.

Must be the darn thing's momma. Hey, everyone's gotta have one, even the filthy, diseased Ugly Things of the world—

This train of thought never had the opportunity to run its course, or to journey into the incriminating sentence he'd intended, vomiting up and out of The Body's flaccid lips. Just as there was no time to pull his hands away or to drop the Coke bottle of his own free will.

No time.

The bottle had landed on the sand, so pent up with carbonated energy that the cap shot off in a squirt of brown lather. Blood among bubbles.

The smaller monkey, the one he'd teased, was now wailing at the sight of its mother with its jaws latched to Matt's arm. He wondered if its cry was fueled by terror or pleasure. He didn't know. The only thing he was certain of was that being in control of The Body came with certain responsibilities, including the ownership of its nerve endings. This was the kind of pain that only biting could bring. Matt was familiar with it, even if he had never gone quite this far. It was the kind of biting that made people bleed. The kind that hurt.

CHAPTER TWELVE

Red against White

1

A RIPPLE OF energy—screams and the smell of blood—crossed the beach, stirring every monkey on the sand. A pulpy beat of silence followed, in which every furred head rose as if on cue. Their eyes were wide and wet.

That stench, those sounds...they grew as solid as the rocks against which the monkeys sharpened their teeth. This solidity was a key that unlocked a door. On the other side of that door was an impulse for which the human brain had assigned a corresponding word, though of course semantics meant nothing to these animals. Those among them who had been trained and burned and beaten by their two-legged masters on the mainland were well beyond remembering the barks demanding they dance or juggle knives.

But a word it was. And it unchained them, united them. Made them fearless.

ATTACK.

2

Three adult monkeys scaled Judit. Their needle-pointed claws dug deep, hooked beneath her skin, and dragged. The weight was incredible, impossible to fight against, and pulled her to her knees. They stunk of shit and soil and rich, untreated wounds. Pus. Slit-open scabs.

She cried in Swedish—random words and exclamations—as one of the animals wrapped a muscled arm around her neck, throwing her off balance. It leaped from her shoulders, screeching shock, as Judit tumbled backward, arms outstretched before her. She landed on the porcelainlike spears of a giant conch shell that had been buried just below the sand's surface.

White-hot light. No agony. Just the sense of her body tensing up.

A memory cracked open, spilling good times with her husband and their friends, back in their apartment. Rolf had brought home from work a four-person Lightning Reaction game that some sicko had given him as a birthday gift. It required the participants to place a fingertip on a little flashing pad, which, as in a game of Russian roulette, would randomly give one of the four people a minor electric shock. It would beep, beep, beep at them, the flashing lights flashing slower and slower until they all knew that at any minute now—any second—one of them would be yelping.

She had been the first to be zapped, and as it turned out, her Lightning Reaction skills were not quite up to par. Everyone had laughed into their glasses of wine and she'd slapped Rolf's arm, telling him that she hated him for bringing the stupid game home in the first place.

Judit wished she'd never said that.

It had been the expectation of the shock that had hurt the most, not the shock itself. Looking back, it hardly hurt at all. The sensations of the shell spikes in her brain were very similar, in a way.

A PLACE FOR SINNERS

That white-hot light began to fade, and through the glare Judit watched the monkeys crawl her length.

They were fast and armed with wide, foaming maws—so many rows of scalpel teeth.

This can't be happening. Not to someone like me.

I'm married. I'm happy. I'm young.

My mama is pressing my bouquet as we speak. It's going to be framed and will hang in the wall of our apartment. Our bed is just down the hall from there, off to the left. Our new mattress is waiting for us to come home and throw ourselves against it. There's nothing like coming home and lying down on your own bed after a long trip, don't you think? After a great adventure.

A monkey scuttled up to her throat and looked her in the face. It inserted its spider-fingers into her mouth and grabbed either side of her lips, as though they were the bars of a prison it was desperate to break into.

This can't be me. This isn't my life.

In a burst of strength that no man, woman or child on that beach could have predicted, the wiry animal ripped the skin from the lower half of Judit's face. There was a pinkish spray of blood; it flecked the white sand. She rolled onto her side, arms flailing, misaimed punches swiping at nothing.

Judit's husband, who at the time of the attack had been busy deleting photos from his camera's memory card, was shocked into immobility. The camera, which moments before had so consumed him, now dropped to the ground. He could see the conch shell nailed into the back of his wife's head in a picture-perfect composition—the contrast of light and dark, the red versus all that white... The whole mise-en-scène was even framed by a low-hanging tree branch that gave the shot some balance.

Did we turn off the power to the television before we left? Rolf had no idea where the thought had come from. A nervous giggle escaped him.

He watched the conch shell crumble as his wife arched her back. The spikes, however, remained embedded in her skull.

Yes, you turned off the power. All is well.

"Judit!"

As he ran, he saw his wife in her wedding dress, the dress that she had debated over for so long.

Piercing hazel eyes through a veil. She had tasted like a peach when he'd kissed her in front of the church crowd. His mother's pearls had glowed in the flash of cameras. Judit's bouquet lay between her knees in the Mercedes after the reception, rocking to and fro as the car made its way down the rocky road. They had been a little high—not much, but enough. A delicate mix of rum and the line of speed the best man had offered them.

Her wedding dress, coiled up at the bottom of the bed. Their intertwined legs as they spooned, tumbling into dream.

The monkey ripped Judit's jaw clean off her face. There was something in that popping sound that reminded him of those flying Champagne corks, the thump of bedposts against their apartment wall on the night he'd asked her to marry him. On the other side of these sounds was the woman who had said yes, sprawled on her back in the sand. Bleeding. Dying. Right before his eyes.

Rolf dived onto her chest, shielding her from the claws that had ripped jagged slits across her throat. He kicked one monkey in the face. It twirled on the spot but wasn't deterred. Eleven of its kindred latched on to him—their reflexes so much faster than anything he could draw on. One of the animals lowered its jaws to him and scissored through the cartilage of his ear. The sensation of being tugged this way and then that way. Caught in a tide.

The remainder of Judit's face was inches from his own. Rolf saw his reflection in what was left of her pupils.

A large monkey, otter-slick with blood, latched on to his hair and flogged his head against Judit's, crushing his nose with enough force to send splinters of bone shooting up into his brain.

But she wasn't dead yet. She lived long enough to watch her husband die through a cruel, red veil.

3

They were a swarm of teeth and claws. Bristled backs. Eyes that didn't quite understand what was happening or what they were doing.

There was only the energy, the screams and cries whipping them further into frenzy. Some were surprised by how sweet and warm the blood was. Their muscles flexed, forearms digging into the sand in readiness to run and then leap. When there were no humans within distance to bite and squeeze and flay, they turned on each other.

Flurries of brown and gray zipping across the beach. Tracks through sand and flesh.

4

"Aban, *courir!*"

The fingers of the child's left hand were now just stubs gushing blood, but as had been the case with the Swedes, the sensation of pain was yet to scoot up through his body and alight his brain. He didn't understand what was going on, didn't understand that he would never again color with his crayons on the butcher paper his papa bought by the roll, that his days of fingering the soupy interior of the cake tin (despite how much his mother—on the weekends that he saw her—told him not to) were over. Aban loved that she always gave in. He missed her.

He watched his father vanish beneath their onslaught.

"*Courir! Courir!*" came a final set of gurgling cries.

Run.

Run.

The swarm thinned and drew together again—just like the birds that sometimes flocked above his papa's house in Beirut. Aban had once inquired as to what breed they were, and his father, who had been leaning so close that the child could smell liquor he more associated with his mother, told him they were *zarzour*. "Which is also a province in Algeria," Papa had added. "Where I once met a pretty woman."

Aban had so often wanted to ask his father who that woman was, but never did. His parents hadn't been divorced for very long, and even at such a young age, he understood that prying into other people's pasts was a bad thing. And deep down, Aban suspected that the woman from Papa's little story was not his mother—that she, perhaps, was the great wound of his life, one that would forever bleed.

A ring of gore. At its center there was the corpse, which writhed and danced in an imitation of life. The monkeys had hollowed out his father's stomach and now played in the cave left behind.

"Papa!" He wailed, shaking his fists as tears began to course down his cheeks, landing on his lips. The scene in front of him didn't make any sense. It scrambled the mind. He could sense his instincts rerouting information within his brain like the telephone operator he'd seen in an old television show once. She was sitting behind a desk with a set of headphones wrapped around her head, sweating in the grainy black and white of the "olden days", yanking cords from the switchboard and stabbing them in other holes. *Click-click-click*. Only these weren't voices that were being directed; no, they were images.

A dead kitten on the road that they had passed on the way to his mother's house. Aban had tried to ask his father what was wrong with it, but had been told to be quiet. To look straight ahead.

This image was now rerouted to the word DEAD.

It made him cry again.

He saw the old DVD player that they used to keep attached to the portable television in their kitchen. Papa often watched old American movies dubbed in French on it as he cooked. But the player just didn't turn on one day. There was only static on the screen; Aban didn't like the sound.

DEAD.

The upper half of the corpse shot upward, a bloodied puppet on a string. The throat bulged and exploded outward, revealing the glossy face of a monkey whose mouth was furrowed in a twitching carnage kiss. It dropped onto the sand and rolled among the grains until it was albino white, reflecting a rare ray of sunshine so bright it appeared as though lit by flame. His father's head cocked to one side and an eyeball slipped from its socket, dangling, swaying on a thread of muscle.

The switchboard operator turned to glare at Aban. There was blood dripping from her nose. He'd done the job for her.

DEAD.

Another monkey ran toward him but stopped short; it punched the ground in a defensive stance, squaring off its forequarters. It hissed at him, losing chunks of meat that plopped onto the trodden shells. Aban glanced down at them—unaware that he was dressed in a pinafore of blood—and saw that the meat was not just meat, but a part of his papa. An important part. The child's stomach emptied itself in a lurch that shocked the creature. The meat was the chewed-up remains of his papa's "boy parts".

Courir!

Aban pivoted and ran toward the shoreline. He could see Nikom, the friendly tour guide, stumbling back onto his boat. Behind him was a horizon lost to stormy haze.

Courir!

The command reverberated through the child's chaos. He could feel the first twinges of pain brushing against the raw nerves of his body, like the wings of the gentle *zarzour* he wished would swoop down and fly him away.

5

Nikom threw the anchor onto the deck in a clash of chain and iron. Panting foul-smelling breath, he dived to the controls, checked the boat was in neutral and that the shift lever was in the up position. He ignored the vomit threatening to spill out from between his lips and ran back to the outboard motor and started to prime it.

Push-push-push-push-push.

Don't flood it, he told himself. *Whatever you do, don't flood it.* His cigarette-stained fingers wouldn't stop shaking.

And through this all, he was thinking, *I knew this would happen.*

Someday, sometime. I knew it would all come crashing down.

He had spent many hours kneeling before the shrine in their house, praying to Buddha that his instincts would be proven wrong. Incense lit and blown through the rooms; whispers in the dimness. But ever since his older brother had approached him with the idea of indulging in illegal tourism trade to Koh Mai Phaaw, which his ever-ancient mother Thaksincha had always warned him against, Nikom had felt plagued by the inevitable. Haunted by spirits yet borne by their endeavor.

He tossed the throttle into start and pulled on the choke, yanking the cord over and over. Icy cold bullets of sweat dropped onto the plastic casing; the drumming sound unnerved him further.

Come on. Come on!

The screams continued to echo from the shoreline, but the roar of the engine and the hum of the proper blades beginning to spin overcame it all. They whoop-whooped through the air. Nikom's relief brought laughter.

Aban slogged through the shallow water, startling fish that had been swimming through clouds of pink blood. His head was beginning to carousel—clashing screeches, spinning, dead-eyed faces—and he felt as though his body were growing heavier and heavier with every footstep. The sand was wrapping around his ankles, as firm as clutching hands, trying to hold him in place. His calf cramped up, and he cried as he pulled his feet from the slush and continued to propel himself onward. It was endless. He'd had nightmares just like this, where some monster from his comic books would be chasing him down a street, dreams in which his imagination would punish him by making all of his movements sluggish, enduring the torture of slow motion.

Water splashed in his mouth. *Ew, salty,* he thought, spitting it out. *Papa always said not to drink water from the ocean, no matter how thirsty you were. It could make you crazy.*

The temptation to glance back over his shoulder and look at the beach was strong, but he didn't let it win. If he saw Papa's body again—all bone and raw flesh and spilling blood—it would all become too real. As of now, this was just a bad dream, nothing more; a nightmare that he could wake from as soon as he was safe on the boat's deck.

Temptation was calling out to him, demanding his obedience. It growled, forming words that wrenched at his skin, that pulled at the sides of his face. *Turn now,* it said. He twitched his eyes in the direction of the beach for half a second, exposing the thick tendons and roadmap veins that kept them safe in their sockets.

No, don't do it, he told himself, knowing full well that he was going to anyway.

But the dream is ugly.

The voice of the temptation was persuasive too. Frisky. It was the same voice that sometimes said, *Why don't you put that bread knife in the toaster, Aban? Boy-oh-boy, imagine what it would be like to stick your finger in that power point. Tee hee hee hee.*

"Pas! Pas!

No. No.

But his pleas went unheard. Aban turned around, and lucky for him, he only saw the long line of blood-streaked monkeys at the water's edge, slamming their hands against the hard-packed sand in frustration as he escaped into an ocean they didn't dare enter. Their faces were feverish scrawls of red.

He screamed.

Thrashing, Aban drew close to the back of the boat. The last thing he saw was the blue paint peeling away from the stern in curly flakes; it reminded him of the wood shavings on the floor of Papa's workshop.

The smell of cut pine. There was a handcrafted rocking horse in his room, the varnish smeared with his little fingerprints. He loved it. Always.

The outboard motor dropped down in an arc of whirring metal blades. They sliced through his scalp and butterflied his face.

6

Nikom wrestled with the motor until it hit the water's surface, and only then, as a six-foot-high fan of spray shot up into the sky, did he realize why the motor had resisted. That spray was bright red, with a finger of sunlight stabbing through it, casting a rouge shadow over his face.

His mouth was opened wide, salt alighting on the tip of his tongue. He didn't register the taste; in fact he didn't register a thing. The sight in front of him rendered him utterly powerless. Lame. Unable to do a thing. Nikom could feel himself emptying out, going pale. An unsympathetic, icy hand touched the back of his neck and squeezed. It was as though he no longer existed.

The boat shot forward, the engine booming its wasplike screech. He saw the bright pink smear left behind in the waves and the black shape bobbing to the surface at its center. It was hard to tell for sure, but something told Nikom that the black shape was the child.

And yet, at the same time, it wasn't. It was Kalaya, *his* little girl, floating there in the churning froth of the lapping waves. Weeping, Nikom wiped his face. It wasn't just ocean brine he saw lathered on his hands, sinking into the creases of his palms. There was so much red.

I knew this would happen.

And yet he had brought them here day after day anyway. The gamble he'd continued to make was etched with cruelty, but the sight of your family starving superseded it all. He couldn't just sit there in their decrepit house, unable to find work, and watch Kalaya's face grow gaunt and tanned.

I just couldn't.

I won't.

His fingers curled around the accelerator stick and shifted the boat into top gear. The bow split through choppy waters. Hands that he couldn't remember controlling gripped the steering wheel, piloting him further and further toward a life he no longer wished to live.

7

"COWARD!"

Caleb watched the boat sailing away, whitecaps red in its wake. "Come back, come back." His voice fizzled, snapping on the plea. He didn't want to fall to his knees, but the shock of being left stranded was overwhelming. He had to fight to keep himself upright. The world was a whirling place of brown blurs, twinkling teeth. The more he tried to convince himself that this wasn't happening, the more real it became.

The more blood he saw.

He was armed with a Coke bottle in each hand that he'd plucked from the sand. One was broken from where he'd smashed one of the monkeys across the back of the head, not killing it, but leaving it a writhing mess on the ground. He couldn't believe that he'd done it. Caleb never thought himself capable of violence.

Back in Danny's cramped office in Lismore on the last of their visits together, Caleb had told his counselor about how he'd once defended himself against a schoolyard bully, Steve Grafton. Steve used to call him Monster

Mash, and would press a finger to his nose and bend it sideways in an exaggerated echo of the wounds Caleb had suffered when trying to save his sister's life. Steve used to think this was the height of humor, and sadly, he was not alone. An entourage of cackling hyenas followed Steve wherever he went. Caleb had told Danny—who'd stared straight into his eyes, perhaps with the knowledge that he was being lied to—that he'd punched the bully square in the jaw.

It was important to Caleb for everyone to think that he was tougher than he was.

In reality, it had been Steve who had punched him, and without provocation. His bottom lip had been split open. He'd fallen flat onto the field, blood beading against the dry summer dirt. Caleb could still see the bully's shadow stretched out across the ground near him, see the shadows of the crows that circled above the school in the hopes of picking at forgotten sandwiches. At any moment, he expected either the birds or the bully to swoop down on him.

Those blows never came.

Caleb had watched Steve's shadow slip out of sight, but he couldn't hear the retreating footsteps over the pounding in his head. He remained there for a full five minutes, despite the green ants biting his arms, even after the school captain had rung the bell that signaled that recess was over and that it was time to go back to class. Only once the school-ground buzz had died did he pull himself up onto his haunches and wipe away the tears. The blood had already dried in the heat. His mouth tasted like he'd chewed on steel wool.

Two of the crows had fluttered down from the sky and landed on the soil in front of him.

"Go away."

The larger of the two black scavengers squawked at him, tilting its head to one side and then another as though scrutinizing him somehow. Its bleat was different from the *ca-aaaws* Caleb associated with the bird. This crow sounded as though it had said the word *fool*.

Caleb entered his classroom and felt the cool air caress his sunburn. He closed the door, slow and gentle, the clicking of the lock making his heart skip a beat. All of the faces turned to stare at him, and he could do nothing but stare back.

"Caleb Collins, what on earth took you so long?" asked his teacher.

Swallowing hard, he crossed the creaking floorboards until he stood in front of her, where he whispered that he'd tripped running back to class after the bell had rung and landed on a rock. He could sense Steve's icy stare burrowing into the back of his head the entire time.

His teacher had escorted him to the sick bay, where he remained until it was time to go home. The bunk had been hard and watched over by an old, rusted fan with ribbons flapping from the guard. Everyone had forgotten about him, apparently, because nobody came to dismiss him. So Caleb picked up his dust-covered backpack and left, even though he needed to pee. Once outside, he looked up at the sky for the crows. They were nowhere to be seen. He left the school grounds and walked home, becoming one with the quicksilver heat waves rising from the road. He found the stray puppy ten minutes into his journey...

The Coke bottles were still in his hands, but they didn't remain there for long. Crouched in a defensive pose, a wrestler in the ring, he was caught off guard by an attack from behind. His eyes blinked almost comically, and a gasp hiccupped from his body. The monkeys ripped, bit and tore as they climbed his skin, raking up his flesh, and climbed onto his back.

Disease.

The word was an iron spoke in his chest. It wasn't alone.

Rabies.

AIDS.

A knot of needle teeth clamped down on his neck, on the place where Tobias had kissed him the night before. He'd laughed and giggled at the time—the memory was barbed.

The creatures stank of spoiled fruit, shit and wet dog fur.

Caleb couldn't understand how something so firmly latched to his body could writhe and fling itself about so without breaking its back. He didn't understand anything—his thoughts were scrambled. Reality was a thin film, and the same claws that had ripped through his back had ripped through it too.

A notion burst in his brain. *I'm losing this.*

The two other monkeys crawling over him snatched the bottles from his hands and dropped to the ground—

(fight back for fuck's sake!)

—but he made this work in his favor. Their prizes, and the momentary distraction they gave them, granted him a stroke of opportunity: just enough time to thrash the remaining few from his body. Two flipped through the air and landed on the sand. There was just one left, and it was dug into his neck. He reached up and grabbed the stinking blur, dug his fingers in its hair. Caleb could feel the layers of flesh yielding beneath his grasp; he pushed through it and latched on to the frail chest bones beneath. A surge of power shot through him. His fingers: pistons flexing down, snapping bones.

The snapping skeleton made a victorious thowcking sound that made his determination burn brighter. "I got you! I got you, you sonofabitch!"

Caleb tossed the animal aside, laughing as it hit the ground and lay there, empty of life.

They're just goddamned Muppets. Watch me as I cut all their strings.

Something hot and syrupy squirted into his mouth; it was bitter tasting. He reached up and touched the half-moon of missing flesh from his neck. Blood coursed down his chest and bruised his cotton singlet top; he didn't care. He was fucking fearless now, hungry for the next attack. To bleed was to live.

"I'm doin' it. I'm fucking doin' it."

Energy exploded in him, forcing his legs into movement, even though his brain tempted him with lullabies. *Wouldn't sleep be good now? Sleep is safe and silent.*

No, he wouldn't give in. Couldn't.

Sleep.

Amity was still out there, somewhere.

Caleb stretched over the top of the refrigerator, shuffling dust and forgotten trinkets—a Vegemite jar full of sewing needles, a ball of twine. He heard the jingle of keys brushing against his fingertips before he saw them.

Gotchya.

He limped down the hallway toward the front door, which he'd left open. There were leaves dancing across the carpet, carried on the wind. One plastered itself against the television set.

Don't go any farther, *said the voice, which, thirteen years later, would tell him to give up and lie down on the beach.* You're going to get in so much trouble.

But he didn't listen, and ran into the still-foggy morning instead. His sister was lost out there, having wandered from the tent where they had been sleeping. Caleb saw the arms of surrounding trees fading out of the gray wash, the sliver of the dark road. The family Holden was still in the driveway; he hobbled over to it and slipped behind the wheel.

"Holy shit!" *he said, looking down at the dashboard, knowing the word was something he shouldn't say. But it didn't matter; the guys at school said far worse. They even dropped the f-bomb sometimes—the dreaded word that got you sent to detention quick smart.*

His fingers were shaking so hard he struggled to insert the key into the ignition. I've seen Ma and Pa do this a thousand friggin' times—it can't be that hard!

"Stop fighting me," Caleb told the car. *He closed his eyes, took a breath and funneled all of his focus into his fingers. And as though the key had been listening, it slid into place with a satisfying click.*

"I did it! I did!"

"I did it! I did!" The sludge of blood and sand in his mouth made his mantra taste better.

His strides dug foot-shaped clods along the shore as he beelined toward the jungle. Caleb stopped.

The sight was almost impossible to handle. It reminded him of those Hieronymus Bosch paintings he'd studied at school, the ones his mother had been so upset over that she wrote to the principal asking if artists of a more "Catholic decorum" could be featured in her son's class. A shroud of embarrassment had wrapped itself around Caleb as a result. Though the school had listened to his mother's plea, they couldn't scour from his mind the images that he'd seen. And this surprised him, as his interests had always leaned toward sports; art was more Amity's thing. Looking back, he was sure his fascination with Bosch stemmed from the fact that his mother had prohibited it.

As he stood there trembling, with his eyes locked on the beach in front of him, he couldn't help but wish his mother were there to write it all away again. "Oh God..."

There were no demons lurking beneath pomegranate trees, or elfish hogs in clam shells. There were no inquisition barristers being stabbed to death with swordfish blades. The scene that was burning itself into his brain was far worse than anything he'd seen in those textbooks because it wasn't an image of the fantastic. It wasn't a work of imagination. It was as authentic as his scars.

Churning clouds of black and mauve stood out bright against the island's canopy. Beneath this there was the strip of sand, which not so long ago had thrilled them all with its sparkle and warmth. Now it was a red carpet laid out to celebrate slaughter, a gala of the grotesque.

They rocketed back and forth at an incredible speed. So nimble, so light-footed. Some juggled pulpy eyeballs, scooped from the faces of the dead. Others were engaged in a tug-of-war over intestines. Some had dipped their grubby little fingers in pools of blood and smeared the mess across their faces in a terrifying echo of their lives on the mainland, where some had been forced to wear lipstick to appease the tourists as they danced, as they begged on their masters' behalf.

Now that so many of the travelers who had arrived on Nikom's boat were either dead or missing, the monkeys' resolve had become less fiery. They had not been bred to kill; they were just mad for frenzy. So with nothing else to do, the males grabbed females by the backs of their necks and mounted them from behind, their hips quivering and their giant testes swinging. Animal mouths spread wide in yawns, stretching the leathery skin of their faces. The noise was an assault. Peppered throughout the scene were Coke bottles streaked with bloodied fingerprints, empty banana peels. This was a place of sickness, a battlefield. And Caleb, standing so very still, hardly breathing, was among it all.

But not for much longer.

"*On your marks,*" screamed a voice from the past. It was as though he were fifteen again at the school sports carnival, the air thick with the sweetness of sweat and hot dogs, at the only place he would ever be cheered.

"*Get set.*"

If he won the race he would be awarded with another certificate and a colored ribbon that his mother would later slip beneath the wax paper of her Memory Lane book. He might even get his photograph in the yearbook! His skinny arms raised in victory, the flash of a camera.

Yeah, that would be just too cool.

"*Go.*"

He ran.

The family Holden backed out of the driveway.

There was no oncoming car to smash the vehicle into submission. There was just the thinning fog, pulling away in ghost layers. It was an invitation to go further into the early morning, to succeed. And succeed he would.

This is what big brothers do. They don't give up. Never.

He tore through the narrow Evans Head streets with a dominance he'd never expected to have over the car. It was as though all this metal, the springs and grease, were an extension of his arms and legs. "I'm coming for you, Amity."

Caleb could see the campsite up ahead and, through the windows, saw the shocked faces of the State Emergency Service crew, the gasping locals who had volunteered to search for the little girl lost in the fog.

It was then that it happened.

The wheel slipped under his grip, and the Holden skidded sideways across the churned earth. His world filled with an almighty crunch. Flying glass twirled through the hub as the car started to roll.

A monkey with an almost humanlike face dropped the fingers it had chewed from a corpse and leaped onto Caleb's shoulder as he attempted to run past unnoticed. Its face burrowed in the already soft and wet part of him, where its kin had already torn, shredded and swallowed.

Caleb hit the ground hard and rolled. The landscape began to revolve. Bloodied sand that had been below was now up; clouds that had guarded them all from rain now under his head.

The car twisted and rolled, the frame turning into a horrific mouth of sharp metal teeth that stabbed into his teenage body. He could see bursts of rock through the spider-webbed windshield as the Holden continued down the incline. There was pain blooming inside him somewhere, but Caleb couldn't pinpoint its origin. It wasn't one place. It was every place.

He gasped as the car came to an abrupt stop. Waves crashed

around him, a cold spray against his face. "Amity, I'm a-comin'."
Words were a bloody chorus. He didn't have long. There were
animals out there in the fog, vicious critters that wanted to hurt
and eat his seven-year-old sister.

I'll save you.

Caleb took off his seat belt and forced himself through the
saw-toothed cluster of shattered car and slipped onto the rocks
outside. The cave was right there, its mouth wide and dark.

He was shocked by the strength of the monkey. It had
shot out of nowhere, bringing with it a well of power that
betrayed its size. Caleb's breath had been knocked for a
home run and his mouth was full of sand again, but he
was alive. That was what mattered. He hadn't given in.

The animal's muscles were threads of force wrapped
around bone. And those bones were frail. Caleb had
found its weakness, and his fear had made him strong.
He crushed its skull with his hands, globs of fish-stinking
brain spewing across his face.

He spat at the remains. "Fuck you." He proceeded to
punch the dead thing's chest. *Crunch.* "I got you, Steve!"
Crunch. "You bastard." *Crunch.* "You—" He ran out of
insults and pulled his fist out of the remains. Vomit
boiled inside him, the bile burning his throat.

En masse, the creatures that had spilled from the
trees in search of sugar were a force to be reckoned with.
Together, they could tear a grown man apart in seconds.
Yet on their own, they were weak. Feeble. Although he
couldn't be sure, Caleb assumed that was why he was
laughing now.

He was a good fifteen yards from the jungle, which,
now that he was closer, was not the impenetrable wall
he'd assumed it would be. It was lush and full of flowers,
almost inviting. And now Caleb was more certain than
ever that his sister had wandered into it.

How could she resist?

Caleb reached the cave before any of the adults had a chance. He'd been faster and stronger willed than any of them, including his father, who he knew must be close behind with his best mate. Not even that surprise sideswipe off the road and tumbling down the cliff had stopped him! He could see the headlines of the local newspapers now, twirling out of the dark as they did in the movies.

TEEN SAVES LITTLE SISTER.
CALEB COLLINS, STAR OF THE SCHOOL.
PINT-SIZE HERO—AUSTRALIAN OF THE
YEAR.

"Amity, I'm here. Just call out to me, bub."

The cave was dark and throbbed with echoes. Waves struck the rocks outside, shaking the briny walls and startling a flock of cartoonish bats into flight. They twirled around him, their wings slapping together in applause. Caleb smiled as his initial fear receded; they weren't scary. They weren't the repulsive, flying rats from the old black-and-white vampire flicks that played on television some Sunday afternoons—the ones that were meant to be scary but, man, were they just so lame. Nope; these bats were happy to see him. Why else would they be smiling at him with their tiny faces as they escaped into daylight? The nightmare was almost over. His heart battered with excitement.

"Amity, where are you?"

There. Now that his eyes were adjusting, Caleb could see her toward the back of the cave, at the rounded place where rock met the barnacled floor. Amity was very still with her back to him; the only movement was the swish of her blond hair in the draft. Her locks shimmered gold, so long they reached halfway down her back. Caleb thought she looked a bit like the Raggedy Ann doll the seven-year-old had left in the tent.

"Are you okay?"

Caleb reached out and set his hand—which shook in spite of itself—on his sister's shoulder. As soon as he felt the feverish heat radiating through the little girl's flesh, Caleb knew that he'd been deceived. This wasn't Amity Collins, the little girl whom he'd taught to tie her shoelaces or braid her hair. The creature under his palm was something else.

It was AIDS. Rabies. Disease.

Caleb's scream caught in his throat as the figure in front of him spun around with venomous speed. It had simian eyes and cheeks of downy fur. Buckskin lips hauled back to bare black gums and rows of teeth, which were marbled with chunks of flesh.

High-pitched mewls. Shallow panting.

The monkey—coming out of nowhere, out of everywhere—launched at Caleb's face before he had a chance to get to his feet. In no time at all, it popped his eyes with the splayed fingers of a single hand and sucked up the jelly in two greedy, birdlike swoops. Claws severed Caleb's nose and lips from his face.

8

Amity glanced at her waterproof watch. She agreed to give herself five more minutes in the scrub before she about-turned and made her way back to the beach. But until then.

Until then...

She felt alive, at one with the jungle around her. The odors were raw and plush, as palpable as the humidity. Wild hands of sight and smell touched her with tenderness that was by turns cruel and arousing.

I'm meant to be here.

It was a living world. There were trees strangled into submission by vine and rot, which, given time, would fall to the ground and become the mulch for further trees, homes to animals so small she didn't stand a chance of seeing their scurrying. Dewdrops floated through shafts of pale light, thrown from the thick canopy overhead. The ferns were doorways that led to additional layers of vegetation. She passed through it all. There were the exploding colors of the flowers—yellow, orange, blue, purple—freeze-frame fireworks that made her skin tingle. And beyond all this there was darkness she couldn't wait to brighten.

Amity came to a giant, half-collapsed tree that resembled a hunched old man with a beard of branches and dangling moss. He appraised her with kind, tropical bird eyes. She laughed into her silence, so happy to be away from all of the RED that haunted her, lost now in GREEN that was so easy to give herself over to.

Oh, Caleb, I wish you'd come in with me. You'd love to see this.

Maybe then you'd understand.

Maybe you'd forgive me for wandering. Again and again and again.

The high she was riding was more powerful than the few times she'd tried drugs. Those three occasions had been with her brother: once at the Lismore Light Festival, another time at one of Caleb's friends' apartments in Ballina, and another time in the middle of the night on the Evans Head beach. Amity and Caleb had dropped the ecstasy pill in the pub restroom, watched the end of the cover band, and, with arms draped over each other, walked to the water, gushing love for one another as they went. There, they lay upon the sand and drew dot-to-dot star pictures with their fingertips.

"*God, the world is so big,*" he'd signed to her.

It was a wonderful feeling. But this was better.

Amity giggled into her clammy hands. She'd spent so many years trying to pinpoint from where her desire to explore nature had sprung. There had been times when she'd given herself a migraine trying to figure it out—to justify it all. And this was why she laughed now.

It so-oooo doesn't matter why. It never did.

A huge butterfly swished through the air on huge wings—a flapping spectrum of color and shape that blurred together to form the illusion of a warrior's face dressed in war paint. It landed a yard away on the old tree man's knee.

The temptation to touch it was strong. Her hand was outstretched.

Its body throbbed against the mossy bark; the wings arched and relaxed. Antennae twitched at its head. *Curiouser and curiouser*, she thought with a smile.

Three plops of RED splashed against the insect. Startled, it dashed off into the air.

Amity glanced overhead as a hot splatter of liquid landed on her face. There were monkeys swinging through the trees above, leaping from branch to branch with Coke bottles curled up in their tails. She jumped up and down, thrilled by the sight—the way their sleek bodies looked against the cross-stitch canopy, which was lit with stars of dimming sunlight. The way their fur glimmered red. Like the liquid. That had been on the butterfly. And was now on her face. In her nose. On her tongue.

She held her hand up to her eyes. Blood.

What the hell?

Strong hands wrapped around her from behind, pushing her flat against the old tree man's belly. Sweaty fingers wormed over her mouth.

9

Robert Mann forced the girl against the tree. "Christ almighty, don't budge an inch!"

He'd been running through the jungle, away from the beach, when he saw her standing there as though she hadn't heard all of those screams and shrieks, and had no reason to be concerned by the monsters. And monsters were what they were. Hell, maybe they were even demons. Robert didn't have a religious bone in his body, but he always figured he had the potential.

One day, it'll be a case of "the straw that broke the camel's back"—someone I just can't bear to live without will die—and horribly, most likely—and I'll go a-running to the Big Book for comfort. He had observed it happen many times over, with colleagues deciding that, *Yeah, I guess it's time to get that suspicious lump on my neck checked out*, only to be diagnosed with cancer a week later. These were grown men who had never once stepped inside a church in their lives, and then jump cut: they're kissing the withered hand of a priest, weeping into his frock, begging him to pull some strings with the Big Guy upstairs to organize some angel to overnight FedEx him some instanta-cure (it's simple, you see: *just add water*).

He could see the ad copy now.

It was an A4 page design that depicted a sledgehammer sealed under glass. The words I KICK ASS FOR THE LORD were burned along the length of the tool's wooden handle. Above the image, in a distinctive font that really made the lettering jump off the page—

(*"Come on, Robert, you really got to make this one pop," was how the marketing team always put it*)

—was written:

BREAK IN CASE OF EMERGENCY.*

The asterisk, of course, related to a thin line of disclaimer text at the bottom of the page.

Assurance is not guaranteed. Guess you'll just have to have a little faith, huh?

Had this advertisement been real and the sledgehammer within reach, Robert would have thrown his fist through the glass and yanked it into his hands by now. He longed to feel its weight in his arms, to grip the inscribed handle so tight his knuckles turned white.

And he'd swing it, he'd swing it hard, and he'd do it for the both of them. Him and the girl.

We need saving.

He had been taking a photo of an infant monkey with a banana in its mouth when the Swedish couple had been bombarded; their screams changed something in the animal. It assessed him with new eyes. Moments before, as he gave it the fruit to chew on, he'd been its best friend. Now he was the enemy. A threat. Something that could, yes, provide it the food and drink as it demanded, but which could also threaten and hurt. Robert had felt a ping of guilt as the infant glared at him, seeming betrayed. He had, after all, witnessed similar expressions on his daughter's face.

That primal urge to seek safety sent his legs into a sprint. His aim was to disappear beyond the tree line and into the cover on the opposite side, but he tripped on an exposed root just before reaching his goal. His hat fell from his head, exposing the tufts of his graying hair. The shadow from the encroaching jungle made the sand here much cooler than that back in the war zone. It was almost soothing. Whatever relief he felt was short-lived, as a splish-splash of scat sprinkled over him. Robert didn't allow himself to react. His body stiffened and he buried his face in crook of his forearm. Monkeys leaped from the trees above, as fluid and graceful as flowing water, and passed over his unmoving form.

Robert kept his prayers to himself.

And then there had been the blood.

The part of his brain that dictated his logic condemned him for not seeking refuge on the boat, for not trying to save those who were under attack. It confirmed in him what he'd perhaps always known but never admitted to: that he *was* yellow.

It was an expression his father, when he was alive, had often used in reference to his drinking buddies—those of them who hadn't enlisted in the army. "They're yellah," he'd say in his clipped Kansas accent, which Robert had made a concerted effort to shake off. "We live in the Air Capital of the World, and some of these guys haven't ever stepped inside a hanger. Sedgwick County's a breedin' ground for cowards." He would fix his glare on his son, lean forward and caress his cheek in a manner that spoke of both comfort and threat. "You ain't *yellah*, are you, Robert?"

It was then, as he lay there playing possum, that his skin had begun to itch.

Yeah, I think I am.

His ex-wife also shared this sentiment. And she'd been right, even then. He hadn't had the balls to tell her that he was drifting. When she asked if he still loved her, he'd said yes. Robert's guilt was deep and bloodied. That didn't stop him from putting his hands on the legs of the women who slipped in through his car door and sat on the leather seat next to him. He was constantly shocked to find how sad they were. Yet this was why he could trust them: they were his mirrors. Robert was always trying to tell himself that *nah-hhh*, cheating's just an elaborate form of masturbation—love's where it counts. Another lie. He was sure it would end the way he wanted, amicably and without notice, though it didn't. He got caught and it ended the way it should have, with his wife busting open his face.

"*Coward,*" was what she called him.

When he was running from the beach—forcing himself through the jungle like a slow-moving blade through flesh—and saw the girl near the tree, the part of himself that he hated the most reared its head.

Redeem yourself, you fat fuck.

This was why his sweaty arms were pinning her against the bark, shielding her vulnerable body from the eyes of the monkeys in the canopy.

Take me! Take me!

There's little in me that's worth saving anyway.

The girl writhed under his grip. "Sh-shhhh, sweetheart. Don't move. They'll see you."

Her beat of stillness was a distraction that worked. She crouched to the side and drove her elbow into his crotch. Roberts swooned, breathless, as liquid pain seared through his lower half. By the time he landed on his knees with an almighty guffaw, almost all of the color had drained from the burst capillaries on his cheeks. The girl stumbled away.

"No." Gasp. "Stay still! I'm here to—"

Help you, Robert wanted to say, but the nausea from

the blow snatched him up again and wouldn't let go. The sudden urge to vomit was consuming. He grabbed one of the tree roots and began to drag himself back onto his feet.

Robert saw the girl. She had plucked a fallen tree branch from the among the deadfall to defend herself with, only to have it crumble into mulch in her hands, spilling white caterpillars down the front of her blood-speckled singlet top. Her fingernails began to scratch at the insects, popping and smearing them, yet tearing up her skin in the attempt.

Robert began to feel the phantom sensations again, those bedbugs that lurked deep down in his flesh. The hairs on his arms stood on end, revealing the threadwork of white scars they had left behind. He knew they were still there, somewhere inside him, even though he couldn't see them. They were building tunnels through his bones, waiting until it was dark again, and only then, once he'd finally caved in to his fatigue and fallen asleep, would they rise. It was horrible the way they burrowed up through the pores in his skin and danced. Robert had no idea how they managed to survive, but they had. The evidence was right there, in the echo of their bites. They were as immune to the pesticides he'd doused them in as they were to his limitless begging.

They had flared just enough to remind him that they were still there—

(*Ha. As if I could ever forget!*)

—and then vanished. Their electricity fled him and he almost collapsed in an anemic faint. Hands of darkness massaged his head, threatening to knead him into sleep. However, they disappeared just as quickly as they had come when he saw the monkey drop out of the canopy and land on the ground behind the girl.

Robert searched inside him, through the burning flares of pain, and found speech.

"Watch out!"

Amity sensed the presence behind her as the last of the repulsive caterpillars peeled off her skin. Those that had survived her assault writhed against the leaves between her feet, baking in the sunlight they had tried so hard to avoid.

She spun around.

The monkey's fur was the same hue as the ashes that coated Evans Head during sugarcane burning season—and it stank just as strongly. Saccharine and soil. It was hunched over with its forearms scratching at the ground and its head arched in her direction. Were it to stand, Amity was sure it would stretch over a yard in height.

Its mouth was as wide as its face. Teeth protruded. She could tell that it was roaring at her, and the sound she couldn't hear was RED. And yet, in a way, she could hear it...

Amity's body tensed.

The sound was the growl of wild dogs—echoing, echoing—within a cave.

She could still see the head bitch now, as threads of rubbery saliva dripped from its jowls. Fleas swarmed through its coat. Even after all these years, the bitch was squared off to leap at her, to bite and tear and covet her bones again, if indeed it had ever stopped.

The monkey shot at her, sending up a spray of dead leaves behind it. It slit through the air, through floating dust mites, twirling bugs, and the day's first rain that had just started to trickle through the canopy. Amity could see every one of its rippling hairs; the sight seized her chest in preparation for pain. Those beads of water exploded against the monkey's face as it soared nearer and nearer.

The lead bitch pounced.

Amity knew that nothing would soften the blow, but she turned her shoulder to it on instinct. Needle claws rooted in her skin and dragged slashes through her flesh as gravity bore the monkey to the ground.

Until that moment, she'd never known what real pain was like. Not really.

It had been so many years since the day her eardrums exploded that the memory of the agony had dimmed. Then, of course, there had been the time she'd lost her footing in a school-run yoga class and landed on her tailbone. *How she had cried*—the ache was incredible. Her friends, all of whom had speech impediments of varying degrees, had huddled around her in their leotards and tried to help her. When one girl tried to haul Amity to her feat, a scream had filled the hall, stopping all in their tracks. At the time she'd thought, *It can't get worse than this, except maybe childbirth.*

But she was wrong. Real pain hit you hard, and it didn't act alone.

It had conspirators. Spiteful memories that smashed at her from every angle.

The lead bitch biting her leg.

Bright blood on her fingers as she pulled her hands from her ears.

Her father's coffin being lowered into the ground.

The faces of the leotard-wearing students huddled around her, their large foreheads bulbous moons threatening to tumble to the earth and crush her alive.

There was the man in the old gas mask; his unheard words fogged the eye glass.

Yes, there was all of this pain too.

The monkey hit the ground and revolved around to attack again. She kicked it in the throat with her foot. There was heat in the impact, in its soft gullet. It revolted her.

Got you, you fucker.

But the monster was quick. Its eyes darted with frightening intelligence.

Christ, what do I have that it wants so bad? I've got nothing, she wanted to tell it. Instead, she roared back at it, hoping to scare it away. No luck.

It leaped again but didn't get far. A slab of brown rock thumped down on the back of its neck, forcing it against

193

the jungle floor in a spray of red. It twitched under the weight, kicking at the air in frantic jabs. It spasmed one final time and then settled. Dead.

Panting and oblivious to her own bleeding, Amity slumped against the roots of the old man tree and watched the stranger in the Hawaiian shirt, who had appeared from nowhere to save her life, reach his soiled hand out in her direction.

I'm so sorry for hurting you, she wished she could say. The humiliation was instantaneous. *I'm sorry I doubted you.* Only then did the tears begin to flow.

The stranger from the boat wrapped his arms around her. Safe. Amity pressed her face against his sweat-soaked floral print. She longed to speak the words she wanted to say, yet wouldn't.

Thank you. Thank you.

Amity felt the man tense against her. Through a stunned blur of tree, earth and rain, she saw the shapes dropping from the canopy and landing around her. They plopped to the ground—one, two, three. Exploding bombs of hair and teeth scuttling toward them.

The man's mouth wrote a single word for her reading. *Run.*

The shock of the attack stripped Amity and the man of their sense of direction. They were sprinting now, hoping against hope that the path they were carving through the jungle would lead them back to the beach.

Amity called out to her brother in her head, and the name ricocheted off the interior of her skull. Her pulse hammered through every limb. Sharp leaves whipped against her face. A bright orange bird shot up from behind a bush and crashed into a thicket of flowers, exploding dust pollen in their faces.

We're going the wrong way, cautioned a voice in Amity's head. *I just fucking know it.*

It was getting darker. The canopy was so thick that even the rain struggled to touch the ground. She glanced over her shoulder and watched the monkeys hurtle from tree to tree in a sloppy choreography of luck and dexterity. They were dark with blood.

The man's hand gripped around her wrist.

You've got to slow down, please-please-please.

Amity's feet were beginning to drag, despite the adrenaline forcing her onward. It came without warning...

There was a sudden dazzle of sunshine and clouds. Weightlessness. One of the monkeys dove through open space beside her head, waving its arms, clutching at nothing. She watched the man fall ahead of her, his Hawaiian shirt billowing. The raindrops were caught in conflicting currents of wind and glimmered—shooting stars. Amity's stomach lifted into her throat.

The ground had vanished from beneath their feet and now they were plummeting off a cliff face with the peaks of trees rushing up to greet them. White birds flashed by, a shimmer of hope before the impact.

10

Koh Mai Phaaw's beach was a red-and-white checkerboard. The monkeys dragged themselves back into the trees, exhausted by the game. Coke bottles were wrapped up in their tails, tinkling against the branches as they went. They left their dead behind in puddles of rippling rainwater and bone shards.

Nobody was mourned.

Wind blew hard. Air full of kinetic energy. Leaves twirled, fell.

There was movement in the red water. Susan Sycamore's bald head, crowned in a halo of pelting rain, hovered above its surface. She blinked, squinting against the sting of bloodied saltwater splashing in her blue eyes. Lightning gashed the sky in a silvery bolt. She was ready.

Sycamore would miss the ocean. It was home to her now. She stepped from waves that churned with gristle, with meat. The water ran down the curves of her body, beaded off her skin. She could feel it all. Her senses were alive, alive in a way that they had never been before. It all had changed, and she was not who she had once been. Her lurches through the water grew heavier and heavier until she was on the beach, her feet sinking into the sand. Deep breaths, so very calm. Sycamore had waited her life for this moment.

Her clothes clung to her limbs, weighing her down. She couldn't believe that there had ever been a time in her life when she had stood in front of mirrors, unsure of what to wear, judging herself so that people she didn't care about wouldn't judge her. *Changing outfits before leaving the house; asking her husband how she looked, knowing that he would only lie anyway.* It made her giggle. The noise sounded foreign in her throat.

She leaned her head back, exposing the long line of her throat. Her mouth was open. She could feel every drop of rain bursting against her face, drumming against her like the fingers of curious children who knew that she was changed, and that she was to be admired. They touched her almost with a sense of reverence. A stone to be kissed. A face to fear.

I'm here, she thought. *It's happened.*

The air smelled of ozone and shit. She pulled her head out of the sky with the aid of muscles that had never been used before, muscles that had been loitering near her bones, waiting for the day when all the bullshit would be stripped away. And bullshit was what it was. That other life, all the fools she'd filled her time with. Like the animals that had fled into the trees, Sycamore didn't mourn those who were dead to her.

She was hunger. It consumed her.

The beach was still there. She wasn't sure when things had gone to hell; it was hard to remember anything anymore. But when the blood had started to spill, turning toward the ocean had come naturally to her, as it always had. It was the right thing to do. There she had been baptized.

In some distant part of her brain, where there were still a few fraying binds tying her to the other life, an image of the Normandy beaches during the Second World War stirred—black-and-white footage from some late-night television program. Or had it been a film? Something with lots of shaky camera work. Sycamore didn't know. All she knew was that the shore looked just like it: intestines and body parts disguising the postcard-perfect stretch of land beneath. She walked among it now. Stopped.

Her clothes constricted her every move. They repulsed her. It was as though the fabric were woven with poison ivy that stood to make her skin blister and itch. A shiver ran down her spine, igniting nerve endings that had never burned before. She began to weep; it was glorious. Her fingers twitched to life, the knuckles cracking. There was such strength there. The power lifted her hands without the provocation of her brain, made those fingers that had once marked students' school papers, ruffled her children's hair, rip at her shirt. It tore with ease. She dropped it between her feet.

"Get off me! Now. Now. Off—"

The clasp of her bra eluded her; it was so fickle. Vile. Another little trapping that she'd forced herself to be ruled by. No more. All of that was gone to her now. Swallowed up by the ocean. Given to the storm. She was the shark, and she had no use for it. So she ripped it off her chest, that little clasp flung through the air. Her nipples hardened under the kisses of the rain. A moan began to build inside her.

"I want. The light."

Another bleat of laughter. Snot ran from her nose. Sycamore hooked her thumbs over the waistline of her cutoff jeans and forced them down her legs. "Let me go. Christ, now." They joined her torn shirt on the sand. She had soiled her underwear at some point, but didn't care.

That was the other woman's problem, the other woman's defeat. Sycamore slipped off the panties, those nerves ringing like a series of bells—

(yes! yes! yes!)

—and tripped as she flung them from her foot in a wet, twirling arc.

She watched the landscape swing onto its side as she fell. The sand cushioned her. There was no pain, just that tingle deep down, building, swelling. She began to quiver, moaning again.

Another crack of lightning boomed through the sky, so close this time it ripped a scream from her, emptying her out. The rain came down harder, pooling in her mouth, blending with her tears. Her smile was wide and manic. She gurgled as the laughter came again, brought on by a tingle that was no longer a tingle, rather a toe-curling sensation that was coming in waves, with each stronger than the one that preceded it. It all crashed—

(now! God, yes. Yes! Yes!)

—against her.

The sky was a cathedral and in its wings there hovered a creature of great size. Its jaws were wide and lined with rows and rows of triangular teeth. It swam down toward her, its great tail moving from side to side in majestic sweeps. Its skin was of the darkest gray on top, unlike its underbelly, which gleamed so white it almost hurt to look at. However, none of this was as penetrating or as consuming as the creature's eyes. They were black, lifeless mirrors in which she could see her old life. Her children and her husband, all of whom she had once despised. Now there wasn't even this. There was just the nothingness. The shark had finally, after all these years, eaten it all.

It had been with her always, right behind her life. Its fin always within sight. Sometimes, when Susan Sycamore had woken in the middle of the night, wanting to destroy the people in her little London apartment, she went to the mirror and saw it swimming behind the glass. The evocative ripples of watery shadows, silken and elegant, over its impenetrable hide. Now the shark, a great white, had caught up with her.

There was a flicker of doubt, as wild as the lightning above her.

"I'm not—

(yes! yes! yes! yes!)

—ready."

But she knew this was a lie. It was the other woman, her last lingering burst of energy. Sycamore smiled because she knew that weak and pathetic *thing* would be gone any second now and would never come back.

The great white's jaws opened wide, seeming to smile. Behind the teeth there was a field of stars, the kind that only a child who isn't burdened down with responsibility and lies takes the time to notice. But Sycamore could see them now because all of the bullshit had been chewed and crunched and swallowed. She was naked in every sense of the word. She was open.

"Now!"

She arched her back against the sand, pushing her breasts up into the air. It was here, right now. The intensity blew out to bright, blinding her. Every muscle tightened and shook. Were it all to stop right now, if the shark were to swim away and choose someone else, she feared she would go mad. It was incredible. She didn't want to be anywhere else. Nothing else mattered. It was delicious, this tightening. All of those teeth, dripping with blood and streaked with strands of flesh and skin and hair, descended over her. Her laughter echoed in the dark as she exploded. Over and over again.

I'm here. I'm here now.

One by one, the stars twinkled to life.

She stood, the eye of the storm above her. All was silent except for the swish of her thighs as she approached the broken Coke bottle lying on its side before her. Sycamore bent down, picked it up and neared the tree line.

Her movements were graceful in their complete lack of self-consciousness: the stride of the free. The wind blew sand in her eyes, yet she did not flinch or blink. Sycamore continued to walk, machinelike and unwavering—she even resembled a storefront mannequin, with her nakedness and shaved head, without the fat that clung to so many women of her age. And like a mannequin, her expression was fixed and empty.

She stopped when she saw the man with no face.

He was still alive, just, writhing in a puddle of shit and gore. His moans were unintelligible, thick with inky blood. Sycamore scrambled to recall what the man had looked like, but couldn't, remembering only that he had sat next to the other young man on the boat and had spent much of their journey gesturing hand signals to the girl with the lovely blond hair. Brother and sister, she assumed.

A deaf sister, no less.

The man kicked at the sand, a beetle on its back. It was pathetic.

There was laughter somewhere inside Sycamore, yet it refused to register on her face. She was distracted by the young man's light as it shone up through the wounds in his skull, through his mangled chest. It was even there, in the bud of bloodied mess between his legs. It made her mouth water.

"I eat you," she said. Her voice was stripped of its accent.

She dropped to her knees and put the broken bottle in the man. She then pulled it out of him. She then put it in him again. Out. In. Out. In. She repeated this until he no longer moved or moaned, until the light was free for her to swallow and chew on and leave to burn inside, with all the others that she had collected. Sycamore didn't have the patience to make this one last, *to last goo-ooooood*. The next one. Maybe.

A PLACE FOR SINNERS

The eye of the storm passed over them all, the living and the dead. It seemed weaker now. Wearied somehow. Sycamore was not disappointed, nor was she happy. She was nothing. There was only the hunger for more food, more light. The desire was all-consuming and brilliant.

Sycamore pulled the shattered bottle from the corpse, and a gasp of bowel gases hissed from the gash. The glass, or what remained of it, was green beneath all the blood. She wiped away the red and studied the color beneath, saw the dim sunlight reflected in its surface.

The sky opened above and let loose a downpour that came in a wave. Sycamore watched it approach from the far side of the beach, tearing up the hard-packed sand as it went. The water petered against the remaining bottles that the monkeys had missed in their raid, drawing tinkling music from their spouts. Some of the bottles were made of clear glass; others were also green or blue.

Bones cracked under her skin as Sycamore rose to her feet again and breathed deep and hard. Her breasts were pert and prickled with gooseflesh. Some part of her brain that she no longer had control over was making a decision on her behalf. She began to walk through the rain, heavy footprints trailing out behind her.

She was a sliver of snowy flesh against the roiling ocean behind her as she searched for bottles of every color. Her eyes didn't register any emotion or flicker with life; they seemed lost within the dark hollows of her gaunt face.

With her clinking bounty of glass, Sycamore neared the tree line once more. There, she reclined on her haunches near a discarded coconut. Crabs scuttled sideways across the sand in front of her. She didn't give them a thought. Some other time, they might have startled the woman she used to be, with their sharp pincers snapping as they ran. Not anymore. It was better this way, being complete.

She began to lower the four bottles. Icy, watered-down soda trickled from their rims and warmed in the tuft of her pubic hair. Ignorant of this, she deposited them against the sand. The rain had stripped them of their promotional stickers, leaving behind a sticky residue on the green, clear and blue glass; and when dirt whipped from the trees when the wind gushed, it stuck to the bottles in crusty rinds.

Pain didn't enter her mind.

Sycamore took each of the bottles and shattered them against the coconut. She got the sense that every time one of them came apart in her hands, she was taking a giant step closer to where she knew she needed to be. Each shattering sound was a herald.

Nearer.

Nearer.

A mosaic of broken glass was spread out between her knees. She shuffled through the shards, picking out the stronger and larger of the pieces, and laid them out in a line across her thigh, seven in total. They lay there, staring back up at her like sharp, colorful arrowheads awaiting the yielding flesh of the enemy; in a way, that is exactly what they were.

Only Sycamore had no intention of taking the glass and attaching it to the ends of sticks. Besides, what would she use for adhesive? Weeds?

Not a chance, she thought.

Her heartbeat began to quicken despite itself. Her trepidation was evidence enough to prove that a little of the other woman lingered. The shark had left a little behind for her to destroy herself, which Sycamore knew was the right thing for it to have done.

Soon the final threads to her old life would be severed.

The wind blew hard again, pelting the last of the storm's rain horizontally across the beach. Waves rolled and crashed in sprays of crimson froth. A confused, solitary seagull rode the breeze, frightened of the carnage below.

"Closer. Closer. Now."

Her fingers did not shake as she picked up the first shard of glass, the piece closest to her pelvis. It was green and caught the light as she lifted it. Sycamore breathed against its surface, fogging the color until it coalesced into a single drop of condensation.

"Pretty," said the part of her that would soon be gone.

Without thinking twice, Sycamore thrust the shard's sharpest point up into her upper gum. It scraped shavings from tooth and bone as it slid beneath the skin and locked into place; it was almost as though it was meant to be there. That it was always going to end like this.

There was heat, but no pain.

Her mouth filled with blood as she stabbed the second, third and fourth pieces of Coke bottle into place. She stopped to cough, fat globs of flesh plopping against the ground, and noticed that her thumb and forefinger had been sliced open. Sycamore glanced at the wounds, each a red mouth puckering up in a kiss, and could see glimmers of white bone. A smile slit her face but didn't last; she wasn't quite finished yet. There were still three more pieces to go. She slid them into her lower gums with a grunt of satisfaction.

The rain stopped falling, the final few drops swirling in the wind, catching the light—lost little fireflies. From somewhere deep within the jungle there came a hollow whistling sound. It carved the air and left a jagged stretch of empty silence in its wake.

It was as though the island were calling to her, to the shark. Was there something in the soil that had drawn them all in, not just her, as a magnet draws in lead shavings? The husk of Susan Sycamore almost found it supernatural the way the stars had aligned to conspire in their uniting. It couldn't just be providence or luck. Within the jungle there would surely be streams that she would eventually bend over and drink from—perhaps it was something in this water, some element that man had yet to discover, that beckoned.

Were there sirens among the trees, she wondered?

Maybe, maybe not.

The shark pulled herself to her feet.

But I've counted the bodies and there are three of them in there. Hiding. Waiting. I can sense the blood pumping through their veins, waiting to be spilled and to slip into my body. Their light is shining on me, will soon be in me. With the others.

I'm so hungry.

Her eyes were buttons punched against her sunken face. She had forgotten to blink and there were tears pooling in her lashes. The shark's naked skin was virgin white, except for the stripe of blood flowing from her mouth; it ran down her neck, down between her breasts and ended in the tuft of hair between her legs. She didn't bother to wipe it away. It was her war paint and would help to shake the meat from the bones of her victims when they saw her coming at them from between the trees.

Every muscle in her body was tensed in preparation for the hunt.

Her mouth was a lopsided snarl of jagged, multihued glass teeth that made chinking sounds when she ground her jaws together. It was good to be alive.

PART THREE

CHAPTER THIRTEEN

Amity

1

"YOU CAN HEAR me, right?" Caleb asks. They are sitting at the kitchen table. The room is dark. Faces lit by moonlight flowing through the back room windows like liquid silver. Her brother's voice is angelic, revelatory.

"Yeah, I can." Amity laughs, covers her mouth. "It's just wonderful."

"If you can hear me it means you're dreaming."

"No, don't say that. Please, Caleb."

"I'm sorry. I really am. But if it makes you feel better, I've got something for you. It's from Pa."

"What do you mean, Pa? What?"

Caleb places a little transistor radio covered in My Little Pony stickers on the table. His hand, his Family Love tattoo slides back into darkness. He is gone.

Amity picks up her gift and switches it on. Static blares. She toys with the tuner dial.

"Hello?" lilts a voice from the speaker. "Can you hear me?"

She figures it must be one of the truck drivers on one of the in-between frequencies, one of the ghosts roaming the highways around Evans Head, desperate to reach out and speak with the living.

"Amity, darlin'?"

No; it is her father. There are weeds growing up through his grave, and she and her brother sometimes go there to remove them.

It is then she sees the length of rope laid out in front of her. It is thick and strong, though its tiny hairs are frayed. Amity thinks it looks like something she would see on a ship. For some reason, this makes her panic.

"Can you hear me, darlin'? Come back if you can hear me. Amity? The rope—"

2

And then there was the vacuum, nothing else. She was one with her silence again. *Breathe, Amity*, she told herself, realizing that she was flat against the ground. *Breathe now or you'll die.*

Mouth opened. Bolted upright. Sucked in as much air as possible.

And still, this was nowhere near enough. If oxygen were solid, then she would have grasped at it and shoveled it down her throat. Tingles fired as synapses that had disconnected in her brain rejoined—sparking, giving off light—just as copper strikes beneath a vehicle's dashboard as the thief hotwires an engine. And that was exactly what she was doing: commandeering the vehicle again. Taking control. Now drive.

That's it. Let it in. Come back.

Casually, Amity lifted her right hand and saw a tree branch speared through her palm. It was a foot long and about the thickness of a 2B pencil. Leaves were knotted up against the skin, partially inside her; the impalement had stripped the wood.

Something whispered to Amity that this should be hurting, that there should be incredible amounts of pain. This wasn't the case. There was just the thumping of the headache behind her temples, that sense of swelling and then release.

Oh, my God. I've been–

Amity didn't know what to say. *Stabbed* was the word she was grasping for, and yet that didn't quite fit the bill. *I've been...speared.*

Was the world beginning to tilt, or was it just in her mind? Amity couldn't be sure. Perhaps this *was* the end, and the island was folding in upon itself like a closing picture book, funneling her down through a crack in the middle. And then she would slip through and disappear, those trees brushing together in an applause she would never hear. End of story.

No. She suspected that things were only just beginning.

Stop. Stop this. Think. Now. I can't. I'm falling.

There had been birds flying through the air as she slid into dreams. And before that, the man in the Hawaiian shirt who had saved her life. Those animals would have torn her apart were it not for him. The thought repulsed her. She wondered where he was now. The world was all trees and mud around her, and she was very alone. Had he hit the upper branches in the fall, pinwheeling off in some other direction? It was possible. Amity wished he would materialize from the trees again, snatch her up in his arms and yank the branch from her hand.

Come one, come all. View the human shish kebab in all her glory, right 'ere! Bring yer cameras. Watch her dance. She won't put up a fight–

Shut up! Just stop.

The world, at least, paid attention and righted itself, though the screeching, manic voice continued.

You disgusting freak show. Oh, they'll come and lay down their hard-earned cash to see you.

A part of her admitted that this concept was as true now as it always had been—Amity and Caleb Collins, a regular Evans Head tourist attraction and gossip fuel. The faces of the local women whispering behind their hands, behind that week's Catholic pamphlet at church, were branded in her memory.

And where is Caleb now, huh? asked that voice. Amity wished—more than her rescuer's return, more than finding the path that would take her back to her brother and the boat—that she could find the source of her self-contempt. And crush it.

So do it. Go on. You haven't got the guts. The freak is weak!

Without thinking twice, Amity grabbed the branch with her left hand and yanked it straight out of the flesh. Her pain had a color and it was the color of the warm blood spurting over her face.

She arched against the ground, rolled and curled into a ball. RED. RED everywhere. It devoured all else, including that other voice. For now, at least.

Amity braved a look at the wound in her palm. It was an unblinking, weeping eye. She willed it to close, to stop staring. *Please, make the blood stop coming!* But the wound didn't listen. Amity knew that in the end, wishing was for the weak, so she ground her teeth and dragged herself to her feet with nothing but her own fiery will.

Spinning. Spinning.

Locks of greasy hair stuck to her face. It itched.

She drank up her surroundings. Everything was fragile, overfocused. Shrieking details. There was the cliff of sloping trees behind her (*that's where I fell, God, I don't even remember landing, did I faint before I hit the upper branches?*); there were the walls of the narrow valley on either side (*I'm trapped, I'm trapped*); there was the shallow pool of water she'd only just missed landing in, and the thin stream running downhill from its birth (*there—that's where I need to go!*). That stream was a small waterfall bouncing off the rocks and shooting droplets through the air. Each drop caught the sunlight, formed a rainbow; its beauty was a betrayal. She had to look away.

Amity's outline was imprinted in the muddy bank. Next to it was the stream, which logic implied would lead her to the ocean, back to the boat where Caleb, Tobias and all of the other passengers were waiting for her.

Go. Go now! Don't waste a second.

She couldn't help but wonder where this burst of determination had come from. Had the dream, only the flavor of which she could recall, left something in her, something as real and firmly embedded in her as the splinters in her palm?

Maybe. But what, Amity Collins had no idea.

Another surge of pain knocked her knees out from under her. Stinking mud squished against her weight. Gagging, she dunked her hands in the water, the frigid bite chewing through her. Tears twinkled through the air and plopped into the pink cloud below.

Make it stop. Now. Make the pain invisible.

Wishing didn't make the RED go away, so she yanked her hands back, stood, and stumbled across sand and slate to the wall of trees and rock where the water trickled, where the rainbow mocked. Broken fingernails gripped a flaking shred of bark, and with a grunt, stripped it from its slimy girth. It dangled in her hands, limp and waterlogged.

It was perfect. She couldn't believe it. Another win.

I'm beating you.

This revelation etched a smile on her face, despite another one of those agony-waves dumping down on her. She wrapped the elastic bark around her right palm. Despite the difficulty, her movements were controlled and even.

Was Caleb there with her, swatting away the pain and threading the bark into a makeshift knot?

No.

It was just she, Amity Collins. Alone. For the first time since the night she'd wandered. *Alone.*

There wasn't enough bark.

I need more. More.

Adrenaline said "fuck you" to sense and worked its magic. It was alive inside her. Was she screaming as she yanked the leaves from one of the palm trees? Maybe. And if Amity was screaming, they were screams that defied the island's mistrust in her.

I played by your rules. I came here with kindness. I fed your children; I appreciated your goddamned beauty. And what did you do in return? Huh? You turned on me, you bitch.

She wanted to hear the island cry as the leaves tore away in her hands. She left blood smears across the bark. A graffitist's tag. This made her feel euphoric.

THE FREAK WAS 'ERE. Deal with it.

Amity wrapped the fronds around the bark, adding an additional layer of reinforcement to her bandage. She didn't know how effective it would prove, but for now it would have to do. Gasping, she stepped back from the pool of water and glared up at the sky. The storm clouds were clearing and she could see the blue beneath.

Caleb, Caleb. Where are you? I need you.

(I don't need you).

I do.

(You don't. He's your drug.)

He's not.

(This had to happen.)

Amity trudged alongside the stream, following its glimmering path. Stopped. Amity had no idea how she could have possibly forgotten. Her left hand fingers inched toward her pocket with tenacious, fearful thrusts.

She felt it, just as she had thousands of times before when she wanted to take a photo, or needed to log into that other world and vanish in that other life.

Like. Favorite. Retweet... Take me back.

(You are.)

Her iPhone was shattered into pieces. Amity was surprised by how little she felt; the absence was its own kind of silence. The screen was webbed with cracks, and in its blank, dead pieces she could make out a jigsaw reflection staring back. It looked a little like someone that she used to know, and that person dropped the machine and descended into the jungle.

CHAPTER FOURTEEN

The Shark

1

THE SHARK TROLLED as she had never trolled before. It was paying off. There was a scent in the air, and it made something stir within her, as though it were offspring in her belly turning their jaws upon each other, biting in the fury of hunger. The hunt was now. Soon, her prey's light would be deep inside her; the offspring would still.

She'd swum through the jungle alleys. There was no direction, for she was being led. She was not lost, for she had found her newest victim. The shark had seen it moving between the trees—just a quick flash of sunlight reflecting off flesh.

Her feet weren't moving, not really. Her gate was a glide; arms moved through the humid air, brushing aside stray leaves. Her snout pushed forward, antsy to put her new teeth to good use. If she could have opened her mouth wide enough to swallow the world, she would, and still it wouldn't be enough.

But it was important not to rush it. It paid to make it last *reaaaalllll gooooooood*.

"Gah-heee-grhu."

(*"I see you."*)

It was a *child*.

She would have smiled, but her mouth was already stretched to the limits of its elasticity. Her skin was taut and deformed now. The shark couldn't wait for her prey to see her bearing down on it, to feel her power. The fear she invoked would shake the meat from its little bones. Fear was golden, as would be its light.

The shark saw undersides of its small feet running, saw its back as it wormed between two fallen trees. So close. This fleeing thing fueled her on, through fatigue and pain.

You've got to go faster. The whisper of the ocean. *The tide's on her side. Overcome it. Speed.*

It was lithe and quick on its feet. The distance between them was growing, though not for much longer. The shark's determination made the machine of her body spin every cog. It was brutal and efficient. Her legs strode wider. Her breath rasped. It forced her into layers of black and green. Pure energy. Beautiful. Admirable.

There! She could see the little one again. It turned its head and locked eyes with her.

It was Susan Sycamore's eldest daughter, only she wasn't a teenager anymore. Something had peeled her back to childhood, back when pigtails were in and boys didn't matter, when there was nothing but love.

The shark didn't falter, despite the shock. She knew it couldn't be the same little girl ahead of her. No. Little Samantha Sycamore was back in London with her father and two younger sisters. Samantha would be lying in her bed, thinking of new ways to rebel against them.

It was pathetic.

If only Samantha knew how close she had come to dying, over and over, at the hands of her mother. *If only they all knew.* There had been so many times when Sycamore had woken in the middle of the night and stood over their beds and watched them sleep with the dirty hypodermic needle held tight in her hands.

She didn't know why she hated them. She didn't know why the very sight of them made her skin crawl. They brought an angry throbbing to her chest with their stupid comments, by leaving something out that she had told them to put away. Her anger was a jug poured to its limit, overspilling.

The needle hovered. It never plunged into flesh and eyes. Some morality had been at play. And Sycamore had resented that mercy. But whatever barrier had existed was no more, which was why chasing her daughter through the jungle with the intention of ripping her to fucking shreds felt right.

Boiling.

Boiling.

Plotting.

It had not just been the needle. Sycamore had come close to ending them many times, and never closer than the letters. Her failure to send them was what had led her to travel. However, there were no regrets. Had she gone through with it, she never would have killed all of these people. That was okay. Deep down, Sycamore felt that her family would not have been worthy of the shark's jaws.

How still she wanted them to be. Their mouths open and yet quiet. Eyes wide and yet not seeing. Gravestone victories.

The letters.

They were typed up on A4 sheets of paper and slipped inside plain envelopes she'd stolen from the work stationery cupboard. None of the content was dated and they held little continuity. This way she could send them whenever she wanted to. There were seven of them in total, each addressed to her husband and herself.

    Stop the lies or you and your family will
    be punished.
    If you continue to live this way, I will find
    you and you all will suffer.
    You haven't listened to me. Continue and I'll

find a way into your house.
My patience is ending. End the lies or I'll
come for you in the night.
You, your wife and your children will die.
Time is running out.
I've already been in your house. Stop or I will
come again.
You didn't listen. You deserve this. Good-bye.

It had been Sycamore's belief that she would not be
suspected of the crime because the letters were addressed
to herself. The plan was to break a window from the
outside of their apartment, which was on the bottom
floor of their building and faced the side fence. It was
important that the glass land on the right side of the wall,
solidifying in the detective's mind that the intruder had
not come from within the building.

She would murder them close to dawn with all of the
knives in the kitchen. How the needle would fit in, she
wasn't sure. But it would. She would write messages on the
walls in their blood that echoed the letters. Her husband
would be the first to die, followed by the girls. There would
be no fingerprints because she had gloves; the bloodied
footprints would match the pair of oversize, secondhand
men's boots she'd bought for the event a year before. She
would then take them with her once the deed was done,
after showering. Sycamore would then go to the gym for an
early morning balance class, as she often did before work.
The river would claim the boots. Upon returning from
class, she would check the bodies, scream loud enough for
the neighbors to hear and then call the police.

None of this happened.

She knew it wouldn't the night she visited her husband
as he slept in his chair in front of the television set. There
were two empty beer bottles on the coffee table. No
coasters. Sycamore had watched him breathing, had seen
how his face was furrowed by nightmares. He moaned.

And just like *that* the spell was broken.

I don't think I can do this.

There had been evangelical nonsense screaming from the television set. The hallway clock chimed. All was still in the witches' hour, still except for her hands, which shook.

I can't.

To make sure, she'd walked into her daughters' rooms and spied on their sleeping. They were ugly and hurtful and made the pain so bright, as bright as the light that escaped from between their lips. Despite this, she couldn't muster what was inside her.

My hatred for you all is my everything. But I can't do this. I'm–

(*say it*)

I'm...

(*own it*)

...not brave enough.

And so the shark had turned its tail on her. She walked away from them and slipped under the covers of her bed. She did not sleep and called in sick to work as the day's first sun crept in through the window to light up the family photos on the wall. Her husband—who never used to drink that heavily—had been curt with her as he shuffled off to the primary school where he taught fourth grade, his hangover having trimmed him of his otherwise finer finishings. The "get better soons" and "I *wuv* yous" were always the first to go.

Susan Sycamore would not miss them.

That final day in her apartment had been a daze. She took the letters, which she'd kept hidden in a shoebox stuffed under the bed, and slid them inside an old handbag that smelled of mothballs and dry makeup. She put the imitation Jimmy Choo to her nose and inhaled. Thoughts of her mother, who had been dead and buried for seven years now, were evoked but didn't linger. She put the handbag behind the crawlspace in their bedroom wall, which could only be accessed from within their closet. Sycamore didn't know why she didn't just burn them. Deep down, she wondered if she liked the idea of her husband finding them while she was away, days or even months from now, and learning of how close they had all come to being ripped open.

There's something not right with you.

I'm fine. It's them who are all wrong and backward.

No, it's you. Mothers, wives, they aren't supposed to think like this. Act like this. They don't dream what you dream and they certainly don't drop everything and leave. What excuse are you going to give them, huh? You went out for a pack of cigarettes? You don't even smoke, you nitwit.

I'm fine.

After booking her around-the-world ticket online, paying from her personal Visa and not the account she shared with her husband, Susan Sycamore walked through their apartment, soaking up the silence. It was like being underwater, and that felt right to her.

She went into the downstairs bathroom, and instead of seeing her face in the mirror, she saw the shark. On some level, she'd known that it had been with her, growing in size and drawing nearer and nearer, for a long time. Its great gray dorsal fin had long ago slit open the surface of her life and chased after her, always with the sun at its back and casting a long shadow over her life.

And it had been *right there* staring back at her, as close as it had ever been.

When she turned her head to the right, the shark echoed the movement. When she nodded, it nodded. Its nose was a swirl of melted ice-cream colors, charcoal and vanilla cream and unnatural pink. The rough skin was threaded with scars and pockmarks. But it was its eyes that impressed her the most—the way they were dead and yet so alive, rolling from black to white.

Sycamore wanted to reach out and touch the mirror but didn't. Not yet. It wasn't time. She still had so much further to go, so much more to do. If it wasn't going to be the light of her family that she was to consume, then it would be those of strangers.

A coward's compromise.

She opened her mouth and the shark did the same. Its throat was dark and bottomless, lined with black gills and strands of half-devoured flesh. The gums were speckled with bloodied diseases, speared by rows and rows of triangular teeth.

They closed their mouths. A link formed. The circle closed.

Bright. I want my bright.

With a single sweep of the shark's tail, it propelled forward, the tip of its nose striking the underside of the mirror and shattering it. Sycamore screamed as a torrent of icy cold saltwater gushed into the room. She stumbled backward and tripped.

"Help!"

It kept coming and coming, forcing her against the wall. The door that led to the hallway outside was closed; no water escaped. Pillowcases floated on the rising tide. Sycamore paddled to stay afloat, gasping for air as she was pushed closer to the ceiling, the room filling to its capacity.

"Help me! I'm drowning! Somebody, please!"

But nobody answered her calls. Nobody could hear. She was submerged. Her long hair floated about her face like seaweed in an ocean's ebb. Fingernails scrabbled at the walls and tore back and cracked. Flakes of paint twirled before her eyes.

I'm going to die.

She couldn't hold her breath any longer; the pain was too incredible. And so she caved. Her locked lips undid in a soundless yawn and the ocean filled her lungs, weighing her down. She began to descend, passing a towel, a compact case, a paperback book with the pages turning to mush and falling out. Everything was blue and soundless.

I'm not dead. I can breathe!

Her feet touched the carpet next to the upended mattress, which was turning on a corner like some giant, spinning domino. The blankets waved, billowed. Panic faded away.

Warmth on her back. Sycamore swished around to face the window. The curtains were partially drawn. Golden luminescence cut through the haze, illuminating tiny dust, sand and ocean particles.

There. Go there now.

She swam toward it, a smile on her face. Sycamore was hopeful, though for what she did not know. The window loomed, warmth strong against her face. There was something on the other side. Her hands moved with nightmarish lethargy, reached up to grasp the curtains and drew them aside.

On the opposite side of the glass there was an atrium of people staring back at her.

They pointed and giggled and looked up with awe. Sycamore knew then that she was more beautiful now than she had ever been before.

There was a little girl, somewhat familiar, standing close to the glass. Sycamore pushed herself flush against the window. It was so cold in the water.

Sycamore didn't know how she could hear what the little girl was saying, but she could. She watched, helpless and unable to answer, as the child turned to the tall man beside her. His giant hand was resting on her left shoulder in some grand gesture of comfort and protection. His face was a bowl of blowing blood that did not spill or overflow, and when he spoke, scarlet bubbles frothed the surface.

"What is it, Daddy?"

"It's a great white shark, Susan. The greatest creature that ever lived. We're lucky, so lucky, to have ever seen one. It's beautiful, isn't it?"

Sycamore allowed the tide to sweep her up and usher her away from the window, away from the warmth, until the people on the other side were just blemishes against the flailing light. The ocean grew dark and her hunger flared stronger than ever before.

"Gah-heee-grhu."

The jungle screeched and shook as she trolled. Fronds and barbed plants whipped her, dragging strips from her flesh. She didn't care. Monkeys called and laughed above, and birds of all sizes and colors flapped and squawked with fear, rising on blind wings and crashing into trees. Even the ground beneath her bruised feet seemed to shake. And why shouldn't it tremble? The shark was coming. It was proud.

The child was there.

It was her daughter after all, dressed in periwinkle blue. She could smell her shampoo.

The shark reached out her hand. Stretched.

I can see your light. Right. There.

Her fingers latched around the running child's hair and squeezed tight. The shark dug her feet into the earth, roared and pulled her arm back with great power. There was a distinct ripping sound as a tuft of hair was scalped from the child, who now fell to the ground in a flailing heap.

The shark moaned through its Coke-bottle teeth as her shadow fell over the upturned face. Her daughter's eyes were twin mirrors reflecting her jaws. There was no thought. No remorse. The shark leaned further and bit away its face, swallowing its incomprehensible pleas.

Small hands scratched at her neck, thumping without direction. It was funny. She had it pinned *realllll gooooood*. Its taste was bitter saccharine. The light was magnificent.

Her prey gave a final kick. And then nothing.

Lungs scorching from her sprint through the trees, the shark pulled herself together and looked down at what remained of the child. *It was not her daughter.* No. Her daughter was a teenager who had nothing but hatred in her heart for the mother who'd left them behind.

The farewell note pinned to the refrigerator door had read: "I have to do this; if you'll love me, you'll let me go; I'll come back when I'm done."

The shark had been mistaken. The child between her knees was foreign looking and tanned by the sun. It wore a skirt of bamboo strips and finely woven vine. It was a little girl, maybe between the ages of nine and ten years. The girl's hair was black. A seashell necklace was strung about her broken neck.

Insects flew around them both. Sunlight poured through the canopy. The island seemed content with the offering it had sacrificed to the shark's greedy tongue. Beneath the layers of trees and animal cries there was a drawn-out musical note, like a mournful ghost.

The shark studied the remains again and in an almost comical lightning crack of understanding knew what she had just consumed. Yes, it was a girl, and yet she was so much more than that.

It was a scout, whose screams echoed still, reaching out to touch unseen ears.

CHAPTER FIFTEEN

Robert Mann

1

"THAT SOUNDED LIKE a kid," he said aloud, knowing that only crazy people spoke to nobody. But it wasn't just talking to himself that led to this conclusion. It was the way he looked—the torn-open Hawaiian shirt covered in mud and blood splotches. Were he to hold a mirror up to his face, he knew he would see a street artist's caricature of straitjacket verifiability. No doubt about it.

And it still went deeper.

The insanity was beneath his skin, in the depths of the meat kingdom where the bedbugs were building their army.

Don't think about them. Think about that sound instead. Think about the girl you tried to help that you lost in the fall. Think about her. It's time to step up to the plate, Mann.

And then he heard the question—which wasn't really a question but an accusation—come again. *"You ain't yellah, are you, Robert?"*

"No, sir." He was close to tears; they teased, as they always teased. "No, sir. I'm not."

He was almost positive that the scream was that of a child and not the young woman he'd tried to save. It was too high-pitched. It sounded young.

The itching came again, dragging him away from his fortitude. Fingernails returned to skin, scoured the red-raw flesh. There was no relief. If he kept this up, it wouldn't just be sweat and grime he'd be pulling away. Soon his fingernails would be gummy with blood.

But would that be such a bad thing? Perhaps, were he to look closely at his fingertips, he would find the crushed bodies of black bugs too. That, at least, would be some kind of triumph.

Don't think like that, Mann. Keep your head on straight. Focus.

He stopped near the thin stream he'd been following downhill, drew back his head and glared at the canopy above. The words

CALM IS AS CALM DOES.

were printed across the sky in a font that "popped" in all the right ways. It was soft and soothing, as opposed to the bold lettering that most advertisements were splashed with. The point here was for the copy to become one with the graphic design, with the cool blues and greens of the foliage, not contrast against it.

Beautiful. It was the perfect melding of word and image, and it was having the desired effect. The itching was subsiding; he could feel his heart easing back into its normal rhythm.

Robert, who was smiling ever so slightly, was tempted to reach up and finger the page to see if the ink had dried. He didn't. He watched the words fade as the scream had faded. Only it hadn't.

It had been cut short.

He glanced at his wristwatch. It was five o'clock in the afternoon; nightfall wasn't far off. That concept terrified him. He was running out of time to find the girl and to drag both of their sorry asses back to the beach—which he was sure the stream would lead him to.

"Girlie! You out there?"

His voice was hoarse and blistering. No matter how many times he called, she never answered. He hoped to a God that he didn't really believe in that she hadn't died in the fall, though there was a good chance that she had. Come to think of it, the fact that he'd survived was nothing short of a miracle. He remembered how the ground had been there one moment and gone the next.

Trees grabbing him with brittle, bony fingers and forcing him into the jungle's gullet.

It had chewed him up, thumped at him from every angle, driving the air from his lungs and blood from his face. Things were hot and then cold. Pure violence that led to darkness. This had continued until he heard the tick of his wristwatch. He woke suspended between the lowest branches of a tree, the muddy soil a yard or two below. There, frozen in time, he spared a thought for Manhattan and the life he'd left behind.

Robert wondered what diagnosis Donald, his doctor of nine years, would cast upon him—other than the obvious aforementioned insanity. A couple of broken ribs? A swelling in his left ankle that could only be the worst kind of sprain? Oh, what Robert Mann would give to walk into that officious bastard's office and have him point out the obvious.

"Girlie, answer me if you can hear *me-eeeeeeeeeeeeeeee!*"

He continued on, choosing to ignore his aches and pains. In addition to this, his balance was questionable at best, and he sometimes found himself veering off the shale bank and into the shallow running water. The sudden cool was not unwelcome.

Robert stopped.

He could have sworn he heard distant grieving. It was brash, unmistakable. And this wasn't like the polite, churchgoing weeping he'd heard stifled behind monogrammed handkerchiefs at his father's funeral. No; this was something altogether different. The sounds he could hear on the wind were primal shouts of torture and heartbreak, bereft of dignity or self-consciousness. He knew the sound because he'd heard his mother scream that way behind her closed door.

The grieving stopped.

Robert stood still, scanned for the source but came back empty-handed. The walls of the jungle were impenetrable on both sides, a prisonlike compound of vibrant, cross-stitched vegetation. Bizarre flowers of yellow and orange rubbernecked at him, almost contemptuously. An azure, foot-long lizard with slit eyes and a crown of spikes spared him a glance and then zipped into camouflage.

There was nothing but the island. It was alive, though there was death within its borders.

Robert's entire body clenched, shooting hot bolts of pain through him as the trumpet began to sound. He gritted his teeth and stumbled in the water. Or at least he assumed it was a trumpet, as it held no tune or melody that registered with his ears. It was a kind of braying. It didn't pluck strings of anger or fear. Instead, that melancholy call sang of defeat.

CHAPTER SIXTEEN

Tobias and Matt

1

TOBIAS WAS SURE that he'd been here before, although he didn't know when. It was an intangible place. Haunted. The landscape was black, and what sights there were to see were carved into its opaque surface. The old roller coaster was a good example of this.

It stood over him, rotting wood groaning against nails, an abandoned relic that signified some other time and existence. He was sure he'd ridden it once with his mother, back when he was a kid. He had been afraid. Yet logic implied that it couldn't be the same one; that roller coaster stood within the walls of a shut-down carnival in Germany.

He was confused but didn't question it any longer. Tobias turned his back on it and trekked deeper into the dark. It was cold here in this nowhere place. He'd never experienced such emptiness.

This must be what it's like to be blind. How horrible.

His longing had teeth that bit and chewed at the back of his neck, in the hollow of his throat, in the deepest part of his belly. He missed the warmth of the sun and, more than anything, the comfort that Caleb's presence brought with it. Tobias had never thought he would ever find someone who evoked such feelings in him, who stood to slip inside the steel of his resolve and stoke the embers beneath.

It was love, he assumed, scorching him raw. And not the love a child feels for his mother, as he had experienced in the past, or that a man feels for his brother. It was not the kind of love that was familiar and bred into his fabric. It was utterly *other*. It was cherry-picked and yet *not* at the same time.

Maybe he did not assume. Maybe he knew.

Drained, Tobias continued on, squinting against clear-cut black. In the hush of the nothingness he could hear his feet tip-tapping across dried, fragile soil. It was like parchment. "Hello? Is there someone out there?" He then translated his shouts into German and announced them to the void.

In answer, another shape began to emerge. It was a tall, white tree.

2

The monkey that had attacked him on the beach had taken with it two of The Body's right fingers. This newfound pain had shocked Matt. Physical torment didn't exist in that other place.

It was invigorating.

"That's it, baby doll," he whispered to his wounds as he bound them in banana leaf and dabbed them with moss. "It's going to hurt like a bitch, but man-oh-man, a bitch's better than nothing, yerrrr-right!"

The bitch had bite. But to hurt was to be alive, and even pain was better than the nothingness below.

As he trudged through the dense scrub, palming off trees that seemed to have minds of their own and tenacious grips, Matt found himself replaying the scene at the beach, wondering just how he had managed to commandeer The Body's legs away from the bloodshed and into the island's murky stomach. He could still make out the animal's maw—those yellow snaggleteeth—as it ripped the Coke bottle from his hands and took the digits with it.

All he'd felt was a tug. It wasn't real until he touched those funny-looking stumps with his other hand, fingered the protruding bone. His scream had sent the animals into fervor, and they had come spilling from the trees to take them all. Except him. He was fast.

I did this, he'd thought to himself as he slid backward toward the tree line. *It's all come together. I'm the great controller, can't you see? I'm in charge here!*

It was as though the jungle reached out and claimed him. *You did well*, its touch implied. *You gave them what they wanted. You were brought here to start this.* They *were born to end it.*

Even with the pain—which, push come to shove, he was tiring of fast—the thrill was outstanding. "Dude, what a rush."

He had rounded a fallen tree and descended a sudden, severe decline. There was light here, cutting through shadow. The dewy ground misted in newfound warmth. Vast boulders formed a V through which he passed, revealing deeper foliage, interwoven vines and aromatic bushes full of flowers. Insects leaped as the clouds opened. Little black flies landed on his back, flirted with the sweaty tufts of his matted hair. He didn't bother to swat the mosquitoes, instead letting them feast on The Body's arms and legs, on the curve of his throat. Their mouths sucked the blood from him. It itched. He stopped to piss against a rock and laughed. Matt was plugged into the ecosystem now; he fed it, and after grabbing a handful of low-hanging berries, it now fed him. They had fucked. Swapped fluids. Without a rubber. What greater risk was there?

His hands rose above his head. "I'm here, you hear me?" He waited for his echo. There wasn't one. "You wanted me, you got me! Woo-hooo!" Matt had danced and skipped back into the jungle on the other side of the sunlit clearing.

Only the rush of not knowing what was behind the next tree, around the next turn in the trail, wasn't enough. It was all too slow. Matt began to sprint, his feet slamming against the earth, ducking below low-hanging boughs. The island cheered him on. And he bled through it all. It wasn't long before he began to feel funny.

The jungle wasn't as clearly defined as it had been minutes before. Things had grown gloomy. There was an odd tingling sensation running through The Body's limbs. He was thirsty.

"This, uh-hh. This is good. This is what it's all about. Right here. Right now."

So he pushed on, even though the foliage was encroaching on him, even though some unseen weight was draping iron arms around his shoulders, making it harder and harder to move. Matt whimpered.

"Push it. Push it."

He was in the thick now. It was damp here. A place of rot and dodging silhouettes. The semaphore blasts of sunlight through the trees were growing few and far between. Fetid stench slapped him across the face.

I'm slowing. I'm dimming.

Only that wasn't all that was happening. Moments before he had run without reason or concentration, and the island had accommodated every misjudged leap and bound by sprouting a root for him to land on, forcing back a thorned plant so he wouldn't slit open his shins. This was no longer the case.

I'm falling.

The ground sloped and he sloped with it. His makeshift bandages slipped off as he reached out to break his fall. Matt rolled and the landscape rolled with him, funneling down into a green carousel-swirl.

Thump.

Matt landed facedown in a putrid sludge of soil and decomposing bird corpses. Leaves pirouetted from above and landed around him with hushed fanfare. Blood spurted from his missing digits and lathered lifeless beaks and empty eggshells.

(This–)

Matt drew all of his concentration into a knot and yanked The Body back into line.

(This is–)

Breathe, you goddarned fink!

(This is peachy.)

He wheezed relief and pushed himself onto The Body's side, that hot blood inky against the jungle floor. A chill crawled up his legs, across his torso. It filled his head.

"Ouch, God. Hurts."

You know you like it. You betchya.

Raindrops pitter-pattered around him, drumming against rocks hidden beneath a blanket of mist that glowed in places where the sun managed to cut through, and even then, it did so as though fearful of this place. Matt spat out a glob of phlegmy blood and swiveled onto his haunches. He could see the hole he'd punched through the vegetation with his fall.

The Body's heart began to race and Matt felt better. He'd almost become detached from his sensations for a moment there. If he didn't keep a firm hold on the flesh, he ran the risk of giving it over to The Others. Tobias, no doubt, would be first in line to reclaim his former throne.

The focus that had eluded him earlier was back, illustrating for him the hollow of silken majesty. Matt was lost for words—a first, surely. He knew, now more than ever, that this was where he was destined to be. He jolted at the sight.

This very spot. The ultimate kick.

Gnarled foliage had been pulled aside, perhaps by the same hands that had forced the island into such tortured poses and peaks. Strung between the walls of this shadowy cave were velvet-thick webs.

3

Tobias looked up at the tree in front of him and was in awe of its albino bark. It looked carved from tusk. He could have sworn that he'd been here before, though maybe only in a dream. The sense of déjà vu was incredible and lent the scene a texture that was both homely and terrifying.

The tree's highest branches blurred into darkness. From that out-of-focus place there now came a thin stream of bright red blood. Panting and eyes wide, Tobias stumbled back a step or two. His feet thumped against something. It was an old ukulele.

The nylon strings thrummed a discordant tone that hung, vibrating, in the air.

A memory wormed through his mind, blinked its single milky eye.

He was alone in the hostel while Caleb and Amity shared a joint room across the road. Tobias had been on the phone to his boyfriend earlier in the night, and once he'd turned off the light and tried to settle into sleep, he'd heard the sound of plucking ukulele strings and children's laughter coming from the hall. He'd crept through the dark in his underwear and pushed the door open. There had been nobody out there.

"Is there anyone here?" he asked the tree in no particular language and yet in all languages at once. "Where the hell am I?" If there was one good thing about this place, it was that all self-conscious clunks of his accent had been stripped away. Here, he felt efficient and impervious to the glares and contempt of those who judged people who were from different places, were of different colors, didn't love as others loved.

"We're here," came a thin voice.

Tobias grabbed his chest, clutched the fabric of his shirt. If only he could dig his fingers deeper, through his rib cage and into the flesh beneath, and settle his thudding heart. It felt as though it were going to explode.

A boy who didn't look as though he'd yet cracked his teen years stepped out from behind the tree, holding the hand of his twin brother. Their physical appearances were strikingly similar, from the chubbiness of their cheeks to their matching denim overalls; it was only in their dim-witted eyes that Tobias could strike a note of difference. "Hallo?" Sigh. "What's your name?"

"My name is Joe. Joe Mccormack. This is Gus. Are you our brother?"

Tobias had been on the gringo trail long enough to recognize an Australian accent, and this kid's vocal tones were unmistakable.

"Me? I'm...no. No, I don't think so."

"But you're Tobias, aren't you?" asked Gus.

"I am, but I don't know you. I don't even know where I am."

Joe took a step toward him, leaving his brother alone near the tree. "You're below."

A little black girl, slightly younger, stepped into sight. "I'm Mariama," she said. Her sunken and jaundiced skin was puckered with weeping lesions. Even her words sounded infected. "Can you play us a song? It makes things nice."

The ukulele scowled up at Tobias from his sand-covered feet. His fingers began to itch, craving something he never knew he wanted. He glanced up again, and the group of children had increased to include another young girl with hair as white as snow and a boy who looked just shy of his toddler years. His pants were wet with urine. Next to him there stood a tallish girl in a ruby-red dress whose porcelain features were misshapen by twitches. She held the hand of another boy who Tobias guessed couldn't be more than two; he was clothed in a Spider-Man onesie.

"Matt climbed the tree," Joe said, tilting his brow to those out-of-reach branches. "He left us behind."

"*Nous sommes effrayés,*" said the girl in the ruby dress between twitches. Tears beaded off her face and plopped against the little boy's costume.

"Wait, did you say Matt?"

The child named Joe Mccormack gave Tobias a single nod.

Blood began to pool among the great white tree's roots.

4

Shadow hands came together, intertwining fingers that blotted out what little light there was. Still, it wasn't pitch-black yet. Matt could still see where he was stepping, could still see the bodies of decomposed tropical insects—the grasshoppers and the butterflies—strung between the sticky webs ahead of him. There were even sparrows trapped there too, their wings splayed in a grotesque pantomime of flight.

Matt's smile was unearthly. The color had drained from his face, drawing dark bags under his eyes. His cheeks were gaunt. He peered out at this tempting scene from beneath The Body's brow. The only sounds were the groaning jungle, the crunch of deadfall beneath each of his steps. The trickle of blood dropping from his mangled hand.

There were no mosquitoes down here.

I'm all alone. For the first time in my life. Man, it feels...it feels...

But the thought wouldn't assemble because he was so giddy with excitement. He spared a thought for Tobias, ole Captain Sensible. He wondered how he was dealing down below with all of The Others, those diseased and pathetic leeches who'd sucked the life out of him for years on end.

Now you know what it's like, Tobias. Now you know.

Good luck trying to make sense of Apolonia's gibberish. Have fun cleaning Mariama, Uwe and Paw-Paw when they piss and shit themselves. Enjoy Maëlle's company, the whack-job. Can you blame me for wanting to go above?

A PLACE FOR SINNERS

Can you, huh?

He'd been abandoned for too long. For too many nights he'd sat on the white tree's largest root and plucked at the old ukulele, to settle them when they grew restless. And who could blame them, really? It was cold and barren down there. An emptied place, devoid of taste and life and sensation. Just thinking about it made his skin crawl, just as The Ugly One, Tobias's younger brother, the one who seemed to descend further and further into some unreachable place where it was okay to drool when you smiled, where you didn't have to care how repulsive you were...

The flesh could be cruel. Hideous. And yet, as Matt had now found out, it could be angelic too, just as he'd always suspected. And his pursuit had been worth it. Climbing that tree, branch by branch, had not been a futile exercise.

There were questions *and* answers in the flesh; faith *and* disbelief. It was so easy to be in awe of its anarchy. The slow and winding road to self-destruction was paved with pleasure and pain, sometimes in unequal amounts. And despite certain fear and possible reward, he would never shy from his pursuit. He had been determined to climb the tree even if it killed him.

In turn, The Body was responding to the thrill he was providing it with. It was all a case of give and take. He was gifting it with sights and sensations Captain Sensible had always denied it, and in return, the nausea was subsiding; it now caressed his groin and was drawing his prick to a blood-filled point.

He and The Others were roller coaster babies, knit from nowhere. Matt was positive that he was meant to be here. Right now. This was how it was meant to be.

So take another step.

And ever obedient, The Body had no choice but to comply.

5

The earth shook, shifting tiles of dry mud and strumming the ukulele's strings.

One by one, they turned toward the thundering crash of the roller coaster. Tobias watched the dim silhouette of the unsound structure crumble to the ground.

"What is happening here?" he asked. He received no response from the children. All of their faces were matching portraits of uncertainty—eyes impossibly wide and mouths slightly open.

The last of the roller coaster's beams crashed and thumped and drummed, and the dark reclaimed its eerie silence. The children held one another, gripped tight in a knot of interwoven limbs. "Tobias, make it stop!" Joe cried. His fear, which was stark and innocent, seemed to age him. In fact, it had aged them all. They were withered and emancipated.

An enormous dust cloud billowed toward them. A great, ashy wing.

"Cover your faces, cover your eyes!"

Tobias rushed over to the group and ushered them behind the girth of the tree, unsure of what reservoir his newfound courage was being drawn from. All he wanted to do was bury his head in the sand and pretend like none of this was happening; and yet it was. Nothing was going to change that, or take him back to that other world, a place where he was happy knowing that none of these people existed or were dependent upon him.

Denial would get him nowhere. This existed. These children, who trembled under his arms, were *his* responsibility, just as Jörg had been his responsibility. Tobias was caught off guard by how protective he was of them. He couldn't explain it, but the kinship he felt for them was immediate and as real as the dust cloud rushing at them from the other end of the void.

The cloud passed over them all, staining the world.

A PLACE FOR SINNERS

A plucking ukulele in the middle of the night. Laughter from a darkened hallway. And even further back, there was Matt, a man who Tobias could have sworn had walked by his side through those winding Thai backstreets.

Go deeper.

The awareness of not being alone, of being watched in classrooms during tests, in open fields playing sports. Out-of-focus and difficult-to-recall dreams of stitching children's clothes and dabbing burning foreheads. All of those alien emotions bubbling up to the surface and expressing themselves in peculiar ways, through art or the singing of songs or random words that made no sense...

These memories were an unfolding flower within him. And they were beautiful—and yet not at the same time, because at the delicate core of the flower, where petal met stem, there was no pollen to be found. Instead there was nothingness, abysmal and endless.

That nothingness was guilt. And it was growing.

Tobias huddled near them, trying not to breathe in the dirt and rust. There, he accepted the truth of the flower. He said the words in this head so they were real.

I think I knew about The Others and ignored them.

I'm sorry.

Everything was quiet except for the clattering of his teeth. The dusty fog lingered, staining the void pale gray. His body loosened and he stepped away from the children.

He remembered that day on the roller coaster as a kid. His parents had taken him to the carnival because he'd been so kind to his brother, who sometimes didn't clean up after himself and who couldn't communicate like other kids could. The fair had been a swirling place of lights and smells and screams of excitement.

The clattering of their carriage rocketing down the tracks. The thrill of it all. The complete and utter belief that at any moment their train would skirt off into the sky and come crashing down among the crowd. His mother had been on the ride with him. She, like he, would die, their bodies burst open against the dusty fairground floor.

But none of this had happened.

His stomach might have lifted up into his chest, his heart might have wrestled with his rib cage in its attempt to flee, but they were alive.

The city lights had not dimmed the glow of the stars. His terror was complete. And now in the carriages behind him there were The Others. Their arms were waving above their heads as they neared another crest. Their laughter was infectious, their cheers unadulterated by sorrow, by regret.

Matt had been there too, dressed in his black leather jacket. His hair had been slicked back in a 1950s quiff. An expanse of possibility was spelled out in his expression. It was then, just as the carriage had descended, that Matt reached around from behind and pulled himself close to Tobias's ear. His words came in a rush, loud and clear over the clattering of wheels against rails.

"You only get one ride." His breath had stunk of grease and cigarette tar. The moon slid out of sight. "One chance! So ride the rap! 'Cause one of these days they'll drop the bomb and we'll all go Rocky Mountain high!"

The children's tears streaked their faces. Their hair was bleached with dust. They looked hewn from the same white tree that had protected them. Tobias ached for them and for the life that had been taken away from him.

"You have to save us," Joe whispered. "Please."

You got to ride the rap. The words carried. *Ride it.*

Tobias wasn't conscious of his nodding head. He looked at his hands. They seemed so strong and no longer shook.

If I don't fight for us, I won't exist. None of us will.

I'll never see my parents again. I'll never get to New Zealand and earn my way. I'll never get home and hug Jörg. Caleb will just be a memory.

Tobias let his eyelids drop and saw his boyfriend, lit in the glow of floating lanterns. Tobias could see Caleb's crooked smile as clear as day, could almost taste the charm and faux-confidence it radiated. There was that slightly crooked nose, a testament to bravery. And there was the tattoo on his right arm. *Family Love.*

Tobias put his hands against the tree and gripped.

"*Ich kann dies tun.*"

("I can do this.")

He started to climb.

6

Matt drove The Body into a run. There was only a single thought in his head at that point. It was stark. It was simple.

This is magnificent.

He dived into the hollow. Twisted. Turned among the webs. The threads latched to his skin as though fashioned from billions of tiny barbs. Everything tugged, knocking the wind out of him. Matt took a huge gulp of air, and for the first time since commandeering The Body, even worse than when the monkey had bitten off his fingers, he struggled. The webs were as thick as wet sheets, suffocating and heavy and dense and unnerving. Fear flickered through his brain.

But then again, fear was what this was all about.

He was going all the way to the edge—over it, even. This was what he was born for. The ultimate kick.

Between bouts of awkward laughter, Matt inhaled the webs and the decayed bodies of insects into his throat, where they scratched at the tender flesh. He flailed his arms, trying to double over. He choked, coughed and became very aware of how hot it was.

"I'm riding it," he growled. "I fucking am! Fuck! FUCK!"

The webs had clawed and cocooned, lifted up his shirt to expose the flat curve of The Body's belly. "Come on! I'm ready. BRING IT!"

And as though the spiders had been listening to his cry, they began to crawl out of their burrows, quick as lightning. They were not afraid of his bulk and thrashing.

Matt saw them coming out of the corners of his eyes, which were upturned toward the *hundreds* of funnels above his head.

Their attack was soundless. The only sounds came from him—that awkward meshing of snicker and yelp, and from the crunching of dead animal bodies beneath his feet.

They were so much larger than he'd expected them to be. Each of their yellow and brown abdomens equaled golf balls in size. Their long, dexterous legs skittered along the whispery ladders, little skull-faces covered with eyes.

Even Matt couldn't help admiring all of those teeth.

7

The white wood was cold and dead; it bore no scent. There had been no life in its branches for many years. Maintaining a firm grip on its bark was difficult, and the exertion was juicing a stream of sweat from every pore. It was as though the tree had been eroded, its surfaced buffered by unseen hands in the gloom. However, this didn't stop the occasional splinter from shooting up into his palms.

Hold tight, Tobias. You let go and we all come crashing down. And all the king's horses and all the king's men will never put us all back together again.

Blood continued to pump down the other side of the tree, forming a substantial pool among the exposed root system. The children stared up at him, their pale faces reflecting some light source he couldn't pinpoint. They only moved when the pool widened, taking careful steps backward and yet keeping their eyes on him.

Dust floated through the void and made breathing difficult.

Come on. Keep going. You can do this—

"Tobias!"

Joe's wail: fingernails on a chalkboard. It made him loosen his grip on the wizened branch. "Tobias, there's something up there!"

Don't tell me that, Joe. That's the last thing I want to hear.

But he *had* been told, and like a seed of doubt that can corrupt without control, the child's cry wouldn't let him be. And even though it took great effort to do so, Tobias lifted his head to where where tree hazed with shadow.

Joe was right.

There *was* something moving up there.

A suggestion of deeper black against all of the black. A sickly chill frosted the breath in his throat. A silvery rope swept past his shoulder. It moved through the air in sluggish curves, a perverted ballet.

Is that crepe paper?

No, it wasn't.

Tobias tried to convince himself that someone was planning a party for them up there in the dark. Somewhere, not too far out of reach, there were glasses being filled with lager, plates being loaded up with pretzels and Bavarian mustard. Yet he knew this wasn't true.

It *wasn't* crepe paper. That lightweight cord was closer to finely woven silk.

The giant spider shot out of the shadows and scurried over Tobias. It had not seen him. Huge pole legs thumped against him, tearing holes in his shirt and splitting the flesh beneath. He gritted his teeth and flattened his face against the bark.

It moved on, and took its icy shadow with it.

Tobias glanced over his shoulder. It took all of his will not to vomit right there and then. The spider's abdomen was the size of a tub chair, cheerful yellow streaks against its gristle-brown hide. He couldn't see its upper half over the blur of lashing legs, and was grateful.

That thing just touched me! It ran right over me! I'm dead. I must be dead—

Another spider, this one slightly smaller in size, dropped in lurches on a taut cord threading from a wet, puckered teat on its rear. Its legs were bunched in close, but not for long. He watched them spread, spanning yards, curling and then uncurling like a teasing hand.

Tickle, tickle, tickle, the act implied.

The children screamed, scattered. Except for little Joe Mccormack, who stood rooted to the spot, a deer in the headlights. The first spider splashed through the pool of blood, scurried across the cracked earth and took Joe in a single sweep.

"No!" The power of the word was as empty as the void. Tobias was sure that a part of him was dying. His grip on the branches grew even stronger. His ear was flush against the bark and he could hear the hollow thumping of another monster's feet as it followed the scarlet stream toward the children on the other side of the tree.

Tobias watched the spider latch its pincers around Joe's face, crushing it in a detonation of flesh and venom. The boy's arms jerked once, took a blind swipe at one of the spider's many gelatinous eyes, and fell to the ground. Dead.

Shock looped around Tobias's neck, a tightening noose. He tried to tell the monsters to stop, to go back where they had come from, but the words were dry and brittle nothings on an already dry tongue, crumbling and dying before they ever had a chance to sound off.

The scream of the girl in the ruby-red dress was sharp and cutting. She had the toddler in his Spider-Man onesie cradled in her arms. The second spider chased them down and snatched them off their feet, tearing them to shreds. A scarlet arc across the dust. Tobias watched the spider's back dance and throb as it sucked them dry and wrapped them in its webs.

8

"STOP!"

A spider had clamped itself to his lower lip, filling the tender flesh with venom. He bit down on its legs and felt them flex in his mouth, lodging in his soft palate. He could no longer see. One eye was swollen in an inflamed welt that had sprung up at a disorienting pace. Added to this, he'd spun around on the spot and thickened his silky prison.

Those tiny mouths continued to bite. Fireballs of pain seared into him. The tears flung from his face were snagged in the webs, diamonds on a thread. The arachnids continued to scurry back and forth over The Body, stabbing every patch of exposed skin.

Matt stopped.

The thought was paralyzing.

This isn't what I signed up for. This hurts.

I've...been misled.

Matt closed his one remaining good eye in defeat. The glory of the flesh had blinded him, and he felt a fool. He knew what he had to do, even though it humiliated him. There was no longer any alternative. The roller coaster, after all of these years, had finally derailed.

9

"Do you think I'll come back here one day and it'll all be just as awesome? Just as special?" Caleb had asked. It had been at night along the beach, and the lanterns had been set to sail the sky. One had caught alight and trailed toward the horizon in a rain of sparks.

"No," Tobias had replied.

"Really?"

"Caleb, it is never the same. I've been to a lot of places more than once, and it's never as good as the first time."

"Gee. That frightens me."

"No; don't be scared. Yes, it is sad, but it cannot be helped."
Tobias had cupped Caleb's face in the warmth of his hands.
"*The only thing that feels as good as the first time is home.*"

10

"Home," Tobias said. The word was wan. Had the fog of
dust followed him here? He was confused. It was hard to
see.

Where am I?

Wherever he was, it was a hushed chamber and was
empty except for the sounds of his own breathing and the
faint clicking of nearby insects. His ears twitched. Were
there rats in the walls of this dimly lit room? He suspected
that there just might be. Something scurried. Something
stirred.

Tobias stood silent, motionless, as though cast in
amber and forgotten about.

Home.

Tobias went to lift his hand but felt resistance tugging
against him. He tried to open his eyes but could only
manage the left, which slit open just far enough to reveal
a gauze of blurred shapes.

*Focus. You've got to concentrate. It's coming back. Can you
feel it? It's rushing at you, like thunder after the lightning strike.*

The analogy was both apt *and* prophetic.

It struck him with brilliant clarity. As his pupil
narrowed with shock.

Knives. Swords. Shards of exploding glass. They were
impaling him. Over. Over and over. In his face. In his
chest and back. Through his groin. His prick. His balls.
Down the lengths of his legs. In the skin behind his knees.
Across his ankles. In his toes. It was everywhere. The
closing spikes of an iron maiden.

And that iron maiden drove further and the pain went
deeper, past unchallenging flesh and splintering bone.
His roar was inhuman.

Tobias was back in The Body.

It was the spiders; they existed in this world too. He was at one with their venom. They were torture incarnate, fraying whatever thread of sanity that remained in him.

Tobias beat at the cocoon. Escaping was impossible. His limbs were heavy, but he refused to give in. Instead, he forced The Body onward. Teeth gritted together and head bent low, he rose, fighting for the surface of whatever horrible lake Matt had left him to drown in.

And he broke through. The webs snapped around him. He tumbled to the ground and heard spiders popping under his weight.

Mindless and robbed of his hatred, Tobias allowed the pain to suck him in on himself. It turned him inside out. The vomit began to flow, gurgling through his mouth and nose in a green spray. Beyond all this was the sweet air, and he welcomed it.

Tobias rolled across the deadfall, blanketing himself in the fetid leaves and water, continuing to crush spiders that refused to let go. Howling, he clawed the webs away and the world of the jungle was revealed to him. However, it was of no comfort. Where two of his fingers should have been, there was nothing but black and weeping stumps. Every inch of his flesh was puckered with purple bites.

Tobias searched inside himself for a name, found it, clung to it, screamed it out loud.

"Caleb!"

Over and over. Again and again. "Caleb! Caleb! Caleb! CALEB!"

This is not how things were meant to go.

(You're going to die here.)

I'm still young.

(Your heart will stop.)

I don't want to be alone.

(Look again...you're not.)

Everything grew vivid, like the moment a dream becomes lucid, and he saw the monkeys sitting near him, perched along the tree branches. Some were cackling at him, amused by his display. Their faces were all manic grins and bared gums and teeth.

Take me below.

Please.

Hello?

Are you there?

Were they all dead, he wondered? Were all of the children ripped to shreds? Tobias could feel his heart breaking. They hadn't deserved to be born into the life they had lived, let alone to die the way they had.

Tobias dropped his head. The pain was fading, and he was thankful. He drew his arms around himself and he wished that it were Caleb who was holding him now.

Did I tell him that I loved him?

It was hard to remember if he had. He hoped so; he really did.

Things were so hard to piece together... How peculiar it was that he'd gone on this incredible journey to begin with, leaving behind all of the people he loved in the hope of learning a little more about himself. In the end he'd discovered someone else, a stranger in some nightclub. Back home, he never would have been so brave in his advance. He was actually quite shy.

"*You got to ride the rap, you know,*" the thrill seeker would say. "'*Cause one of these days they'll drop the bomb and we'll all go Rocky Mountain high! You'll all be burned away, just like me. Nothing but ash'll be left.*"

Tobias's body stiffened. He was oblivious to the spider that was weaving its web inside his mouth, feasting on his withered tongue.

"*You make me feel like comfort.*"

That, at least, he knew he'd told him. But it wasn't enough. No, not even close.

A noise danced through his ears. It was an insidious sound.

The gentle plucking of ukulele strings.

Tobias tried to smile, though the numbness made it impossible. Maybe, just maybe, some of the children had survived and were there among the roots of the white tree, listening to that melody. It boiled down to hope.

Hope was all that he had left, and so he prayed for them, not for himself. He was beyond that.

The monkeys came at him. They carved him open and ate him alive.

CHAPTER SEVENTEEN

Amity, Robert and the Shark

1

AT NO POINT did Amity think she was going to die.
She couldn't. The moment she did was the moment
she would fall apart.

(The rope. The rope. Hold on.)

If she began to wonder what would happen to her if
she didn't find her way back to the beach and onto that
goddamned boat, things would come undone. So she
couldn't let her imagination get the best of her—even
though it already had.

Amity is sure there are shapes moving through the jungle.
Stalking her.

She distracts herself by grabbing handfuls of fruit
from a tree branch. Scoffs it down. It has no taste except
for water, but that's enough. It is amazing. The moment
the food hits her stomach, she wonders if the fruit is
poisonous. What if eating those berry-looking thingies
left her writhing on the ground, easy pickings for the
monkeys or whatever other hungry critters the island was
home to?

It's way too late for that. You've got to stay focused. Stay here, in the moment.

One footstep. Two footsteps. Think it through. Now repeat.

Amity was not walking through the jungle, even though she was. She was walking the hallway that led to her mother's bedroom, to the labyrinth of swelling trash. Her hand was outstretched before her, the fingers splayed against oak, pushing, pushing. And there it was: the aisles and piles, all in slow-motion decay. Heat waves rippled up through the floorboards, flaking old newspapers into ash. And there was her mother, but not really, perched on a hill of blankets knit out of love by old ladies, who gave these gifts to ungrateful offspring who only ended up giving them all away, perhaps because they were warm enough already, loved enough.

Amity's mother scooped it all up. She was greedy for it. *Waste not, want not.*

This was what she saw, and yet what she did not see.

Twin lives running in parallel, each threaded with threat, loss—

Water splashed up onto Amity's ankle, dragging her back to reality, and reality was what it was, no matter how much her mind refused to admit it. Even though she could still smell the ashes from the labyrinth, the bitter musk of melancholy, there was no escaping the island's heat, its orchardways. The taste of those berries.

I'm not going to die out here.

She studied her foot below the water's surface. She was no longer walking through the plant life that had ripped open her shins in little red smiles. There was sand underfoot.

Sand.

Not weeds. Not shale.

Sand.

She felt it. The curious sensation that optimism brings. It quickened the pulse, made breathing a task. Amity

Collins continued to stare at her foot, afraid to look up and see what lay ahead.

Be brave, Amity. You've got to be. You're breaking. You got to hold on—

(to the rope)

—and look. You realize that it's just the broken part of you that's afraid to know the truth. Either the jungle is thinning and the beach is within striding distance...or it's not. It's simple.

I know.

Fight it. Fight giving in like you did before, when you bandaged your hand. Who was that girl?

I don't know, in all honesty. She wasn't me.

Yes, she was.

But it couldn't have been me. I'm terrified. I feel like I'm falling apart. All I want to do is curl up and bawl my eyes out. I wish I'd died when I'd fallen back there. I wish I'd snapped my fucking neck. That'd be a mercy, at least.

Strong, fatherly hands—that were not there, though maybe they were—grabbed her by the chin and silenced all voices, both good and bad. Those fingers forced her head to rise, up-up-up to face a landscape she'd feared for no good reason at all.

The jungle *had* opened up into a ravine of towering boulders and sand. Trees still soared above her on both sides, like sentries waiting for the right moment to open fire, but they *were* thinner. The sight brought a smile to her face. The stream was thicker too, flowing harder and faster toward the thin V of light at the end of the ravine that appeared to veer to the right and led to sunlight.

This is it.

When she closed her eyes and focused her senses, she could taste the fresh and tangy salt being carried on the wind. Yet that wasn't all. There was also the smell of dead fish, brine and minerals, the ocean's unmistakable perfume.

I'm here. I'm really here.

Seaweed hung from the bulks of the jagged rocks standing between her and the jungle's exit—they were clashed together to form an almost impassable terrain. *Almost.* When the wind blew, the seaweed flapped like streamers strung across the finishing line of a school carnival field track. She'd never been very good at such events; this was Caleb's forte, not her own. Winning had rarely been within her reach. Finishing, on the other hand, was. And to prove it, somewhere in her mother's Memory Lane albums, between her brother's colored sports ribbons, were her certificates of effort and achievement—pride pinned beneath wax paper.

Almost impossible terrain. I can do this. I know I can.

Amity sensed the movement before seeing it. She tensed up and almost fell over. The relief that followed was as sweet and cool as the water splashed across her thighs. The animal was above her, behind the boulders, at the jungle's edge. The deer was tenacious, if a deer was what it was. It radiated age, wisdom, despite its pygmy size. It bore no antlers and its chestnut body dwarfed peg legs, but she knew it was strong. Its eyes were not complacent with its face, and instead furrowed with intelligence. Determination.

How on earth did you survive out here, sweetheart?

How do you do it?

How much do you fight and how much do you give in to?

Aren't you afraid, like I am?

Without seeming to judge or show pity, the deer turned its tail on her. Amity watched as it was welcomed back into the arms of those sentries, and was gone for good.

The man who had grabbed her chin earlier now leaned in close and whispered in her ear.

Go. Go now and don't look back. Run!

A PLACE FOR SINNERS

2

Robert had given up on chasing the scream and the trumpet's blow. The jungle had swallowed both up. It had tricked him into thinking that there might be people here, and if there were people, then there would be shelter, food—hell, a motherfucking radio. But no. The jungle was tricky. It fed on hope. Robert sighed. Now he doubted if he'd heard anything at all. It wouldn't surprise him.

Crickets and birds competed against one another, stitching the air with an impenetrable thrum. It rose and fell in pitch, in sync with the wind moaning through the trees. The island was breathing, and he was nothing more than a bug caught in its throat. Robert had gone too far down to be spat out, so he was scrambling, pained, as it slowly swallowed him whole.

It was too much. All of it. He allowed himself the indulgence of exhaustion and sat down on a nearby rock. Once upon a time, he never would have done such a thing. *I laid out sixty-five big ones on this set of hiking shorts, and I'll be damned if I'm going to go and get them all soiled over nothing.* That person was distant now, if he still existed at all. He tried to weep, but nothing came. Dry.

The pain in his guts was fierce, and he was worried he needed to shit again. Before hadn't gone so well. Robert didn't know if it was something he'd eaten or if it was the stress of this whole situation or if it didn't matter in the end. Either way, he'd been crippled by it, forced to squat like some pathetic animal. He'd learned a valuable lesson: unlike toilet paper, jungle leaves were not measured in ply.

Huddle in kids. Today was brought to you by the letter "H". As in humiliation! Oh, ain't life grand? Robert couldn't help but be a little disturbed by his laughter. He might not be able to cry, but he could still be a wiseass. This godforsaken place couldn't take that away from him. Not yet, at least.

The stream had petered out again. Robert bent down and scooped water into his mouth, wiped the back of his neck. Its coolness trickled between his shoulders, ran across the late-night scratch scars.

Even though he knew it was of no use, he reached into the pocket of those sixty-five-dollar hiking shorts and pulled out his iPhone. Somehow, it had survived the fall intact, a fate unshared by the bones in his rib cage, which he was reminded of every time he inconvenienced himself with a breath.

There was no reception, just as there had been none the thirty other times he'd checked since waking up in the mud. Those little bars. *Ha.* They meant nothing when they were there on the screen and meant everything when they weren't.

There ain't no reception in hell, big fella. Get used to it.

Robert was the kind of guy who would tongue a sore tooth, regardless of the somehow-pleasing discomfort it awarded, so it came as no surprise to him to find that his fingers were now scrolling through his photos, revealing faces he knew deep down he would never see again.

"Fuck you," he said to himself, looking away. "Why are you doing this? *Christ.*"

He knew the answer to that one. He wanted to look at the photos because hurting could be pretty damn sweet. Sometimes hurting yourself was the only thing you could do; it convinced you that there was something better, a less painful alternative worth fighting for.

Don't do it, Mann.

And yet he was. His fingers were moving over the touch screen, fat fingers with a life of their own. The same could be said for his eyes, which scoured all that should be avoided. His daughter. His wife. A scanned reproduction of a photo he'd found in a shoebox featuring his parents when they were young and happy and so very, very alive. He missed them all. His thumb continued to swipe, revealing further variations of lives he was no longer a part of.

She was in there too, even though he'd sworn he would remove all traces of her. All *visible* traces at least. Her fingerprints, it was hard to deny, were still imprinted on him where they once counted. After he'd broken off their relationship—which was to say, after being caught— he deleted all of her emails from his computer, wiped the messages from his phone in a rage. But were someone to ask him whom he was angry at, he wouldn't have been able to figure a reply. His pain was a lot of things, but mostly it was of the unfocused kind. And pure. Regardless, he'd torn it all up. Stripping her from his hard drive was hard, but the sickness hit harder. Control, Alt, Delete.

And it *had* to be a sickness. There was no other reason for it.

He knew his wife and daughter would never forgive him, and he knew that he'd ruined whatever had been sacred between them, but that other life had to vanish.

Which was why he figured being lost in this jungle was his punishment. This is what he deserved. And he deserved it because he was *yellah*.

A coward's penance lies in remembering his cowardice. His father had taught him that. This was why there was still that one photo of her on his phone. Just one. *She.*

He dared speak her name. "Bonita."

The jungle did not reply.

The photo didn't do her justice. Her brown skin looked too dark, her smile not quite wide enough. It had been taken on his iPhone. In it, she had a mean case of bed hair lit in morning light and spread across the hotel pillow. The elegant simplicity of the shot hinted at the life inside her.

Bonita. Once a wonder, now just an ache.

Robert rubbed his face. "Why are you doing this to yourself? Like this all isn't fucked up enough as it is." He shook his head and laughed; if he didn't, he might break again. "Stop talking to yourself."

"*Look at me again, Soldier,*" Bonita said from beneath the screen.

Soldier, her little nickname for him—*'cause you make me feel safe*. She often had bad dreams. In them, there were endless telephone calls, white noise from a muted television. Her dead husband scratching at the window of the bedroom they had once shared, his body made of ash.

"I don't want to look."

"But Soldier, you got to. It's meant to hurt. Isn't that what your old man used to say?"

"No." But Robert Mann looked anyway.

She was smiling in the photo. She had that look about her, frisky and a little wounded, which he'd found so damn attractive in the first place. They had met at a magazine launch in Chelsea; there, his work was on display in a series of highly awarded articles. The accolades were going to the photographer and design team, not him, of course, which was why his wife and daughter never came to these events. He was okay with all of this, both with their absence and his well-paid inferiority. He was a ghost between the written lines, a machine whose purpose was simply to complement and sell. That would never change, but he liked that Bonita thought his words had some weight. She had been leaning forward, scrutinizing a sentence on the blown-up one-sheet when he approached her. Their conversation started out innocent. Being charming wasn't as easy as it had once been; he was out of shape in more ways than one.

She didn't care.

The guilt he'd felt the following day was poison, and just like poison, his body tried to eject it from his system. The creative director stepped up to his desk and eventually told him to go home and rest. "Don't sweat it, Mann. You look like crap. Hell, alcohol doesn't sit well with me like it used to either."

Ha. The man was twenty-five.

Robert went home, spun his lies. More copy.

"Look at me, Soldier," Bonita said again. Robert did, despite himself. Her blades drove deep and carved her name against his bones.

It felt good. It always had. He'd long ago embraced the torture.

The memory of her kisses: cuts upon cuts. His father's words: an echo that would not stop. His wife's slap: an award he deserved. Imogen's tears on the shoulder of his shirt: acidic.

The bedbugs.

Her sing-song voice, rich as honey, came again. "Look. At. Me."

Robert Mann looked, and in doing so welcomed it all. He didn't know why he'd fought everything for so long. This was the way it was supposed to be.

"*Let them come,*" Bonita said, nodding. Her beautiful brown skin was now the hue it was meant to be, the glass and years separating them having dissolved away.

The phone went blank. Robert stood. "What the goddarned fuck?"

He'd drained what little power remained in the battery by looking through the old albums. The machine in his hand was as dead as the men and women he'd left behind on the beach.

Let them come.

Fury gushed through him, splashing disgust into his head. He opened his eyes and hated everything around him. The island was paved with trees, and in the bark of every one there was the face of someone he'd hurt or let down. Without thinking, he threw the iPhone that he'd bought at the Apple store on West Fourteenth Street into the green. As soon as it flew beyond the reach of his fingertips, there came that oh-so-familiar regret.

"You stupid sonnofabitch! Fuck. FUCK!"

Robert slouched through waist high ferns, heading to where he thought the phone might have landed. The vines from the trees—which continued to stare and trace him with ever-open eyes—wrapped around him. He fought them off. Sweat coursed his length. The anger hadn't receded. Everything was his enemy, and the fact that he couldn't *hurt* the island only frustrated him more. For every branch he thumped and broke, there were millions behind it waiting to pull him into a splintery cuddle.

Moving faster. He could smell his own stink; it was sickening. Finding the phone would probably make no difference, dead was dead, but having its weight resting against his leg would be comforting, a thinning bond to a life he'd been so desperate to escape from.

The irony was not lost on him.

"Yeah, so fucking funny, right? You sick cunt. You bastard. Holy Christ on the cross, goddamnit!" However, it wasn't him saying these words. No. They came from the man trapped beneath the bark of the tree in front of him. *That's so weird*, Robert thought.

That fella looks a little like me.

Light.

It was dazzling, even though he knew the sun must have been close to setting. Robert let the moments roll by, sensed the anger in him evaporating as dew steams at daybreak. The breeze touching his cheeks was cooling and clean, sensations he'd suspected he would never feel again. The truth was that Robert had expected to wander in the jungle until he dried up, collapsed and died, assuming some critter didn't knock him off first.

He had come from darkest dark to *this*.

Three words bloomed in his mouth. "Oh. My. God."

He'd found himself at the apex of a small ravine, and there was a decent-size river ten yards below. The decline was steep and paved with boulders—giant dice tossed by powerful though careless hands centuries ago. There was nothing neat in their design; each rock clashed with another, creating pockets of darkness in between. A gust of wind blew, sending seaweed streamers into a flutter. The sound reminded him of when he was a kid, and of the discarded plastic bags that would snag on the barbed-wire fence separating his family's property from that of his neighbors. They hissed. There was something hypnotic in the sound.

The river led to a bend in the ravine. The ocean was on the other side of it. He could hear crashing waves.

But that wasn't all.

There she was, the young woman he'd saved earlier. She was running along the uneven riverbank, tripping occasionally in the sand and diving over the rocks. Her blond hair was a beacon calling out to him: SAVE ME. SAVE ME.

It all became clear. *This.* This was why he was here: to answer her call. And saving she most certainly needed, because Robert understood better than most what it was she stood to lose were she to go unfound... as he had already lost it.

It wasn't just a stranger running down there. She was everyone. She was his father, his wife; she was Imogen; she was even Bonita. The girl he was sent here to save was every single spoke on the cog that had turned his whole life through, pushing him closer to this exact point in time—through lies and bullshit and bloodshed—to right now, right there at the ravine's highest peak.

"HEY!"

Robert waved his arms.

"UP HERE! STOP! WAIT!"

Goddamn it, what is she, deaf or something?

Something caught the late afternoon light and shone up at him from between his feet. Robert followed its Tinker Bell glow and saw his iPhone lying there, dangling on a thatch of hickory grass. Not even the screen was damaged. Had someone snatched it from the air and gently placed it down on the ground in full view? Were that the case, then, *thank you very much, Senior Invisible, you've sure earned your tip!* He laughed. This discovery spoke of chance—only chance of the *good* kind, the kind that worked in your favor as opposed to that which fucked you over, again and again. Yeah, Robert considered himself an expert on the subject.

So without a second thought, he bent down and snatched the damn thing up. He lifted it to eye level and gave it another once-over, praying that the same magical hand that had carried it to its resting place would also herald the return of those elusive blue reception bars, especially now that he was so close to the shoreline. But he was out of luck; the screen was blank.

He caught a flicker of movement in its opaque reflection. And that's when he felt it. The breath on the back of his neck.

Robert made as though to turn, but his feet slipped on the weatherworn boulder under him. The man who had crept out of the jungle was now just a diminishing blur as Robert's view gave way to a sky in agonized twilight with all the reds of the sun splashed across the clouds. A galactic crime scene.

The ravine was only ten yards steep.

It seemed far more severe to Robert, who tumbled backward and frontward and sideways down the picket-fence slope. The world rushed at him. Bones rose up through flesh, spearing him from the inside out. His jaw dislodged from his face. Teeth shattered.

He thumped against a boulder and felt himself starting to slide. He scrambled for something to cling to. There was nothing there but that paper-thin seaweed, which exploded into green dust the moment he touched it. Energy emptied out of him. His fingernails clung to the barnacles and snapped backward as gravity took control and dragged him between two of the giant rocks, down into one of the black pits he'd seen from above. There was a withered tree branch at the bottom, and it was its wooden point that broke his fall: impaling his leg, thrusting upward, and then embedding itself in the underside of his right arm.

Robert was already dreaming by then.

His cold and empty apartment was just as cold and empty as he remembered it. Time had been elastic; he hadn't been out of the

United States for all that long, and yet it seemed so much longer. Stretched. Like in The Wizard of Oz, Robert thought. When Dorothy woke up and the world was black and white again. It turned out she'd just been sleeping the whole time, dreaming of walking scarecrows, witches and flying monkeys. Hardly any time had passed at all.

The significant difference between the end of the film he'd loved so much as a kid and the world he had stepped back into was that there was nobody there in his apartment with whom he could share an "And you were there...and you were there too!" moment.

There was just the room; a morgue with a view.

He sat at the kitchen table. The sun was setting. Robert's shadow stretched across the Formica, the tiled floor, and rested against the door leading to the bathroom. There came a flushing noise from inside.

"Hello? Who's there?"

Robert was as still as stone. There were sirens wailing in the streets below, and the sound made all of the hairs on his arms stand on end. It was growing colder by the second, with steam puffing out from between his lips to cloud his vision.

The metal handle turned with a delicate metal scrape.

"Please, no."

The sun time-lapsed behind the Manhattan skyline, giving the city back the darkness it thrived off and hungered for during the day. The cold took over.

Light flickered beneath the bathroom doorjamb.

A tear slipped from Robert's eye, froze on his cheek.

Bonita fell into the room; smoke and flames were close behind. Robert tried to stand up and rush to her but he couldn't. It was as though he were trapped inside his own body. His former lover's curly black hair was singed to the scalp. Her hands were blackened bones, twitching and then falling apart on the floor. The floral skirt she'd been wearing (the one that he'd picked out for her from the boutique she liked on Fifth Avenue) was melted against her skin, a sinewy grafting of flesh and fabric.

Robert screamed out to her from inside but nothing escaped. He could only watch as she lifted her head to reveal molten eyes, her once beautiful, widening mouth.

She'd tasted like caramels.

"Soldier!" *Bonita shrieked, gurgling blackness that dribbled and ran down her chin.* "Soldier, he-eeeeelllp me-eeee!"

Small. Damp. Closing in on him from all sides.

Breathing was difficult. His skin felt too tight. When he tried to move, all he could see was white light. Dreaming was better, even with the nightmares.

Everything tasted coppery. Robert knew he was drowning on blood. Salt water rushed in from the cracks between the rocks. The tide was rolling in from the sea. Soon this crevice would be submerged and he would die.

He imagined that might be a nice turn of events.

It was colder here than it had been in his apartment, only he sensed that the cold was not on the outside of his body but *inside*. The pain was more than he could have ever imagined. The rocks offered no comfort. They were immovable and alien.

Look up, he told himself. *Search for the sky.*

Water continued to trickle and bubble around him. It was so loud.

He let his head snap backward. The white took over. In it he saw black dots swirling, imperfections against immaculate agony. It faded and he saw that other world above, so very out of reach.

The sky was painted a vivid purple and was freckled with the evening's first stars. Robert had read somewhere that it took hundreds—or was it thousands?—of years for the light from a single star to reach human eyes on Earth... How disappointing it must have been for the star itself, to travel millions of miles through space and time, only to embrace a place where grace had never touched. Robert sighed. Even if this were true, he selfishly liked the idea that those stars were pinprick gateways back into some other time, light from nowhere reaching down to usher him back into nowhere. In some strange way, this idea made him feel less alone.

Perhaps the light came from stars that had died long ago.

If he could have cried then, he would, but even crying took energy, and Robert Mann had none to spare. So he lay there instead and watched as three words began to fade into form against the award-worthy backdrop. They were printed in bold though elegant lettering.

Yeah, they really *popped*.

Three words. They sounded familiar; Robert no longer knew why.

LET THEM COME.

Drained, Robert allowed the simple sentence to sink in. It haunted him, stirred something in him that had been waiting for the right moment to come out of hiding.

Don't fight it anymore, Robert told himself. *It's just not worth it.*

Let them come.

And so they did.

The bedbugs rushed out from beneath his skin with all the strength and determination of the sea. They carried themselves on tiny legs, blinded by a hunger that could only be satisfied with misery. Robert was certain now that he hadn't contracted them on his trip to Florida, as he'd at first suspected. No; they had always been with him.

Robert didn't fight them. It didn't even hurt. Not anymore.

Instead of swiping and scratching at them with his broken fingers, he focused all of his attention on the ancient glimmering above. His smile was weak, but like those faint stars, it was there.

A man stepped into Robert's line of sight.

The stranger leaned forward to peer down at him. Beams of sunset orange doused his body. Robert hadn't really seen him back up there near the jungle's edge, but there was no doubt in his mind: it was the same man who had crept up on him and breathed down his neck.

"Help...me," Robert tried to say.

The stranger simply stood there. He was Asian, his skin all tanned and leathery. It was difficult to tell his age, although Robert guessed close to thirty. Those eyes peering down at him were a dusky gray and burned with contempt. A rabid stare. His hair was matted into waist-long dreadlocks that were tied into a bunch at the back of his head. A hand-span of dark, curly beard was plaited beneath his chin, tied off with vine.

But it was the stranger's clothes that unnerved Robert the most.

He wore a pair of cut-off jeans that might have once been blue but were now seagull-shit white, serving only to make his muscled legs look darker. They hung loose about his waist, fastened to his hips with a snakeskin. His upper half was dressed in a patchwork T-shirt that had been carefully stitched together from other, smaller T-shirts, all of which featured *Star Wars* iconography. Robert could see fragments of Chewbacca, Luke, Leia and Han against red, blue and white backgrounds. The thread holding the pieces together was Frankenstein-stitched with reed.

The man breathed. His barrel chest rose and fell with the throb of the ocean rushing in between the rocks. It was up to Robert's breastbone now, which meant nothing to the bedbugs, which continued to feast.

Why doesn't he reach down and help me out?

Why is he staring at me like that?

Robert tried to speak. It was too difficult. *Help me, goddarnit,* he wanted to say. *We've got to save the girl. Don't you get it? That's why I'm here.*

There were tears flowing from the stranger's eyes, shimmering beads caught in his whiskers. His mouth opened in a grimace of exasperation, revealing rotten teeth webbed by saliva.

The stranger began to shake his head.

No.

And with that, Robert watched him turn away.

Wait—

Robert didn't let his head drop back against the stone; that white pain frightened him. So he remained motionless, knowing now that he was being left here to die. He knew he deserved a lot of what had happened to him, but he honestly didn't believe that he deserved this.

He gawked up at the sky for a final time. The three words that had seemed so important to him before were gone, and he didn't care. The stars were still there, they were all that mattered. It was to them that he spoke.

"I'm...not..." The final word hurt too much to say aloud. It charred inside him.

Yellah.

Bedbugs wormed across his eyes and ate away at the corneas, but the stars' dead light continued to shine, growing brighter with every throb of his veins. The coldness had him in its grip and there was no going back.

Robert held his breath until it hurt. After that, there was no choice. No alternative.

He let them come.

The water rose and rushed inside him, filling him up. It made everything heavier. Total pain ignited, reminding him that he still had a choice. Robert could snap his limbs from his torso and propel himself to the surface; he could double over and chew through the wood that impaled him, wearing what few teeth he still had down to nubs in the process if he really wanted to. He didn't do either of these things. Robert did nothing.

And slowly, the pain went away, and there was calm silence on the other side. Screams he'd been unaware he was voicing were cut short. He was abandoned. Those stars shimmered a final time, dimmed, and then there came a beat of blackness. Exploding purple crystals bloomed, fireworks upon fireworks of refracted light and what looked like multifaceted shards of glass. It was astounding. It made him feel like a kid again—the marvel of it all. But like those passing years, this display started to escape him too. There was no stopping it.

Robert Mann closed his eyes and was happy to feel the insects that had plagued him for so long leaping from the kingdom and into the dark. The heaviness that had filled him when the ocean rushed in was gone now. It was as though he were naked. *Free.* The bedbugs had taken all of the guilt with them. He was happy.

Floating. Tipping into black—almost. A peculiar noise jolted him awake. It was a strange, comforting hiss. Robert could smile now. Everything was okay. It was the sound of plastic bags, caught on the spikes of an old barbed-wire fence in a small Kansas town, blowing in the wind.

3

The shark could feel daylight slipping away. Oncoming night didn't bother her. She was not afraid. Her fearlessness was what gave her power, and without it she suspected she would falter. And so she continued through the jungle.

The mosquitos were out in full strength, carpeting her body in stings she didn't feel. Theirs were burning itches upon itches upon flesh that was numb, and no longer her own. A shark's hide is tough, and of that she was thankful. But that didn't stop the hundreds of insects from trying their best; they bit and sucked, tiny mouths ripping through skin. Sycamore would swipe at them occasionally, out of habit if nothing else. Faraway tingles.

She began to grind her jaws and could hear her glass teeth scratching together. Heat boiled between her bloodied lips. Sucking oxygen into her lungs was getting harder and harder to do, but it was worth it. Every wheeze was copper flavored, reminding her of tastes yet to come.

Soon. *The light.*

The shark's hunger bore no comparison. It was as complete as anything she'd ever known or witnessed, if not more so. And so she let the mosquitos feed and was unbothered; she understood their purpose in the world more than that of her children, who over the years had fed with similar greedy mouths.

Light.

She could feel it now. It was growing stronger as the land stretched into an incline. Even the constant, electric whine of the insects started to fade with this immaculate warmth. There was a new sound now: a hush, like distant waves or rushing air. The branches before her unsewed themselves and in turn put together a jigsaw sky. The temperature dropped, sending the mosquitos rushing back toward the island's humidity. Sycamore stopped; her copper-breath held at the sight.

The landscape had driven her to one of its many peaks without her even realizing it, and now she stood on a tongue of rock overlooking a chasm that was wide enough to accommodate her entire London apartment.

Standing there with evening wind drawing water from her eyes, the shark wondered who else had stood on this rocky outcropping. Whoever it had been, they had dreamed of building bridges, had been the owner of strong, committed hands. But that was not all. Whoever the man was—and somehow she knew it was a man—he'd also had an undisciplined brain within his skull. This fact was illustrated in the demented architecture in the chasm.

Something foreign, yet familiar, began to penetrate her skin in a way that neither mosquito nor mercy had managed to do. It was a flicker of disquiet, a sense that there were other great powers and jaws and teeth in the waters through which she swam.

The chasm was filled with unfinished bridges. It wasn't as though they had collapsed and the engineer had simply continued building upon the broken remains. *No.* That wasn't it at all. Each foothold ended in a violation of gravity. One bridge ended in the birth of another, which would then stretch up or sideways at a contrasting angle.

As a result, wooden pathways crafted from jungle debris reached higher and higher, instead of straddling the chasm and making a direct route to the other side. It was all pure ambition, thwarted by an inability to think straight or with clear purpose.

It was insanity. A puzzle to which there was no resolution.

Something inside the shark was crushed.

The knot of bridges was old. Spiderwebs quivered in every joint. Dead leaves caught at its angles. This was a forgotten place. And that made sense in a way— the combination of such hands and mind didn't seem compatible with completion.

How sad, thought the woman who had once been Susan Sycamore. *Imagine living a life without getting what you set out to find.* This misery was echoed in the sound the bridges made when the wind blew: old wood groaning against old wood. It was a moan some part of her brain associated with empty pirate ships in movies some child had once watched in a carpeted living room with her father. It was the groan the child's house made when storms came a-knockin' against its walls. These were the sounds of desertion.

I'll get what I want. What I need. Her thinking was in defiance of the bridges themselves. Sycamore gritted her jaws together and tasted the red, red, red.

4

Amity dropped to her knees.

Her lungs burned with the effort of sprinting. And all along, she'd been thinking, *Yeah, this is it. It's finally here. The beach. The boat! It's over. Caleb. I need you now. I want you to just hug me for a while. I want us to cry against each other and know that everything is going to be okay. Because it is. It is.*

This train of thought had continued the entire time she ran, as the sand beneath her feet grew colder and wetter, as the salty wind churned with more force.

I'm saved. We're saved.

She'd even struggled not to laugh; doing so was so easy, so tempting. Victory was close. And yet she had held herself in check, driven onward toward the bend in the ravine. She didn't want to jinx herself, even though she knew that—yes, yes—she was right and goddamnit, this was it!

I'm about to be saved and things are going to be different, I just know it. I promise they will. There's so much that I've learned. Truly. And I know how fucking trite that sounds, but I'm being serious. I'll never wander again. From anywhere. And I'll stand by family to the end. Family Love. Ma, too. I can't wait to go home and care for her. I want to dig her out of the grimy hole she's buried herself in. I swear all of this is true; I just hadn't realized it until now.

How fucking juvenile can you get, Amity? You weren't traveling the world. You were running away. Say it. Own it. How the fuck could you have ever been so selfish? Ha. I can see Ma right now; she'll sit there and scream at us, stating our sins. She'll say that we gave up on her. And she may be right.

Her monologue ended as she slid between the V of boulders separating her from the torture any kind of hope brings. On some level she'd known everything would go wrong.

Amity dropped to her knees. The sand was cold. Lifting her head required the summoning of strength she didn't think she had in her to lend, and yet she forced it to come. It was so important that she torture herself with just one more look.

Sinners get punished, Amity reminded herself. *Ma was right.*

It wasn't the beach where she and the other tourists had docked. It wasn't really a beach at all. It was a cove of jagged rocks facing the cool blade of the horizon. Seagulls rode the wind. She watched their mouths open and shut like scissors cutting through the veils of her deafness to allow a distant screeching to slip through—Amity didn't know if it belonged to the birds or if it was her own. She suspected the latter. *There were vibrations.* Every time the waves crashed against the rocks, both the ground and her body shook. A tide of realization, of truth, pounded her head with all the force that moons muster.

Amity leaned back and called out to her mother, to her brother. She was way beyond caring how she sounded—it was real and raw, the way it should always have been and so often wasn't. The thorns of her lies had dug deep long ago, and in some strange way, airing at least this truth brought relief.

It happened.

The body of a young girl slammed against a boulder five feet to her right. The seagulls worked themselves into frenzy, diving toward the rocks and then swooping back up again. Their eyes were as red as the blood in the air.

Another wave splashed against the cove, covering the corpse in a sheet of bubbles.

Whatever heaviness had been hovering over Amity vanished. There was only weightlessness and a fever's ache. No words. Nothing.

Waves retreated, taking all of their bubbles with them. The child was revealed.

She couldn't have been much older than eight. Her naked body was impossibly twisted to accommodate the curve of the rock it had struck. A small hand lay outstretched, the fingers curling inward as though in invitation. Her head was twisted to face Amity, eyes rolled up, revealing the whites, so blanched in comparison to her heavy tan.

Even through Amity's confusion and shock, a weird buoy of rationality floated by and she had no choice but to cling to it—*she's not Thai. Japanese, maybe. Chinese.*

I just don't know.

But not Thai.

It was almost as though another voice was announcing this fact to her, and Amity couldn't understand for the life of her why it was so important—but it was. And the voice just might have been right, too. The child's face was longer and a little more oval shaped than those she'd seen on the mainland; her nose was a little more pronounced. It was Amity's artist's eye that noted these subtle differences.

Or maybe it was that focusing on the dead child's nationality distracted her from the slit throat. The ocean had cleaned the wound, but there was more blood below the skin to replace it. A tide of a very different kind.

Before Amity had a chance to glance up to see where the girl had fallen from, another corpse thumped against the sand right at her feet. Clods of flesh and gray matter splashed over Amity's legs, her chest, peppered her lower lip. Its taste was in her now.

The second child was a boy, a little older. Thin. He wore a bright blue *Star Wars* T-shirt. Han Solo's and Chewbacca's faces were stern and severe as they brandished their pistols. The boy's shorts were stitched together from other shirts.

Brother and sister.

There was no mistaking it. They had the same features, the same broad nose structure. Not to mention his-and-her matching throat slits.

Vibrations brimmed. Amity was screaming.

There were sounds now coming from deep inside her. Their echo grew and grew. Amity's hands inched toward her ears. There, they gripped the cartilage, pulled.

Go away! Go away!

It was the sounds of feral dogs growling in preparation for attack.

Vibrations ran dry.

You've got to breathe. Don't and you're as dead as them.

It was easier thought than done. Had she forgotten how? Something that had come so naturally to her all her life now required extreme concentration. So she lifted her head and let the oxygen pour in through her lips.

The sky boomed with the day's demise. Epic cumulonimbus, as imposing and majestic as atom-bomb clouds, flared purple and orange and red. Against this backdrop, a hundred yards above, Amity saw the peak of the cliff. Between her and it there stretched the island's rocky throat, exposed and vulnerable to the horizon's blade. Two silhouettes stood at the peak. One was taller and hugged the smaller figure from behind. Their embrace ended with a flurry of movement, and then the silhouette in front began to fall. Amity watched it arc across the clouds headfirst, its small arms outstretched. An upturned crucifix.

These sights had a color and that color was RED.

The third child hit a boulder near the breakers, exploded and tumbled into the water. The makeshift knife that had been rooted in its neck slid free, snagged against a crop of oyster shells. It sat there until another wave slammed the cove and snatched the evidence away.

It was sunset, and the day was darkening with each death.

The vibrations came back.

Crying, Amity swirled around to face the way she'd come. The shadows that had lurked in the jungle—the ones that had threatened to close in on her minutes before—had now fulfilled their promise. The way was strangled by darkness. Her tears mingled with blood; Amity swallowed it all down. She didn't know if she was strong enough to go back that way. It would be pitch-black in there.

That was a lie. She *did* know.

She *wasn't* strong enough.

Amity turned to the left. To the right. The small cove was nestled against the island's edge. There were rocks and jagged boulders in both directions. Soon they would be indistinguishable from the sky. There would be no lights flickering on at dusk as there were along the Evans Head streets. Once the sun dipped beyond the cliff, the shadows would claim all.

It made sense that if she kept on rounding the island's perimeter, then she would come to the beach where they had arrived. Eventually.

Go left, said a voice. Amity listened to it because it sounded friendly. Right now, anything that drowned out the dogs' barks and growls was an ally. She scrambled toward the first set of boulders and pulled herself up their barnacled girth. The wound in her right palm screeched pain, but she pushed through it. Fingers latched on to a clump of weeds. Salt flakes filled her nose.

Don't sneeze. Sneeze and you're a goner.

Amity pulled herself upward and onto the rock. Gasping, she drew herself into a ball. Now that she was on her side, it required no effort to glance up at the cliff.

She watched the final figure leap into the air.

It even gave itself a running start.

"No-ooo!" Amity screamed, unhearing the word but feeling it just the same.

She reached out for the falling silhouette as though she could catch it. There was nothing to do but watch it tumble. The arms thrashed. The legs kicked. *It was a woman this time.* Amity knew it was the mother of the children. She watched the woman land on the sand near her boy in the *Star Wars* T-shirt. What had been an intact woman one moment—so very alive, as her children had not been—was an accordion collapsing in on itself the next.

As to what lay between? Amity had no idea. She just hoped it was painless and quick.

The sun dipped behind the cliff. Those cold fever fingers were back to stroke her.

What's happening here?

What the fuck?

This couldn't be a dream. But it couldn't be reality, either. On this island, animals attacked and families fell from the sky...

Amity studied the clump of dead grass between her fingers. *Let it go*, she willed herself, but her fingers weren't in a listening mood.

She wondered if she was dead and if this island was some kind of purgatory, or worse, hell. Even that made more sense to her than what she'd just witnessed.

Let. It. Go.

Her fingers relaxed and the brittle strands of grass blew away. The world slid into further darkness. She had to get up and keep on climbing. There was no way she was going to make it around the island and back to the beach before dark, but she couldn't stay where she was.

So even though it hurt, Amity dragged herself up onto her haunches. Grime coated her body, clung to her clammy skin. Spray misted her face. Salt against salt.

Move. Leave this horror behind. Leave it or you'll go mad. Don't think about it. MOVE!

Amity steadied herself and shuffled to the next rock. It was slippery, but not too bad. The higher she got, the better it would be. She soon found her rhythm. But night, like panic, was impossible to escape.

OhmyGodohmyGodohmyGodohmyGod—

Shut up. Keep going.

So much blood. What happened to them? Why—

MOVE. Don't kid yourself into thinking you'll make it back to the beach tonight. You've got to find somewhere to hide. You're safer out here than you are—

(Hold on. Hold on. Hold on.)

—in the jungle. Trust me. Even if you just jam—

(Hold on to the rope.)

—yourself between two big rocks, it's better than nothing. You need to stay warm. Stay out of sight. Stay—

There it was.

A cave.

Shadow inched across the rocks, cold on her heels. Its dark, clammy fingers were quick but she was quicker. Though not by much. Every plunge drained her of energy, made her journey to the cave harder and harder.

The cave.

She watched its mouth growing slowly larger. Images of her bent over wood pieces within its walls, chafing fire into life, danced in her head.

Amity suspected that drawing flame from sticks wasn't as easy as she hoped it would be. Not like in the movies, anyway. But then again, nothing ever was. The idea of temporary warmth and shelter did give her comparative comfort. And that was enough. Enough to keep her going.

I need to put as much distance between the bodies and me as possible. I want that even more than warmth. So lunge. Lunge. Lunge.

The shadow was the dread that knowledge brings. The knowledge that she *was* going to die out here, that she would rot and become food for the animals in the sea.

A memory.

There had been a large fish tank on the way to the headmaster's office at Saint Catherine's School For Hearing Impaired Children. Inside were five forgetful goldfish swimming in constant circles of rediscovery. She envied them for their simplicity, that they would never know what it was to be haunted. But it wasn't the fish themselves that unsettled her. *It was the ceramic skull at the bottom of the tank.* The way the top of its head would lift off to allow a stream of bubbles. Little goldfish puckering kisses through the eye sockets.

Please, no. Please, not that.

Amity glanced at the ocean. She'd read somewhere that it was the one thing on this planet that you should never turn your back on, and she could see why. It boiled with contempt for her. It was hungry for *her* skull.

Never.

The dread wouldn't be shaken.

Why? Why on earth would a mother kill her own children? And to do it like that...

Her breath was ragged. She felt sick.

The shadow was persistent as it crossed the island, a slow-moving scythe.

Every time she blinked, she saw the dead family on the beach, their faces turned toward her. Their blood churned in the water. Everything was RED.

Why commit suicide?

She didn't want to blink again, and yet there was no choice. She was a slave to her flesh.

The mother's knife caught on the rock. It looked as though it was crafted from wood and bone, one edge whittled down to a point. The waves lapped away the blood, hungry for it.

Amity was sure if she went any farther her lungs were going to explode, so she stopped and crouched on an uneven rock that was puckered with potholes. Each brimmed with seawater, reminding her of how thirsty she was.

A palm-size octopus rounded the walls of the shallow pool, its legs a spectrum of neon hues.

What pushed a mother to destroy not just herself, but her whole family? What in God's name could have pushed her—literally—over the edge?

Amity's headache continued to beat at her head, growing behind her eyes. Adding to her discomfort was the fact that her throat had grown so dry it was almost impossible to swallow. She rested her palm against her cheek and counted breaths—questions just weren't distraction enough.

What happened here? What?

Amity's eyes shifted from the octopus in the pool and focused on her manic expression rippling across the water's surface. It took a moment to realize that the person staring back was *her*. She sighed. She'd been thrown off by the look of *understanding* in the reflection's eyes, by the intuition carved into that face. It was primal. It was chilling. And then she knew.

We're the reason they've exterminated *themselves. We've penetrated their home and they'd rather* fucking *die than have us here—*

"Oh, Amity."

The whispering voice was silky and smooth. It was intimate, a voice that sounded as though it knew every one of her secrets—even the ones about the man she had met on the Internet—and still loved her for it. This was why she wasn't afraid. Besides, this stranger's breath must have been nothing short of magic to slice through her deafness the way that it had done.

Gooseflesh prickled her body. The darkness was over her now, cutting her in two. Her own shadow stretched out long before her, warped by the step and steep of the terrain. She followed its length, arching her neck, and saw the mystery speaker.

It was a man.

He was tall and his clothes changed with the shifting light, a kaleidoscope suit. Formless and undefined, he stood at the mouth of the cave, beckoning to her with both hands. A sheet of cardboard was strapped to his head—a printed black-and-white face. Two holes had been punched out for the eyes, but there was no twinkling to be found behind them, just blackness. It was her father's face, taken from the photograph that sat on her bedside table in Evans Head.

"Keep going, Amity."

Something clicked. She almost felt it. Something had turned *on* inside her, somewhere in the backstreets of her brain. She wasn't certain, but she thought it might be—

(she probed for the word, reached through the dark. Found it. Held it. Owned it.)

—*acceptance.*

It *was* her dead father standing there and calling out to her. This fact couldn't be disputed because it felt so damn right.

She smiled. "Pa." The word was stripped of her usual self-consciousness. The vibration was sweet. It was not RED. It was PALE BLUE. Amity laughed.

"Don't give up, sweetie. You're so close. Push yourself. The cave is dry."

He beckoned again. The gesture tugged at her chest; she gave herself over to it and followed. Dean Collins had her, hook, line and sinker, and she gave herself to him willingly.

A flower of memories, blooming at an impossible speed.

Sitting on her father's knee at a barbecue in their backyard. He was bouncing her up and down. She was wearing her red slicker, the rubber squeaking. Her mother was there too. There was sauce dripping from her sandwich as she leaned forward to take a bite, splattering across her gown. It was dusk and the barbecue smoke was keeping the mosquitos away. A man whose name she couldn't quite remember sat across from them. He was broad shouldered and black. He held a beer in one hand and a cigarette in the other. His face was a bowl of kindness; she could see it in his eyes.

Then it came to her: this was Clover, the man who had killed the dogs on Chinaman's Beach with her father's shotgun. In saving her life, he'd burst her eardrums. Her mother kept his obituary in one of her Memory Lane albums.

She was crying in her bedroom. Her father had a wooden spoon in his hand. He looked so disappointed in her. Amity couldn't recall what she'd done to elicit such a punishment, but it must have been severe. Afterward, lying on her bed and sucking on her thumb, her father came into the room and hugged her. "I'm sorry, little luv," he said. "Please don't do that again. I hate hurting you. I just don't got it in me."

Another petal.

Amity going up to her parents' bed late at night, her Raggedy Ann doll tucked under one arm. "I think I feel sick," she told them moments before vomiting across their legs. Afterward, her father lay in bed with her, stroking her forehead with a wet cloth.

Another.

Another.

She burned for him.

It seemed appropriate that he was clothed in a kaleidoscope of shifting density and hue; it reminded her of all the shirts that he used to wear, and how they had defined him.

Shirts.

Each one was an event that he'd never had a chance to attend with her.

Birthdays, Christmases, her graduation from Saint Catherine's, the day her grandmother passed away.

All of those missing days were spelled out in this flickering weave, which was undoing and reknitting itself before her eyes.

Take me back, the kaleidoscope seemed to say. *All of those missing years are waiting for you. You just have to want it. Come to me.*

Amity broke in to a run. "Pa! Pa! Don't go."

She wanted to hold him and tell him who she really was. She'd long ago grown tired of pretending to be someone she wasn't. Her Facebook and Twitter presence had filled just some of the space he'd left behind—places where her whining was accepted, where she could cheapen herself, where the boring and the mundane were slotted between flickers of honesty.

Amity wanted—strike that, she *needed*—a father. Or at the very least, she needed what even Facebook claimed to have: a moderator. Binary code just wasn't going to cut it.

Amity's foot slammed against something. She hardly felt it at all. Looking down, she saw an old, splintered tree branch whitened by sun and salt. It rocked against her sandals. Amity looked back up. Her father was gone, as she had known he would be.

It was the crushing feeling of waking from a dream in which you won the lotto or finally found Mister Right. Yes, it was just like this. Only worse.

You're a fucking idiot, Amity.

I know...

Do you like torturing yourself, is that it?

No, of course not.

You just like making bad situations worse.

That's not it at all. I–I–

You're losing it. You can feel it, can't you? It's like a rope–

(Yes, the rope!)

–tying us together, everything together, and it's fraying. I'm going to fucking drift away; it all is. And you're going to be left behind. Stark raving mad. There ain't no loony bin out here, girl. There's just the dark.

Amity stood at the threshold to the cave.

You've got to keep your smarts about you, okay?

Okay.

Go inside. Get out of this god-awful wind. The shadow's almost here. Now. Now!

Wait.

Amity bent down and picked up the long tree branch she'd almost tripped over. It was heavy in her hands yet lighter than she'd suspected it would be. The weather had drained it completely dry over time. Mother Nature could be a vampire, and Amity had no intention of becoming her next victim.

Her fingers gripped the smooth surface; the branch was like bone. She shivered.

Good, girl. That's the Amity I know and love. Keep the rope strong. Keep it strong.

She cradled the wood with both hands, holding it the way action heroes held their weapons in the movies her brother sometimes made her watch (Caleb had to explain to her why Arnold Schwarzenegger's subtitles were always written in broken English—"No; that's how he *actually* sounds!"). She was locked, loaded, and could already feel herself growing stronger. Or at least this was what she told herself.

The shirts Amity's father used to wear were not the only things she remembered from her childhood. There were other things. Other events... There had even been this one time when she'd wandered from a tent where her pa and Caleb had been sleeping, and she had fallen through some trees. She'd been spat out on a landscape similar to the one she currently stood on. In that place, long ago, there had been monsters with fleas in their fur waiting for her. Foam dripped from their mouths.

The lead bitch had bitten her. *Coveted* her. She had the scars to prove it.

Amity tensed and peered into the mouth of the cave. The last time she'd found herself in this position, she'd almost died and all sound had been seized from her ears. Amity would be damned if she would allow anything like that to happen again.

6

At first sight the cave didn't seem much bigger than a single-car garage. It was divided in two by a gradient of light versus shadow, and even then, shadow was closing the gap. Soon there would be no illumination at all.

The branch was slick beneath Amity's palms. She extended it out in front of her, ignoring the searing sensation from the wound in her right palm. A trickle of blood ran to her elbow, grew fat, and plopped onto the ground. The rocks on which she stood were worn and almost looked glassy, covered in patches of white moss and bird shit. She could smell damp, wet earth and something like rotten fruit.

It was impossible to tell how far back the cave stretched—or if it narrowed down in size like a funhouse forced-perspective room—without stepping further into the dark. And she didn't want to do that, not even if her ole pa was in there somewhere.

Stomach knotted. Teeth clenched over her lower lip. Her eye twitched.

Maybe it wasn't too late to go back and find somewhere else to hide out. She glanced over her shoulder and saw the final rays of light arching around the cove, silhouetting the cliff the woman and children had fallen from. This was answer enough for her. If night fell and a storm rolled in off the ocean, she'd be royally screwed. The decision had been made for her. Like it or not, this was her home for the night, and all things considered, she could have fared worse.

But why was her skin prickling? Why the butterflies of anticipation fluttering in her bowels? Why did she feel like she was being watched? And it wasn't for the first time either. She'd sensed it before, back in the jungle.

You're being an idiot. Calm the hell down. Sit. You need to rest.

Now when she blinked it was not *just* the faces of the dead family she saw. There were wild dogs prowling there. They inched forward on gnarled legs, eyes glinting. Each swipe of her eyelids brought them closer.

Closer.

Amity gave another minute's pause and then exhaled. She loosened her grip on her makeshift weapon. It hung, clublike, at the end of her left arm, dragging against the rocks. Her muscles unwound.

There were no eyes watching her from the dark, and yet she *felt* them. And there were no hands reaching out to touch and turn her head, and yet her head *was* turning without her seeming to have a say in the matter. Amity's eyes locked on the right-hand side of the cave— the side still exposed to the dwindling sunlight.

What the hell?

She took a step toward the wall, the stick's point carving a line through the grunge underfoot. Her eyes were wide and absorbed it all.

Amity knew that her mouth had dropped open, a habit that she had always been self-conscious of—

(*"Close your mouth or the flies will get in,"* her mother used to tell them when they were kids, although in what cadence or pitch she'd long since forgotten, as was the case with all voices. Her own included. Amity guessed that it was the image that had stuck with her more than the expression itself: that of black flies swarming around the kangaroo roadkill that paved the road into Evans Head. Those flies would feast, fuck and leave their larvae under envelopes of flesh, and then, unsatisfied and pregnant, they would wait for her little lips to part.

Her mother had many expressions, though only some still rolled about in her head. But by far, "close your mouth or the flies will get in" was the worst, simply because it didn't just speak of bad habits. It told a tale of death-starved things squirming in the throats of children.)

—but she was way past caring now.

Amity stepped close enough to the cave wall to inhale its chalky loam. She brushed the rock. It was cool, submissive to the shifting sun. Scratched into its face were etchings, carved by a delicate and controlled hand, some time ago from the look of it. The dust and salt and grime were thickly coated, but the illustrations could still be clearly seen. It was almost like a primitively drawn comic strip spelling out a narrative she wasn't sure she was brave enough to read.

There were threads of writing here and there. Amity had seen many of the signs up and down the coastline and scoured countless menus to recognize the basic shape of Thai script, which was distinguished by arcs and gentle curves. These cave scrawls bore no resemblance to what she'd seen since arriving in this country. These words were harsh and jagged, violent strokes against stone.

They're not letters, Amity told herself. *They're characters. Japanese.*

She took a step back, composed herself. The scythe of shadow was drawing on the cave and soon the story would be hidden. But did she really want to know what cards the island kept close to its chest? She already knew they weren't alone—*wasn't that enough?* She honestly didn't think it was, which was why she took another step back so she could view the drawings in full, even though she was worried that reading on would reveal her guilty part in these peoples' destruction.

Are you sure you want to do this?

Yeah. I think I do.

And what if you learn that those people back there—that woman, those children!—didn't jump? What if you learn that they were pushed? They had lives before we arrived, didn't they? We've done something to set them off. What if you realize you are the one who slit those kids' throats?

Amity closed her eyes, a deliberate move. The faces of the dead were revealed to her.

Their eyes were open. They looked into her. Mouths moved. Goldfish pleas. Amity crossed the cove and kneeled by the mother's side. *The waves didn't dare touch them. All was still. The sun had frozen over.*

"Whatever it is we've done," she began, "I'm so, so sorry."

The dead mother continued to speak, unheard.

"I want to take it all back. All of it. But you need to tell me what crime we're guilty of. Please."

Blood filled the woman's mouth. The waves coveted them.

7

It spoke to the artist in her, this sometimes chaotic but always-intricate carving. And her eyes, accustomed to drafting professional works for money, could see that what stood before her was a testament. A confession. Amity had never felt so shallow as a creative soul. Never in all of her years had she *ever* come close to making something half as pure or honest as this. It shamed her.

She leaned in and blew against the wall, swirling dust captured in the shaft of yellow light. Enough details were revealed for her to tell that the narrative ran downward in right to left columns within a lanky rectangle, a frame of horizontal text.

The first drawing in the top right-hand corner was of a man. He was bent on his knees, though in pleading or thanks she couldn't quite tell. Yet. The limbs were well defined, the face a rough scraping of dashes—the eyes, the mouth. But she could see that he was *strong*. More than anything else, that was what she took from the rendering. Above the figure was something that looked like a bird, or maybe even an airplane.

This same man appeared in the next drawing below, which like them all was separated by another Japanese symbol. The man was standing this time and was holding an old laborers' pick—an inverted T with the top slash curved to a point.

So he's a worker. Doing what?

Beneath his feet were deeply etched ladder rungs. No. Not ladder rungs. A railway track.

Amity swallowed. She imagined kneeling on this very spot with a blade in her hand for *months* on end—because that is how long this would have taken. Whoever did this had had plenty of time to spare, not to mention patience, and whoever they were, Amity suspected they were angry about something. Furious. You didn't just kneel down and make work like this because you were bored, or *just* determined. She could sense the tightly held frenzy between the carvings, a blade that must have slipped so many times. There would have been cramped hands. Cuts.

Lots of them.

The next drawing was of a bridge. It was wide but unfinished. There were more of those bird-airplanes above it. Three wavy lanes were engraved below.

Water.

Next, the strong man was on his knees again. The pick was by his side. Standing behind him was a tall stranger with broad shoulders whose body was divided by an angry streak across his hands. Amity didn't just suspect this was a rifle; she *knew* it was. That incessant chill, which she'd felt before, grappled with her again.

The memory of a noise, and that memory was RED.

The same bridge was obscured by angry slashes in the next drawing. It was hard to tell what this signified. Rain. Fire? Amity reached out and touched the gashes in the rock.

Not rain. Flames. Explosions.

Christ, what went on here?

Next, the man was running. The image reminded her of the pedestrian crossing sign that lit up at the main intersection in Evans Head. She used to have to touch the buzzer to feel it vibrate, the sound to walk lost on her.

The pick was still in the man's hand.

Six depictions in the clay and she was already invested in the story.

Next, the man was standing beside a second figure. This second person's hair was shoulder length, the legs long and thin—a woman. Amity could see that this companion had been sketched with considerably more care than the man had been, as though in *respect* to a precious memory. Cramped hands and spilled blood just might have been worth it for this particular artist.

Next, the man and woman were in a boat crossing more wavy lines. Her head rested against his shoulder. The boat seemed small, and although it had a mast, it bore no sail.

Next, the boat was docked on a straight line, the water behind them now. The two figures were standing on that line, at the end of which were trees. Amity's mind animated the sequence.

The man and woman stepped onto the sand, relieved and exhausted. It must have been murder out there on the ocean in a vessel of such diminutive size, but somehow, perhaps even surprising themselves, they had survived. They had arrived on a beach—and it made sense that it was the same stretch of land where Amity, Caleb, Tobias and the other tourists had docked.

Amity couldn't even begin to imagine how happy they must have been. Their sense of safety couldn't be measured in scratched stone.

Next, the man and woman stood among those trees, holding a baby. A boy, as indicated by a small dash between his legs.

Next, the man and woman sat on a rocky outcropping. There were two children now, the second noticeably dashless.

The following two columns were dedicated to an incestuous lineage of second-generation children mating with each other, resulting in the birth of further children. Following the little crosses and circles and zigzags that were meant to differentiate each offspring from the next was growing confusing.

Amity rubbed her head.

It was also becoming harder to distinguish the first-generation children—now taller and broader in adulthood—from the versions of themselves in their younger days. It was like a slow-moving zoetrope, only instead of smooth transitions lending to the impression of passing years, there were distinct gaps and repetitions in the design. It wasn't as though the artist had lost track of how many grandchildren and great-grandchildren the first arrivals must have had, it was just that Amity was in no state to keep up with it all. It was all blending together, just as their time on the island must have done.

She imagined that it must have been a demanding life living off the land, made harder by the defects that must have plagued the children as a result of their muddled bloodlines. For all she knew, some of them had been born without eyes or with extra toes. Maybe some of them had even been deaf.

Amity sank to her knees. The weight of the narrative was dragging her down. Her many wounds cried protest—so insignificant in the face of the story being told.

There were deaths inscribed, too. The second-generation girl, now grown into a woman, gave birth to a son on one occasion and triplets on another, but she died during that final labor. A solid, unmarked stake, kind of like a fence post, marked her grave. The delicately carved shapes next to it had to be flowers.

Amity held her breath as she continued, lives lived and ended in quick succession. There were more such posts, more graves. The third-generation children gave birth to a total of four others: a son (again, the dash said it all), another set of twins (a boy and a girl) and a final girl.

Another life over, the flowers as carefully drawn as the rest.

The children sat around a dead animal. A deer.

A family held hands under a full moon.

And yet through it all, over however many years had passed (by working backward, Amity estimated that the original man and woman must have arrived on the island almost...*seventy* years ago), the first man remained. It was easy to track his increasingly passive role in the story, because unlike everyone else around him, he didn't seem to age. He remained the same throughout, and he always had his laborer's pick by his side.

The scythe of shadow was almost fully drawn. Amity looked through the cave's entrance and saw the final twinkle of the sun on the cliff peak. The day, like the story itself, had finally drawn to a close.

The final chapter was laid out before her.

For reasons not described in the pictures, the first man (albeit a little more hunched than he was before) left his surviving family. Amity squinted in the dimming light, bent forward again. Yes; he now appeared to be *leaning* on his pick for support.

Hmph. So not immortal after all.

Amity sat back on her haunches and couldn't help but sadly smile. The first man—who long ago created bridges at gunpoint—had grown old as all men eventually do, despite always being young of mind. She interlaced her shivering fingers and tucked her knuckles under her chin. It was obvious now. It was the original man whose strength and artistry was on display here.

This isn't just a story. It's an autobiography. And it ends here.

Amity's eyes traced the final carvings. The author had left his family behind. They watched him go and huddled close to one another for support. Her heart ached for them. These were people who cared about one another, who appeared to act with respect, loyalty and integrity. Though their faces must have been misshapen, their DNA strands as knotted and confused as the island's many paths, they were as human as she was. They hurt as she had hurt, perhaps even more so.

They loved.

They feared.

It had grown colder, and Amity knew she should take her makeshift spear and break it into pieces for kindling, yet the promise of the final drawing held her in place. She doubled over, placed one hand against the rock for balance, and studied the bottom left-hand corner.

The first man was walking into a large circle. A *cave*.

8

Amity could smell him before she saw him. It was a wet-skin-beneath-the-Band-Aid stink. An aroma she would quickly have dismissed as disgusting, although this would have been a lie. It was one of those repellent self-musks that she guessed were normal to tolerate, or even secretly relish.

And why?

Because it didn't just signify decay. It was the sweet smell of evolving flesh. It was rebirth.

She swiveled her head to the left and watched him materialize out of the dark. Time kicked, thrashed and seemed to stop. Everything did—the throb of her pulse, the vibrations of the crashing waves.

Everything except him.

He walked into the last wheeze of light—it glimmered against the milky corneas of his blind eyes. The man was ancient, more skeleton than skin. His mouth was opened in a shuddering sneer of overgrown teeth.

Amity was too startled to move. She stood there, lapping up the sight of him. Bile rose up her throat and stained her tongue. It was bitter, warm.

A shawl of knitted seaweed was draped over his shoulders. His jaundiced skin appeared so thin in places that Amity could have sworn she saw his inner heat radiating through, giving him an ethereal glow that prickled her flesh—*a man who shone like the moon.* A shit-stained beard cascaded over his chest, half-obscuring cancerous caves of flesh scooped out of his body.

Time bucked again, time enough to scream. Her hand clenched against the rock wall.

Something *stirred* in the man's flesh caves.

As a candle burns brightest just before it blows out, the sunset bloomed and stretched out to illuminate the lives living on and in him. Crabs lived in his cancers, and ran back-and-forth sideways paths across his chest. Their multicolored shells were wet, as though dabbed with splashes of paint. Only it wasn't paint—it was shreds of flesh in various states of decomposition. Putrid sequins. The crabs—the parasites—continued their dance as their host took another step.

His foot struck the cave floor—only there was no foot, just a withered stump of jagged bone and wilted skin. The moon man, still glowing, lurched with every movement and kept his balance with the aid of an equally ancient laborer's pick. The blade was blunt. When it struck the ground, a cloud of rust stained the air.

Amity tried to yank herself up off her haunches but her hand slipped again, fingers running across the engraving and scouring her skin. She landed on her back. Time caught up with her and propelled the man at her with a speed that belied his years. He extended a hand to her, and she saw that his fingers were curled up on themselves, that they had fused to his wrist. There were long flints of shale embedded in the flesh where his digits should have been. Some were dulled, some not. And Amity knew that if they were sharp enough to carve through the clay walls, then they would have no trouble slitting her open gullet to groin.

Her scream ran dry. Darkness threatened to swish her away. She wasn't so lucky.

There was a shadow on the wall beside her.

Amity moved as though in slow motion, giving herself enough time to wish that the intruder were her brother, or Tobias, or any one of the other tourists. Long enough to imagine the kisses of gratitude and relief that she would plant on their cheeks as they carried her down the rocky slope to where a rescue crew was waiting.

It wasn't her brother. And it wasn't anyone from the boat. She could tell this from the shape of his silhouette. The last ray of sunlight caught his hair, and she saw its matted length stretching back against his skull and down over his shoulders in loosely bound dreadlocks. His hand was upturned before his face, as though waiting for a priest to lay down a wafer of blessed Eucharist.

Hold on to the rope, said the voice in her head. *Don't let it break.*

Amity Collins gripped it as tight as she could, despite the rest of the world dragging on it from every opposing direction. She could feel them tugging at her, those great, unseen hands—and she knew who they belonged to, had seen their dirty work lurking in every twist of her story. They were the hands of the cruel and insane.

The world was a color and that color was RED.

Keeping a firm hold on the rope was hard; it was greasy and slick. She was trying her best, as she always had. Her teeth were gritted together, the vibrations out of control now. There were thick, velvety growls of wild dogs boring down at her, working her terror into new heights.

She wanted it all to end. Was that so bad? Couldn't she just slip away now and have it be done with? There was no mercy here; there never had been. That struck her as so terribly finite and unfair.

What was it that I did to deserve all of this? What crime am I guilty of?

What is my sin?

Tell me. Tell me, please.

The dark man blew against his palm and sent a spray of powder shooting into her eyes and mouth. It filled her nostrils and she dragged it into her lungs, burning all the way down. It reeked of earth, of mushrooms, and was a strange kind of sweet.

The cave was colder now, far worse than before. The scythe had fallen.

CHAPTER EIGHTEEN

The Last Son

1

WIND GUSTED THROUGH the island, rattling trees both dead and living. It cast sand across the corpses on the beach, where nightfall made the blood seem black. This wind drove through the jungle, up its slopes, down its valleys. It sent spider into hiding, monkey into play. It was feral and fleeting, and unlike the rising and retreating tides, it had no master watching over its every move.

That hallowed wind. It created music at the island's heart, a long drawn-out note. Nearly all that had heard its tune were dead now. *Almost.*

The island was not a place of ghosts, though it *was* haunted. It always had been.

2

The last son carried the girl over his shoulder, her snores in his ear. She smelled unlike anyone he'd ever held before—the scent reminded him of the rich and creamy deer milk his mother used to give them. He let her bleed into his patchwork shirt, not caring; this one was beginning to fall apart and there were plenty of materials below with which to sew together a new one.

He took her from the cave and down to the cove where his brothers, sister and mother lay dead. The ocean had swallowed them one by one and, finding their flavor unsatisfactory, had spat them back out again. They hung on the rocks, the youngest of their number facedown on the sand.

The last son never lost his footing on his journey down that rocky slope, his eyes having grown accustomed to seeing in the near pitch-black years ago. His movements were spry and nimble, despite the weight he lugged along with him.

He put the girl down, watched her shudder. She would not stir from sleep for many hours yet, and that was good. Her eyes, nose and mouth were sticky with the dust. It always worked. She might even come to like it, in time.

There was little in the way of moonlight, just enough to give the plankton something to glow about, enough for him to see how much his life had changed. The last son was alone now, and he knew he would *never* visit this part of the island again.

He took their bodies and dragged them to the jungle's edge. There, he held them close and wept. There had never been pain like this before, not even when his father died. Agony threatened to rip him to pieces with all the violence the island could muster, which was unimaginable. And yet he faced such power head on. Just holding them was an attempt to keep them a part of his life, even though his efforts were useless. They were as cold as the water spray on his back. The island always won.

It wasn't meant to be like this. This place was meant to be safe.

War had come back to claim them all, just as the old one had said it would. The belief that they would be untouched by the evil men forever had not proved strong enough. It was a truth he'd known since he'd found his kin dead in the jungle, torn apart by one of *them*. He'd sounded his horn. It had been *he* who let them know of the intrusion. And as the old one had said, it was better to kill yourself than to live under their watch.

His regret defined him now. It would have been better to track down the intruders—who had ventured too far—and to have slaughtered them all, one by one, instead of going to his mother with his brother's blood staining his hands. But he knew he didn't have it in him. That was the problem.

The last son's tears patterned their broken faces. He shrieked on their behalf. They were still so beautiful. Death couldn't rob them of the poetry in their eyes, in the cusps of their lips.

His howling echoed far, making snakes hiss, sending fruit bats into alarmed flight. There came a point when it mingled with the island's hollow musical note, contaminating its loveliness with misery that had never been heard here before this day.

The last son glanced up at the rocky slope he'd just come down, at the cave overlooking the ocean. It was a dark eye against a dark face, but he could still make out the opening. The old one was still in there, as he had been for seasons on end, having retreated because he prophesied such a day would eventually come.

He hated the old one, now more than ever. And not just for his madness.

The old one had cheated death and escaped its guns and orders and whips. The old one had fled and, with the old woman, had claimed this land as their own. But death had come back for them as he had always known it would.

The last son left the girl on the beach, but not before covering her body in wet sand and mud, keeping her mouth and nose unobstructed. This way her heat would be contained within her body, but she wouldn't draw insects or animals. He stripped a tree of its palms and covered her up. Before leaving, he took more powder from the pouch around his wrist and sprinkled it across her lips, tipped some into her partially open mouth.

Once he'd finished, he dragged his kin—two at time—into the dark by the locks of their hair. He had no idea how long he was in there, burying them next to the others. It was the pain that kept him going. All he wanted to do was sleep; this could not happen. They had to be in the ground tonight or else the island's many animals would pick at them, and they would not stop until even the bones were gone. Tomorrow he would craft a marker with the old one's tools.

There was still so much to do.

Once the job was done, he patted the graves flat and sat under a tree. Spiders played in his hair. The blade that he'd used to dig up the earth was still in his hands. Its edge was hot. He knew what he was supposed to do, knew that putting its serrated edge against his throat was what needed to be done. And yet he didn't have it in him to go through with it.

Unlike his kin, the last son wasn't bred to self-destruct. Even animals—which was all he considered himself—feared death. Though living would be torture, it must be better than death. Or maybe it was just that he *was* the coward the old one had predicted he'd grow into.

Yowamushi.

The birds were yet to cry. There was still time to go back and get the girl. He'd sensed the innocence on her, which was why he'd claimed her. She had betrayed them by coming as far as she had, and likewise, he would betray her by never letting her leave. This would be their symmetry.

3

The jungle had no design to it and was as fragmented as a night's worth of dreaming, but the last son always knew his way. If forced to, he believed he could find a path by touch alone. The land was a part of him, just as he was a part of it. They mourned.

He sat in the fork of a barren tree. It had stopped bearing fruit seasons ago, but he'd been scaling its heights since he was a child. There was comfort to be found in its old, dead limbs.

The girl was on the ground at the foot of the tree, tucked between two of its aboveground roots. She was asleep, as he knew she would be. He studied her deathly stillness in gloom as the island's corridors writhed with life making the most of the night. Snake wrestled snake, lizard fed on slumbering butterfly.

A hot wind played with the last son's dreadlocks. The island's song could be heard from here, and he would return to its heart with the coming of the sun, but not before. And he would not be alone. Between now and then there was much that needed to be done.

The last son was not alone in the tree. He was surrounded by monkeys, perched in waiting. They occupied themselves by picking the fleas from each other's hides and feasting. Their little faces were alike, distinguished only by variations of disease and blood splatter. One sat on the last son's shoulder; it was dressed in the remains of a pink tutu. Its marble eyes were sad, downcast. It, like the rest of its kind, seemed to understand the gravity of their failure.

Their cowering before him was nothing new. They feared him as they had the rest of his family. He had killed many of them out of example. The twisted bodies were below the girl's head and shoulders.

Warm, furred pillows.

It began to rain without warning, the drumming sounds of sky against sand. The last son watched the mud peel away from the innocent's face and body. She looked frail, beaten, but strong and well fed. And so unlike anyone he'd ever seen before. Sure, there had been times when he and the others had watched visitors come and go, but it had always been from great distances.

Her skin was the color of tusk. It stirred him.

Water dripped down the monkeys' faces. Blood washed from their bodies, staining the dead tree in inky rivers.

The last son lowered his shoulder and let the monkey in the tutu crawl down his arm. It grabbed on to the bark and turned to face him. It was sleek and frail and hungry for sugar; the monkey had no idea that there would be no more boats bringing them drinks and fruit for quite some time.

Staccato light silvered the island as lightning tore the clouds apart. The air was thick with burning ozone. The last son raised his head to the rain and let it fill his mouth. He swallowed and then began his descent.

CHAPTER NINETEEN

Nowhere, Here

1

SHE STANDS BEFORE the burning sugarcane and listens to the wicker-crack of the flames. Lightning thrashes somewhere, so bright it hurts her eyes. Amity is naked but not alone. She can see people running back and forth ahead of her, between where she stands and the field of fire. Nobody stops to see if she's okay. Their steps are mistimed; some fall. Some stop to stare before going on their way.

Something moves between her feet. The ground is covered in fur, not grass. It reaches up between her toes. The ground is breathing. She can hear its wet rattle. Amity wants the sound to go away.

The rain comes. She wants to go back home, knows that Evans Head isn't too far from here and that she can probably make it. Sure, her feet will ache and she'll maybe catch pneumonia in the attempt, but at least her mother and brother will be there on the other end.

And yet she does not move.

Amity looks at her hands. They are red. It isn't rain falling from the sky.

Even though she can *hear* her surroundings, her own voice is lost to her ears as she begs for help. There aren't any vibrations. The heat from the fire grows hotter and hotter against her skin.

There are no more silhouettes running back and forth. She is alone. She is *not* alone. There is another presence, and it's lifting her up into the air. Her stomach knots.

Put me down, God, now, please!

Nobody listens because nobody can hear her. She isn't as naked as she had at first thought. There is something over her head, hot and clammy as a wet sheet—and just as suffocating. Even though she can't see it, Amity knows from the chalky smell that it's the old World War II gas mask the man she had met on the Internet had been so fond of, the one he kept in his "bag of tricks".

She remembers going to his house and knocking on his door. It opens. He stands there. She goes inside. He makes her a drink and soon after makes a move. She is repulsed by him. He says he is different from other guys. He shows her his bag, pulls out the mask. He says that he wants her to wear it, and if she doesn't, he will tell everyone online who she is and what she came here for.

Amity runs away from that place. She lives with the fear he put inside her for a long time. He never contacts her again. Her secret is sown.

But the mask is bound to her head now, a rubbery embrace growing tighter and tighter. She sees the world through its two bug eyes, watching as the ground shrinks beneath her. There is another man down there, dressed in a kaleidoscope suit and wearing her father's black-and-white face. He's waving to her as she rises up in the air.

Lightning fills the sky. Every drop of rainwater glows, a sea of stars.

There's tightness between her legs. The pain is *instantaneous*, a thing of its own. It plows inside her, filling her up. The wind whips her naked flesh.

Something is on top of her, up here in the sky. They're spinning together, weightless in the storm's frigid heart. Sweet-smelling smoke from the fire below churns around her, takes shape. She sees a blurred face bent close to the gas mask, close enough to block out all else. And then it's gone again. There's just sky. Another flash of lightning.

It's a dog on her, fucking her. Thrusting. Tearing her open. It's jaws glimmer with teeth. The rubber squeaks against her face, her panting as loud as crashing waves. If this is what sound is like, then she doesn't *want* it back. She wants the silence again. Needs it more than anything else. This is horrible. This is the hell her mother has convinced her children they will one day end up in.

The pain has a color and the color is RED.

It isn't one of the wild dogs in her. It's a blur. No. It's a man, only she can't see his face. He's too close to the mask and is hazing over the glass. However, she can see what's behind him, perched on his shoulders. It's a monkey. Its strong hands thump against the man's neck, rabid with exhilaration. Its mouth is open in a wide yawn of exposed teeth. The monkey isn't alone. There are others all around her, watching and screeching and pulling clumps of hair from their heads. She can smell mud and crushed leaves and the foul richness of his soured breath.

Another blaze of lightning.

Amity tries to fight him off but her body is heavy. The mask is sucking the energy from her body and it's getting darker again. Even the strobes of light in the clouds seem to be dimming. The pain in her is subsiding. She can feel herself slipping away. There's a strange odor. Strong, but very clear. Mushrooms.

Take me home, she asks the sky. *I want to see my room, the one I was so desperate to get away from. There will be the calendar on the wall. The crack in the plaster, the one I like to trace with my fingers. My phone will be beneath my pillow, full* of messages from all of my friends. Ma will come in and check on me soon, even though she secretly hates us. She'll make breakfast for Caleb and me.

We will be pretend-happy again.

Together we'll go to Pa's grave and pull up all the weeds. Even though the weeds will grow back.

CHAPTER TWENTY

The Final Day

1

A CAUL OF mist painted the world a dull, headache gray. It was so bright it blotted out all else, and was every bit as consuming as the suffocating blackness she'd woken to once or twice through the night. It took a few moments for the light to dim and she watched, panting, as her hand began to fade into view.

Concentrate, Amity told herself. *Concentrate harder.* Her pupils cranked, once, twice. It wasn't an easy task, but she did it. The next step was to digest *what* she was seeing.

There were black things stuck to her skin, wet, matted leaves...maybe.

Wrong.

Amity sat upright—every muscle in her body pleading with her to stay put and punishing her for her disobedience with thumps of stabbing pain. What she had mistaken for leaves were leeches grown fat on her blood. Black elastic bodies did contortionist flips as she flailed about; their mouths were latched tight to their food. Nauseous and still half-blind, she screeched as she yanked them off.

Some exploded in her hands, others dropped off and plopped back into the puddle between her legs.

She was nestled between the enormous roots of a tree. Finding a sturdy hold on the bark was hard, though she managed, and used this grasp as leverage to yank herself up off the ground. Her head swayed into disorientation, and she didn't stand a chance of stopping the vomit from ejecting from her system.

Her head boomed and she stupidly thought, *Oh man, I've really got to pick up some aspirin from the shops. And some Gatorade. And food–God, that more than anything else.*

What the hell are you talking about?

Amity wiped her mouth. Everything tasted like dirt, like the dusty flavor of old mushrooms. She continued to gag as she scrambled away from the tree and dived into her misty surroundings, plucking at the leeches as she went. Her hands quivered with revulsion and she danced on the spot, too afraid to crush them beneath her sandals despite the gluttonous way they had fed on her. She slipped her shorts down over her hips and found, just as she'd suspected she would, two more leeches attached to her pubic bone.

She swatted them without thinking twice and squealed as they popped.

2

Amity gingerly pulled her shirt back over her head, confident now that she was parasite-free. Her fingers wouldn't stop shaking. The sensation of her saturated clothing slipping over her skin repulsed her; it clung, weaseling against her like unwanted kisses. Despite this, she put it on. Right now, a little bit of something was better than a shitload of nothing.

She broke down. Buried her head in her hands.

The reverberations of a dream sneaked up on her, amorphous and indistinct. It wasn't images she was recalling, rather a weird, niggling sensation of being soiled and frightened. Some obscenity had filled her mind during the night, as though Freddy Krueger, or something equally vile, had paid her a visit. This pervasiveness dimmed enough for her to take in her surroundings.

The mist didn't seem to have any end.

It all struck a familiar chord, even down to the way the morning light was slanting through the canopy.

Her headache was a living thing and was punching holes in her concentration. It was far worse than the one she'd woken with after her big night out in Phuket, on the night they had met Tobias.

Tobias.

She allowed herself a quiet sigh. Amity wanted to will herself to blame him for everything that had happened, for setting them on the course that had led them to this place. She didn't have it in her, was too far gone to hate. Wishing, on the other hand, was very immediate and within reach.

Wishing that she weren't lost in the jungle, wishing that she had never bought their tickets out of defiance, wishing that Caleb and she had never left Evans Head.

Amity crouched down against the dewy grass, more afraid and confused than she'd ever been in her life. The last thing she remembered was being in the cave, where she'd been running her fingers over the wall carvings. After that, there was only unfocused, nightmare dreams of crabs and dogs and monkeys and lightning, a vicious whirlwind of assault.

BOOM.

Her hands shot to her groin. An unexpected burning sensation flared between her legs and spread across her thighs and into the contours of her abdomen. Her knuckles whitened as her fists clenched, squeezing blood out of the back of her right hand, where her makeshift bark bandage was starting to come loose.

Amity started to count. *One, two, three*–groan–*four*–breathe–*four*...

The jungle stared down at her; it had no end. Trees loomed above her, motionless and indifferent as the birds in their branches. Humidity drew what little water remained in her system out through her skin. The pain withdrew, the fire extinguished.

A minute passed. Her head buzzed. She didn't feel like she was *just* having a hangover; it was far more like coming down. Everything had a shimmering hyperreal quality to it–the light shimmering on the wet leaves like liquid mercury, the pinpoint swirls of dew flying before her eyes. And her thirst... *God, her thirst!*

Shaking her head worked a little. She rose to her feet again, limped on.

All she could think of was that her brother was out there somewhere, and he was waiting for her to come back to him. Family meant everything. She had no intention of letting him down.

I'm not giving up. I'm holding on to the rope. See, I told you I would. Aren't you glad?

Hello? Are you there?

3

Amity continued through the mist, although where it ended and the unfocused haze of her mind began was blurred. Her thoughts were becoming *slippery*; they were running away on her, and she was too numb to reach out and snatch them back.

Through it all she didn't let go of the rope. That was what all of her strength was focused on now. Keeping a firm hold on it would get her to safety, or so she hoped. The notion of letting it go terrified her. She sensed that doing so would plunge her into a murky place she stood no chance of escaping from, an island within an island. That couldn't happen.

Hold on.

In the meantime, there was nothing else to do but continue taking steps, one after another, over and over, repeat. Even though it hurt, even though the jungle refused to relent, she kept on assuring herself that she'd be damned if she would give in. Amity was maybe even starting to believe herself. A little.

She stopped to pass foul spurts of shit and then wiped herself clean with handfuls of grass. The act made her cry. The island had stripped her of so much that the loss of even basic humility came at a cost. Even though she was trying so hard to fight it, Amity was weakening.

More steps. Rubbery blades brushed her thighs. The slick sensation reminded her of where she was, despite seeing nothing but the cave with the carving in front of her. Two places at once. In no places at the same time. There had been something in there with her, back in the cave, but she couldn't remember who or what it had been. It was a mental itch that couldn't be scratched, no matter how she tried.

She stopped near a plant with trashcan-size leaves cupping bowls of rainwater. Amity saw her reflection in one: a bruised and battered skull framed by hair that looked as though it were turning white. She'd aged years in the space of a day. Amity splashed her hands into the water—

(it isn't me it isn't me it isn't me)

—and lifted them and drank in great, greedy gulps. The moment the liquid touched the pit of her stomach, her senses grew more distinct. Things became more vivid. Tightened.

The mist didn't appear quite so thick. The heat wasn't as oppressive as it had been moments before. Her duel with the headache began to swing in her favor.

You're not dead yet. And don't you forget it.

She splashed more water over her head and let it run down between her shoulder blades, oblivious to the eyes watching her. It was so cold she started to cough. It felt good. Hell made heavens of the smallest things, she realized, and in this place even water could be divine.

4

A held breath. The stalker's gaze held strong. So close, so close.

5

The wind picked up, sieving the mist. A curtain drawn. There were more trees beyond trees beyond trees. A funhouse carnival mirror trick going on and on. Amity had never felt so claustrophobic, despite being outdoors. She was discovering that the very nature of being on an island was to have all ways barred to you. Surrounded by water, cut off from the world.

Trapped.

Tropical birds flapped through the air—blurs of brilliant color shedding feathers. A bright green snake with yellow eyes slithered the length of a fallen branch beside her, a sight that should have sent her into girlish wails but evoked little more than a raised eyebrow. Bugs teemed. The wind continued to blow, soothing her skin.

Nothing. Everything.

Hold on to the rope. Squeeze it tight.

Slippery thoughts.

Amity stopped, a breath held tight in her lungs. It almost hurt. Release.

There was a fallen tree. Prior to the wind shaking it to the ground, it must have stretched thirty feet into the air. But now it was just another something once grand now something spent, and she was sad for its defeat. The great branches looked strong. *Looked* being the operative word. They were obviously no match for the gusts blowing in off the ocean. Amity traced its bulk, which lay against the uneven ground, and she saw the animal pinned beneath it.

She stepped closer, winced. Her arms folded in against her chest, an involuntary, slow-moving chest beat. It hurt to look. She did it anyway.

The creature was familiar—something that she'd maybe seen on a late-night television documentary, though it had been so long ago that the possibility of naming its breed was impossible. It reminded her of a pig, and yet it wasn't. The skin was black and wrinkled with age, except for what she could see of its rear half, which tapered off to white. Its hind legs and quarters were beneath the branch. Amity sighed for the animal, saw the pain in the meek geography of its face. It didn't have a nose in the traditional sense; instead it bore a lengthy proboscis. She pictured it rummaging for ants or scrounging between low bushes.

An herbivore. It's a friendly animal. Something of the earth.

Its twitching ears were like that of a hippopotamus, not that she'd ever seen one, of course—not in real life; all she had to draw from were boredom-induced YouTube trawling. But its eyes were universal. Yes; those she didn't need any reference for. They were small and round and brimmed with tears, matching pits of misery and pain.

The stocky animal was still alive, and although Amity couldn't hear its braying, she knew that it was. It was screaming for help.

Amity stared down at it and was reminded of the baby elephant she'd seen back on the mainland, the one whose legs had been bound in leashes of barbed wire for the enjoyment of passing tourists like herself. Blood absorbed into dirt. The flash of a camera.

She walked away.

Stopped.

The rock in front of her looked deliberately placed there for her to see. It was so obvious in a way, as though this were a test on some elaborate reality television show. Only where were the cameras? And what kind of audience would watch such a cruel joke? Amity wondered who in their right minds would find entertainment in the cries of an animal caught beneath the weight of a collapsed tree, or in the sight of a young woman with the rest of her life ahead of her lost in a jungle designed to destroy her.

There were no answers. There was only rock.

Test or no test, she picked it up. It was the size of the football her brother used to kick around the backyard when they were young, the one that had—as all well-loved footballs do—ended up going through a neighbor's window. Caleb had denied that he was the culprit until he was blue in the face, even though they all knew it was him. Amity could still remember her mother closing the door to Caleb's room, the flash of her brother's crestfallen face before the lock slid into the jamb.

She'd put her hand against the door and closed her eyes. There were no vibrations to be found. Whatever scoldings were going on in that room were worse than her mother's usual yells and threats.

They were whispers.

Amity held the rock against her stomach. Small, colorful bugs that had been hiding beneath it fell onto the leaves like M&Ms slipping from a bag. Only these M&Ms had legs and were scurrying for safety. Her stomach rumbled.

Don't worry, little guys. I'm not here for you. Yeah, I'm starvin' like Marvin, but I'm not here for you. Not yet... God, I hope it doesn't come to that.

She limped back to the fallen tree, to the strange animal she couldn't name. Its eyes peered up at her and she wished it would look away, that more than anything. Her fingers gripped the rock's jagged surface as she lifted it high over her head. Amity bit her lower lip.

You can't back out of this now. You got to do what's right. Do to it what you would want someone to do to you. Mercy.

Mercy.

A PLACE FOR SINNERS

Dirt from the underside of the rock pattered across her head. Her body rocked to and fro under the weight, forearms quivering.

The jungle grew still for her. Winds died. Both bird and butterfly were nowhere to be seen.

It took a great deal of will power to do what needed to be done. But she did it.

It all came back to her the moment the skull shattered, when the animal's forelegs thrashed for the final time. Her mind *kicked*.

She saw the decrepit man in the cave with the crabs in his cancers, creeping toward her on his laborer's pick, remembered the way he had reached at her with shale-claws. There had been a second person then, whose shadow had been cast across the wall of stories.

Amity had spun around and seen his form: the outline of dreadlocks writhing about his head like Medusa's snakes, two eyes glimmering within all that shadow. This stranger had held out his hand and blown a Eucharist of mushroom-scented dust into her face.

And then the darkness.

She dropped the rock and stumbled away from the dead animal. The island's stillness evaporated and the wind picked up again, swirling the fog into thinning and thickening curls. Birds dived from tree to tree, casting shadows over the ground.

It's not just me, Caleb, Tobias and the other tourists out here. There's other people. People who were either too stubborn or too damn afraid to kill themselves like all the others.

I've got a savior out here somewhere.

The sensation of being watched returned. The jungle itself peered down on her with pitying eyes, just as she had peered and cast pity over the trapped animal. Her headache flared again, and yet it was nothing compared to this new unease.

Why did the stranger save me only to set me loose again?

Her heart started to race again. The heat was more cloying.

Maybe I'm wrong on that last point. Maybe I'm not alone.

Amity raced ahead, past the fallen tree, and watched a bamboo field emerge from the fog. Each ridged stalk swayed under the bulk of its foliage. The ground was soft with pine needles and moss. It would be so easy to lie down and fall asleep against it, to simply give in and let the island take her at last.

"No," Amity said. The vibration in her throat was silent music to unhearing ears.

Her jaws were clenched. At the foot of the field there were snapped, scattered stalks of bamboo. They were white and bonelike, and the piece she picked up felt incredibly strong despite being so light, just as the stick she'd dragged into the cave had been. This new find was well over a yard long and was tapered to a sharpened point, perfect for swishing through the spiderwebs strung between the trees. But then again, she imagined it would come in handy should anything more threatening *dare* come her way.

Before continuing on, Amity turned around and looked back at the way she'd come. It was hard to see with all the fog, but she could have *sworn* there were shapes moving back there. Scavenger shapes.

Wild dogs teeming with fleas and dribbling ropes of saliva. Twinkling teeth and eyes rolling around to peer at her before the feed.

Amity could *hear* their growls.

CHAPTER TWENTY-ONE

In the Night, the Shark

1

THE NIGHT BEFORE. Her exhaustion was as thick and clinging as the darkness.

She came to a thin stream, lit up by sporadic twinkles of lightning, and rested. She sensed that she had been here before. It was hard to tell if the imprints in the mud were footprints made by herself before or by an animal. Either or, they were full of water, struck by rain slicing through the trees, bubbling and spitting like oil in a pan. She drank from it. Her face hurt, pounded as a bruise will pound. Only it wasn't just her face, it was *everywhere*. In every limb of her naked, shivering body.

The cold was inside as well as out.

She lifted her head and saw a universe above, strangled by tree-hands. She bathed in the tears it shed. All around her the island continued to scream its song, as she sat there in the dead water. Every time she gritted her teeth, the jagged shards of broken bottle dug deeper. When she touched her upper lips with a fingertip, she felt points through the flesh.

The woman who used to be Susan Sycamore had never thought it possible to be so tired. It was like insomnia, that screeching urge to sleep despite the breaking point nudging you awake every time you threatened to dip below. No comfort. No light.

There were moments when the shark receded in a way she never thought it would, and the woman she once was would clamber to the surface. It took even more energy to keep her under control.

Insects crawled over her. Played in her wounds.

There was a wet rattle in her throat, the sound of sickness breeding sickness.

She spat into her palm and in a flash of lightning saw a dollar of blackish flesh. Sycamore didn't know if it was hers or if it belonged to something she'd eaten. It washed away and sank in the water. It had weight.

There was no right way to go; there was only the urge to keep moving. *If you stop, you'll die*, she thought. *If you stop, the hunger will take over and the pain will getchya. It's trolling you now. Can't you see?* So she stumbled on.

An image slipped through: of Susan in her little Volvo in Crouch End, edging into a drive-through car wash. There had been the suds spray, a speckling of color turning to slush. And then came the washers. They thumped against the car, against the glass. She'd been afraid of them for some reason. They slapped and scrubbed like something wild. Fingers clamped against the wheel. Knuckles turned white.

The jungle around her was just the same. Every shadow was full of leathery leaves sluicing up and down her body. They grabbed her, wrapped around her. She had to push them aside, sometimes ripping at them to break through. It wasn't enough. The jungle wanted her, and worse, her fatigue was letting it win.

Her hand reached up into the air, the tendons so tight it was hard to make out where arm began and vine ended. The island pulled her under.

A PLACE FOR SINNERS

2

Susan Sycamore holds the gun in her right hand. It's a semiautomatic, sleek and brutal. It's heavy—not just with the weight of metal but also with intent. She is about to open the world with a wound that will never heal. The halls of her school will run red.

She drives to work and parks in her normal space. Her handbag is slung over one shoulder, a briefcase in one hand—she looks just as she does on any other normal day. She passes the kids running through the schoolyard gates with an enthusiasm that will fade, especially after the first class bell rings. Her high-heeled shoes clink against the hallway linoleum, the clickedy-clack of normality, of sowing what you reap. In the staff room she sits with the other teachers, a little more indifferent than usual. She speaks to her coworkers in brief, birdlike sentences. Squawks of acknowledgement and half-laughs at their stupid jokes. They all think they are so clever, so unique, but she knows that they all look the same on the inside. They are just guts bound in skin, with a light burning somewhere down beneath the shit.

First period goes as planned. Her writing on the whiteboard is sloppy. It's cold in here. The heaters must not be working. The kids act as they do any other day, except for one or two who stare at her as though they know they are going to die.

The walls are covered in drawings on cheap budget-cuts butcher paper. These are the My Dream Holiday assignments that the kids turned in at the end of the prior week and hung with pride. They ripple against the wall as though touched by ghostly fingers, so she guesses the heating must be on; she alone feels the chill.

Sycamore glares at the drawings again. Skeletal renderings of children riding bikes and playing football. The colors are bright. But not as bright as the exploded faces bursting across them.

She can smell the gun smoke, even though she doesn't remember the semiautomatic going off. The surviving children scatter, stumbling out into the hall. Some of the My Dream Holiday drawings tumble to the floor under the weight of bone

315

fragments and brains, a red carpet for her grand appearance. Her heels do not click anymore. She is barefoot now.

The dream is always like this.

She goes barefoot into the corridor with the weapon still in her hand. The transition from being inside the classroom and outside strips her of her clothes, and she stands there under the flickering fluorescent lights as bare as the day she was born.

3

Her eyes opened to blackness. It was still night, and she was still living, even though the dream had died. It had fully slipped away by the time she sat upright. Sleeping helped a little, helped to tease her with energy enough to stand. It was easy now, or at least by comparison.

Things got a bit hairy back there for a while.

No, not hairy. Leathery. A shiver scuttled through her.

The jungle vine and leaves and branches that had wrapped around her before the dream had fallen away, were flaccid in the moonlit curvature of her muscles. To say that she was replenished would be an exaggeration, and she was convinced there was still more fuel in her to burn.

Got to keep on moving. Got to do what I'm meant to do.

It didn't take long, though, for this confidence to waver. A sugar high at its peak, and the drop on the other side was severe. Every step she took was closely followed by a stumble; behind every breath there was a choke creeping up on her.

"No." Gasp. "No, not ah-ghan."

Troll. You have to find more food. If you stop, you'll die. You know this. You've always known this.

Now that the rain had stopped, the mosquitos had returned, and she could feel their stingers sucking away at her. *Susan* could feel their stingers.

Her hands slapped at them, and for every insect exploding under her palms there were five more swooping in to take its place. It was like walking through a field of hypodermic needles, each drawing blood through diseased little points. Something snagged in her head.

It was the memory of taking out the trash, racing along the side of her apartment block as though trying to outrun the trail of bin juice splashing across the tiles. She'd reached the general waste bins near the fence, facing a street that always seemed wet with rain, and had seen the spiderweb strung between the two dead trees. The spider was nowhere to be seen, but the silvery threads were freckled with beads of water. One droplet fell to the ground and she followed its path, watched it splash against a hypodermic needle lying on the tiles.

"Tell me that's not what I think it is," she had said aloud. The bin juice, stinking and warm, was pooling between her toes. And yet it was what she thought it was.

A junkie's throwaway, right there in front of her.

Her mind told her to say things like, "I could have just stepped on that! What if one of the kids had come out here and trod on it? What diseases would they have contracted? AIDS? Hep B, or C, or whichever one dealt out that rumored death sentence?"

These were sane and rational thoughts, thoughts that any sane and rational mind would listen to.

Susan Sycamore had ignored them. But she did toss the garbage; to have left it there in front of the bins would have attracted squirrels or maybe even one of those foxes people sometimes reported seeing in the city. She wasn't silly.

Then she picked up the needle by its plunger and skittered back into the apartment block. Her movements were conspiratorial, as though she were a secret agent in charge of important documents, not a housewife with a used, blood-speckled syringe in her hand.

She had no idea why she kept it. Just as she had no idea why she sometimes took it out of the handbag she kept in the crawlspace behind the wall and held it to her husband's face as he slept.

No idea.

Moonlight splashed the ground in an atlas of blue continents filled with civilizations of swarming mosquitos. That wasn't all. She saw mud. It was everywhere.

She bent down and scooped up handfuls of it, pressed the cool muck to her breasts. A little yelp escaped her; it was *Susan's voice*, distorted by the mosquitos inside the glass-toothed mouth. Fingers sluiced wet soil over skin until she was covered from head to toe. The insects that had been too greedy to fly away were drowned, and those that had lost the sense of heat radiating from the flesh beneath gave up and become one with the cloud dancing through the trees.

The new cool sunk in. Her smile speared her gums; the pain was sweet.

Mosquito wings continued their electric whine until it was more than just a whine. It was a plea.

Please come down again. Please. Please. I've missed you.

The sugar high ended and the ground kissed her good night.

4

"Be my little superstar.
When day turns to night.
Be my little superstar.
Shed a little light."

Her third child comes screeching into the world and tears her up. Sycamore knows she'll need stitches, and the pain is so bad she blacks out. Only no, it isn't black. It's blue. Sand swirls around her in delicate, slow-moving somersaults. It's beautiful here. She's alone and there isn't all the screams of children, or the encouraging, clenching hand of her husband, whom she hates more than anyone else on this planet for sticking his cock in and out of her, over and over again, trying to fuck her into some kind of meaning.

The ocean is calm.

Things are good here. Home.

She thought she knew what that was. Home was safety. It was her husband, leaning in close to give her a wet one on the lips. Maybe she had loved him once, way back in the dark of his college room, beneath the sheets, even though she sensed that he sensed something evolving within her, even then. He'd gazed at her with some kind of understanding, a look that seemed to say, I know I'm playing with fire here, but I'm going to do it anyway.

Every burn an understanding. A gift.

Burning. Light. A half-remembered song from her childhood, something her mother had sung to her. It comes to her at night, sometimes.

"Be my little superstar..."

5

"...When day turns to night.
Be my little superstar.
Shed a little light."

The words jingled through her head as the world began to wrench itself back into focus again. It was still night, but the moon was alabaster bright. She lifted her face off the hardening mud and felt the layer of grime cracking across her face. The humidity was back in full force.

She pushed onward and stopped when she came to the trees where her victims were hung.

They are snagged and speared by branches. Hung like pictures on a wall. A testament to all of the good times, captured neatly in a frame.

Her hands were stretched up before her. She formed a rectangle with her thumbs.

Click.

"Be my little superstar," she sang, her throat hoarse and dry. "When day turns to night. Be my little superstar—"

The corpses begin to burn for her, their light shining up through their cuts and slashes. There is the girl she hit with the brick. The child she snatched up here in the jungle. There are the two overweight American women and the waspy man she trolled in Nicaragua, her final stop before landing in Thailand.

They are all here.

"Shed a little light."

She could taste them even though her tongue was numb. Each had been different. Unique. Each had made her wonderful. It reminded her that there was *still* so much light yet to be swallowed on the island, so much more illumination to be shed.

The junkie's needle.

The plan to slaughter her family, those seven hidden letters.

The recurring dream of taking a gun to work, of making the halls of the school run red.

All of the others whom she had consumed. All of those long hours spent trolling.

What were all of their shimmering life-lights revealing to her? What did they illuminate? She had wondered about this before, but the question had never been more persistent than it was now.

There was no answer.

The light could shine as long and hard as it wanted to, but it would only ever shine on farther layers of nothing-upon-nothing. She'd long ago given up on finding out why she did the things she did, of discovering why her hunger had no end.

She watches her victims melt into the dark until there is little more to see than the moon-washed branches they had been hung in. The shark moves toward, among them. There is more light out there somewhere. The running girl.

Out there.

I'll never give up. Never. I'm gonna make it last. Gonna make it last rea-aaaaalll good.

The air thickened with fog sometime between then and dawn.

6

The birds and other animals sang for the new sun, perhaps with gratitude. They had escaped the fate of the food chain for yet another night.

Ca-caw! Ca-caw!

I live. I live.

Most of the mosquito cloud had dissipated, replaced now by moths dodging trees, grasshoppers escaping the shark's swishing legs. Everything smelled like wet woodchips, the kind someone she'd once known had sprinkled in a square patch of garden in their apartment block's shared yard. It was rank, honeyed.

The land sloped beneath her feet. She stepped over rocks covered with moss. To the shark, the ground itself was indefinite and inexact, as though carved from barely controlled fear.

The shark's senses jackhammered.

A hiss threaded through broken bottle teeth, bringing with it a fine red mist.

There was movement among the trees at the end of the downward slope: a thin figure, hazed by layers of velveteen fog. The shark watched it walk, unaware that it had been seen. Her heart hammered, sending every scar and scrape across her body into weeping cries for food.

CHAPTER TWENTY-TWO

The Last Day (Continued)

1

AMITY HAD BEEN trekking toward the dawn; if she kept on walking into the shafts of light haloing through the trees, then she would eventually come to the eastern side of the island. That, at least, was the plan.

Her legs stopped moving. She brought her bloodied hand to her brow, shielding the glare.

Amity couldn't believe what she was seeing at first.

The shape had bled out of the white, millions of vapor drops coalescing midair in the shape of a human being. It came without warning, and there was no ceremony to its arrival. She wondered if it was a mirage.

If it's not, then it's a miracle.

It was real.

Amity waved her arms, the bamboo spear slicing through fog. It was impossible not to smile, let alone break down. But she would not do that. Not yet. Sure, she wanted this newcomer to be her brother, or Tobias, or any one of the other tourists from the boat, but at this point *any* sign of life was welcome. Even if it was her mysterious savior from the cave, the man with the Medusa dreadlocks and sandman dust, it was something.

The visitor just stood there.

Her arms fell by her side. There was a distant ping of alarm in her head, though it was not yet loud enough to make her fear or to make her smile any less wide.

"Help me," Amity called out. She could only hope that her words made sense. "I'm deaf and I'm lost. Help me."

The silhouette advanced.

Despite a tortured limp that looked to have skewed the very architecture of the stranger's bones, Amity knew from the curve of the hips and the swish of the legs that it was a woman. And now this woman was not just advancing, she was breaking into a run.

Amity clenched the bamboo spear, an unconscious tensing that didn't stop at the wrist. Her entire body was knotting itself into painful locks. Soon she was as immobile as stone, a forgotten statue in an endless green garden.

Something's not right here.

You need to turn around now.

Despite this caution, nothing responded. Nothing except her knees, which rattled and shook with such violence they threatened to topple her.

Oh, my God. I'm going to die. This person is going to kill me.

This final thought materialized just as the stranger had materialized from the fog. One moment there had been nothing and then the next—*pop*—there it was. It was simple, really, like any one of the hundreds of thousands of facts and rules that kept the world spinning on its axis.

The opposite of up is down. Day follows night. Boys like girls. Dads don't cry. The world protects its children. If you're good, you go to heaven. If you sin, you go to hell...

These were just some of the many things that had knit her universe together, back in her early years before she wandered from the tent, leaving her Raggedy Ann doll and her sleeping family behind, the night of the lead bitch and the gunshot. But unlike these facts, the realization that she was going to die—that this stranger was running at her with the pure intent of ripping her to fucking shreds—seemed impervious to critique.

I'm going to die and it's going to hurt.

The woman ran in great, unbalanced leaps, her breasts swinging from side to side. Her head was shaved and her mouth was a pit of RED and giant teeth. She was covered in cracked white mud from head to toe. The island parted before her, trees and vines pulling aside to let her through. Flocks of insects shot from their hiding spots among the knee-high bushes and blinded themselves in the sun.

She was as unstoppable as lightning crashing from the sky to strike you down, boiling blood and melting your brains. She was cancer, the kind that came on quick and took you without remorse. She was *deafness* that no doctor could cure. She was a great white shark swimming up from the cold waters, making jelly of your flesh and swallowing you alive.

The woman was all this and more. And she was coming at Amity. Only death would stop it.

Hold on to the rope, whispered a voice in her ear. A man's voice. A strong voice.

Pa?

Things have gotten slippery again, little girl. Hold on to the rope.

The woman was right *there*. Her teeth were not teeth at all but jagged shards of broken glass stabbed into the gums.

All Amity could hear now were the roars of wild dogs layered on top of one another. A chorus of rabid screams building bright and blinding.

Hold tight.

Amity listened. Without even really thinking, she stuck the end of her bamboo stick into the earth between her feet and let it drop a little. It now pointed outward at a forty-five degree angle in front of her.

There was nothing in Amity. No fight. No defeat. Just a moment of empty waiting, in which she had enough time to fill the time with the faces of the people she loved and wanted to see again. Her eyes widened, a hastily drawn breath. Amity watched the woman rushing at her. Watched her *trip* at the final moment. Watched her begin to tumble.

Inertia.

The end of the bamboo spear punched in to her attacker's left shoulder. The wood buckled and bent, but it did not break. It jolted under her grip, vibrating like a guitar string.

Amity exhaled, stumbled back a few steps. The moment had passed.

The woman fell to her knees. It was awful to watch. Amity covered her mouth with her hands, as though attempting to catch her gag. There was nothing to do but watch in shock as her attacker writhed against the spear.

Their eyes locked together. Amity saw herself reflected against the black.

A mangled red mouth opened wide to reveal those long glass teeth again. Her silent cry thrummed the air and made butterfly vibrations against Amity's face. It was a melancholic sensation, and one that wasn't alien to her. She was frightened to think of what they shared.

Whatever it is, I want no part of it. Not now and not FUCKING EVER!

It was Amity who was screaming now. She couldn't help it. Of all the things she'd expected the island to throw at her, this certainly wasn't at the top of the list. It was impossible to her that she'd first plucked the bamboo stick from the ground with the purpose of protecting her from animals and sticky webs. It was almost funny.

Amity stood there long enough for the familiarity of the insane woman's face to form, but she didn't hang around to put two and two together. Just the sense that she'd seen those black eyes before was enough to crush

326

her a little, the fact that she'd once looked upon that very same face and *not* feared for her life was disturbing enough.

Horror.

The world was full of deceit and lies. Amity had known this for a long time, though it hadn't felt real until now.

She ran.

2

The shark howled human cries and human words. "Agh! Fuck. Fuck. Hurts. Fuck. Fuck! Christ!" It spilled out of her, as fluid and raw as the blood running down her breasts, threading through the veinlike arteries of cracked mud.

Breathing was a struggle. Tears burst from her. She glanced down at her left shoulder and saw the bamboo stick embedded not just in but *through* her flesh. Retching a little, her head continued to stretch, over her shoulder, until she saw the rest of the stick poking out of her back.

Breath. Choke. Breath.

Her twitching hands rose to her chest, as though she were going to pray. Instead they came together and curled around the bamboo, as close to the base as she could manage. It felt strong and brittle at the same time.

This isn't how it was meant to go.

I need the light. I've got to have it. She's getting away.

"Come back, you—" Again, another one of those body-wracking coughs, followed by a deep and raspy breath. "—CUNT!"

The jungle screamed insults back at her. Those birds that never seemed to stop; the distant cries of monkeys. Beneath it all there was the snakelike hiss of the wind and that long, drawn-out musical note—a hollow tooting sound that she'd heard so many times on the island.

Just fucking shut up. All of you. All of you.

"Oh, oh—please, hurts."

She knew what she needed to do, and was afraid.

The shark studied the ground where the end of the stick was staked. The earth did not bleed as she did, even though she understood it lived. A strong image whacked at her senses: *Paralyzed people lying down, end to end, across an empty field. Huddled over their chests were men and women just like herself, who stabbed them all with junkie needles. Over and over again.*

Her bloodied smile was short-lived. Agony stripped it away.

She looked up. The girl with the blond hair and so very, very bright light was running away.

"I'll. Get—" The last word didn't form in her mouth. It survived in her mind, as she knew it always would. Even if someone cut off her arms and legs, or poked out her eyes, or pulled the teeth from her mouth. Because some kinds of determination had no end. This was one of them.

—You.

And with each of these words, both spoken and unheard, the shark forced her shoulders against the bamboo, away from the earth. Knuckles splashed with blood. Each wooden rim, a ring of fire. Everything around her exploded into fragments of luminescence and then contracted back in on itself, like an underwater explosion. Her thoughts began to bleed.

3

The wind was a knife slitting the fog's throat, but instead of blood spilling out there was just Amity Collins. Her face was a manic portrait smeared with brushstrokes of emotion and fresh cuts. She'd plowed through trees that had clung at her hair, yanked it out by the roots, branches that hardly seemed like branches at all, but daggers.

Her left eye was a pool of blood from where a twig had torn the lid.

Wet leaves stuck to her skin.

Each step was a brutality she endured. She survived. There was no more screaming out for help—Amity was convinced she was *far* beyond finding it. It had even gotten to the point where she was questioning if the man with the mushroom dust had not been an elaborate dream, like the crab-man, too.

There was only one reality.

This.

She was being chased by something that was more monster than woman—and for whatever reason, perhaps simply because Amity still breathed, the woman wanted her dead. It was as simple as that.

I won't let that happen. I swear to you now. I'd kill myself first.

The ground's surface changed beneath her feet. Grass and moss gave way to rocks. She felt them shift under her weight, almost tripping her over. She skidded to a stop, hair flailing around her face and slipping into her mouth— it tasted of copper and mildew. Her hands scrambled to find the perfect weapons. They didn't come away disappointed. She heaved two fist-size rocks into the air.

They fit perfectly in her grip. They felt right.

Again, it was as though they had been put there with the deliberate intention of her finding them. She was positive now that the island was conspiring against her, and for the first time since leaving the beach, she truly feared that such tests were not being cast against her alone. Amity wondered what her brother and Tobias had had to do in order to survive while she'd been lost out here.

What had they been chased down by?

What weapons did they find and have to defend themselves with?

I didn't deserve this, she told herself. *But that doesn't mean I'm not going to fight you to the bloody end. Even if the rules keep changing on me. Even if Koh Mai Phaaw insists on cheating.*

She was from Australia, a country full of creatures great and small that lived with the purpose of harming those they crossed. Spiders, snakes, centipedes, scorpions, sharks. The list went on. Not to mention the climate, which could chill your bones or burn you alive, given Mother Nature's mood. And yet all of this paled in comparison to the island. Australia's tendency to want to murder you was strangely inconsequential; you knew these dangers were there, lurking below the surface, and you either got out of their way or you suffered the consequences. That wasn't the case here. Things didn't lurk; they crawled out from their hiding places *to get you*. A creature under the bed that had *plotted* to have its victim within its reach.

It was hell, only with a surprising tropical twist.

Amity persisted. Every face in every tree was laughing at her pitiful attempts to outplay the game. She could almost hear them and hated them for it—perhaps even more than she hated the crazy woman with the glass teeth.

I don't even think I hated anything or anyone before coming here. I was different. You've changed me, you fucker. You've whipped me into something that I don't want to be.

I despise you, truly. It's pure. What you've done to me is unforgivable.

I'm not myself because of you. I've been reduced to a character in some sick horror survival flick. So fire the director. Call cut. I'm not going to let you take me.

Amity twirled on the spot—jagged rocks in hand—and faced the direction she'd come from. Her mouth opened and vibrations shot out; her war cry did not go unheard.

The woman with the glass teeth was in pursuit—

(holy shit, doesn't she even feel pain? Anyone else would've been crippled by now!)

—and drawing closer. The fact that one entire side of her body was covered in blood had not slowed her in the slightest. And worse: *the woman was not alone.*

It wasn't just doubt Amity was feeling. No; it was worse than that. It was panic. It undid her, fraying the rope she'd been trying so damn hard to hold on to.

Wild dogs bounded through the trees, through the whitewashed fog. There must have been over a hundred of them, thundering like a tsunami of fur and teeth and dribbling jowls and fleas. Amity could hear their barks and growls.

They were the madwoman's army.

Amity tensed; there was nothing to do but cling to those two rocks even tighter. She wouldn't let them...grow *slippery* and escape her.

Teeth clenched, catching silent curses. Beyond crying. Amity blinked. A moment cut in two. Everything changed.

The dogs were gone. There was just the woman closing in on her with jaws so wide her grimace stretched off her face. Raggedy Ann doll eyes burned just for her.

Amity didn't turn, didn't run. She held her ground, her stance wide.

I'm ready. COME AT ME.

The woman stopped five yards short. Blood pulsed from the wound in her shoulder, a ruby river that slithered over her panting chest, all the way down her leg. Each of her gasps for air fluttered her ripped lips.

Recognition hit Amity like a thunderbolt.

This wasn't some stranger from the island, like the man who might or might not have saved her, or the cripple who might or might not have lived in the cave... No, the woman was *one of them*. Sure, it looked as though she'd been dragged through Hades with every demon along the way stopping to whisper in her ear, but there was no mistaking the shape of her skull, the contour of her cheekbones. This was the woman who'd been sitting across from them on the boat ride to the island.

It was the woman who'd probed Amity's skin with greasy looks.

What happened to you? What has this island done to change you like this?

Am I at risk of going the same way?

Oh, Christ.

Is it already happening?

Amity had no answers to any of these questions. She had nothing, nothing except the rocks, chippings from the island's shark teeth.

That's not true. These are knives. They're bazookas. They're AK-47s. They're weapons of fucking mass destruction, you crazy scrag. They're everything you hoped I would never find, 'cause you know as well as I do that I've got the fire in me to use them right.

I'll do it. Trust me. Take one more step and prove me wrong. I dare you. I double-dare you.

As though the crazy woman had been listening to Amity's thoughts, she took more than a step. She leaped through the misty air, arms outstretched. Amity saw her open mouth, watched the tendons and veins rising up through the mud covering her body.

She didn't need to feel the vibrations to know that this was what screams looked like, and that such screams had a color, and that color was RED.

Amity matched her note for note, leap for leap. The rocks were high above her, swinging down in an arc that connected with the woman's injured shoulder. As soon as their jagged edges snapped through the skin and shattered the bone beneath, Amity was repulsed by her actions.

This isn't like putting some poor animal out of its misery. This is murder.

Amity gave the woman exactly what she needed: a moment's worth of hesitation.

The same injured arm swung wide, bringing all of its dead weight with it.

Wrist hit face.

Fireworks in the sky outside of their hostel window. Dog's teeth chomping down on her thigh. A firing gun in the dimness of the cave. Caleb shaking her. A storm emptying itself over her. Stars, so many stars.

Hot blood squirted through her nasal cavity and into her throat. Eyes frosted with water. Amity flailed, squealed and almost lost her footing. *Almost,* but not quite. The rocks tumbled through the air and vanished among a thicket of thorny branches.

The woman dived again; Amity assumed she must feel no pain at all. A blow like that didn't go unfelt. It shredded ligaments and dislocated shoulders. Pretty agonies wrapped up in a bow.

Nothing.

The woman's jaws widened.

Amity watched, appalled, as the skin on either side of that mangled mouth gave in to the bits and pieces of broken glass and burst like a child's birthday balloon.

Pop.

Of course, Amity couldn't hear the sound, assuming there was any noise at all. But her mind drove a road of memory linking the now to her past. The destination: a single remembered noise.

Pop.

The woman's mouth now stretched from ear to ear, a jack-o'-lantern's grin casting blood down the front of her body. A red petticoat. Her eyes were small and focused, darker. The irises had absorbed all else.

Amity made to move again. Wasn't quick enough.

That grin of blood and grass descended on her. *Fast.* The jaws latched on to the flesh of her right forearm and scissored through the meat until glimmering points struck bone.

The lead bitch had her by the leg and shook its head back and forth, swinging her this way and that. Little fingers lashing out. Thumping against fur.

Amity didn't feel a thing. She had stepped outside of herself, disconnected and removed. It occurred to her that no, that couldn't be her arm with the elastic, fatty skin tearing open like rubber. What she was seeing was some gory special effect.

Totally gross, really.

Because there was no pain and because it all looked so damned stupid, she pulled her arm away from the woman—and in doing so snapped glass shards from the woman's gums. That jack-o'-lantern smile was ruined now. She'd also inadvertently dug away a handful of real teeth in the process. They were sailing through the air on a blood bubble, leaving behind dark, empty spaces in an already darkened hole.

That hole was open. Growing. It was like Amity was falling into it. Those remaining glass teeth were shooting close to her with the intent of slitting her open *rea-aaaallll good.* So Amity did what felt logical to her. She shot her hands up in front of her and watched as her fingers slid inside the woman's cheeks, peeling back the flesh. It was warm under the woman's face.

4

The grass was long. Whipped Amity's shins. A chaotic beat against dimming nerves. Wet rot and brine in the air. She tumbled along, slower now than she'd been before. Face throbbed. The pain was vast. Branches scratched at her wounds.

Amity knew the madwoman was still behind her. She'd caught glimpses of her through the trees, glimpses of that impossible, inhuman force. And yet her disbelief was idiotic; there was nothing that had happened to her over the past twenty-four hours that belonged in a rational, fair world.

The impossible was not just possible anymore. It was happening. It was now. It was right behind her. *Slippery thoughts.*

There was no direction. Aimless. Drawn into a game of Pin the Tail on the Donkey—spun around, blindfolded and set free. It was a game she'd always hated playing after losing her hearing, the dark of not being able to see combined with the darkness of deafness was too much to handle.

A PLACE FOR SINNERS

The ground ran beneath her in a staccato of textures—long grass, rocks, sand, rocks, bamboo shoots, rocks. There was no rhythm to be found and yet she somehow didn't miss a beat. Her aching feet, bleeding into her sandals, always landed right—until the ground conspired against her.

A hideous image sketched in her vision: *a tablecloth yanked out from beneath a setting of fine china, followed by the inevitable cleanup that failure brings to those who second-guess themselves at the last moment.*

If Amity hadn't been running, she would have dropped into the canyon, but due to her speed, inertia cradled her through the air. This saved her life. Her stomach lifted into her throat, that dropping-elevator feeling that always curled her toes and made her wince.

She crashed onto a bamboo bridge. Her ankle twisted again. There were flashes of makeshift bindings and hinges. The force of landing drove all oxygen from her system. Unconsciousness beat its great wings again, churning its siren breeze. She resisted. It was then she felt the entire foundation she'd landed upon shifting beneath her.

Amity rolled. Her eyes scoured the landscape like someone doing a grave rubbing, the charcoal revealing the fate beneath the paper.

It was a small canyon, though certainly wide enough for someone to fall into and die horribly on the rocks below. There, they would become food for the animals that always waited in the wings. The scavengers. *The dogs.* On the opposite side of the canyon, the landscape continued.

Amity's hands grabbed at the planks. She was on one of many interconnecting bridges that spanned the distance between each ledge. Only this was unlike any bridge she'd ever crossed before. The entire scaffolding looked as though crafted by unstable minds and hands, a life-size, giant game of Snakes and Ladders with bridges upon bridges, ladders leading to nowhere. It was all built upon stilts that kept the whole infrastructure suspended in air.

Her ledge slid to the left again and then swung on a massive hinge bound together by ancient vine. She gripped the bamboo rungs, watched them fracturing under her grip. It was like being swallowed by a skeleton. Amity rolled and snapped against ribs, rolled again and hit the spinal cord.

Everything skidded, snapped into place, deposited her on another bridge, and this one extended out over the canyon. Her scream must have carried into the turbulent air; there was no way it couldn't have.

Huffing for breath, Amity reached up to grab an overhead rafter. Her injured arm was exposed to her in full daylight, and for the first time, she understood that it was not a special effect. It belonged to her. It was *her* pain, this distant burning. Mottled flesh dripped blood. Mosquitos layered the scab.

One of her mother's old expressions popped into her head.

It has to hurt if it's going to heal.

Scraped knees, broken toes, a father who had been shot in the head and buried beneath the ground... After all of this—and more—Amity wondered if healing was fucking worth it.

She hefted herself up onto the next bridge as the wind swept around her, battering her with dirt and leaves. This didn't stop her. Amity rolled onto the next level and crawled along its length.

I can do this. I can do this. It's just like being on one of the old jungle gyms back at Saint Catherine's—

Everything trembled. She glanced up through the crisscrossing bamboo rafters and saw the madwoman strung between them like a spider in its web. The bitch had jumped, only from the looks of it her landing had not been as neat as her own.

There were old birds' nests perched among the architecture, and they fell apart with all the commotion, raining down over them. Branches strung across the ladders from past storms came loose. Some snagged between rib cages on their way down, others pinwheeled into open air. Amity watched them shrink, shrink, shrink and explode against the rocks.

That horrible shaking again. *The woman was on the move.*

Amity dragged herself onto her haunches and quickly mapped out a route that would lead her to the opposite side of the canyon. She dug blood from her eyes and studied.

If I go along this footbridge and climb up that ladder, it'll take me to that other one, and if I follow it I'll get to that bamboo tunnel over there...

It was adrenaline alone that gave her the confidence to start. She knew that the young woman she'd been two days before would have clammed up with stage fright. There was no time to feel proud. The whole structure was growing more and more unstable by the second, and now with two considerable weights pulling and tugging at its bindings, things were *literally* starting to fall apart at the seams.

The bridge she was climbing across began to give way. Two wooden planks snapped inward and her leg tumbled through the gap. Amity scrambled. Her fingers latched on to whatever they could find, which wasn't a hell of a lot, just a tumbleweed snagged between two crossbeams.

A part of her was dangling over the canyon, swaying through the air. The sense of weightlessness sent her into tingles.

Hold on...

Bamboo fragments shrank down to nothing below, shattering into pieces.

Sweat dripped into her eyes. Teeth ground together. Every muscle had to work overtime. Gravity was ripping at her skin with its tenterhook hold. *Come on, little girl*, it seemed to snigger at her. *Let me work my magic on you. Just let go and I'll take care of the rest.*

Whaddaya say?

That thicket of tumbleweeds was strong enough to lend her some counterweight—though only just. As soon Amity hefted herself back onto the track, the tumbleweed crumbled. She could already feel more planks beginning to buckle. A splinter shot up, twirled and landed on her chest.

A quick look behind her. The woman's great white and red arms were spanned out on either side, hugging the view, trying to draw her into a bloodied hug.

Christ almighty, what will make you stop?

I can't beat you.

The revelation was eventual. She was going to die; the woman was going to kill her. Perhaps it was better to let gravity have its way, and let it drag her down. If the monster got her hands on her, God only knew what kind of pain she'd endure before all of her questions about whether or not there was *really* anyone "up there" were answered.

I'm not ready. I'm not strong enough. It's just too scary.

Hold on, girl. Hold it. Hold it tight.

Amity's groan vibrated back into the bridge, and she propelled herself onward. Every stretch of her arm made that burning sensation grow stronger in her wounds— there were so many of them! But now was not the right time to let her beaten body win. The flesh would just have to wait. She stretched again, groaned.

Sorry, you psycho-cunt. You've caught me in a surviving kind of mood.

More sand and dust blasted. It was in her mouth, pelting through her tightly closed eyelids. And as quickly as it had come, it was gone again. The wind dropped. It was as though the twister she'd so feared as a child had finally caught up with her, the one from the movie she'd seen.

A PLACE FOR SINNERS

The father had been sucked up out of his storm shelter in front of his screaming children.

This kindergarten fear stoked in her again; it had been lurking there all through the years, waiting for the right moment to surface and undo her for good. She forced it back, a storm of her own. Amity coughed and continued to climb, determined not to let everything that was against her claim victory.

The skeleton rattled again.

Amity hefted herself up a five-foot-tall ladder that was angled in the right direction: toward the other side of the canyon. She was close.

I'm doing it. I'm fucking doing it!

All around her there were slivers of sky—brilliant and blue—and sunlight booming through what little fog remained. In front of all this, the barrier of interconnecting hinges and poles and directionless bridges built up and over one another. Vertigo swooned. Her depth perception was shifting.

She watched her hands reach and grab, reach and grab, as if they were somebody else's hands reaching and grabbing, reaching and grabbing. Every so often her vision would blur as grit and blood slid across her corneas. That same hand rose into air, lingered, and then came thumping down.

Something crushed beneath her palms, something wet and thick as syrup.

Twigs and dead grass catapulted into her face, landing on her lips. Amity shook her head from side to side, trying to shake it loose, but between the blood and grime her face was flypaper-sticky.

A speckled blue egg rolled across the footbridge and came to a stop between the two planks in front of her. It sat there, rocking back and forth as the small crack across its surface widened.

Amity was transfixed.

All of her focus contracted in on it.

An iris drawing down into a tight circle, and at the very end of it, nothing but the egg she'd thrashed from a nest. Her mouth was open, breath probing the shell as it split in two.

The two halves broke away like a cartoon heart, and deposited the almost-fully formed bird on the bamboo. It sat there, kicking in shock, covered in slime.

Of all the horrible things Amity had seen since the moment everything went to hell, this was the one that undid her the most. *The rope frayed a little.* The bird spoke to some deep, primal part of her being. She, too, was ripped open and was exposed.

The eyes were welts against featherless skin; they weren't even formed yet. Just a blood bubble under all that pink. *The beak parted with a cry and she heard it screech the growls of wild dogs.*

Amity reached out for it, not knowing what she would do once she had it in her fingers. But she wasn't quick enough. The bird slipped between the crack in the footbridge and vanished.

It was as though she were falling with it. Helpless. Confused. Suspended in a horrible nowhere between not quite born and not being aware enough to know that it would soon be dead.

This all had a color and the color was RED.

Hot, wet liquid splattered across the back of Amity's neck. It dribbled around into her collarbone—it was like a slithering tongue. She flipped over. The woman was on the footbridge above, reaching down through the gap. Her long white arm, with its broken and bleeding fingernails, was inches from her face. Swiping. Swiping. Amity saw a mouth full of messy flesh strands, strips of gum and glass fragments, and beyond all that, a throbbing throat constricting and releasing.

That hand slithered farther and reached Amity's hair. The fingers curled upward and heaved. Instant heat shattered through Amity's scalp; her skin went taut.

The woman continued to pull as she allowed herself to spill through the gap, bones popping out of joint and spine arching. Human origami.

A lifeless arm slapped against Amity's head. The dark mouth widened. Blood rained over Amity's face, ricocheted into her nose. It glooped onto her tongue, but she was too preoccupied to vomit—which wasn't to say she didn't want to.

Having just a small part of that woman *inside* her violated Amity deeply. She was sure those little warm drops were changing, mutating. Sprouting legs and running around like the crabs in the ancient man's cancers. And these blood critters would feed on her; they would rape her until she bled and died, corrupting everything they touched...

(*Slippery. So slippery.*)

She could already feel them. They were there with that *other* pain in her abdomen. That sense of being filled and torn. The blood critters were there in the deep.

Amity had no idea where the shadows came from.

They came out of the fog, took aim and dived.

White wings fluttered around her. Scratched. Amity thought there were three birds in total, though she might have been wrong. She watched one of their yellow beaks razor through the crazy woman's nose, watched as one of her Raggedy Ann eyes *burst* open.

And yet Amity didn't really see any of this.

All of her focus was on those loose feathers twirling on the air in gentle, soothing contrast to the carnage above.

It was time to keep moving. Time to cling to the rope and live.

5

The game of Snakes and Ladders resolved itself in a single stretch of bridgework, only it didn't really look like a bridge to Amity. It bore a closer resemblance to railroad tracks, and stretched directly to the lip of land on the other side of the canyon.

Seaweed and vine dangled from the beams in between, fluttering in the wind. Dust flared again, fell. Amity crawled on, watched the semaphore peekaboo of the canyon floor between the planks. Each time she saw those rocks staring up at her, there was pain between her legs.

All of those little vibrations. She didn't dare look behind her. Not yet.

Keep going. You're almost there.

The bamboo knot swayed on its stilts. The railroad shuddered. She winced.

Amity extended her arm and watched her shadow spill over the outcropping. It was only now, just as she was about to crawl back onto land, that she almost gave in to her fear. A weaker person would have given in and stalled. And it was so tempting too.

Amity didn't give in.

She kept on going and dragged herself across the threshold, felt the bamboo rafters scrape against her knees for the last time. Grass brushed her cheek. Soil had never smelled so rich.

A hand grabbed her ankle.

Amity couldn't believe the strength still in it. Yet she *had* to believe. The madwoman whom Amity had never wronged—never offended or picked a fight with—was right there, continuing her senseless, blind chase.

If only she could rationalize it, Amity thought she might be able to defeat it.

There were no answers here, only evils so pure they burned like the sun.

The face—split in two by its impossible smile—was covered in mottled feathers. Her one remaining eye did not blink. A severed bird's head rested on her tongue.

The woman came at her fast.

Amity pulled away with such ferocity that urine flooded her pants. The hand slid away, fingernails scraping divots through her sweat.

Running. Lungs filled. Emptied. Filled. Emptied.

(The little bird's beak. Opening. Closing. Opening. Closing.)

The stink of salt was stronger on the opposite side of the canyon, which meant she was getting closer to the beach. There was safety in numbers. She believed that her brother would be there, waiting for her with the others, and that he would protect and shield her from the horror, just as he'd always done. Caleb Collins was the answer to it all.

He *was* the rope.

6

The shark watched the light in the girl. Its rays made crystals of the air, frozen bubbles of refracted color. She followed it all, oblivious to the reality of her body's shutdown. The light bore heat and that heat was marvelous.

She trolled like she'd never trolled before, down a tunnel that was closing in with every lurch. And lurching was exactly what she was doing. Her meat was going slack; even the bones themselves were splintering. Food was the only solution. *Food.*

Half of the landscape was gone. She had to shift her whole head to see anything right of her nose. It was ocean black, which was why she wasn't afraid of it.

The island continued its insults. Every animal in its trees stopped to scold her with high-pitched squawks. Even the wind sucked. Leaves exploded like pom-poms, reminding her of a place where children went to learn, of people who were there to teach.

Lost places. Nowhere lives.

Shit cascaded down her legs, leaving a winding trail behind her. This was her ground now; she could mark it as she saw fit. Blood spluttered from her mouth with each exhalation, none of which came easily. But this was the cost of trolling. Of making it last *re-aaaaaaallll good*, though the shark didn't really understand the meaning of that. Not anymore.

She heard another noise too. It was impossible to miss.

A long, drawn-out musical note.

It occurred to her that she'd heard it many times in this feeding ground, even back when there were still threads tying the shark to the woman who cried when she was alone, who hid secrets in a handbag behind the crawlspace in the hope that someone would find it and end her life.

The sound was *lyrical*. Hollow. Now that she was closer, she realized it wasn't a single note at all. In fact, it was thousands—a chorus blending together to form a single lament.

Were the mountains weeping in awe of her hunger?

No.

Was it coming from the food?

The shark didn't think so.

The only sounds the food made were screams.

They always screamed, didn't they? The knowledge that they were going to be consumed stripped them of whatever lives and personalities and problems they thought defined them out there in the world. What was left behind was raw and ready for her teeth. The shark made everything equal. Ground zero.

She didn't know how many people she'd taken. Once, she had. Long ago. Some images remained.

Grains of rice floating from a girl's slit-open stomach. The crushed face of a child she'd slaughtered with a piece of broken brick.

No.

Not a face. A wound.

She'd worn Christmas lights to dazzle them. Used cunning to earn their trust. She'd spun lies to gain access. In between were stamps on a visa, the pages bleeding.

So many people, and yes, they *did* all look the same on the inside. Split open like rotten fruit, and every bit as sweet. But that wasn't even the good part. It was the light she sought out; it illuminated all of that underwater darkness.

And the girl up ahead burned bright. Oh, did she ever.

The shark gained some ground and snatched glimpses of her through the sway and swish of trees. But now the girl looked different. It was a man. He seemed familiar—

(*A lifting veil reveals the smiling face. There are tears building in his eyes. He is lightly freckled. He burns in the sun during the summer. She makes fun of him for this. He loves her. He makes love to her. He has something to do with why this happened. An agony in her body.*)

—but she couldn't say why.

The shark was wrong. It wasn't a man. It was a teenage girl with purple streaks in her hair.

(*"What's wrong with you? You weren't always like this. What changed? You're all fucked up in the head; you know that, right?"*

"Don't you dare talk to your mother like that."

"Oh, please. Dad, you're the biggest pushover of them all. Everyone says so. Even the kids at school think it. She's losing it and you're letting her. You're afraid of her. Admit it."

"Go to your room. Now. You stay another bloody minute and you'll live to regret it for the rest of your life."

"Dad, you're spineless. She's leaving you. Us—")

A flash of leaves and the person changed again. This stranger is not so strange. Again, the shark finds a likeness in the dark, wavy hair, the long white face.

(*She glares at her reflection in the mirror and struggles to see a resemblance between the person staring back at her and the person she always assumed she was. This person's hair was falling out in clumps (it began with a hairbrush coiled with silvery strands); her eyes were darker and one pupil was larger than the other. The reflection looked as though it were nothing more than a skeleton dipped in wax.*

Susan takes herself and her reflection to her local bulk billing medical center. She catches sight of it in the sliding door. There are gaps in her teeth. So much rot. It stinks. She stinks. Especially when she sweats, when she has her period.

The receptionist calls out her name.

The doctor is a thin man with a lisp. She watches his face begin to smear, the expressions and definitions blurring into one, like Dick Van Dyke's pastel street paintings in Mary Poppins (a film her children loved when they were little), running in the rain.

Her headache makes the walls of the medical center crack open. Water floods in. Health brochures with titles like TODAY'S CHECKUP IS TOMORROW'S HEALING rise with the tide, all of the happy faces in the photographs turning to mush.

There is a shadow over her back. It has come for her again–)

The woman is the girl again. Her light is so bright it almost hurts to look at.

The shark salivated; pinkish threads trailed across her chin. Her left arm was lifeless, more distraction than anything else. She wished she had the time to chew it off, running with the red rainbow.

It would terrify the girl. Fear makes them burn brighter, and they burn brightest just before they're wiped out. I'm gonna make it last. I'm gonna make it last re-eeeeaaaaalll good. You're special. You're Christmas and Easter and birthdays all a-rolled into one. You're mine.

Mine.

7

Amity couldn't believe what she was seeing. The jungle was thinning up ahead.

Her excitement expressed itself in the quickening of her pace. There was salt everywhere; it was even beginning to sting her eyes. She refused to close them. No. Closing them would yank the foundation out from under the hope she was building inside her.

A PLACE FOR SINNERS

That couldn't happen. Not this close.

It looked like a bomb crater, or one of those meteorite landing sites she'd seen on television. The land was scooped out, yet shallow. There were no trees in this valley, just raw soil. She wondered if a fire had ripped through this place, but wasn't convinced. She'd seen enough fires around Evans Head—controlled backburning or sugarcane leveling—to know that even scorched earth gave birth to new shoots of green regrowth. White flowers against the black.

There was none of that. Life was too afraid to grow here.

My God.

There were hundreds of old glass and plastic bottles stabbed base-first into that soil. They covered the entire valley. It looked like an illustration in a kid's fantasy book, a picture of a king's treasure, which she knew was usually guarded by dragons.

The bottles were every shade of green, blue and clear glass. The ones closest to the center of the valley were older, while the less grimy ones edged right to the end of the path she was heading down. And yes, it was a path; Amity hadn't realized it until now.

This part of the island had been landscaped. Just knowing this made her feel lighter.

There would be men leaning on their shovels enjoying a break. They would turn around to face her. Their faces would be kind and strong, as would be their arms. One of them would have a gun, which would be used to slay the dragon.

Wait a minute. What is this place? Some kind of art installation out in the middle of fucking nowhere? Don't fucking think so.

A memorial?

Nope. Please try again.

There were no answers, except for one. She knew where all of the bottles had come from.

347

Tourists.

The monkeys had approached them, week after week, year after year, and had taken their shiny, sweet offerings. And after they had fed—the sugar giving them that much-needed buzz—they had taken the bottles with them. Amity was sure she'd actually seen some of them carrying the bottles, wrapped in their tails, as they leaped from branch to branch. Tokens.

Each bottle was filled with varying heights of rainwater. Every one was unique, these gifts from the men who piloted the boats.

No, not gifts.

Amity's stomach constricted on itself.

A means of trade.

Here, take this sweet. Enjoy it, and in return let us walk along your beach. You'll like the drink, all right. See, I ain't lyin', little monkey. It's sugary and full of bubbles. Tickles your throat, dontchit? And guess what? We'll come back with more, multiple times a week if you'll let us. See, this is a great deal for you and all your little friends. Why, you won't ever have to hunt for food or water again! We'll give it to you over and over until you forget how to pick your own fruit, how to drink water from puddles.

Aren't they shiny, the bottles? You can keep them if you like, a little reminder of who we are...

...and how much we own you.

Amity was so close to it all. She did not make it. Her foot landed on the edge of a hole and she began to slide along the muddy decline.

Everything tilted sideways.

"No!"

It wasn't a hole, just a half-dug pit of five feet's depth. The sides were slick with crushed, veinlike roots. Amity grabbed at the earth, but there was nothing there to hold on to. Her fingers raked rows of finger tracks through the grime. She hit the bottom, her shorts having ridden up around her crotch. There was mud on her tongue, grit between her teeth.

Flies filled the air. Tiny wings brushing, brushing. They crisscrossed in front of her, weaving insane routes through the stinking air.

The stink of shit. Grease. Unwashed skin. Infection.

Amity's foot was flat against a young woman's face, the tip of her toes resting on the upper lip. A worm crept through the eyeball, exposing the pool of pus it had been swimming in. Where her lower jaw should have been, there were only flies. There were leaves and twigs through her hair, as though she'd been dragged a mile. And of course she *had* been. There was sand in her nostrils, clutched in her hand.

This corpse was not alone. There were others.

A death pit.

Amity saw the twisted hands. The exposed knees raked with cuts. The ripped-apart faces obscured by inky rainwater. Their flesh was cold and hard beneath her.

Water and bile fought its way up Amity's throat. She began to scramble at the pit's walls, but they were *slippery*. Revulsion made her weak. She slid onto all fours, squealed. Every time she shuffled off someone's chest, she accidentally pressed against someone's exposed brains.

A shadow fell over them all.

8

The shark was on her hands and knees, crawling to the edge of the pit. Her ears were filled with the sound of hundreds of bottles tooting in the wind. *This* was the sound she'd been hearing.

It was *empty* music, and this emptiness was like that of an abandoned house on a run down street. The kind of emptiness that passing children fill with stories of mystery as a way of culling the unease the absence of life evokes. It was the sound of the haunted, and it was now reaching out to cut the energy from the shark's body. Its singular pitch made the base of her neck throb, as though the

349

children had gifted their fictional ghost with a fictional dagger, and was forcing it between her vertebrae.

But the shark had no choice. The blade had to be ignored. So she peered over the edge of the pit instead. Focused. Blocked all else out. The girl she'd been chasing sat down there on a throne of corpses. There were flies everywhere, a haze of black static.

She watched the girl's light, just beneath the skin, so bright every freckle was projected on the pit's walls. It was stunning to look at, and even though the shark's face had been torn to ribbons, making a smile near impossible, she could still appreciate beauty. And humor, too. A giggle escaped. It was funny how the girl was trying to escape all of that blood, trying to untangle herself from coils of busted intestine.

"I...see...you," the shark said.

She raised her hand, leaving behind a perfectly formed print in the mud. Shaking fingers framed the pale face below.

Click.

Bones cracked as she stretched farther, dragging her empty breasts across the jagged roots. Her giggle was gone; there was only roaring. A tooth tumbled out of her mouth.

Gonna make it last rea-aaaaaalllll good.

The girl was still. All of her color had drained away, making her blood seem much brighter than it was. Her eyes were coals pushed into a snowman's face. Cold. Wide. They no longer seemed to blink.

The shark could see that there was little fight left in her, just a savage stare.

"Whaa ugh euew chashin?" the girl asked.

The shark withdrew her hand a little. Wavered.

Brightness shone from the girl's mouth and eyes with each slurred word. Her light was no longer white, but vivid blue. The hottest and most pure of flames. The shark could feel the heat from where she lay.

"Whaa ugh euew chashin?" the girl asked again. Even though the words were difficult to decipher, the shark knew it was a question by the way it was spoken. The voice—fragile and sweetly pitched, honeyed in its own raspy way.

"*Whaa ugh euew chashin?*"

The woman who used to be Susan Sycamore cocked her head.

What are you chasing?

She didn't care. And that was the point.

I. Just. Don't. Care.

Hands grabbed the shark by the shoulders. She felt herself being lifted up; the pit slid from view. Trees flashed by—a swirl of green and gray. Raging sunlight. The island's song continued to howl. She landed facedown at the foot of the glass bottle valley.

9

The last son was hurricane-strong, and the island watched him display his power. It parted the fog, allowing more illumination over the scene. Each shadow revealed was a testament, slashes of dark pride over her soil.

He was not weak as the others had been.

Winds whipped the trees into leathery claps, a thrum of applause.

The island watched as the monster he'd pulled from the edge of the pit—where he'd thrown the bodies before dawn—landed at the threshold to the clearing. Flesh thumped against sand. Drops of blood on the bottles.

The last son shook his head, dreadlocks flailing in an echo of his movements. It looked like he was trying to shake off his weakness, a weakness that was as well-defined in him as the scars of discipline beneath the patchwork shirt.

10

The shark lifted her face from the sand. The man who had thrown her was just out of sight. He was *roaring*, just as she had roared. Only it was a more primal cry.

For the first time since that bird—a flash of feathers and yellow beak—had shot out of nowhere and snipped one half of her sight into blackness, she sensed the narrowness of her vision and felt pain bashing around inside her skull. Yet it wasn't *just* that.

She was beginning to feel afraid.

And it wasn't the kind of fear a kid experiences when Mom or Dad switches off the bedroom light and all the shadows in the bedroom look like people in waiting. It wasn't that uniquely adult fear of change, either—of having to switch careers and lifestyles, or accept that the special someone in your life doesn't love you in the special way he or she once did.

No. This fear was more sincere. It was *elemental*.

It was the fear of dying. She imagined that being born could be the only thing that equaled this—the collapsing of a world, blinding light, the hands of giants.

Susan Sycamore suspected she would be leaving this world the same way she had come into it: screaming.

The man's roar had the shape of a word, but it was unlike any she'd ever heard. That wasn't to say she didn't understand its connotation. It was a command through and through, and it split the air with all the force of an arrow—only she was not the intended target.

Susan floundered on her stomach and watched as the monkeys came spilling from the trees around the clearing. Every thump of clawed hand and foot threw up explosions of sand. She saw their little pink faces dancing, their mouths full of junkie-needle teeth. Some of the monkeys were deformed—snouts run into eye sockets, ears webbed with furry neck. They looked like toys after the child had grown bored and added a little fire to their playtime.

Susan had done this herself, as had her own kids, whose names she could no longer remember.

I don't know if I ever did.

The animals came at her from every direction. They screeched and chattered as they leaped over the bottles, bounding with great speed.

She tried to command her arms to move. They wouldn't. Her legs were leaden. The wiring between her brain and body had been severed. Panic molded with pain, making hot piss squirt down her thighs.

The shark in the mirror opened its mouth and words spilled out. *You've got to get up. Get up now and fight.*

They were closer. It was impossible to tell how many of them there were, though Susan guessed the tally would number the bottles one for one. On every monkey's manic face she saw something recognizable.

Hunger.

Their black eyes seared the air, charred her wounds.

Hurt. It contorted her expressions into those she'd seen on her victims time and time again. The widening eyes as they filled with the knowledge that they would soon be dead; a laughterless Joker's smile. And, of course, there was the twitching.

Nerves firing. Joints constricting. It was the body's way of reminding the brain that it was still alive, *goddammit* it!

Susan knew that the monkeys could see the lights she'd collected, swirling around in her system. They were reflected in their peepers.

The man continued to roar from behind her, animating the animals even more. They squealed back in reply.

Susan grabbed the nearest Coke bottle.

"Come at me, you clever fucks!"

She hefted it as high as she could, which wasn't very far at all. Rainwater ran over her wrist. She drew her left knee up under her stomach and briefly saw all of her blood absorbed into the sand.

The wind screeched the bottles into screams as the animals closed in. Susan could smell their musk as they shat with excitement. There was a terrible choreography to the way they moved.

Depraved grace.

The monkey in the lead was dressed in the remnants of a pink tutu and its cheeks were rouged with layers of cracked, red earth. There was a broken bottle in its hand, glimmering shards pointing outward like a knife. Rubbery lips pulled back. Its gums were black. Rotten teeth glimmered.

"You can't have me!"

Her heart was beating so fast and hard she thought it might literally clam up and give in. She had stopped moving, and as anyone knew, no shark could survive without the sea rushing through its gills. To do otherwise was to die.

And neither Susan nor the shark was ready to go down that route. Not yet. There was still so much more light to be swallowed. So many more photographs to be taken, click after bloodied click.

You're a fool. You know what's happening here. The writing's on the wall.

Yeah, the writing *was* on the wall, but that didn't mean she had to read it. In a way, she was thankful the monkey in the tutu and all of its little friends moved with such speed... There would be no time to beg.

The monkeys were within striking distance. Each wore a Frankenstein's monster mask of skins and stitching, binding together all the faces of all the men, women and children she'd slaughtered. It made her happy to see that there was no light behind the sockets.

It was all inside her.

I won, remember? I got you all. And each of you was fucking pathetic. You were all just wasted wax. The only thing that was good and special about you, I took and made my own. That's what I was born to do. I am the big bang.

I am cannibal.

Susan's heart stopped. All sound was gone. The sky darkened. She was in the ocean again, back where she belonged. Down here she was innocent. Here, she was not victim to her nature. She just lived. Her hunger was normal; it was in her bones.

Gills opened for a final time. Water rushed in. Her black eyes rolled to white as she breached the surface, jaws widening in readiness for attack.

Teeth met teeth.

The monkey ripped Susan's face right off her skull.

11

Flies covered every inch of Amity's body, a second skin of twitching hands praying and rubbing together. It took all of her energy to hold on to the one thing she had left.

The rope.

She almost laughed when she thought about all the things she and Caleb had filled their travelers' backpacks with—a perfectly allotted solution to any problem that might arise!

Look, everybody. See how smart we are?

There had been her clothing in the plastic drawstring bags. Toiletries in a rubber case. Chap Stick. Her USB. Kindle. Camera. The first aid box, filled to the brim. Tampons in a waterproof carrier. Bottle opener. Passports. Pocketknife. Laundry powder.

The list went on and on, dwindling down into an ellipsis that wasn't worth punctuating.

(Going, going—)

And yet it wasn't just the contents of the bags that had been taken away from her. She'd lost her phone and the world trapped beneath the touch screen—her other personalities and the alternate realities in which she was normal and could hear and was just like every other young woman her age. She'd lost her family.

(–gone.)

All that remained was the rope, and even now she could feel it fraying.

It's hard to hold on to something when you don't exist.

This was true. She no longer had a body, or at least that was the way it felt. It was as though someone had pulled the life support cord out of the wall, only she continued to live on. Disconnected and yet alive. And it wasn't so bad. There wasn't any pain.

Amity floated.

Her eyes were half-open, half-closed. Things drifted in and out of focus. The flies warmed her body as they drank and shat and planted maggots in her clefts of exposed flesh. They were raping her, and she strangely sensed that this wasn't the first time things had gone this way.

But it was too hard to tell reality from dream. The two had wed and eloped in sin. Her mother would be displeased.

And what sin was it that she had committed, she wondered again?

What did I do wrong?

What did I do to deserve this?

She became distracted by one of the bodies in front of her. A layer of wet leaves and coiled intestines obscured it, but she could make out one muscular shoulder above the muck, and one extended arm. It reached up as though caught in perpetual waiting, waiting for someone to pull it up out of the death pit.

The skin was opal white. Two fingers were bent at an unnatural angle.

Amity found herself leaning forward; the flies flew into the air, buzzed and then resettled on her. It was a man that she was looking at—that, at least, was a given—and there was something on his forearm.

She dragged herself over dead mouths, exposed spines. Closer.

And still in the back of her mind there was that gnawing question.

Why did I deserve this?

Why?

It was a tattoo on the man's skin. Amity blinked, unsure if she was seeing what she was seeing. She was.

There were just two little words on the flesh, and each bore great weight in its own right. Yet when combined to form a sentence, the power was unrivaled.

The words were *Family* and *Love*.

Amity's hand dropped back onto the ground, fingers slipping into a young child's mouth. She disturbed the cockroaches that had been wriggling around in there. They ran up her arm, leaving little red scuffmarks.

Family love.

"Caleb?"

Deafly muttering her brother's name distracted her from the one thing she knew she had to do: hold on to that rope. The already fraying cord slipped over her calluses, scraping away flakes of dried skin. It burned. And even worse, she could *almost* hear the sound of the rope whizzing away, and that sound was the same color as the words inked into her brother's forearm.

The color was RED.

Amity Collins watched her brother's fingers began to curl inward and cling to the wall of the pit. He grabbed an exposed root and pulled himself up out of the bloodied water. The flies swarmed and reformed around them like something going to liquid and then coming together again, just as the sparrows seemed to do when they flocked above Evans Head.

When she and Caleb were young, they watched the sparrows from the roof of the house. Together they would sit there on the corrugated iron, their knees pressed close together as they pointed at the shapes the birds made as they dipped and dived. They would laugh, even though they knew the laughter would be short-lived, because soon their mother would find the ladder against the side of the house and they would be discovered.

Tanned hides. Banned games. Confiscated pencils and footballs.

But climbing up there was worth it, even with the loss waiting in the wings. Always.

Caleb stared at her with understanding. Amity heard his soft voice for the first time in many years. Pain throbbed between her legs again.

"*Amity, your sin,*" he began, exposing his bloodstained teeth, "*is the sin of survival.*"

Her brother's breath stank of mushrooms.

12

There were little punches of light in the dark. They shone enough for her to catch hints of swinging dreadlocks, sweaty arms. A melancholy face. Amity didn't think she'd ever seen anything so sad. A flash of white sky. Fog. Clouds.

She was being cradled, could sense her weight against his.

Another blade of light cut through.

There were hundreds of bottles all around them, sliding by as he carried her to the center of the clearing. Amity could tell that the earth was raised here, raised like a great chest holding in a lungful of air—and for all she knew, perhaps it was. The island was alive. She knew that now.

The bottles petered off at the top of the crest. She saw an upturned boat. The hull was worn and scraped and whatever paint had covered its boards had peeled away long ago. It looked like a wooden igloo the way it was just sitting there, upside down. That made her laugh a little.

She was lowered onto sand. Dreadlocks scrubbed against her.

It was hot here. She didn't like it. Her skin was going to get burned.

I need some cream to protect me. It's in my backpack. In a baggie. So it won't go everywhere if the lid comes off. Don't want that. Nope.

No-oooopppppe.

Amity watched the man push against the boat with one of his enormous hands. A door opened inward. He bent down and stepped inside. She thought of a story she'd read once, or maybe it was a movie–she couldn't remember which–but whatever it was, it featured a scene in which people went through miniature doors leading to even smaller rooms with even smaller doors, and on this went until everything had shrunk down to the size of a thimble.

Funny. Ha-aaaaaaaa.

The same hands that had carried her before now materialized out of the dark doorway. They curled around her ankles and dragged her underground.

PART FOUR

CHAPTER TWENTY-THREE

Beyond the Last Day

1

JANINE COLLINS WALKED up Yarran Street. It was quarter past five in the afternoon. A Thursday. The day had been hot and restless for the most part, threatening to split open and storm at any moment, only those rains hadn't come. The skies teased in this part of the world, a place where crops, livestock and livelihoods were dependent upon the turn of the weather.

She waddled along the path, dandelions chasing after her.

Her thoughts were of her day at the Saint Vincent de Paul Opportunity Store where she worked. Memories rang like bells and were just as deafening. She didn't see the waving neighbor and was almost run down by a boy pedaling his bicycle as though it were going out of style. No; all Janine saw were the faces of the customers she'd served; all she heard were the echoes of their stupid questions, the *ca-ching* of the old-school register.

Under her arm was a green cotton Woolworths shopping bag full of odds and ends, the kind of stuff that nobody actually buys in those stores. Old soda streams.

Limbless children's toys. This was the stuff she just couldn't get enough of.

Sighing, Janine stopped to drag a wad of mail from the box out the front and then continued toward the verandah. Only her shoes were laid out near the door; a twisted tinge of sadness threatened to make her go to water again. She did her little juggling trick with the brick of letters and the bag as she jimmied the house key into the lock. Success. She entered the dimly lit hallway, leaving behind the squeals of children as they chased after the ice cream van on its final block for the day.

The house was overflowing with bric-a-brac, further piles of unread books and old records that she knew she would never end up listening to. They didn't even own a player! That wasn't the point, of course; owning them was enough.

She knew the place was starting to stink. Didn't care. Janine kind of enjoyed it—newspapers and mice and all things nice.

There had been a time not so long ago when all of the mess had been confined to her bedroom. Now it had finally broken down the door and vomited through the rest of the house, spreading like a disease. And Janine refused to accept that there was a problem. *Diagnosis diverted*, thank you very much.

It was impossible to see the living room floor anymore. It was easier to climb over the treasure—

(and treasure was exactly what it was)

—than it was to clear it away when she wanted to make her way to the television set. Changing the channels had become an ordeal since the room had swallowed up the remote.

Janine didn't put on the ceiling lights, deciding instead to run all the ornate lamps she'd collected. Their luminescence made everything softer. Fewer shadows that way.

Jingle-clank of the keys against the kitchen table.

A wisp as letters and catalogs fanned across other forgotten letters and catalogs.

The three grandfather clocks continued to tick away around her. The phone rang just as she set the kettle over flame.

She shuffled to the receiver and snatched it off its wall holster, flicking her long, unwashed hair from her eyes.

Probably one of those damned telemarketers again! Haven't they got anything better to do than bother me?

"Hello." Impatient. Stern.

"Why hello, Janine. It's Father Lewis here, returning your call. From the way you answered, I guess you were expecting an unwanted sale."

"Oh, Father! It's so nice to hear your voice. And you're right. Those buggers always call right around dinnertime. Don't *they* eat too, I ask you?"

"It makes you wonder, dontchit? So how are you? I've got to admit, it's been a while. I haven't seen you at church for almost—what would it be, well, a month now."

"Has it been that long, really? Good golly; time gets away on us, doesn't it?"

"It sure does. How have you been keeping? Is all well?"

"What's well is well. The rest? The rest is a bit of a slow slog, really."

"Janine, would you like to organize a house visit?"

"Ah, no. No, I don't think so. Not yet. *Soon.* I'll be coming to church this weekend. I'd love to talk to you after the Saturday night service, assuming you've got the time."

"Of course I do, Janine... Are you sure everything is okay? Excuse me for saying so, but you don't *sound* okay."

"I, *augh.* I guess I'm just missing my babies." An awkward laugh.

"I see. Oh, that'd do it, all right."

"Not that they're missing me none, of course. They don't even bother to try and get me on the Skype anymore. Would a text message hurt, I ask you?"

"True. True. And on Skype, you say? I've heard about that. It works fine?"

"It works when it works, but what good is it at all if they never get on it to call me?"

"How long has it been since they've touched base?"

"I don't know. A month, maybe."

"Janine, you know what kids are like. They're off having fun, and well, you know how it is."

"Yeah, I know all right. I'm finding out the hard way."

"It's not easy. I think coming to see me on Saturday would be a good thing. We've all missed you. Everyone has been like, 'where's Janine?', 'where's Janine?'"

"Have they? Oh, that's nice."

"It's true. You're missed... Dear, I can hear you *thinking* from here."

"Gee, Father. You can read me like a book. I'm a right royal mess, God's honest truth."

"They really should be keeping in contact more, not that I need to tell *you* that. I mean for safety reasons. Security. They'll call when they run out of money, mark my words!"

"You said it, all right. For all I know they could be lying dead in a ditch somewhere, or off selling drugs."

"Janine, you shouldn't say such things—"

"But it happens, Father. It happens all the time. Don't you watch those current affairs programs? It's always about kids getting caught up in trouble overseas. I can't watch those things since they've been gone. It gives me the horrors. I'm not sleeping."

"Are you sure you wouldn't like a visitor tonight? I'm free at the moment. I've just had Maureen Templeton swing by the rectory with one of her blue-ribbon raspberry pies. I didn't have the heart to tell her that I'm watching my weight and won't touch it. I'm sure you'd enjoy it. Well, even I could be tempted. When the company's right, as they say."

"Thank you, Father. You're a gem."

"That's what I'm here for, Janine. It's important you don't forget that. I've helped you out before. I know I can help you out again. I come with reinforcements, you know, and I'm not just talking about the pie!"

She laughed; she began to cry.

"Janine?"

"I'm sorry. I'm so sorry. Oh, this is just ridiculous! Don't mind me. I'm being a *nong*. Silly, really." She stirred the air with one of the catalogs.

"I'll be there in half an hour. I'll come by in the car."

Janine slumped against the kitchen chair. The telephone was hot against her ear. She sat there, dolorous eyes swelling. "I need help. Things have grown ugly over here. I—I—don't know where my rosary beads are, either."

"I'll be there soon."

"I need my kids back. They're breakin' me with silence. I can't stand it. It's all wrong. *All wrong.* Something's missing. I can't put my finger on it." Janine put the catalog down and rested her hand against her forehead. "I can't *feel* them no more. I can't feel my babies. A mother knows these things."

"Janine. I'm leaving now. Is that the kettle screeching in the background?"

"What? The kettle? Yeah."

"I thought as much. I'll be there before it cools. Janine, I take my tea with two sugars. And light milk, assuming you've got it in the fridge. If not, that's okay. I can handle full strength, will allowing."

"Thank you. *Thank you.*" Janine stood and surveyed the room, drank up the sight of all her treasures spilling across the floor. "I'm afraid you're going to hate me when you come."

"I don't hate anyone, Janine. That's not how it works."

She turned away from the table and walked through the doorway, into the back room with the big bay windows overlooking the yard. She nodded and smiled in reply to the priest's words and hung up. The phone made a pleasant beeping sound and then went dead in her hand.

Janine stepped over a carpet of magazines, the kind that populate doctor's surgeries worldwide, and stopped near the window. There was a delicate chill beaming off the glass, despite the heat. A little transistor radio hung from a nail driven into the wooden frame on her right. She couldn't remember the last time it had been turned on; for all she knew it was the day she'd come home from work and found Amity and Caleb packing their big travelers' backpacks.

Janine swallowed her regrets. They were dry. They were bitter.

Amity's postcard, sent from Hua Hin, was slid between the letters and catalogs on the kitchen table. It sat there, unread, as Janine Collins switched on the radio and swayed to songs that made no sense to her and watched sparrows by the hundred dance against the thunderheads.

2

Amity's eyes open to the darkness that is her home now. She is not alone. He is in here with her. It is his odor—all cooked meat, smoke and sweat—which woke her in the first place. She'd been dreaming, though of what she can't remember. She has been in the dark for so long that even the bright glare of dreams unsettles her.

The man chews on his roots and leaves again, slops it from his mouth and slides the mush over her almost-healed wounds. She doesn't fight him like she did those first few times. She has come to find it warm, comforting.

Afterward, he gives her more mushroom dust. Amity snorts it straight off his palm.

He lies against her side, reaching around to touch the curve of her stomach. They lie on a bed of matted cotton and grass he picked from his most sacrosanct soil—the graveyard. She has animal skins to keep her warm. It's often cold down here in the tunnels. And she knows these are tunnels because the man sometimes comes down here with a torch of charred wood. It glows red against all that black, and when it starts to dim, he blows with his foul breath and lends the embers the oxygen required to glow.

His face is hard and emotionless. The dark is better.

Yes, the dark is better.

The man's fingers trace her navel. It tickles. Amity knows she is pregnant, although she struggles to remember when it happened. It had something to do with a storm. A child born of lightning.

She does not feel sick anymore.

3

Amity can hear the dogs growling. They are waiting for her to die, at which point they will claim the bones they've coveted for so long. In a way, their patience is admirable. Sometimes she thinks she can see them moving around. Sometimes she thinks she's just being silly.

They run away when the man comes down to give her food and drinks.

Today—if it is day; she can't tell—Amity is feverish. She shakes. Her breasts and back ache. She knows she's moaning because of the vibrations.

Fear, agony...both are memories of memories. She is beyond it all. These are sensations she associates with some other time, some other place. Aboveground, up where there were blood and teeth and jungle hands clawing.

Her eyes are wide and yet she does not see a thing. Blind. Deaf. She is a worm in the innards of some dead thing. Feeding. Sleeping. Shitting. Building something inside herself. This routine is deeply comforting; it wedges a space between who she is and what she used to be.

There are moments of lucidity: times when she screams and tries to run away, scratching at the cave walls, yanking at the wooden planks that reinforce the narrow tunnels.

This is when the man comes down with the dust. He blows it in her face—a hot gust of air, the inevitable sting. Things always get better after this.

Amity's father rubs her shoulders.

"It's going to be okay, Amity. You're tough as nails. Trust me. You will be okay."

A voice like velvet.

4

Dawn broke and the island shook from its sleep. The birds cawed as light inched through the trees, spiders dragged dead butterflies back into their funnels. Through it all, the island's musical note was unrelenting.

The monkeys were on the beach.

They sat there, panting deep breaths, picking the bugs from each other's backs and eating them alive. Their eyes didn't burn with the intensity they once did. Some were missing clumps of fur from their hides. Little mouths opened wide in a pantomime of eating. The animals fought on occasion, though with little viciousness; territory and mates were the only things that were worth lashing out over, and even then, it was halfhearted.

Waiting. Waiting. It was as constant and rhythmic as the waves.

They came to this beach with the coming of every sun and studied the horizon for hours on end. Though their brains were small, they understood that their starvation was killing them. The babies, which usually clung to their mothers' backs or shoulders, had been the first to sleep forever.

Yes; even these creatures knew of hope, even if the woman down below did not.

The boats did not come that day. Or the next. Or the next.

Amity walks through the tunnels. She hasn't ventured this far before, but she's restless and can't help herself. Her abdomen, hands and the soles of her feet have been itching. Walking doesn't make the sensations go away; it makes them bearable.

The tunnel fills with blue neon light when she runs her hands over the cave walls.

Thousands of miniscule insects live along the rock face and glow when disturbed. Touching them is like skimming water, ripples of light that allow her to see the bulb of her stomach and the uneven ground ahead.

She licks her palms. The taste gives her heartburn.

Amity continues, her father beside her. Weeds grow up out of his shirt. His face is a cardboard-cutout mask strapped to his head. Behind the cut-out eyes she can see flies twitching their delicate wings.

"You shouldn't go too far," he tells her. *"You don't want to lose your way down here."*

"I'm fine, Pa. I just can't sit still. I've got to move. I feel like I'm on fire."

"If you get lost, he won't be able to find you. Don't forget, he has your medicine. All good girls need to have their medicine when they're under the weather."

"I'm not sick, Pa. I'm not."

"Yes, you are."

They come to a large cave. The air is cooler here and it makes her nipples harden. Amity squints, realizing that the room brims with hazy luminescence. The insects are in here too. They twirl through the air like spores.

"It's beautiful," she says. "Don't you think?"

"Yeah, kiddo. It's lovely. Do you see that stuff up there?"

"Where?"

"Looky here."

Her father points.

There are crops growing from the ceiling of the cave. Amity smiles, raises her itching hands to the hollow of her throat.

"Wow!"

It is like corn, or maybe even sugarcane—only it is neither. She inches closer and looks at the dangling stalks, which sway in whatever breeze filters through this space. Each arm of vegetation looks like a deformed hand and is ridged with rows of festering mushrooms.

The cave has a distinct smell: moss and wet rocks. Water drips from above, dotting her body in cold splashes. Each strike against her skin brings a smile to her face. Amity drinks it, bathes in it. It is wonderful here, below the downward-growing crops, in the blue glow.

She goes to tell her father how happy she is, but he is not there to listen.

6

The man comes to feed her. Today the food is cooked. It's a nice change. Either or, Amity is grateful. She clings to him. Her father tells her that it's okay to need him, that holding him is better than being alone. He changes her dressings. There are scars.

Amity watches the dogs drawing nearer.

7

Life below is a string of tableaux in a vacuum. Swirling shapes against the nothing, tricks of the human eye sometimes disturbing the illusion of the calm. Amity gets distressed when this happens. When it does, she opens and closes her hands, opens and closes her mouth, like a dying fish outside its bowl. Doing this helps, but it doesn't make the stillness any more still.

Sometimes her heart races.

Ba-da-boom. Ba-da-boom-boom-boom-boom.

Fear. It recedes. The nothing returns.

She is beginning to feel love for the thing inside her, so she doesn't want her heart to stop beating. If she dies, the child will die, too. She wants to share her doom.

She continues like this for long stretches of time, not that time exists below. There is just the throb of blooming life interrupted by visits from the man, who always comes with fruits and meat. This, and the occasional dreams.

An overweight woman with long hair in a room of towering junk.

The dream has a familiarity to it, a taste like dust. Perhaps it is the woman herself, sitting there on her bed of bloodstained cloth and Memory Lane albums. Amity wonders who she is and what *her* sin was. But she does not get a chance to ask. The woman always lifts her head to stare with eyes that are not there. Her face is sand.

8

The dogs know about her baby. She wonders if they can smell it. Sometimes she wakes up to find them in the insect glow, sitting on her chest and slobbering over her. Amity yells at them, swipes at their snouts. They flee like the cowardly scavengers they are.

Lies back down. Tries to sleep. Impossible.

Differentiating pain from pleasure isn't as easy as it used to be.

Amity rolls onto her side and tries to talk to the man, but he does not reply. He just stares at her in the same numb way he always has.

A sigh. The rejection is infinite.

She wonders where he goes when he is not with her.

Her fingers reach out to caress his smooth, warm back. He flinches at her touch. "Hello, are you there? Please say something to me. *Please.*"

The man gets up and leaves. She can tell from the way he carries himself that his wounds are deep, and few of them are physical.

9

The island was empty of life, a place of gothic shadows and stillness. Little moved and nothing cried out. Its trees shook in nervous expectation of the next storm, those systematic beatings that only a seasonal change could stop. The sky was a giant welt.

Dawn was no different from those that had come before it.

There were monkeys lying dead along the overgrown orchardways, faces frozen in rigored grins, drawing flies. Their emancipated chests bloomed in decomposition, spilling maggots. Mist swirled and wandered like lost souls in constant searching, only there was nothing to be found—nothing except the surviving monkeys, who dragged themselves through the jungle on slow-moving legs. Such easy prey for larger animals.

And through it all, the music played on.

The monkey in the tutu was listening. It sat on top of the upturned boat in the middle of the clearing, the conductor of an invisible band, and limply tapped at the hull with a human jawbone.

10

"Pa?"

"*Yeah.*"

"I've got a brother, don't I?"

"*Yeah, you do.*"

"I don't remember his name."

"*You will.*"

"Can I see him? I'd like to, if that was okay with you."

"*You can't see him. Your brother isn't here.*"

"Well, where is he?"

Her answer is impervious silence.

The baby kicks. She can't comprehend how it can be so energetic when she is so fatigued. It doesn't seem natural.

Amity walks the tunnels, restless again. Her back twinges. She's constipated. Not even the mushroom dust eases the discomfort like it used to.

She is used to getting around in the dark and isn't afraid to wander farther than she has before. Exploration comes to her very easily. The dogs skulk close behind, snapping at her heels. When she spins around to throw stones at them, they dissolve into the dark and are impossible to find.

"Doggy, don't!" Shrill. Hands clenched tight.

The quiet falls again, an iron shroud.

She comes to another large cave. It is similar to the one where the crops grow, only there is more light here. Tiny cracks in the rocky walls, spearing the air with gold slashes swarming with mites. It is an alien warmth, and it isn't unpleasant.

Amity glances around and finds four large wooden crates. The sides are covered with stamps and ornate text she doesn't understand. Each has been opened, the wooden tops ajar. Her fingers latch on to the first and push it aside, revealing the contents of the box.

It is almost empty, but along the bottom there are stacks of shirts wrapped in plastic. Amity leans into the crate and grabs one, feels the brittle crackle of the covering. It is artificial; it is odd to her. Amity holds the package up to the light and reads the words printed in bold type across the shirt.

STAR WARS.

Beneath these words are faces that she must have dreamed about once, because she could swear she has seen them before. This strange nostalgia makes her dizzy, and she drops the package back into the crate and hurries away, stops, kneels against the ground and sweeps dust into her hands. She eats it straight off her sticky fingers; the craving is insane. It seems to satisfy the baby. Her tongue goes dry and it's hard to breathe again, yet it's totally worth it.

Sitting there in the semidark, content. She coughs and spits three rotten teeth from her mouth. They glitter in her palm like promises.

12

The island watched its last son as he whittled wood among the slate gravestones marking where his fallen were buried. This was *revered* ground to him, and his visits were frequent.

It was midmorning and he'd been hunting since the sun crawled out of hiding. His kills—three mouse deer, four fish—were laid out on a bamboo sled. Once he finished whittling with the rocky blade his brother made for him two seasons ago, his plan was to drag the food back underground. There he would prepare another meal for himself and his mate. Maybe on the way he would stop and pick berries from the shrubs near the sacred trees his mother had harvested. Some juice would be nice, something they both could enjoy together.

The blade carved through soft wood and stopped. His ears pricked.

There were monkeys in the trees around the clearing, perched along the extended lengths of gothic branch. The last son stood up, pulling taut the thinning fabric of his patchwork shirt, and watched the animals jump up and down, screaming and dropping scat.

Now they were leaping from tree to tree, zigzagging toward the shore. The last son's eyes grew wide. He blazed—the heat of expectation—as he followed close behind.

He ran through the jungle and stopped where the scrub began to thin. Sand whipped at his shins. The winds were strong and carried with them the stink of the approaching boats.

The last son began to weep. He'd known that the men and women with the fruit and drinks and laughter would come back, given time. All creatures sought retreat in the end.

13

Amity has nightmares that make no sense, and they carry over into her waking life, like the heavy light of blind stars. It makes her pain all over. The fever is back. Sweats come on quick. It's so *hot* down here. Her stomach continues to grow and the baby shifts, content. The two of them, mother and child, live similar lives of dependence and darkness. Each would die without the other, a snake eating its own tail.

Her father comes to hold her. He smells of the ground. *"You're going to be a good mother."*

Amity asks him what that means.

14

The last son threw his shoulder against the door and climbed up out of the boat. Wind blasted, throwing him off balance and sending him over the hull. He landed on the sand. The sky was a heavenly bruise of yellow and green. All of the colors were wrong. His hands didn't look like his hands. They couldn't be, just as his suffering simply couldn't be *his* suffering.

It was another mega storm brewing. The reek of ozone suggested that it would be one of the biggest of the season, or at least the most aggressive. A westerly gust sent the man's dreadlocks into knots; dust blew against the blood lathering his face, hands and thighs. It stuck. It stung.

He arched his back and cried until he had no air left in him. The scream was filled with everything that made him who he was. It was an exorcism. He grabbed the collar of his patchwork shirt and tugged, splitting stitching and exposing the gaunt chest beneath. The material flapped between his fingers.

Even with the wind as it was, he could *still* smell traces of her womanly stink on him. So nauseating. Once the rain began to pelt down and scrub him clean, he was thankful. His body ran red, pooled pink against the sand. The island drank it up.

There had been so much of it. Blood.

The last son flung his shirt against the nearby bottles, tipping them over. They splashed and clattered. There was no music in their whistle anymore; it had become nothing more than a constant, high-pitched wail. It hurt to hear, and yet that hurt was nothing compared to the shock of what had happened, or his regrets.

It was gone.

He drove his fists against the ground as though *it* were to blame—*and not her.* Knuckles snapped, dislodged. Bit his lip so hard blood spurted in his mouth. Spat in the storm's face. It spat back with icy fists of water. The sky's strength was frightening. He watched, impotent, as trees fell around him; one swirled and landed in the clearing.

The wise thing to do would be to rush back underground. After all, that was what they always used to do, back when they were a family. Together they would close every portal— and there were many—and then reinforce the tunnel walls. But the last son did no such thing, not this time. Down below was dead to him now; it was a tainted place.

She had bled so much.

Lightning blades carved sky, speared earth. Everything shook. The thunder was outrage that matched his own. It was hard to see his tears in the rain, but they were very much there, pouring like clouds, spilling truths and purpose and life.

He ran through the clearing and did not bother to close the door to the old boat. It drummed against the hull.

Crack-thud.

Crack-thud-thud.

Its wooden planks had sustained far stronger beatings.

He glided into the scrub. Snakes scurried across his path, searching for cover. Most of them would die, but pity cost effort and there was none in him to spend. He continued on, not knowing where he was running to until he arrived.

The air was cold and burned; his lungs felt like they were close to exploding. He'd lost much of his muscle mass since the death of his family, who in ending their lives ended most of the routines and responsibilities that kept him healthy. Nursing the woman in his warren was an undemanding chore, and his body had taken a toll as a result, though he'd assumed it would be worth it.

Whipping wind. Squinting against a storm in full force.

Leaves covered the last son's chest and legs, bright green and brown jungle tattoos. The rain was horizontal up here. Birds tumbled from the sky with broken necks, thumping into puddles around him. He recoiled; they were such beautiful creatures when they were alive, elegant and inspired, but death made them ugly, repellent. One gull thrashed in the water, its matted wing flapping once. It died screaming.

It was over. Everything.

He stood at the cliff face where his family had fallen; their smashed-in faces and slit throats were branded into the dark behind every blink. This was the way he remembered them, not as they were. The horrible reality of their death-promise had been the last thing he'd seen before burying them in dirt. It was impossible to shake. He missed them. And their absence had turned septic, poisoning him.

The assumption that they would always be with him?

Wrong.

The assumption that he would live to tell his own child of their bravery and cunning?

Wrong.

Theirs was the heritage of the misled.

The line separating ocean from sky was no longer present, having melded into a dark wall that was as impenetrable as the blackness of the tunnels. The last son was so feeble in comparison to the storm's power, and he knew it. But he stood tall—the final, defiant spike standing between heaven and hell's battle to claim ownership of the island.

He cringed, the truth having been made apparent to him. *Survival was worse than death.* And he suspected that the woman knew it too.

The last son had not killed himself as his family had done because he was afraid. This was his shame. He'd been raised to believe that the violence in his heritage would one day return, and he'd been foolish enough, self-righteous enough, to think that these tales were a falsity. *They* had come, passing through to his home's inner circle, shedding blood over sacred ground, slaughtering one of his own: their little scout, so loyal and so loved. She'd worn the seashell necklace he'd made for her, even into her grave. Her laughter had been sweet. Her corpse, ripe.

And even after all of this, still, he thought they were wrong.

He'd been sure there was kindness and dumb understanding in at least one of the invaders: the woman. Incorrect.

Screams echoing through the tunnels. Blood on their hands.

Her deceit equaled the cruelty of his elders' prophecies.

The rain drizzled out. Winds backed away. Everything calmed in hushed reverence. The last son, still panting, pushed his dreadlocks off his face and glared into the eye of the storm. A dim sun stared down on him. It was warm, forgiving.

Lightness swept through him and his knees went weak. He didn't fight it. There was no point. He was tired, so very tired. He allowed his body to cartwheel through the warm tropical air, and the sense of weightlessness was a little like relief, though it wasn't. It didn't take long to reach the bottom. Waves washed his corpse off the rocks and dragged him into the sea.

15

The woman is slouched against the rock. She licks her lips and tastes rat, her last meal; the air is different here. It's sweeter, saltier. Her smile is faint. There has been nothing but damp rot and wisps of natural gas since the water flooded the warren.

It had been a storm. A big one. So big that the tunnel walls had moaned great vibrations into her hands when she clung to them for balance, as the pain reached its heights. She had expected the entire structure was going to come crashing down on them, but the reinforcements held. The woman thought that maybe, just maybe, she would be better off if it did collapse and they died.

Their child was dead.

The pain had taken it away from them. And *he* knew it. This was why he slapped her across the face and ran.

She has not seen him since.

There is no more movement inside her anymore, just heaviness she has never experienced. Her hands knead at her exposed stomach.

Red eyes burn in the dark. *The dogs are close.* They growl as they lap up her vomit.

There is another noise down here. It is a little like the sound of an old transistor radio caught between stations. Ghost voices filtering through. Something in the back of her brain triggers, and the woman knows that she owned such a radio once.

"Pa! PA! Are you out there? Pa! I need you. I *need* you!"

He does not come. She thinks she can see him shuffling through the shadows, but it's not him. It's a stranger in an old gas mask. The glass bug eyes shimmer for the briefest of moments and then are gone. But she knows that he is still there. He is like a great spider lurking in the darkest part of its funnel, waiting for the perfect moment to jump out at her and drink her dry.

She does not know for how long she has walked into the island's bowels, past the crops and far, far beyond the room where the man kept the crates that washed up on the shore. The flood has forced her farther than she ever expected to go.

Now she is here, where there are no reinforcements on the walls and the ground is rising. And of course there is the new breeze brushing over her, bringing with it the terrifying smell of the outside world. The dogs follow her as she pulls herself off the rock and continues up the slope. She slips. Picks herself up again. Slips. Picks herself up again.

The insects are against the rock. The wind blows and they glow, lighting the way in drawn-out moments of blue exposure. It's just enough for her to see where she is going. There are even weeds growing here. Cockroaches. She is close.

The walls narrow and she comes to a barricade of rocks. Either part of the ceiling has collapsed or the rocks were wedged there by someone in the hopes of keeping her trapped in the tunnels.

Even though she is close to collapse, even though it hurts, the woman who no longer remembers her name, grabs the rocks and begins to shift them. Some of them are small and come away easy, though the bigger ones require all of her strength. The cooler wind on the other side lashes against her face; it makes her feel alive.

Insects glow and swirl. It is a throbbing light, matching her heart, beat for beat. She stops pulling at the rocks and watches them with fresh eyes. Sweat drips down her face. The insects are a sea of stars, and upon each there hinges a single wish.

It takes a short while for her energy to ebb back her way, but it does. She grabs one rock with both hands, and when it comes loose she falls with it. The woman leaps backward and narrowly misses having her foot crushed.

She reaches into the hole in the barricade and pulls herself through to the other side. The insects follow close behind, spreading across the wet, narrow walls like ants from a nest.

That cool sweet air...

It is now that discomfort strikes. There is no warning, and it climbs in waves, each stronger than the one that came before. She moans, vibrations on her cracked lips. The insects—her only allies since the man left her—sense it too, and sparkle.

It isn't a pushing pain, more like having knives driven into her abdomen. Her gasps are deep and scorch down her throat. The muscles in her back boom so hard that she has to roll onto her side. Cramps take hold of her, grip, and don't let go. The dogs are on the other side of the barricade and are jumping up and down with excitement, barks echoing through her head.

"Go ahwhayy!"

With this, her first contraction passes.

The woman is too exhausted to move, and even with the growling dogs climbing over her, sleep manages to snatch her away.

16

It is as though every ounce of oxygen is being compressed from her body. This is almost an *industrial* pain. Her system is firing pistons and cogs, mercilessly turning, pushing her closer to birth. It grows, holds, withdraws, leaving behind a faint sting. Her back is so bad she's convinced her spine is contorting, stretching ridges of bones driving up through her skin.

She wishes she had some of the mushroom dust here with her. It numbs. It heals. She wishes this even though she knows, on some fundamental level, that each time she has it, some part of her is corroded away. It is a price she is willing to pay. Anything is better than *this*. If taking the dust means that this pain will be gone, then she will happily sell her soul for the chance—assuming she still has one.

Another wish: that her father was here to hold her and to tell her that everything is going to be okay. He does not come when she screams.

The woman touches her stomach and finds it as hard as the rocky floor she writhes against. Her legs thrash. She still doesn't completely understand what is happening to her. Her terror is primitive, drawn from a well shared by all who have been in such situations, stretching back through the warren of history to the very first woman, whose screams echo through these same dark corridors. They come together, chiming in a single reedy shrill, just like the Coke bottles in the clearing where the upturned boat still lies. That tone is the *unknowable* made music. It is both the divine and the destroyer.

She feels as though her body is conspiring against her, putting her through all of this because pain reminds the living that they are not dead yet. Even though they *want* to be dead.

Fingers reaching between legs. There is something there.

Her scream comes again. It is not for her father this time. She does not know where the name comes from, only that it *feels right*.

"Caleb!"

The baby slides into her hand. Insects swirl and fall and fly again.

It is then that she realizes that every one of those wishes on the stars around her were wishes she'd spent on this child. A wish that it would live. A wish that it would one day find someone to share silence with. A wish that it would not die alone.

The woman lifts her cupped hands and sees what unheeded wishes look like, garishly lit in neon. It is almost amphibian, strung with a net of tissue. Little hands lie still. It has fingers. Legs dangle. It has toes. It is like a featherless bird taken from its shell well before it was supposed to be—this image aligns itself with something from her past, though it's impossible to place... The child's head is the heaviest part of its misshapen form. A delicate face glares at her with shut eyes, and she can't help but think that this is some kind of mercy.

She reels. Cries. Holds it high above her.

Twisted hands shoot out of the gloom and snatch the child away. The insects scatter into chaos so bright there are shadows cast in the crevice.

The woman crumples in on herself, dazed, exhausted. Everything spins, blurs. Her ears ring with the snarls of dogs that have grown sick of waiting. There are gunshots and crashing waves thundering against her ears. The skittery ghost voices between the stations go to static.

She tries to push herself up off the floor. Slides in her own mess. Her vision fades. The fog is coming. The fog is *here*.

It is the ancient man from the cave. He is familiar to her, like an image from some recurring dream, and she knows that he is worth fearing. His flesh is pocketed with caves, and in them crabs scuttle and fuck. Their tiny pincers are wet. His foot ends in a stump of bone and empty skin and he keeps his balance with the aid of an old workman's pick. He moves with a jolting, twitching quality—not dissimilar to the parasites that house themselves in his pus-filled cancers. He holds the baby in the crook of one elbow; the fingers of that hand are fused to his wrist. She sees the flints of shale embedded in the flesh where his digits should be, and recoils.

Dead hair hangs over his face, but his black eyes can still be seen through the knots. Those eyes lock with the woman's, wracking her to the core. Insects buzz. Some land on his lips; they make his rotten pin teeth shine. His head arcs down. Jaws clamp over the child's head. The skull yields. A stream of black blood paints the rock wall.

The man stands tall, rips her son from his mouth. The remains dangle from his one good hand. He drops them, and the sound of their slopping against the ground has a color, and that color is RED. The dogs leap forward and snatch up the mess, fight over it. They *covet* it, patience having paid off.

She watches, her hands still outstretched in front of her, as the man scuttles up the incline and into the dark, where the wind is strong and the insects do not go. His pick scrapes against the rock with every jagged step, sending up sparks.

The woman is alone with her vibrations, but even those fade. Insects settle and the dark reclaims her. The dogs are chewing. Her mouth opens. Closes. She tries to remember her name again. If she can only remember it, then maybe there is something here worth saving. It does not come to her. Not yet. But she does allow her hands to move of their own accord, dictated by something she does not quite understand. A memory shining through the fog.

Palms up. Thumb to fingers pinched together. The knuckles of each hand just touching. And then letting them go and drop.

It is the sign for "lost".

AUTHOR'S NOTE

It's worth noting that *A Place for Sinners* features a gigantic number of real locations, from Yarran Street in Evans Head to the numerous Thai provinces, all of which are described in specific (and accurate) detail. These places, whilst factual, are used fictitiously. The island of Koh Mai Phaaw, however, does not exist. And even if it did, I wouldn't recommend you visit there. For, um, obvious reasons.

So until next time, happy travels.

AARON DRIES—Australian author, artist, and award-winning filmmaker Aaron Dries "helps lead a new generation of Splatterpunk for a new dark age" (Brian Keene, author of *The Rising*). His debut novel *House of Sighs* was written whilst backpacking through South East Asia, including Thailand, where inspiration struck for *A Place for Sinners*. Aaron won the Leisure Books/ChiZine/Rue Morgue Magazine Fresh Blood contest, and later released *The Fallen Boys*, described by filmmaker Mick Garris (director of Stephen King's *The Stand* and *Masters of Horror*) as a "beautiful but brutal book". He collaborated with Mark Allan Gunnells on the apocalyptic thriller *Where the Dead Go to Die*, and recently published the novellas *And the Night Growled Back* and *The Sound of His Bones Breaking*. His short fiction has appeared in numerous horror anthologies. He is currently at work on a new novel and multiple screenplays.

For more information visit aarondries.com or contact him on Twitter @AaronDries

ALSO AVAILABLE FROM
POLTERGEIST PRESS

BRIAN KEENE
DARK HOLLOW
(RUSSIAN EDITION)

ROBERT FORD & MATT HAYWARD
A PENNY FOR YOUR THOUGHTS
(ENGLISH EDITION)

MARY SANGIOVANNI
THE HOLLOWER
(ENGLISH EDITION)

www.poltergeistpress.com

CPSIA information can be obtained
at www.ICGtesting.com
Printed in the USA
FSHW010651111219
64729FS